NEW EVERY MORNING

NEW EVERY MORNING

Ann Purser

Thorndike Press
Thorndike, Maine USA

This Large Print edition is published by Thorndike Press, USA.

Published in 1998 in the U.S. by arrangement with Harold Ober Associates, Inc.

U.S. Softcover ISBN 0–7862–1152–0 (General Series Edition)

The text of this Large Print edition is unabridged.
Other aspects of the book may vary from the original edition.

Set in 16 pt. New Times Roman.

Printed in Great Britain on acid-free paper.

Library of Congress Cataloging in Publication Data

Purser, Ann.
  New every morning / Ann Purser.
    p. cm.
  ISBN 0–7862–1152–0 (large print : sc : alk. paper)
  1. Large type books. I. Title.
[PR6066.U758N48 1998]
823'.914—dc21   97–23293

New every morning is the love
Our wakening and uprising prove,
Through sleep and darkness safely
    brought,
Restored to life and power, and thought.

The slight figure of a young woman stood in the early morning light, one hand on her hip and the other shading her eyes, looking over the village spread out before her. She had crept out of her husband's bed without waking him, silently left the house, warning the old sheepdog to be quiet, and vanished through the field behind the big barn and up into the woods.

At the top of the rutted track, she had stopped and turned, and now gazed in awe at the scene before her.

The sun was just up, and its refracted rays had bathed everything they touched with an unearthly rosy glow. The air itself had turned pink. A cluster of old stone houses, usually the mellow ochre of ironstone, burned richly red. The young woman's delighted gaze took in the squat church tower with its four crumbling pinnacles, the sharply pitched outline of the village school, and the many-chimneyed roof of the Hall, all transformed by the same fiery light.

She smiled a little, took a deep breath and

1

relaxed, sitting down cross-legged on the cold ground. It was scarcely possible, she thought, that so much had happened in such a short time. She looked around the panorama of Round Ringford spread out so picturesquely before her, and reflected on a community which had grown naturally over hundreds of years, filling a hollow place, making use of the clear water of the River Ringle, shallow and swift. Wooded hills on either side of the valley sheltered the village, and a stranger—as this young woman had been, until really quite recently—could easily drive in and think he had found a lost community.

It wasn't lost at all, of course. Round Ringford was rooted in its agricultural past and proud of its traditions. But its teenagers left each day in a bus to attend the comprehensive school in nearby Tresham, and young families of incomers had moved into its new development of desirable executive dwellings with ideas of how to bring Round Ringford into the twentieth century.

The young woman smiled again. They soon learnt, she thought. Ringford bides its time. But the core of villagers who had lived there for generations had a way of asserting themselves, of quietly putting the incomers right. It was usually the incomers who found they had changed.

Still, she thought, they'd have been in a bad way without us incomers this year, that's for sure. With this comforting thought, she stood up, brushed bits of twig and grass off her skirt, and

2

began to walk back down the hill. The sun was higher now, and all traces of the magical pink had gone. It was a perfect winter morning, clean and bright, with spring not too far away, and the young woman smelled frying bacon in the air. Hope it's like this for our school trip tomorrow, she thought.

She broke into a run, and kept going through wet grass and prickly thistles until she ran straight into the arms of her husband, who had come out to look for her.

CHAPTER ONE

'It won't go no further than you, Peggy dear, I know that,' said old Ellen Biggs, leaning confidentially over the counter of Round Ringford Post Office and General Stores.

Peggy Turner, formerly Palmer, was never a head-turning beauty, but she had the kind of attractive pleasantness that made everyone glad to see her. Always well-turned out, even-tempered and with a sympathetic ear for customers like Ellen Biggs, Peggy was saved from being a paragon by an unexpected sparkiness in an argument and a tendency to make impulsive decisions, sometimes leading her into trouble. Recently married for the second time, this was her first day back in the shop as Mrs Turner, and her feet were still not quite touching the ground.

She smiled at the bent old woman on the other side of the counter, and waited for momentous news.

'It was Ivy what told me, and she's nearly always right—specially if it's bad news,' continued Ellen. Miss Ivy Beasley was Ellen's best and most difficult friend, and Peggy Turner's unfriendly neighbour. She was a wicked gossip, and only a fool made an enemy of her.

'Come on, then, Ellen, out with it, what did

5

our beloved Ivy say?' said Peggy, smoothing down her blue and white checked overall.

She had been reluctant to open up the shop first thing, not wanting her honeymoon idyll to end, deliberately not noticing the sweet wrappers and crisp packets piled up in heaps in the gutter outside. But finally she had been forced to acknowledge a steady stream of water pouring from an overflow pipe high above her head, and knew she'd have to get up a stepladder and fix it.

Then she'd remembered Bill. There he was now, back from the Hall, wearing her frilly apron and washing left-over lunch dishes with his big capable hands. Bill would put it right in no time. Dear Bill...

Ellen Biggs started to speak, but began to cough. 'Take it easy, Ellen,' said Peggy. 'Wait a few minutes—take some deep breaths.' While she waited for Ellen to recover herself, she glanced out of the window. Why had she always thought that winter in the country would be grey and colourless? Living in a Coventry suburb all those years with Frank, both of them from town-dwelling families, she'd had a child's-eye view of the countryside. Winter was always grey, muddy and lifeless, or deep in thick, cold snow. There would certainly be bare trees, brown fields, heavy dull skies.

But now Peggy saw a village bright with life and colour. There was indeed mud everywhere. Great clods of yellowish clay spun off tractor wheels and made tracks along the street. A heap of sand on the roadside, ready for icy patches on narrow roads, echoed rusty red ironstone bands in the stone walls of the village's oldest house. Thin parallel rows of green wheat showed already in the field that sloped up from Hall Farm to the edge of the woods. A sudden wheeling flight of sharp black rooks against the sunlight, rising and falling in the clean wind, suddenly made Peggy glad to be back. This was home, and now there was Bill, and that made it more home than ever. She fetched a glass of water for Ellen, who was still unable to utter more than a croak, and patted her knobbly old back through the thin, tweed coat that had seen better days on someone else.

'Well,' said Ellen, finding her voice, 'well, if you promise your lips are sealed...'

'Ellen,' said Peggy firmly, 'no living soul shall hear this whatever-it-is from me, so please get on with it. Or perhaps it would be better not to tell me ...?'

This smart move on Peggy's part did the trick. 'No, no,' said Ellen, her voice firm now, 'you'd be better hearing it from me, and not some garbled version from them village gossips.' It was a piece of hypocrisy that left Peggy speechless, and she waited for Ellen to continue.

'It's Miss Layton, her at the school. She's given in 'er notice, and is goin' to retire. Soon as possible, Ivy said.' Ellen shifted her feet and stood back from the counter, leaning on her stick and looking triumphantly at Peggy.

'No!' said Peggy, with a suitably shocked expression.

Blooming, that's what she is, thought Ellen Biggs indulgently, bloomin' with love. Romance hadn't figured in Ellen's life much beyond those early flirtations with grooms and under-gardeners, and then that more serious business with the gamekeeper she'd rather forget. 'You're lookin' a treat,' she said to Peggy, with real pleasure. She remembered very clearly Peggy's devastation at her first husband's death, and her subsequent courageous determination to carry on at the Stores. 'And you deserve to, my dear,' she added, envying without rancour Peggy's smooth skin, the colour in her face rising a little with embarrassment, her soft, fairish hair, never neatly in place but escaping from behind her ears in tickling wisps. A good-looking woman, thought Ellen, and a good woman too, never mind what anybody says.

'Anyway, Ivy's always right,' she continued, nodding in satisfaction. 'That'll put the cat among the pigeons. Miss Layton's bin there so long she's part of the furniture. Still, nothing lasts for ever, does it, dear?'

Peggy looked at Ellen's lined face, at the big dark smudges under her rheumy eyes, and her knobbly, arthritic hands, and knew for sure the

8

truth of what Ellen said.

'Well, I'm off 'ome,' said Ellen, struggling down the shop steps with her bag of shopping. She declined Peggy's offer to help—'a quarter pound of butter and two oranges don't weigh nothing!'—and set off over the Green to her small, damp and draughty Lodge. She lived there rent free with few comforts, but it was home for an old woman with few savings after a lifetime's service for two generations of the Standing family. And Ellen had been more than a servant. She had provided an open-hearted and eccentric presence for anyone who needed a refuge from the rigours of life above stairs. She could tell a tale or two, she said repeatedly, but to give her her due, she never had, not about the Hall.

Peggy locked the shop door behind her and called through to the kitchen, from where she heard Bill clattering about on the tiled floor. It had been Peggy's kitchen that first lured Bill into the Palmers' home. It was always warm from the Rayburn, its cream enamel chipped and scratched from years of use, and always welcoming with shelves full of blue and white crocks, red-painted chairs made comfortable with gingham cushions, and the old shelf-clock clunking away with its irregular beat. Even when Peggy wasn't there, Bill had never found the kitchen empty, with her imprint so strongly on everything he saw.

'That makes six,' she shouted.

9

'Six what, gel?' said Bill, standing in the doorway, his eyes warm as he looked at his newly wedded wife.

'Six times I've been told in absolute secrecy the confidential news that Miss Layton intends to retire.'

'Well I never,' said Bill, 'and I was about to be number seven.'

CHAPTER TWO

Round Ringford was almost exactly in the middle of England. It was the proud boast of old Fred Mills that you couldn't get any further from the sea than his old person's bungalow in Macmillan Gardens. Fred hadn't set foot outside the county since a disastrous coach tour of Wales, when he had seen nothing but sheets of rain outside the steamed-up windows of the Luxury Roadcruiser. 'Luxury my arse,' Fred had said on his return to a delighted audience at the Standing Arms, 'no room for me knees and not a single game o' dominoes from start to finish.'

The Standing Arms was a solid, ironstone building, so old that no one knew its origins, but cunningly placed by long-forgotten builders at the junction of Ringford's narrow main street and the even narrower lane which led over the hump-backed bridge to Bates's

End. In this strategic position, it welcomed villagers and visitors from all directions—from Ringford's nearest big town, Tresham, from its district administration of Bagley, from nearby villages of Fletching and Waltonby, and most magnetically of all from the houses and farms of Ringford itself. A number of these were situated round the spreading Green which had been the heart of the community since it had been commonly grazed three hundred years ago.

It was a very small community. Now that the farms employed at the most a couple of men, and families were reduced to a neat and manageable size, the total population hovered around two hundred. The increasing number of weekenders buying up old cottages and farmhouses had made the village seem even smaller. During the week it was common for the main street to be empty of any living thing except the Jenkins' terrier on the loose and perhaps old Fred stumping down the Gardens to the pub.

But there in the centre of the village, just to one side of the Green, and with its playground fronting the street, stood Round Ringford Church of England Primary School, its foundation commemorated on a stone plaque high up above a classroom window: 'Erected in 1868 by Charles William Standing, Lord of the Manor, for the Education of Children in the Faith and Practice of the Church of England.'

There were still Standings at Ringford Hall, and the vicar visited the school regularly every week to give a generally inattentive schoolroom a modern version of the faith and practice of the Church of England.

The school was the heart of the village. The children swarmed into the playground first thing in the morning, shouting and fighting and swapping insults, and at intervals during the day the quiet village was enlivened by children at play, children playing netball, children galumphing through country dances that their parents had done before them, and finally children rushing out to meet waiting mothers like long-term prisoners newly released. Numbers were small, averaging twenty-nine or so, but their comings and goings set the routine of the village day.

Miss Layton, the school's headmistress, was a small grey-haired woman with plain-rimmed spectacles and a thin, fine-boned face which managed to maintain a stern expression until she smiled, when she revealed the truly pretty girl who had come to Ringford thirty years before. She lived in the next village, Fletching, from choice. There was a pleasant schoolhouse available in Ringford, but Dot Layton had moved away from it when pressure from too close proximity to parents and children in her free time had made her life a misery.

Now she stood in the small school cloakroom, with its instantly recognisable

12

smell of old sweaty sports gear, disinfectant and assorted packed lunches in a pile of multi-coloured plastic boxes. She settled the children as they arrived, with coats to be hung on the right pegs and boots to be changed into soft shoes from drawstring shoe bags. Each child had his own wrought-iron peg, chipped and pitted from a hundred years' bashings from daily use, but recently freshly painted scarlet and bearing its tenant's name.

'No, no, Mrs Jenkins,' Miss Layton said coolly to a large, frizzy-haired woman standing on the doormat and blocking the entrance for others queuing up behind her. 'No, it's not a secret. I am retiring soon, but not leaving the area. I shall still be in my bungalow at Fletching, staying in touch, I hope.'

Dot Layton was respected not only for her legendary ways with recalcitrant small children, but for her uncomplaining devotion to a wheelchair-bound elder sister, who without doubt cramped her style and restricted her lifetime's ambition to travel to foreign lands.

'That's nice, anyway,' said Jean Jenkins, feeling pressure from behind and moving to one side of the narrow porch. 'But you'll be missed here, Miss Layton, that's for sure,' she said. 'Especially by our Mark.'

Dot Layton sighed. Mark Jenkins was a slow child, overweight like his mother, but with things going his way he had a pleasant nature

13

and an eagerness to learn, both of which she had carefully nurtured. She knew only too well both could disappear at a moment's discouragement. But Miss Layton was tired, fed up with increasing educational bureaucracy, and determined to explore life further while she was still able.

'I am sure the Governors will think of all the children when they appoint a new head, Mrs Jenkins, including your Mark,' she said firmly.

'Excuse me, Mrs Jenkins.' A slim, blonde woman, younger-looking than her thirty-eight years, squeezed through the porch and into the cloakroom.

'Sorry I'm a bit late, Miss Layton,' she said breathily, 'but Octavia couldn't find her music and we had a great panic before the school bus arrived.'

Parents, some reluctant to let go, eventually left the school playground, and the children found their places in the big classroom. It was ecclesiastical in feel. Tall windows at each end followed the arch of the roof, and the lofty interior was cool in summer and difficult to heat in winter. The old coke stove, which previously filled the room with fumes and a cosy warmth, had long been abandoned in favour of electric storage heaters, and these were not always adequate. Mothers had learned to wrap up their offspring well in really cold weather.

Each morning the children stood for a brief

14

and appropriate assembly, with Gabriella Jones, part-time teacher and mother of the wayward teenager, Octavia, playing the day's hymn on a jangling piano. This morning there was shuffling and whispering in the far corner where Mark Jenkins sat.

'Mark!' said Miss Layton sharply. 'If you have something urgent to say, please say it to all of us, otherwise be quiet.'

Mark exchanged a knowing smile with his neighbour, and shook his head. He had been about to confirm the rumour of Miss Layton's departure, but now sang the first verse of the morning hymn with guileless innocence.

The overheard conversation between his mother and Miss Layton would wait until playtime, when it could be released to a chosen few.

CHAPTER THREE

Bill Turner was a Round Ringford man, born and bred. He had done well at the village school and Tresham Grammar, but family fortunes had dwindled after the early death of his father, and he had left school at fifteen to work for the Standings at the Hall, giving most of his meagre earnings to his mother. A tall, steady man, healthy-looking, with salty blue eyes and a shock of thick grey hair, he had a good sense of humour and an air of reliability acquired early as the man of his family. He was a popular and essential part of Ringford, and he was very much in love with his new wife Peggy.

The fly in this apparently pleasing ointment was Bill's ex-wife, Joyce. For most of their married life, Joyce and Bill had led a miserable existence. After an early miscarriage, Joyce had become depressed and reclusive, blaming Bill for everything, and becoming obsessively jealous as the years passed.

As Ellen Biggs had said to her great friend and sparring partner, Miss Ivy Beasley, 'It were the final straw, Bill havin' it off with Peggy Palmer.'

Ivy Beasley, in her sixties and every inch a spinster, pretended ignorance. 'Don't know what you mean, Ellen,' she had said. But she had watched Joyce Turner return from psychiatric treatment at Merryfields Hospital, restored and in balance, and had had to admit that Joyce's decision had been the right one, to leave Bill, and surrender him to Ivy's arch enemy and neighbour, Peggy Palmer at the shop.

But Joyce was not far away, living with her sister over at Bagley, and now that Peggy and Bill had returned from the magical limbo of honeymoon, Bill began to glance up Macmillan Gardens as he passed, seeing the empty council house he had shared so

16

unhappily with Joyce, and find himself wondering where she was, what she was doing, whether she was happy.

Peggy, too, could not help thinking about Joyce. She had appeared only once in the shop, and had caught Peggy off guard. Cool and contemptuous, she had reduced the embarrassed Peggy to a stuttering mess, and Peggy had been greatly relieved when Joyce moved away out of the village.

Now Bill stood outside Fred Mills's house in the Gardens, his back to his forlorn, curtainless former home, chatting to the old man who was tying up a clematis which had been blown awry by the recent gales.

'Ad a good honeymoon, then, boy?' said Fred. He was muffled up in an old duffel coat, with a scarf knitted by a charitable Ellen Biggs wound several times round his scrawny neck. He was very old, so old that he could not remember his exact date of birth, and did not care. Bill looked at the wizened, pixy face, and felt a pang of anxiety that the old boy would not make another winter.

'Wonderful, thanks, Fred,' he said. 'Good weather, good food and a good wife. And plenty of good bird-watching, too. What more could a man ask?'

'That were the right kind o' bird-watching, I 'ope,' said Fred with a disgusting cackle.

'That's my business,' said Bill good-humouredly. 'Come on, you old devil, I'll buy

17

you a pint to warm you up. Then it's back to work for me.'

Fred Mills was out of his gate with surprising agility at this suggestion, and the two of them set off down the Gardens to the Standing Arms. As Bill glanced compulsively at the empty house, he was surprised to see two men coming out from the side gate. He stopped, but Fred was stumping on, a frothing pint squarely in his sights. Bill thought of asking Fred if he knew who they were, but decided against it. One question was enough to set off a train of gossip all round the village. He'd find out somehow else.

'Yep,' said Bill, 'the Scilly Isles are very beautiful, Fred, but look at that. Round Ringford takes a lot of beating.'

He was looking down Macmillan Gardens and over the Green to where the River Ringle flowed fast with winter water, glinting between its fringe of willow trees, disappearing under the stone bridge that led to Bates's End. Beyond the river lay the Hall park, dotted with sheep and spreading oaks, with the great house at its centre, solid and impressive.

'Just look at them kids,' Bill said. A line of scarfed and booted children, two by two, girls holding hands and boys deliberately not doing so, wound their nature studying way along the footpath leading to the bridge.

'Butter wouldn't melt,' said Fred. 'Takes you back, don't it. Though that school ain't nothing like it were in my day.'

'Just as well,' said Bill, pushing open the heavy door of the Arms, and ushering Fred into the warm, beer-smelling interior. The Standing Arms had originally been a humble alehouse, but generations of landlords had added their penn'orth of ambition, and now the main bar was a long, low-ceilinged room, well spliced with dark oak beams, and decorated with every conceivable brass or pewter object it was possible to acquire. Horse brasses, of course, but also bits of ancient harness, hunting horns, ale measure, candlesticks and candleholders, mugs and jugs of every size, dented and beaten plates and trays, all were polished to a cheerful twinkle by Bronwen Cutt, the landlord's sturdy and energetic wife. A row of terrifying guns—all clean and apparently ready for use against marauders—hung from the beams, and the bar itself was a great slab of oak adorned with a generous array of beer pump handles.

Bill Turner greeted Don Cutt, and turned to his companion with a smile. 'Now then, Fred,' he said, 'what are you going to have? Same as usual?'

*   *   *

'Sorry I'm late, gel,' said Bill, coming through the shop and into the cheerful kitchen, where Peggy had set out a crusty loaf and fresh

19

Cheddar. They had decided to have a quick snack at lunchtime, and then linger over a hot supper when the shop was shut and Bill's working day over. Although very comfortably in tune, physically and in shared experiences, good and bad, they were novices at living together, and new routines had to be established. This was a house where the business ruled. The shop was open all day, and the customer was always right.

'Don't worry,' said Peggy. 'There's nothing to spoil. Did Mr Richard find you? He was in the shop earlier, saying they'd got trouble with a tree fallen across the lane.'

'No—I mean, yes, I got it cleared away. No, it was old Fred. He was out in his garden fiddling about with his clematis, blue with cold. I took him down to the Arms for a pint to warm him up.'

Peggy looked at Bill. 'Very noble of you, I'm sure,' she said.

'Glad you see it that way, gel,' he said.

'So you'll not be wanting anything to eat?'

'Just a quick nibble before I get back to work,' said Bill, approaching Peggy and putting his arms around her.

The shop bell, jangling loudly, demanding attendance, split them up and brought Peggy into the shop, where to her surprise she found Miss Layton. It was not often the headmistress left her post during the day.

'Hello, Mrs Turner, welcome back. Did you

have a lovely time?' Dot Layton had been on many honeymoons in her dreams, always with the good-looking young airman to whom she had been engaged before he crashed out of her life one dark night so many years ago.

Peggy nodded. 'And what's this I hear about your retiring?' she said.

'That's why I'm here,' said Miss Layton. 'I thought if I told you the hard facts you could set the gossips straight and everyone would know exactly where they stand.'

Peggy had quickly accepted her role as sorting office for not only the village letters but also the stories which went round and round, greatly embellished as they went, bearing in the end little relation to the truth.

'I am taking early retirement,' said Miss Layton. 'To tell you honestly, Mrs Turner, I am really looking forward to it. Soldiering on to the bitter end is not my way, and I am not so old and incapable that I cannot see a useful and enjoyable retirement ahead.'

'And your sister?' said Peggy. A wheelchair-bound woman, not able to do much for herself, could cramp anyone's style.

'She is quite determined to go into Tresham House, if they'll have her.' Miss Layton turned away and looked out of the wide shop window and across the Green. The children were returning from their walk, crowding through the narrow iron gate into the playground. The wind blew their scarves and pony-tails, and

21

they were all colour and life. Miss Layton was silent for a few seconds, and then turned back to face Peggy.

'I've spent nearly a lifetime doing my duty, Mrs Turner,' she said, 'and now it's time to please myself. That probably sounds very heartless to you, but my sister is insistent, and I am accepting her decision with gratitude.'

This outburst from the heart touched Peggy, and she reached across and patted Miss Layton's small hand resting on the counter.

'Quite right,' she said. 'Absolutely the right decision. The village is right behind you, from what I've heard. Mind you, you'll be sorely missed.'

'Well, that's the next thing,' said Miss Layton. 'There'll be a new head appointed, probably younger and keener than myself, and I hope everyone will give her the support she'll need. It's not easy in such a small community, you know, and with so few children.' She recalled Mark Jenkins, slowly blossoming under her tender care, and felt a pang of guilt.

'That'll be the Governors' responsibility, then,' said Peggy. 'No doubt they'll bear everything in mind.' Bill was a Governor, and took his duties very seriously. She wondered if he was still in the kitchen, listening to all this.

'So there we are,' said Dot Layton, picking up a packet of part-baked croissants which were her regular treat on Sunday mornings, making her think of France, sunshine and sparkling seas. 'It will take a few months, but things are in train already, and I hope the changeover won't be too disruptive for the children.'

Bill came through from the kitchen, and nodded politely to Miss Layton. 'Afternoon,' he said. Miss Layton paid for her croissants and left, hurrying across the road and into the school playground. She picked up a small, red knitted glove from a puddle by the flagpole, shook drops of water from it, and disappeared quickly from sight.

'The children'll not be the only ones to feel disruption,' he said. 'What goes on in that school affects us all. Always has.' He kissed Peggy, shrugged on his work jacket, and left.

Peggy watched him retrieve his bike from the footpath at the side of the shop and set off across the Green, jolting up and down over the bumpy track, his hair wilder than usual in the keen wind. Some strand of her thoughts must have caught up with him as he skirted the big chestnut. He turned and waved in the general direction of the shop, wobbling and putting his foot down to the ground to steady himself.

See you tonight, Bill, said Peggy to herself, and felt the comforting warmth of his presence still with her. And, in spite of herself, she wondered why it had not been enough to comfort Joyce.

CHAPTER FOUR

Victoria Villa was a square, uncompromising red-brick house, detached and separated from Bill and Peggy Turner's Post Office Stores by a narrow strip of garden and a fence. Double-fronted, with shallow bay windows either side of the green-painted door, the house belonged to Miss Ivy Beasley, who kept her three steps well scrubbed, making sure that rainwater collecting in the worn hollows did not stay there long enough to turn green and slimy. A fierce sisal doormat defied visitors to forget to wipe their feet, and a shiny white china button on the doorframe said commandingly PRESS.

Miss Beasley was the latest and probably the last of generations of Beasleys who had lived there since anyone in the village could remember. Her parents had been in their forties when Ivy unexpectedly came along, and they brought her up in the fear of God and of offending their many rules and strictures. When they died, she had the house, good solid furniture and a nest egg in the bank, a small field to bring in a steady rent—small but useful—and a position in Ringford society. Ivy Beasley lived a blameless life. At least, that is what she frequently told her two friends, Ellen Biggs from the Hall Lodge, and Doris Ashbourne, previous owner of the Stores and

24

now living in an old person's bungalow in Macmillan Gardens. But as a renowned gossip and mischief-maker Ivy Beasley was feared and avoided by most of the village for the damage she could wreak. The three women met for tea each week, regular as clockwork, taking it in turns to be host and indulging in a certain amount of rivalry in the matter of home baking.

Today it was Ivy's turn, and Ellen Biggs was the first to arrive. She struggled up the steps and paused just inside the front door to take several deep breaths.

'I don't know, our Ivy,' she said, '’ow much longer I shall be able to carry on with these teas. It's all I can do to get over the Green, not to mention your steps—perfection as they are.'

Ivy frowned. She worried about Ellen and her increasing frailty, but would not show it. An ounce of help is worth a pound of pity, her mother used to say. Still did, on the occasions when she voiced her opinions, usually tart, inside Ivy's head. But this was when Ivy was alone in her quiet house.

Now she put her hand under Ellen's bony arm and helped her along the narrow hallway and into the immaculate, chilly front room. It was cheerless, in spite of good, heavy furniture and thick curtains which kept out winter draughts. But they excluded a great deal of light as well, as did lace drapes which were there to shield Ivy from inquisitive eyes.

25

Photographs of her late parents stared down at her from elaborate frames, alongside gloomy, mist-shrouded views of the Lake District and the Yorkshire Dales. In the bay window stood what Ellen Biggs called Ivy's 'watching chair,' which did indeed command a very fine view of most of the village.

'Is this all you got to heat this room, Ivy?' said Ellen crossly, warming her hands in front of a one-bar electric fire. 'What's wrong with yer fireplace, then? Got it blocked up for economy?'

Ivy was saved the need to match this by a knock on the front door, followed by a 'Yoo hoo!' and the appearance of Doris Ashbourne, a neat, smallish woman in a dark blue coat and Paisley headscarf. She peeled off navy leather gloves and untied her scarf, revealing short grey hair and a pleasant expression.

'I'm last, then, am I?' she said. 'It was that old Fred. Caught me on me way down, and I couldn't get away. I shall have to go down the other side of the Gardens in future. Brrr! It's cold in here, Ivy. You could do with lighting that fire.'

'Don't you start, Doris,' said Ivy Beasley. 'I haven't got money to burn like some, you know. Here, give me your coat, and then I'll make the tea.'

She disappeared, leaving the door open so that the other two couldn't discuss her without her knowing, and brought the kettle quickly to

26

the boil. She was back in no time at all, with delicate china cups and saucers, milk in a silver-plated jug and lump sugar in a matching bowl. Her mother and father had been prudent with their savings, stingy, some said, but old Mrs Beasley had prided herself on keeping a nice home.

'What you bin bakin' for us today, Ivy?' said Ellen. She turned to Doris Ashbourne. 'Not a bad cook, our Ivy. Mind you, she don't come up to Hall Lodge standards.' She laughed hoarsely, slapping her knee with a gnarled hand, knowing that Ivy and Doris would not have the heart to contradict her.

Ellen had been cook at the Hall for many years, finally moving to her grace and favour Lodge cottage. Not that there was anything graceful or favourable about it. It was damp, cold and smelled of the brick and earth floors on which her lino and threadbare carpets were laid. To give him his due, Mr Richard Standing had done his squirely duty and offered to improve her conditions, but she resisted all suggestions. 'It'll see me out, dear,' she had said cheerfully. But Ivy and Doris feared that it might well hasten her exit.

Ivy poured and handed round the tea. Ellen put in three lumps of sugar and stirred long and loudly.

'Leave some pattern on that cup, Ellen Biggs,' said Ivy.

'Don't nag,' said Ellen. 'Anyway, what you

got for our delectables today?'

She was beginning to feel a little anxious. There was usually a feathery light sponge sitting on a cakestand ready for their arrival, but today no sign of cake of any sort.

'Ah,' said Ivy with a bland look. 'Supposin' I didn't have time for baking today?'

'Oh, go on Ivy,' said Doris the peacemaker. 'Don't tease the poor old thing. Go and get it, whatever it is.'

Ivy sniffed and stood up. 'I'll have a look in the tins,' she said. 'Might be something left from last week.'

'Miserable old devil,' muttered Ellen, quite depressed. Her pension never seemed to stretch to luxuries of any kind, and she looked forward to Ivy's baking as her weekly treat.

'There you are, Ellen,' said Doris. 'Look at that!'

Ivy had returned, a small smile warming her stern face. She bore a large tray with a plate of perfectly risen scones, a dish of home-made strawberry jam, and a generous bowl of rich whipped cream.

'Ivy!' said Ellen, a dark red flush covering her deeply lined face. 'Well, you are an ole twicer!'

They were on to their second cups of tea when Doris dropped her bombshell. She had been waiting for the right moment, and judged it had come. Old Ellen had her swollen legs up on a footstool, and Ivy had drawn the curtains

28

across darkening windows.

'You know the Turners' old house,' Doris said.

'We should do by now, we've lived here long enough,' said Ivy sharply.

'Don't take no notice of 'er, Doris,' said Ellen. 'What was you goin' to say?'

Doris ignored Ivy and addressed herself to Ellen. 'Well, there were two men going in and out this morning, and I thought to myself it might be burglars, so I ought to go and make sure.'

'Very public-spirited of you,' said Ivy.

'They were very nice and said I'd done the right thing,' said Doris defensively, 'and said they were just checking what had to be done before the next people moved in.'

'What next people?' said Ivy quickly.

'Well, this is the bit you're never going to believe,' said Doris.

'Doris!' said Ivy warningly.

'It seems the next tenant of number fourteen is going to be the very same as the last.'

'Don't be ridiculous,' said Ivy, putting her cup down on the saucer with a rattle.

'Yes, they said for sure,' said Doris.

'Oh do get on with it, our Doris,' said Ellen, losing patience. 'What d'you mean?'

'Joyce Turner, Bill's ex-wife. That's who I mean. Except when she moves back in, she'll be Joyce Davie. Mrs Joyce Davie.'

The full dramatic effect of this news was lost

29

as Ellen Biggs choked on her last mouthful of scone and had to be sat up and thumped on the back by Ivy until she recovered.

'Well I never,' she said, finally finding her voice.

'I said so,' said Ivy smugly.

'No you never, Ivy Beasley,' said Ellen. 'You knew no more about it than I did.'

'I mean,' said Ivy, with exaggerated tolerance, 'that I knew she'd marry that Donald Davie, him she met in the hospital, soon as she'd got her divorce. I saw him once, when I took her shopping in Tresham, and it was there then, plain as a pikestaff.'

'What was there?' said Ellen.

'That look in their eyes,' said Ivy triumphantly. 'There was no mistaking it.'

Ellen shifted in her chair. 'I shall believe it when I see it,' she said. 'And as for looks in people's eyes, Ivy Beasley, I wouldn't put no trust in you to recognise true love if it stared you in the face. Which ain't likely. Now, Doris, are you goin' to see me 'ome?'

CHAPTER FIVE

Chairman of Round Ringford Church of England School Governors, the Reverend Nigel Brooks sat at the head of the long vicarage dining table. Not much dining was

30

done here now. The room had been designed for more gracious times, with a vicar who had private means, the younger son of neighbouring gentry with little religious conviction but an eye for a comfortable sinecure. Here grand supper parties were held, the food prepared by the vicarage cook and served by obedient maids. When Nigel Brooks and his wife moved in, they had spotted the spacious, high-ceilinged dining room as a place at last for the ancestral dining table that was much too big, but also too beautiful and valuable to send off to the saleroom without family consultation. But they had yet to eat a meal off it. Today, Nigel sat up one end, papers laid out neatly in front of him, glancing down the shining, polished length of mahogany.

Middle-aged and a little vain, a latecomer to the cloth, former solicitor Nigel Brooks had settled into the village after a somewhat shaky start. In common with many in his profession, he had taken on a new parish with plans for change and improvement. With little experience of village ways, he had come a cropper over the Christmas concert, organised by him and attractive Gabriella Jones, choir mistress and now part-time teacher at the school. But this had been put behind him, and he mistakenly thought all was forgiven and forgotten. It was neither, but the village had other concerns and had filed away the episode for future reference.

He had suggested the Governors' meetings take place in the vicarage in the winter to save on school heating bills, and Miss Layton had wholeheartedly agreed. With small village schools constantly under threat of closure, she had pursued a canny policy of spending only on essentials, never exceeding the budget and inviting no special attention from the county Education Department in Tresham.

'If we keep our heads down,' she had explained to Nigel Brooks when he first arrived in the village, 'we are more likely to escape notice. If the school balances its budget, makes no unreasonable demands, and does a good job, no authority in their right minds is going to close us down and give itself the headache of finding alternative places and expensive transport arrangements.'

So far this had worked. Round Ringford, along with a number of other small schools in the county, was under review, but although the Governors had supplied facts and figures asked for, nothing further had been heard for months.

Now Nigel Brooks looked around the table and was pleased to see that he had a full complement of Governors: Bill Turner; Jean Jenkins, parent nominee; Colin Osman, newly elected district councillor; Doreen Price, farmer's wife and church representative; and Mr Richard Standing, squire and hereditary owner of Ringford Hall. John Barnett, former pupil and now farming a sizeable chunk of the parish, had been co-opted for his common sense and local knowledge.

A little prayer for guidance in this turning point of the school's life opened the meeting, and a number of small matters were dealt with quickly before arriving at the main item on the agenda.

'I suppose there's no hope of persuading Miss Layton to stay on?' said Jean Jenkins tentatively.

Nigel Brooks shook his head, and Colin Osman, tall and fresh-faced, keen, brash and insensitive, interrupted vigorously.

'Time the old thing went, in my view,' he said. 'In many ways this school is fifty years behind the times, and a number of parents have spoken to me about the possibility of bringing it in line with current educational thinking.' Colin's first priority was always to have the right jargon, the fashionable phrase.

Bill Turner turned to look at Colin's eager, confident face. ' "The old thing" is not the way we describe Miss Layton here in Ringford,' he said quietly. 'She has been a wonderful teacher and more of a good influence in the village than people like yourself could possibly know.'

'Hear hear!' said Jean Jenkins stoutly. 'Well said, Bill. You and your friends, Mr Osman, would do well to look at results. Of course, with you havin' no kids, and that Walnut Close lot sending theirs to snobby private nurseries, or whatever they call them, you ain't likely to find out that our village school has an unbeaten record in results when they get on through Tresham Comprehensive. Just ask Mrs Price here, she'll tell you.'

Jean was hot with anger. She tried hard to be nice to the newcomers to the village, invited them along to the WI and other village activities, but again and again she found herself prickling with indignation at the nerve of the likes of Colin Osman.

Doreen Price, whose now grown-up daughter had spent happy infant years in the benign atmosphere of the village school, supported Jean Jenkins, but attempted to be fair.

'Miss Layton herself says it's time for somebody younger,' she said, 'so I don't think we are in total disagreement, Mr Osman. And anyway,' she added with her customary good sense, 'she's going. So we'd better get on with planning to appoint her successor.'

The Reverend Nigel Brooks sighed with relief. Good old Doreen, she could always be relied on to set things straight. He had followed his training in keeping quiet and encouraging the village to make its own decisions, but now he felt it was time to take the lead.

Advertisements in the right papers would be taken care of, and then short-listing and the all-important interviews must be arranged. It all took time, and the moon was up on a crisp, starlit night when the small group emerged onto the vicarage drive, buttoning their coats and winding scarves to keep out the chilly wind. They passed the dimly lit window of Ellen Biggs's Lodge and noticed the curtain pulled back a fraction as they went by. The end of the chestnut avenue up to the Hall was dark and shadowy, and Jean Jenkins tucked her hand through Bill Turner's arm with a shiver. They were soon out on the moonlit Green, and Colin Osman remarked that the witches were riding tonight—'Look,' he said, 'see the trails across the face of the moon.'

'Silly bugger,' said Bill, but only for Jean Jenkins's ears, and as she shook with suppressed mirth, he branched off on the footpath which led to the Stores.

CHAPTER SIX

'Move over, gel,' said Bill, easing a sleepy Peggy over to one side of the bed to make room for his own lanky frame. He was designed for a different kind of room, not this simple upstairs chamber with one small window, low-beamed ceiling and sloping floor made of wide, highly polished elm boards. Peggy had loved it the very first day she and Frank had come to see the Stores. With its view over the Green, and strange, lingering scent of geraniums, she had planned to have it all white—walls, bedcoverings, white curtains with small sprigs of forget-me-nots—and the low ceiling hadn't mattered to Frank. He was a small man. But Bill had to stoop through the latched door, and several times he had hit his head on the beam above their bed.

'Long meeting?' Peggy said, reaching towards him without opening her eyes.

'Went on a bit,' he said, kissing her gently, her forehead, eyes, the end of her nose, her mouth.

Wide awake now, Peggy tasted beer. 'So you ended the meeting in the pub, as usual, I suppose.'

'Naturally,' said Bill, feeling the wonderful warmth of her enveloping him. 'Most important part of any Ringford meeting, that is. Bit like the vicar saying grace.'

Peggy laughed aloud at this, and Bill knew he was on to a good thing.

A few blissful minutes later, an irritating intrusion in the form of loud, discordant catawauling caused Peggy to sit up in alarm.

'That was Gilbert!' she said. Gilbert was her she-cat, mistakenly named when very young, and she had been Peggy's chief comfort and companion in the bleak months after her first husband's death. Gilbert was very precious to Peggy, but Bill had known many cats and felt differently.

'So what?' he said indistinctly. 'She's out on the razzle and good luck to her, I say. Come on Peggy, she's fine. Pity she can't be a bit quieter about it, but she wouldn't thank you for interrupting.' The last bit sounded heartfelt.

'I'm sure you're right, Bill,' said Peggy, 'but I think I'll just nip down and make sure.' She pulled back the covers, and Bill groaned. He could hear her slippers clacking on the stairs and then the back door opened and shut.

'No sign,' said Peggy, jumping quickly back into bed and snuggling up. 'But old Ivy's bedroom light's still on. That's unusual, isn't it? Do you suppose she's all right?'

'How should I know?' said Bill, moving into top gear. 'Perhaps you'd like to bring her in with us, my lovely gel. Old Poison Ivy might just enjoy a bit of an orgy...'

*   *   *

Nigel Brooks sipped the cup of coffee his wife Sophie had handed to him as he came into the vicarage kitchen and slumped down in the old armchair by the Aga.

'Usual marathon?' she asked. Sophie was small, sharp-featured, with dark red hair liberally streaked with grey. She came from a well-heeled family in Yorkshire, had been happily at home in Nigel's legal world, but had not easily adapted to being a vicar's wife. There was an air of reserve about her that had kept the village at arm's length, an even longer arm than was usual in the circumstances.

'Oh, not too bad, thanks to Doreen,' Nigel said. 'Young Colin was his usual bumptious self, and Jean Jenkins rose to the bait as always. But they're a sensible bunch. Could be a lot worse. Imagine having Ivy Beasley on the Governors' board.'

'Poor Ivy,' said Sophie. 'I bet there's a heart of gold in there somewhere. She cares a lot about old Ellen Biggs, you know, though she hates to show it. I think she's really worried that Ellen is going downhill.'

Nigel nodded, but his three parishes were well supplied with old people in various stages of decay, and he was always deceived by Ellen Biggs's cheerful front.

'We shall see,' he said. 'Meanwhile, I have to prepare the village for a new headteacher. No easy task, I suspect, if things prove anything like as traumatic as when we moved in here.'

'Needn't have been that traumatic,' said Sophie quietly. But Nigel was rummaging in the kitchen-table drawer and did not hear her.

'What did you do with those pitch pipes Millie used to have when she was learning the guitar?' he said. Their daughter Millie was now married and living in Paris, but she had tried most musical instruments at school and relics of those days were to be found in odd corners around the house.

'I thought I saw Eddie Jenkins playing with

38

them when Jean brought him up last week,'
Sophie said. 'Anyway, what do you want them
for?'

'I promised Octavia Jones she could have
them,' said Nigel, his face turned away from
her and shielded by a cupboard door. 'She's
having a go at classical guitar.'

Sophie stared at him, trying to catch his eye.
But he didn't look at her, and she contented
herself with saying, 'Just watch it, Nigel. That's
all. Just watch it.'

* * *

Mr Richard Standing had said little at the
Governors' meeting. He was anxious to get
home and report on the new deal he had fixed
up with his brother over at Fletching. They
dabbled in property development, selling off
parcels of family land here and there to raise
enough cash to keep the estate going.

Ringford Hall was one of the county's
loveliest grand houses. Built in the local yellow
mellow stone in the eighteenth century, it had
weathered to a warm dark ochre. A stone
terrace ran along the front aspect, and long
windows looked out on to the pleasant park,
dotted with beech and oak trees placed
apparently at random, but with artful care by a
long-dead landscape designer. Rumour was
that the great Capability Brown had had a
hand in it, but Richard Standing never

confirmed or denied the rumour. The possibility sounded good, and if it wasn't true, what did it matter? At one time the entire village had been employed in the Hall or on its land, and there were still memories in the old people's minds of a benevolent, patriarchal family, who knew them all and cared for them throughout their lives.

'All right,' said Fred Mills, 'so we 'ad to live in tied cottages, and relied on the Standings for just about everythin' we could expect in life. But you felt safe. You knew there was always someone over you. We looked up to them, yer know. Never thought nothing of it. None of your equal rights in them days. Lookin' back, it were better all round, I reckon.'

He had been talking to Colin Osman in the pub at the time, and the younger man had given him a lecture on poor conditions in the agricultural classes of the eighteenth and nineteenth centuries. But Fred's attention had wandered. He was keeping an eye open for a chance to get in on the dominoes school in the corner.

Members of the agricultural classes now at the Hall were restricted to Bill Turner, who managed the estate, Foxy Jenkins, husband of Jean and father of five growing children, and a few young lads from the village who were glad of some occasional work during the busy seasons of lambing and harvest. Mr Richard himself loved the property and felt very strongly the family's historical connections with the village. He kept up a lively interest in the management of the gardens and tenant farms, but he was well aware that it was Bill Turner who ran the place and made all the decisions.

When Richard reached home, he found his wife Susan in a comfortable armchair under a brooding portrait of one of his ancestors, deeply immersed in a television programme. She held up a hand to him as he came in and he kissed it gallantly.

'Hello, darling,' he said. 'All well? Poppy asleep?' Poppy was their late and much loved last child, and had cemented the two together after years of a somewhat rackety relationship.

Susan nodded, and Richard said, 'Saw James today. I think the Waltonby deal will go through...'

Susan held a finger to her lips and continued to watch the screen. 'Just got to the exciting part,' she said. 'I would really love a nice creamy cup of cocoa, darling.'

Richard nodded, and went off down the long passage and through the green baize door to the kitchen, where he filled the kettle and began to heat a small saucepan of milk. As he waited for it to boil, he looked round the great, empty kitchen and remembered it as it was when Ellen Biggs was Cook and he a small boy sneaking in for a snack from her stack of cake tins in the larder. His parents had been hospitable, and there were always weekend parties, with the guest rooms full of secret squeals of laughter. He sighed. Those old copper saucepans would fetch a good price at auction, he thought. We never use them now. And Susan was always nagging him about replacing the deep stone sink and heavy cupboards. He'd resisted, reluctant to erase all traces of his childhood. Thank goodness now they'd got Poppy, Susan seemed to have given up for a while. The hissing milk, boiling over and bubbling on the hot stove, brought him rapidly back to the present, and he made one cup of cocoa which he put on a small tray, alongside a heavy crystal glass half-full of whisky and water.

*   *   *

Doreen Price found her husband Tom fast asleep in the sitting room of Hall Farm, in front of the same television programme. She quietly switched it off and planted a kiss on top of his balding head. He grunted and woke up, muttering something unintelligible as he surfaced.

'What did you say, dear? Were you asleep?' said Doreen. Her square body filled the armchair opposite, and she patted her neat brown hair into place needlessly. It fell obediently into a short, wavy bob that had been Doreen's style since she left school.

'Course not,' said Tom, 'I was just thinking.

Heard you come in ages ago. How did the meeting go?'

Doreen could not be bothered to say she had only just returned, and what's more, deep, reverberating snores usually indicated someone sound asleep. She gave Tom a quick outline of the meeting and then went on to what was really bothering her.

'Do you know, Tom,' she said, 'when I came past Ivy Beasley's house, there was a light on in her bedroom.'

'She's every right to put her bedroom light on, ain't she?' Tom had a bad taste in his mouth, and was hoping Doreen would go and make a last cup of tea.

'It's not usual,' said Doreen. 'Ivy Beasley is always in bed by ten o'clock, and it struck half past on the church clock as I went by. It's not at all usual,' she repeated, and went off, frowning, to lock up the heavy oak farmhouse doors and fill hot-water bottles for their large and comfortable bed.

*   *   *

In her tidy, clean bedroom, Ivy Beasley sat bolt upright, scarcely wrinkling the perfectly ironed sheets. It was the same room she had had since childhood, a narrow cell-like space with an iron-framed bed, a long thin wardrobe with no looking-glass and a glass-topped dressing table which had no adornments except for a large pot of multi-purpose cream and a tortoiseshell-backed hairbrush given to her by a long-dead aunt. She could easily have moved into her parents' front bedroom and the high double bed, but she had not even considered it. The only frivolous item in Ivy's bedroom was on the narrow mantelshelf over the black cast-iron fireplace: a china figure of a lady in snood and pink crinoline, bought from a jumble sale by Ellen Biggs and received with bad grace by Ivy Beasley one Christmas.

Propped up on a couple of pillows, her hair pinned up and anchored with a hairnet, Ivy had put on her late mother's pink lacy bedjacket and opened her book. But tonight she could not get into the plight of dark and lovely Sheena, trapped in a gaunt castle on the coast of Ireland, with no one but the seagulls and mysterious, cleft-chinned Sir Clive Fitzgerald for company. Ellen Biggs kept entering her thoughts, and the tired old face, with its pain lines around the mouth, swam up before her and obscured the print.

I shall have to speak to Doris, she thought. Much good that'll do you, said her mother's sharp voice in her head. That Doris Ashbourne was always one for keeping herself to herself.

That's not true, Mother, said Ivy. She tried hard to help after you'd gone and that Peggy Palmer—I mean Turner—speaks very well of how Doris helped with the changeover at the shop.

44

Ivy would not have admitted virtue in Doris to anyone but her mother, and then it was in retaliation. But she did respect Doris's judgement, and resolved to sound her out on what they could do to make Ellen Biggs's lot a bit easier.

Silly old devil won't accept any help, though, that's the trouble, she thought. Who does that remind you of, said her mother.

Don't know what you mean, said Ivy, and focused once more on her book.

This time it was Joyce Turner, soon to be Davie, who took her place in Ivy's tired brain. Could be awkward, Mother, Joyce coming back to Ringford. Mind you, that Bill and his floozy wife deserve a bit of trouble to muddy the waters. Too happy by half, they are.

I'm sure you'll think of something, Ivy, said the sly voice.

And then there's Miss Layton going. Some new flibbertigibbet will come in her place, I expect. And that'll be more trouble, no doubt.

Ivy Beasley, if you don't put out the light and go to sleep you'll feel the rough end of my stick.

'Don't be silly, Mother,' said Ivy aloud, as she reached for the light-switch. 'Don't think I don't know perfectly well that you're dead.'

CHAPTER SEVEN

Joyce Turner sat on the bus which wound its way from Bagley, through quiet, empty villages, bleak, winter fields and tunnels of bare, wind-blown trees, to Round Ringford, where she intended to live with her second husband, Donald Davie. For years she had been a slovenly, unattractive recluse, caring nothing for her appearance. In fact, she had deliberately become a slattern, often not bothering to wash for days, to revenge herself on Bill for all the sins of which she imagined he was guilty.

But now, as she stood up to leave the bus at Ringford Green, she looked a different woman. Thin still, but with good legs and neat ankles, she was dressed in good, quiet taste, and her pepper-and-salt curly hair had been cut to flatter her well-shaped head. Her hazel eyes were everywhere, taking in the small group of people waiting for the bus, the children out for playtime, shouting and screaming as they linked arms and skittered round the great sycamore tree in the playground. She noticed Jean Jenkins emerging from the shop, firmly holding a squirming Eddie, and saw Doreen Price driving off in her battered Vauxhall estate, the spattered mud all but obscuring her rear window.

'Morning, Mrs Biggs,' Joyce said, smiling to herself at the astonished look on old Ellen's face.

Joyce stood on the pavement looking around, in no hurry, the whole day ahead of her to plan exactly what she was going to do with number fourteen, Macmillan Gardens. Donald had not been at all sure that it would be right for them to live in the house where she had been so unhappy with Bill, but Joyce was quite determined. 'We shall be fine, Donald,' she had said, 'and anyway, I have unfinished business in Round Ringford.'

Donald, a widower and a mild man, had been drawn to Joyce in Merryfields Hospital where both had been patients. He thought Joyce's remark a little odd. But he was so glad to have a quiet companion who knew what it was like to be alone and totally unable to cope, that he humoured her and went along with negotiations with the Council, and her plans for redecorating and furnishing.

'We'll start again, Donald,' she had said. 'Let's sell all your furniture, and mine, and buy new. It will be a fresh beginning for both of us. Please say yes...'

Donald Davie had some good pieces which he and his late wife had collected and looked after with loving care, but he hadn't the heart to deny Joyce, and anyway, he thought she was probably right. Joyce could be very persuasive, he'd already discovered that. Joyce took a final look up and down the street, and crossed the road, hesitating outside the Stores, reading the posters in the window. Then she said, 'No, not yet,' to herself, and walked off towards the Gardens.

*　　　*　　　*

'God, was that...?' Peggy strained to look out of the shop window at the retreating figure, small and neatly dressed and vaguely familiar. Her only customer in the shop was Ivy Beasley, who came out from behind the display of biscuits and followed Peggy's shaking finger.

'Ah, yes, Mrs Palmer—I mean Turner—' she said, 'that was indeed the other Mrs Turner. But then you'd not be too familiar with her, would you, except for what you've heard. And there are two sides to every story, you know,' she added darkly.

Why did Poison Ivy have to be in the shop just now, thought Peggy. She tried to collect herself, and put Miss Beasley's packet of chocolate biscuits in a white paper bag. I'll have to get rid of her as quickly as possible and see if Doreen knows why Joyce is here, she thought.

'Is that all then, Miss Beasley?' she said, pushing the biscuits across the counter.

'Giving them away today, are we?' said Ivy.

'Oh no, sorry,' said Peggy, confused. 'That

will be seventy-five pence, please.'

Ivy Beasley handed over the exact money, and turned to go. Then she stopped and looked hard at Peggy.

'I expect you've heard,' she said.

'Heard what?' said Peggy, her heart sinking.

'That Joyce Turner is getting married again, and coming back to live in her old house in Ringford.' Ivy paused, allowing time for this to sink in. Then she continued. 'Folk will be pleased about that. We don't like to see a house standing empty.' She was rewarded by Peggy's shocked expression, and smiled a small smile to see her grab at the counter with shaking hands.

'Good morning,' said Ivy brightly, opening the door and stepping out into winter sunshine. She nodded at a passing car, transferred her shopping bag from one hand to another and shaded her eyes from the sun. 'It's turned out quite nice after all, hasn't it,' she said, looking back at Peggy with what could only be called a smirk.

CHAPTER EIGHT

Joyce Turner had walked deliberately slowly past the shop, intending to be seen. She had glanced up at the window and noticed a poster for a Village Auction coming up shortly. She made a mental note of the date. Could be useful, that, she thought, and took a short cut across Macmillan Gardens, avoiding a large puddle and sinking into wet grass before she reached number fourteen on the other side. This square of grass and flower-beds were maintained by Fred Mills, had been for years, but now he was finding it difficult to cope. The long, matted tufts should really have had one last cutting before winter set in. In the flower-beds, dead antirrhinums drooped over rusty, flowerless cushions of alyssum. Who'll do it when Fred's gone? thought Joyce, and realised she was thinking like a Ringford woman again.

She pushed open the small iron gate which led into her front garden. It swung to behind her and she was immediately assailed by memories of Bill slamming out of the house and riding off on his bike to get away from her hysterical nagging. The memory was so clear and sharp, and yet seemed to have happened to someone else, not Joyce as she was now.

But that Joyce is still inside me somewhere, she thought, and shivered a little. Please God, don't ever let her come back. All Joyce's counselling and treatment had enabled her to see what an appalling situation she had created for Bill and herself. And yet, deep inside, she was still quite certain that it had not been all her fault. Nothing is ever just one person's fault in a failed marriage, she said defensively to herself.

The key turned easily in the lock. Bill must

have oiled it. In the bad old days, when she never went out, not even into the garden, she always knew when Bill was coming in, from the scraping sound of the lock, the key turning reluctantly.

An unpleasant smell of damp plaster and drains greeted her. Well, she thought with irritation, you'd have thought he'd have kept an eye on the place, just for the sake of the next people. I wonder if he knows the next people are us? Bill had never met Donald, and she could not imagine two more different men: Bill, a great hefty countryman, cheerful and quick-witted, capable and popular with everyone; and Donald, small and slender, gentle and shy, leaving all decisions to Joyce and wanting no one but her for company.

It will be quite a meeting, she thought, and smiled. And then she nearly jumped out of her skin when a voice from upstairs called out 'Who's there? What do you want?'

Ah, thought Joyce, well, that's neat. I know who you are, Bill Turner, I'd know that voice anywhere. She said nothing, waiting for him to come clattering down the uncarpeted stairs.

'Joyce!' His face seemed to get thinner as she looked at him. All his ruddy colour drained away, and he put his hand out to steady himself on the banister.

'Oh dear,' said Joyce. 'I'm sorry if the sight of your former wife has this effect on you. I didn't mean to startle you. The Council man

51

said I could come in at any time.'

'But whatever for?' said Bill. He looked at Joyce standing in the middle of the empty sitting room where they had had so many fights, where she had thrown ornaments and pictures and crockery at him. She was quite collected, smiling a little, neat and attractive, and no longer anything to do with him. But no, that was not quite true. Those years would never be erased, could never be totally forgotten.

'What for?' said Joyce. 'Haven't you heard, Bill? Donald and me are coming to live here, after we're married. The happy occasion is next week, but I don't suppose you'd want to come. Wouldn't be proper, would it. And I'm sure your lady wife Peggy would not think much of it.'

She wondered if Bill would ever speak. The silence stretched on, and she heard the church clock strike, the old familiar sonorous chimes, and a shout of laughter from Eddie Jenkins next door.

'Well, Bill,' she said, smiling, 'if you'll excuse me I've a lot to do here. Donald and me intend to gut the place, get everything fresh and clean, have everything new. You won't recognise it, I can promise you.'

But I'll always recognise you, Joycey, Bill thought in private distress. This is how it should have been, you and me living sensibly in peace, growing old gracefully together.

'Oh, shit!' he said, and turned on his heel.

Joyce heard the door slam and gate clang shut, just as it always had. Her smile was still in place.

*   *   *

'I can see you've heard,' said Peggy. She watched Bill walk slowly into the shop, his face troubled.

'Yep, I've heard,' he said, 'from the horse's mouth, in a manner of speaking.'

'You saw Joyce.' It was more of a statement than a question.

'Yes, she came into our old house. I was upstairs fixing a dripping tap in the bathroom, and I heard somebody downstairs. When I came down, there she was, standing there. Smiling.'

Peggy was silent for a moment, and then came round from behind the counter. She put her arms round Bill, holding him close. She buried her face in his broad, comforting chest, smelled the wood he'd been sawing for the Standings, a sharp, living smell, pleasant and clean.

'It'll be hard, Bill,' she said. 'Joyce living in Ringford, coming in and out of the shop—at least, I suppose she will, with nothing more for us to hide—passing me in the street, sitting behind me at the WI. Always there, always a reminder. Why? Why does she want to do it?'

Bill shook his head. 'Search me,' he said. He hugged her tight, unable to give any optimistic explanation for what seemed such contrary behaviour. He kissed the top of her head, and she stroked the back of his neck in mutual consolation. The bell over the shop door sprang into life, and a rush of cold air heralded a customer.

'Oops!' said Joyce. 'Perhaps I should go out and come in again. Sorry to interrupt, I'm sure.' But she still had that smile on her face, and didn't look in the least sorry.

CHAPTER NINE

The Village Auction had been Colin Osman's idea, like many innovations in Round Ringford since the Osmans had moved in. Initially, like his other bright ideas, the auction had been greeted with scorn and apathy. 'Who does he think he is?' said Ivy Beasley. 'Good question, Ivy,' said Ellen Biggs, as they studied the poster together. 'Reckon he fancies himself standing up there with a gavel in his hand, raising the bidding with a few merry quips,' said Doris Ashbourne. 'Merry *whats*?' said Ellen Biggs, bringing the conversation to an end.

Pat Osman had counselled caution. 'People are funny about their belongings,' she said.

'You're bound to get trouble. Some of these village folk think just because their tatty furniture is old, it must be valuable. I blame those antiques telly programmes. Now everyone thinks they've got buried treasure in their attic.'

'Funny way of putting it, my dear,' Colin had replied, not at all sweetly. It seemed to him that whatever he suggested, Pat criticised. Still, she usually came round, worked with a will and conscripted her friends where necessary. Just had to make him suffer first, he had thought grumpily.

Now, a week before the event, the Village Auction was meticulously planned and prepared. Colin had worked out percentages and rules for minimum fees for anything to be auctioned. 'Should make a nice little profit for the playing fields,' he said, collating papers and lot numbers. All items for auction would be handed in on Friday. He'd decided to take the day off and be there at the Village Hall to receive the lots. All had to be numbered and listed, and he and Pat would work like the clappers all Friday evening typing and stapling the catalogues. He had no idea how many lots would turn up, but from the enthusiasm which had grown steadily since he put up the posters, he hoped it would be a good show.

Friday was fine, but cloudy, overcast. Colin collected the Village Hall key from the shop, acknowledged Peggy's good luck wishes with gratitude, and went to open up. Yesterday had been more than gratifying. Contributions for the auction had begun slowly—first to arrive had been old Fred Mills with an ancient wood-framed tennis racket. 'Bin up in the cupboard for years, boy,' he'd said. 'Might be good enough for a beginner, d'yer think?' Only place for that is in a museum, thought Colin. But he smiled and gave it lot number one, and listened to Fred's reminiscences of tennis tournaments in the village long ago, which was the real reason Fred had brought the racket in.

The hall had gradually filled up, and some curiosities had emerged. With seventy-five per cent going to the seller, all they needed was a good audience and a few dealers, and people should be more than satisfied. A lovely glass-fronted cabinet had been brought in by Tom Price's cousin from Waltonby, and old Ellen Biggs had mysteriously produced a very delicate china jug, Crown Derby it said on the bottom. 'An heirloom?' Colin had said. Ellen hadn't answered, just looked sly. Colin had heard of her habit of collecting up trifles from the Hall, things turned out by the Standings, and sometimes items not quite finished with, but not readily missed. There'd been a rumpus at a jumble sale two or three years ago, when a valuable vase had appeared on the bric-a-brac stall. Richard Standing had been apoplectic, and Ellen had kept her head down, but she'd been behind the whole thing. Colin found himself hoping the Standings wouldn't come.

It had been soon after lunch that a woman walked in, a stranger to Colin, with a small, scholarly-looking man with glasses and a worried expression. 'Good afternoon,' Colin had said encouragingly from his reception table. Things were going well, the hall more than half full of all kinds of items already, and Colin was feeling benevolent. 'Do you have something for the auction?' he said.

'Afternoon,' said the woman. The man hung back a little, glancing fearfully around the hall. 'Yes, we've got quite a few things outside in a van. Can you give us a hand?'

When the van had been unloaded, the Village Hall was completely full. Chairs and tables, glass, china, cutlery, bedlinen and ornaments, all had been lifted from the van and grouped together for Colin to list. It was as if an entire houseful of belongings had been turned out. Perhaps a relative had died, thought Colin. He didn't like to ask, especially as the woman seemed so cheerful. It could have been the man's mother: *he* didn't look so happy. And there were some very good things amongst the lots.

'Right,' said Colin, making out the receipt and addressing the woman, who seemed to be in charge. 'Now, what name is it?'

'Turner,' said the woman. 'Joyce Turner. At least, it is at the moment. But perhaps you'd better put Davie—that's Donald here—to save confusion.'

She was well aware of the effect this had on Colin Osman, and smiled broadly as she took her receipt and left, with Donald Davie in tow.

*　　*　　*

'It was extraordinary,' Colin said to Pat, when they finally got to bed that night. 'Where do you think it all came from? Loads of it, and all clean and good. Some of the old pieces were real antiques, and should make good prices.'

'Did you say "Turner"?' Pat said.

Colin settled into his pillow and grunted. 'Bill's ex-wife,' he said, 'and the little chap would be her intended. All very odd ...' He relaxed and began to whiffle gently.

Everything had been done. Colin was an excellent organiser, and Pat had typed until the ends of her fingers were sore. The thick pages of the catalogues were laboriously stapled together, the lot numbers stuck on, and the hall safely locked up for the night. Viewing would be from nine o'clock next morning, and the sale itself would begin at one o'clock. 'But everybody'll be having lunch,' Pat had protested, but then agreed that if they were to be finished at anything like a respectable time, they'd have to start early.

'Doreen and her WI ladies are doing tea in the hall kitchen,' Colin had replied. 'People'll just have to bring sandwiches.'

The bedroom was dark and peaceful. With the pleasant exhaustion of one who has worked hard and knows a good job has been done, Pat began to drift. And then Colin suddenly sat bolt upright. Cold panic had penetrated his sleep. He clutched Pat, warm and sweet-smelling beside him. 'Oh God!' he said. 'Suppose nobody comes! All that stuff, and nobody to buy it—what shall we do?'

Pat put her arms round him soothingly. 'Don't be an old silly-billy,' she said. 'They'll be queuing up.'

*   *   *

Colin woke at five o'clock and tried not to disturb Pat as he turned to and fro in an effort to get back to sleep. Was that rain he could hear on the window panes? The forecast had been good. Rain would certainly put some people off turning out for the auction. Or was it birds in the eaves? He tried relaxing, starting from the top of his head, then his face, shoulders, arms, just as he had been taught by that idiot at the yoga classes. That had been one of Pat's many enthusiasms, but he had found the relaxing technique quite useful on occasion. Such as now. But it didn't work this time, and he very carefully put one foot on the floor and eased himself out of bed. He had to look to see if it was raining.

It wasn't. There was a brisk wind blowing

the poplars outside the bedroom window, and the sound was like rain. Colin crept to the door and very carefully opened it without a sound.

'Where are you going, Colin?' Pat raised her head from the pillow and looked blearily at him.

'Sorry, Pat, just need a pee.'

'You don't fool me,' she said. 'Been awake for hours, haven't you. Well, you might as well go down and make us a cup of tea. I don't suppose I shall go back to sleep now.'

Colin disappeared, and Pat propped herself up on the pillows. She could see it was quite light outside, that cold, unwelcoming light of early morning. The bedroom was warm and friendly, with pink light coming from the bedside lamps, and all their familiar things around them. Just us two, she thought. And then unbidden Joyce Turner came into her mind. How could she dismantle her home, without a backward look? Still, I suppose if life had been awful with Bill, those things would hold nothing but unhappy memories. But they must have been happy once...

'Here we are then,' said Colin, coming in with a tray.

'You are a love,' said Pat. 'Don't ever leave me, will you.'

Colin looked at her, astonished. 'Why on earth do you say that?' he said.

'No reason,' said Pat. 'Well, nothing much.'

Colin got back into bed, and they sat

companionably drinking tea and chatting idly about the auction. 'Anyway,' said Colin, 'thanks to Joyce Turner we have more than enough to make a really good sale.'

'I know,' said Pat. 'It's a bit sad, though, isn't it.'

Colin looked at her, and leaned over to kiss her cheek. 'Ah,' he said, 'now I know why you said that.'

*   *   *

'You go down to the viewing,' said Peggy at breakfast. 'If there's anything you fancy, we can hurry down after the shop's shut—or you can go down first—or we can leave a bid.'

'Any of those,' said Bill, smiling at her fondly. 'And anyway, there's only one thing I fancy . . .'

'Bill Turner,' said Peggy, 'it's twenty minutes to opening time, and I've a business to run.' But she smiled. Goodness, Frank had never said such things, or done such things, come to that. Poor old Frank.

All morning in the shop, Peggy's customers had come in with tales of fantastic bargains to be had down at the auction, so long as no one else knew their worth. 'Tom says the dealers'll be there,' Doreen had said, putting trays of new-laid eggs carefully down on the counter. 'Ten dozen there, Peggy,' she said, 'and more on Monday if you need them.'

'Hope the dealers won't cream off all the

61

good things,' said Peggy. 'Bill's gone down to look, but we really don't need anything. All his furniture and things—what was left after Joyce's smashing sessions—went to Joyce. And of course Frank and I had everything we needed here.' A shadow crossed her face for a fleeting second and was gone.

'We collect a lot of junk over the years, Peggy,' said Doreen gently. She was the only one who could see that Peggy's happiness was not totally untroubled. It was Doreen who had stood by Peggy during the awful time of Frank's death, and she had grown fond of her, got to know her very well. 'Well,' she said, taking empty egg trays from Peggy, 'I shall be there for a bit of fun. Shan't buy anything, mind, but it should be good for a laugh.'

As she turned to go, the shop door burst open and Bill stalked in, a deep frown on his face. He walked straight past, seeming not to see Doreen standing there, wide and solid, smiling at him. 'Morning, Bill,' she said, took one look at his face, and left.

What's upset him? she thought, going down the shop steps. And then the sight of Michael Roberts chasing one of Tom's sheep, escaped from the field and going at full trot, put everything else out of her mind.

*   *   *

'It was such a shock,' said Bill. He sat in the

62

kitchen in front of an untouched omelette, his hands held tight in his lap.

'Are you sure they were yours?' Peggy said.

Bill nodded. 'What's more,' he said painfully, 'some of that stuff was Mum's. Not that any of it was worth anything, but, well ...' He tailed off, his face full of hurt.

'Why did she have to sell it here?' said Peggy. She could not believe anyone could be so insensitive. Maybe Joyce had her reasons for getting rid of her furniture, but why here in Round Ringford, where Bill was sure to recognise it? The only conclusion was a tough one. Joyce had calculated the whole thing, Bill's pain and all. It was revenge, and it was pretty nasty. Peggy felt totally powerless. All she could do was persuade Bill not to go to the auction.

'Oh no,' said Bill. 'I'm going. And if Joyce is there, I'll make sure she sees I'm not upset.'

Peggy reached out and put her hand over Bill's clenched fist. 'Then I'm coming with you,' she said.

CHAPTER TEN

The Village Hall was already full when Peggy and Bill pushed their way in at the back. With so much entered for auction, there was little room for bidders. This was something Colin had overlooked, in spite of all his planning, and he rapidly pushed and shoved chairs under tables, piled a coal scuttle and a rosy jerry on top of an apparently new washing machine, moved garden tools and a rusty wheelbarrow out into the yard to be brought in at the end of the sale, and finally squeezed everybody in. Pat had been right. There had been a queue, all village people and their friends and relations jolly and teasing, to greet him when he arrived at the hall at twelve thirty prompt.

Dogged and immovable, Fred Mills had settled himself in the most comfortable armchair, and Ivy, Doris and Ellen were perched on a row of dining chairs which Ivy had recognised instantly as formerly belonging to Joyce. There had been some muttering between the three on this subject, and now their eyes were everywhere, spotting other items from the Turner home.

Joyce herself stood to one side of the hall, close to Donald, whose face was expressionless, like someone in shock. As Bill and Peggy settled a couple of rows from the front, Joyce stared at them and when Bill met her gaze she nodded her head a fraction and her eyes narrowed.

Raised up on a very solid dining table—not a Turner one, this, but from the same Price cousin at Waltonby—sat Colin Osman, papers on a rickety card table in front of him, borrowed gavel in hand, and having every

64

appearance of a man who did this kind of thing every day.

'Lot number sixteen,' he said, looking round the assembled crowd with a satisfied smile. His only regret so far was that there seemed to be no dealers present. Still, he'd heard there was a big country house sale over the other side of Fletching, so they were probably there. 'A very fine chamber pot, made in Staffordshire, like all the best ceramics, with a design of cabbage roses. Now, ladies and gentlemen, what am I bid for this very fine gazunder?'

'What's he on about?' whispered Ellen Biggs to Doris Ashbourne. 'Just an ordinary ole jerry. My ma used to 'ave one just like it.'

'Come along now,' said Colin. 'Who'll start me off at a pound?'

'Fifty pence,' said Doris Ashbourne, and her face flamed a hot scarlet.

Ellen stared at her. 'What you want that thing for, Doris?' she said loudly.

Doris ignored her, concentrating on her bid. 'Any other bids?' said Colin, his hand in the air. He couldn't waste time on small lots which were unlikely to make much money. 'Got to get on, ladies and gentlemen,' he said. 'No more bids? Then lot number sixteen is going ... going ... gone! Sold to Mrs Ashbourne, over there on the left.'

'Never know when it could come in handy,' said Doris, subsiding like a deflated balloon.

Pat sat below Colin at the table, writing

furiously, keeping an accurate record of bids and bidders. Lots came and went, and some made ridiculously small amounts whilst others rose and rose until there were gasps of amazement as Dot Layton's old oak chest made enough money to finance her first retirement trip abroad.

Peggy's face was blank. She could feel the misery in Bill, standing like a ramrod at her side, but she said nothing. Colin's jokes—some of them quite funny—left both of them stony-faced. Peggy slipped her hand into Bill's as the lot numbers crept towards the symbols of his and Joyce's married life. He squeezed her hand, and she heard him sigh. He looked down at her and smiled, a wan effort, but a smile all the same.

'Now, we come to a number of lots which will, I know, create some confident bidding,' said Colin. He could not help glancing at Joyce, and heard Pat sniff loudly behind him.

'A fine three-piece suite,' said Colin. 'Chintz covers in good condition, and cushions to match. Will someone start me off at a hundred pounds?'

Silence. Not a single bid. Joyce's face fell, and she looked quickly at Donald. He remained staring straight ahead.

'Come along, now,' said Colin, puzzled. 'Let's get started, ladies and gentlemen!'

'Five pounds,' said Peggy Turner, and felt Bill start. He turned and stared at her. 'Peggy!'

he said.

'Did you say five pounds, Peggy?' said Colin, playing for time.

Peggy nodded her head. 'Right,' said Colin, 'now let's get going to something a bit more realistic for this fine sofa and chairs.'

But there were no more bids, and the suite was knocked down to a bland-faced Peggy Turner. Bill frowned furiously, and tried to pull Peggy out of the hall. But she stood her ground, signalling him to stay put.

One after the other, in an atmosphere charged with tension, Joyce's furniture, ornaments, linen, all her worldly goods whilst married to Bill, came under the hammer and were knocked down for ridiculously low amounts to Peggy Turner, Doreen Price and occasionally to Sophie Brooks, the vicar's wife. The very nice antique pieces which were Donald Davie's made very respectable sums commensurate with their worth. 'After all,' Peggy had said to Doreen on the telephone, 'fair's fair, don't you think.'

Colin struggled on, his heart sinking as he saw what was happening. The village Mafia had struck again, he thought. Well, he'd just have to get through these as quickly as possible and get on with the rest. Still some good stuff to go, and plenty of people were now drinking cups of tea and settling down for an afternoon's entertainment.

At last the garden equipment was brought

under the hammer, and the crowd began to disperse. Joyce and Donald Davie had left immediately their lots had finished, and with a face like thunder Joyce had scrambled into Donald's car and slammed the door.

Bill finally managed to manoeuvre Peggy out into the car park just ahead of the rest. 'Now then, Peggy Turner,' he said fiercely. 'I'd like an explanation. And it had better be good.'

But Peggy began to laugh. 'Oh Bill,' she said. 'Did you see her face?'

'Never mind about that,' he said. 'What the hell are we going to do with all that stuff?'

'Oh, that,' said Peggy, turning to greet Doreen and Sophie as they approached.

'Very good sale, Bill,' said Doreen. 'Couldn't have been better, from my point of view.'

'All right,' said Bill, sitting down heavily on a garden roller which had been lot number two hundred and thirty-six. 'Go on, tell me what you three have been up to. I suppose I'm the last to know?'

'Wasn't time to tell you, Bill,' said Sophie. 'It really was a last-minute telephone call from Peggy that fixed it. And then, of course, Doreen spread the word round the hall. Most of them are related, one way or another.'

Bill knew this was true, and light began to dawn. 'So it was a buyers' ring? I suppose you know that's illegal?' he said.

'Not here in Ringford,' said Doreen,

chuckling.

'And anyway,' continued Bill, 'that doesn't solve the problem of what we're going to do with it all.'

'Holiday cottage,' said Doreen with a seraphic smile. 'Tom's doing up our old cottages on the Tresham Road. Knocking two into one, and making a really nice job of it. That's where all your ex-wife's bits and pieces are going, Bill, and very good use will be made of them, I can assure you.'

*   *   *

'Could've taken quite a bit more money if it hadn't been for Peggy and Doreen,' said Colin. 'I can't understand why so few other people put up bids.'

'Most of them had got the message,' said Pat happily. In spite of feeling grubby and tired, she had cooked Colin's favourite lasagne smothered in a rich cheese sauce, and they sat either side of the kitchen table, sharing a bottle of Chianti.

'Yes, but even so,' said Colin. He had an uncomfortable feeling that for a while things had been out of his control. Still, the total takings had been excellent, and the only dissatisfied customer had been Joyce Turner, who spat at him as she departed, 'I'll be on the phone about the money.' He had watched the eyes of the village on them as they left. It was chilling, a demonstration that rough village justice could still be called up when needed.

'Mind you,' said Pat consolingly, scraping up the last of her lasagne, 'second-hand furniture like that stuff of Bill and Joyce's doesn't fetch much, you know. There was nothing really good there. I reckon the nice bits were from Donald Davie's home. But why should he sell those? It's all still a bit of a mystery.'

Colin stood up and took his plate to the draining board. 'Village ways,' he said, 'are still very deep. Real village ways. We'll never get to the bottom of them, that's for sure. Still, we made a nice little sum for the playing fields, and that's what we set out to do.'

He opened the kitchen window, and breathed in the cool night air. 'I've had a really good idea, Pat,' he said. 'You know the pavilion needs extending...'

CHAPTER ELEVEN

'I've just remembered something,' said Sophie Brooks to her inattentive husband. She had given an edited version of the auction to Nigel, who'd been at a Deanery meeting in Tresham, and hoped he wouldn't ask too many questions. He was certain to have disapproved of what he would call collusion. Now she flipped a duster round his untidy study, and remembered Miss Layton's delight at her coup over the oak chest. She deserves a happy retirement, dear old thing. But who would take her place? Who did they know who might be suitable for the job? Sophie had been brought up in a family where personal connections were all important.

Nigel was working on his sermon, as usual trying to strike a happy mean between some real and useful thoughts, and sufficient simplicity and brevity to keep his congregation awake. In the heart of the large old vicarage, Nigel's study was a beautiful, oak-panelled room with large windows looking over the long garden and far away to the end of the Ringle Valley. It was always a temptation to leave his sermon notes and watch blue tits on the swinging nut-feeder and rabbits invading from the Glebe field to eat Sophie's vegetables. Sometimes he was lucky enough to spot the arrows of wild duck flying down the valley with such remote and graceful ease that he pondered like some nineteenth-century cleric on the hierarchy of evolution in man and the rest of God's creatures. 'Are we, we sinful, muddled creatures, really superior to those brilliant, gentle birds?' he could hear himself saying passionately from the pulpit.

'What have you just remembered, Sophie darling?' he said absently, shifting his papers back to where they had been before she

71

whipped over his big, leather-topped desk. Jean Jenkins came once a week to clean the many high-ceilinged rooms of the vicarage, but Nigel would not allow her into his study. This annoyed Jean Jenkins, who was quite intelligent enough not to throw away valuable papers, or disturb the pattern of books and texts which Nigel had laid out before him.

'The Drinkwaters—do you remember them, Nigel?' said Sophie. 'The old man was an accountant in Harrogate, and Father played golf with him occasionally.'

Nigel shook his head. He wished Sophie would hurry up and finish her half-hearted cleaning. A good theme for Sunday had come to him while he was shaving, and he wanted peace and quiet to develop it.

'You *do* remember,' Sophie persisted. 'They came to dinner when we were in Yorkshire one Christmas. She was very managing and self-opinionated, but Gordon Drinkwater was a nice kind man.'

Nigel sighed. The best way to get rid of Sophie would be to pretend he remembered and get her quickly to the point.

'Ah yes, the Drinkwaters,' he said, 'and what about them, darling?'

'They had a daughter at Eastleigh College, training to be a teacher. The apple of their eye, don't you remember? Couldn't get them off the subject, I recall.'

Now Nigel really did remember, and began

to see Sophie's drift.

'And you think she might be a suitable candidate for Ringford School?' he said, hoping to take a short cut.

'Oh, goodness,' said Sophie, 'I don't know about that. But I do remember them being very proud of how well she was doing. It was just a thought, really. I expect we shall have hundreds of applicants.'

The letters from potential replacements for Miss Layton had indeed been coming in steadily, and Nigel had postponed serious consideration of exactly what they would be looking for until the next Governors' meeting. Now he felt his sermon slipping away amongst thoughts of references to be read and decisions to be made on qualities required, and the inevitable disagreements which would follow.

'Dear Sophie,' he said, with slight edge to his voice, 'it all looks lovely and clean now. Why don't you go and make a cup of coffee and have a well deserved rest.'

And why don't you just get stuffed, thought Sophie, irritated by his lofty tone, and wondering for the umpteenth time why being a vicar had brought out the hitherto unsuspected pompous side of her charming husband.

*   *   *

'Round Ringford?' said Gordon Drinkwater to his wife. They sat at opposite ends of the breakfast table in the comfortable affluence of leafy Harrogate. 'Isn't that where Sophie Brooks ended up?'

'Yes dear,' said his wife. 'This letter is from Sophie Brooks.' If only Gordon would occasionally pay serious attention to what she said, it wouldn't be necessary to say everything twice.

'Nice woman,' said Gordon. 'What does she have to say?' His wife told him once again that Sophie had sent details of a vacancy at the village school and wondered if their daughter Sarah might be interested.

'It is a headship, of course,' she said. 'Tiny school, but a headship, even so. Could be of interest to Sarah, do you think?'

'No harm in sending her details,' said Gordon, jiggling his car keys in his pocket. He was anxious to be off to the golf course, to the convivial companionship of his chums, and the daily challenge of the small white ball. Now that he was retired, golf had become a full-time occupation.

'Right,' said his wife. 'As usual, I am spared your overwhelming enthusiasm. I shall write to Sarah today.'

'Send her my love,' said Gordon. 'See you later—be a good girl.'

His wife bristled, but it was too late to retort, and she sat down to write to her beloved only daughter.

*   *   *

Miss Layton had stayed on after school to sort out some books for tomorrow's lesson on growing rice in India. She was down on her hands and knees, reaching into the book cupboard, when she felt a twinge in her back and straightened up painfully. Better sit down for a minute until it wears off, she thought.

She sat in her old teacher's chair behind her desk, and rested her hands on the smooth wooden arms, polished to a sheen by constant use. It was very quiet. The thick stone walls insulated the classroom from the street outside, although there was very little noise there, once the children had gone off home. Traffic through Ringford was light, increasing twice a day as cars drove off to Tresham and Bagley in the early morning, and then returned at the end of the afternoon, their owners slamming car doors and vanishing with relief into welcoming homes.

The big clock high up on the wall, so high that Miss Layton had to stand on a chair to wind it up, ticked slowly, a comforting sound. She looked around the classroom, tidy and productive, with colourful splodgy paintings on the walls and ingenious constructions set out on shelves, each a development of some project she had given the bigger children to do. A Stone Age settlement made of cardboard painted to look like rocks sheltered Plasticine

75

figures crouching round a red paper fire. A grand puppet theatre, painted in bright poster paint colours, stood on a table by the window, and carefully cut out puppet figures rested in neat rows, idle until animated into life by clumsy little hands.

My world, thought Miss Layton. My little empire. Here I am monarch of all I survey. How shall I feel when I abdicate, hand over to some Pretender who will sweep away all I hold so dear, introduce all kinds of new methods and ideas ... someone who will steal my children. And then there's the review. If it's been put on one side, maybe my resignation will make them take it up again.

She was suddenly overwhelmed with panic. What on earth am I doing, giving it all up before I need to? Then she felt another twinge in her back, and was reminded of how tired she felt at the end of each day, so exhausted at the end of the week that she spent all weekend sitting in an armchair recuperating for the tasks ahead. No, it was time to go, and she would go gracefully. She would school herself to expect the worst, and then whatever happened she would not be upset. If her help and advice were needed, she would give it gladly; but if not, she had plenty of plans for using her freedom.

The sound of a tap running in the cloakroom brought her to her feet. She went quickly to see who was out there. Some child not yet collected, lurking around and hoping to be unnoticed? Or an intruder?

But how silly of me, she thought, seeing Mrs Roberts, the school caretaker, with her cloths and brushes, cleaning round the small basins and replacing fallen shoe bags and forgotten scarves. Renata Roberts's efficiency and pride in her job never ceased to amaze Dot Layton, who had been very apprehensive about her appointment. The Robertses lived in Macmillan Gardens in some squalor, and their garden—to give it a name it did not deserve—was a disgrace to the village. 'More of a rubbish dump,' Fred Mills said, very often, and loudly, as Michael Roberts went past Fred's house on his regular way down to the Arms. Their house, too, was a jumble of battered old furniture and the remains of bringing up a family, most of whom had gone away at the earliest possible date, leaving only two boys at home, William and Andrew, who were counting the days to the time when they, too, could escape from their violent father and weak, defeated mother.

But for Mrs Roberts, the school was different. It was hers, hers just as much as the children were Miss Layton's, There was no Michael to push her around and blame her for everything that went wrong, every breakage or spillage, or worn-out appliance. Here she polished and scrubbed, and hummed softly as she worked. Miss Layton had to admit she'd been wrong, and had grown fond of Renata Roberts and tried to help her in a number of small ways. Andrew was still in her school, and she encouraged his quick intelligence and channelled his inherited cunning into what she hoped would be legitimate interests in the future.

'Just for a moment I thought you were a burglar!' she said to Mrs Roberts, who smiled and shook her head. She continued to work, but chatted as she swept and dusted, offering to help Miss Layton look for the elusive book, beaming when she found it.

'Any news on a new headteacher?' she said, moving desks aside to get at slivers of paper and silver foil left from the afternoon's art session.

'Not as far as I am aware,' said Miss Layton. 'But we shall know soon enough, I dare say. I hope it won't all be too much of a shock for the village. I've been here so long they think I'm a fixture.'

'Talking of shocks,' said Mrs Roberts, leaning on her broom. 'I had one this morning.'

Miss Layton looked at the clock. She was hungry and desperate for a cup of tea. She hoped this wasn't going to be one of Mrs Roberts's rambling tales.

'I was just goin' down the shop,' said Renata, 'with my head down against the wind—it was very cold this morning, wasn't it—and I damn near bumped into Joyce

78

Turner.'

'Oh dear,' said Miss Layton, opening a tall cupboard door behind her and pulling out her coat.

'And you'll never guess what, Miss Layton. She's moving back into the Gardens with a new husband.' Renata Roberts waited for a duly amazed reaction and was disappointed.

'I think I knew that already, Mrs Roberts,' said Dot Layton. 'The school's a great place for picking up the latest news, you know.'

'Huh,' said Renata Roberts, 'and I suppose I'm the only one who didn't know?'

'No, no,' said Miss Layton consolingly. 'It has all happened rather quickly, I believe. She was at the auction, with her fiancé. He looked a very nice person, I thought.'

'More'n she deserves, in that case,' said Renata sulkily. 'What does she want to come back here for? Too many bad memories, I should've thought. And anyway, it'll do nothing but harm.'

'Possibly,' said Miss Layton. 'I suppose it could put several cats among the pigeons.'

And should take the heat off my retirement for a bit, she thought with gratitude. She pulled on a woolly hat, collected her bag full of books, and made for the door.

'Bye, Mrs Roberts,' she said, 'don't forget to lock up.'

'Do I ever?' said Renata Roberts under her breath, and bent down to prise a sticky piece of

79

chewing gum from under a desk lid. 'Dirty little devils,' she muttered, unaware that the desk belonged to her youngest, most promising son.

CHAPTER TWELVE

Ivy Beasley walked smartly along the street, turned into Macmillan Gardens without slackening her pace, and was nearly sent flying by Eddie Jenkins on a skateboard.

'Just watch where you're going!' Ivy collected herself. 'Why aren't you in school, Eddie Jenkins? Does your mother know where you are?'

Eddie looked at her dumbly. On his own he was scared of her, like all the village children. There was safety in numbers. Groups of cheeky boys had been known to answer back, and then run off laughing when Miss Beasley gave them the rough end of her tongue. But now Eddie reached for a good excuse. 'Bin sick,' he mumbled, and picking up his skateboard, scuttled off across the Gardens to his house.

Ivy pursed her lips and continued on her way to tea with Doris Ashbourne. 'I thought it was Ellen's turn, until I got your message,' she said, stepping over Doris's door mat and into the small hall of her old person's bungalow in Macmillan Gardens.

'Well, it was, strictly' said Doris. 'But I called in to see her this morning and she looked so poorly that I suggested coming here instead. Where were you, anyway? I knocked and knocked.'

'So I heard,' said Ivy. 'I was in the smallest room if you must know. And by the time I'd got downstairs you'd gone. And I found that scrap of paper on the mat. Which is why I'm here instead of down at the Lodge.' Ivy took off her grey tweed coat, belted for extra warmth, and the felt hat she had had for the Bates's wedding, now without its pink rose.

'Takes you a long time to get downstairs from your toilet, doesn't it,' said Doris mildly.

'Depends, Doris, it all depends,' said Ivy. 'My father always said ...' She paused, remembering that what her father said wasn't all that suitable for a ladies' tea party. And he only said it once, when her mother had gone round to Granny Price's for tea.

'Come on, Ivy, what did he say?' said Doris.

'No, no, I can't remember,' said Ivy, staring down the Gardens and willing Ellen Biggs to hobble into sight, which, in answer to Ivy's prayer, she duly did, using her stick to help her along, and clutching a peeling rexine bag which banged against her hip as she moved slowly up the pavement.

'I see I'm last,' she said, sitting down heavily on a chair in Doris's hall. 'Let me get me puff back. Then I'm all yours.'

'No hurry, Ellen,' said Doris, helping her with her loud green and orange-checked jacket. 'Is this warm enough? You could do with a good long winter coat.'

'I'll get me one at 'arrods next autumn,' she said, shaking with laughter and coughing at the same time.

'Harrods nothing,' said Doris. 'Them clothes you get at the Jumble Sale are worn out already. There's no warmth in this thing.' She hung it up on her hall stand, and Ellen looked at it appraisingly.

'But it's lovely colours, our Doris, you 'ave to admit that. Mind you, that wind's a killer today. Don't you think so, Ivy?' Ellen had seen Ivy through the sitting-room door, standing in front of Doris's hissing gas fire, warming her wide bottom.

'Ivy was just telling me a saying of her father's,' said Doris.

'No, I wasn't' said Ivy Beasley, her lips pursed.

'Right, lets's 'ave it, then Ivy,' said Ellen. 'The wonderful words of Arthur Beasley. What were it?'

Ivy was fed up with all this, and glared at them. 'If you must know,' she said, 'I can only remember the last bit, and that was "and when she got there, there was nothing but air, and that wasn't worth a penny, was it".'

There was a suitably shocked silence. Then Ellen began to chuckle. 'What on earth were you two talking about afore I came in?' she said.

'Toilets,' said Ivy defiantly. Doris settled Ellen in a comfortable chair in front of the fire and made for the kitchen.

'That's quite enough, Ivy Beasley,' she said. 'I shall put the kettle on and then we can talk about something sensible.'

'You did ask,' said Ivy, and sulkily straightened Doris's wedding photograph in its silver frame.

The light was going quickly outside the big window. A grey, leaden sky over Bagley Woods looked ominous, threatening snow, and old Fred Mills, bent nearly double, disappeared into his front door with a crash that Ivy could hear clearly. 'Old fool shouldn't be out in this wind,' she said. 'That gets into every nook and cranny if you aren't properly wrapped up. My ears were singing when I come in here.'

Ellen started to speak, but a violent coughing fit stopped her. 'Better get this hot tea down you,' said Doris, appearing with a loaded tray. She put three spoonfuls of sugar in a steaming cup, and handed it to Ellen, who gulped it down gratefully.

Ivy still stood at the window, and said gloomily, 'It's starting. There's a few flakes settling on your grass, Doris.' She watched the Jenkins twins run up the path and into their gate, shrieking at the solid figure of Mark, their plodding brother, who never hurried for anything or anybody.

'Them twins is uncanny,' said Ivy. 'They talk to each other without speaking.'

'Don't be ridiculous, Ivy,' said Doris.

But Ellen, for once, agreed with Ivy, 'No, it's right, Doris,' she said. 'It's spooky, the way they do it. I reckon that's why their Mark don't say much. They freeze you, them two.'

'Miss Layton's done wonders with their Mark, though,' said Doris. 'He's come on no end lately.'

'Well, he'll have to make do without her soon,' said Ivy. 'Who knows what kind of a useless drip we might get next in that school. If you ask me—'

'We do, Ivy, we do,' interrupted Doris with a sigh.

'If you ask me,' repeated Ivy, very deliberately, 'we could do with a man.'

'Speak for yerself, Ivy,' cackled Ellen, more her old self.

Ivy did not bother with this, and continued. 'Some of them kids is very difficult to control—like that Eddie Jenkins, for one—and a good schoolmaster, not too young, would be just what's needed.'

'The Governors decide, Ivy,' said Doris Ashbourne. 'With one or two from Tresham to keep an eye on them. And the vicar, of course, he's involved, it being a Church school.'

A strangely soft look came into Ivy's eyes.

'That's one good thing,' she said. 'Reverend Brooks will have a say this time, and stop that Colin Osman bringing in a young miss with no experience or sense.'

Ellen looked at her over the top of her teacup. 'But Ivy,' she said, 'you can't deny your precious Nigel Brooks has a bit of a rovin' eye. Don't you agree, our Doris?'

Doris stood up. 'Enough of that, Ellen,' she said. 'Now, if you're aiming to get home without a sledge, you'd better be on your way.'

*   *   *

By the time Ellen reached her front gate, the snow had formed a misty surface on everything. The hedge tops looked like currant buns dusted with icing sugar, and as she walked up her cracked concrete path, delicate prints of birds' feet advanced before her, like some coded message from Hansel and Gretel. She gazed out of her cold kitchen across the park. White flurries, driven by the icy wind, tumbled across the meadow behind Ellen's garden, and black leafless chestnuts, not yet softened by the snow, stood out bleak against the twilit sky.

Ellen shivered. She turned clumsily, carrying a kettle full of water to heat up for her bottle. She intended to go straight to bed, the only place she could get away from the chilling draughts which whistled through the cracks under and around her doors. As she put out a hand to steady herself on the rickety kitchen table, her feet, clad in boots two sizes too big and slippery from the snow, slithered across the cold tiles, and she fell heavily to the floor.

CHAPTER THIRTEEN

Andrew Roberts and Mark Jenkins should have been on their way home from school, but were not. They had decided at afternoon playtime that they would skive off very fast, before either of their mothers saw them, down to Bates's End and then along the footpath by the Ringle to the den of thorn bushes where generations of children and lovers had conducted private affairs out of sight of the village.

'Come on, Markie,' said Andrew, thin and quick, wriggling with no trouble under the wire which shut off the old, collapsing footbridge from public use. The Parish Council had discussed what to do with it many times. Should they repair it? Or get rid of it all together? Usually they voted to repair it, and then got bogged down in discussions about who should do it, and whether they should get tenders, and wouldn't it be better if Bill Turner just took it away in his van.

'Wait fer'us, Andrew,' said Mark, staring down apprehensively into the cold, swiftly-flowing water. Strands of water-weed stretched out beneath him like trembling green fingers, and he skipped over the rickety bridge as quickly as his bulk would allow.

It was odd that although most boys in the top class had nicknames, Andrew Roberts was always accorded his proper name. He had a kind of gypsy dignity about him, with his dark intelligent eyes and wiry body. 'Takes after my Italian grandmother,' Renata would say. But Michael Roberts, square-jawed and burly, denied any virtue in Renata's family, and declared Andrew was the image of his cousin in Suffolk, reputed to be descended from Romany gypsies. 'It were known as Little Egypt in the old days,' he said confidently, 'so that just shows yer, don't it.' 'Lot of old tinkers, more like,' said Renata, and ducked.

Mark followed Andrew into the centre of the thorny den, and looked around. There was the usual detritus of crisp packets, empty drink cans and discarded evidence of alfresco passion.

'It's cold,' said Mark, reluctant to join Andrew in sitting on the sparse wet grass. 'Mum said it would snow before tea-time.'

'Your mum ain't right about everything,' said Andrew. 'Here, have a fag and shut up.' He had pulled a packet from his anorak pocket, and with a damp box of matches was trying to light up. Finally he blew a cloud of smoke in Mark's face, and grinned.

'Get on with it, Markie,' he said. 'Tell us what you saw.'

Mark Jenkins repressed the usual feeling of nausea which attacked him as soon as he had a lungful of cigarette smoke. He had hinted to Andrew that he had something juicy to tell, but it had been a ploy to get him on his side in the playground, to deflect the Chargers on to some other victim. Mark Jenkins was not allowed to be a member of the Ringford Chargers, the playground gang of bullies, and more often than not he found himself up against a wall being taunted by boys smarter than himself. Now he had to do some quick thinking.

'It were that Octavia Jones,' he said. Andrew looked disappointed. 'Not her again,' he said. 'That's nothin' new. Who's the lucky boy this time?'

Mark knew what he meant, all the boys knew, from the telly and researches in their dads' magazines. But for the life of him he couldn't think of a convincing pairing for the wayward Octavia. It had been Robert Bates, young farmer and now husband and father, who had been in Octavia's sights for a long time. But now she was living an apparently blameless life, and the lads in the village were frustrated and puzzled. This had filtered down to the younger brothers, and Mark pounced on an idea which would add glamour to his own

88

stature as well as satisfy Andrew Roberts.

'She's after our William,' he said, with a knowing leer. To his discomfort, Andrew rocked on his heels hooting with laughter. 'Your William?' he yelled. 'He's only thirteen, you berk, she don't even know he exists!' He got to his feet. 'Well, if that's your hot news for today, you can keep it to yourself. I'm off,' he said. He inhaled deeply, squashed out the cigarette under his scuffed trainer, and pushed his way out of the bushes.

Mark followed hastily, scratching his hand and snagging a strip of fabric from his dark blue anorak. Oh God, more trouble from Mum. His face set into a depressed expression, and he trudged after Andrew, who, after all, did have the decency to wait for him by the bridge.

'Race you up to Bates's farm,' said Andrew. 'I got to ask Robert if my dad can borrow the chain-saw.'

'Who's 'e goin' to saw in half this time?' said Mark, with a rare flash of wit.

'Oh, ha ha,' said Andrew. 'Come on, race you up there.'

It was an unequal match, and Mark puffed along behind without trying. The message given, they returned slowly, scuffling their way through dead leaves already sparkling with snow, which was falling rapidly now. As they passed the Lodge, Mark stopped.

'Here, Andrew,' he said, 'old Ellen Biggs's front door's open. That ain't right in this weather is it?'

Andrew danced about on cold feet. His trainers were worn through, and he could feel the damp penetrating his socks. 'Most likely gone visitin' and forgot to shut the door,' he said. 'Come on, Markie, I want me tea.'

But Mark hesitated. His mum would know what to do. But then his mum would be in the middle of getting tea for the twins, and himself, and Eddie, and his dad coming in hungry and tired.

'I'll just take a quick look,' he said. 'She 'on't mind. 'Er barks worse'n 'er bite, my dad says. Come on, Andrew, you come too. Won't take a minit.'

A reluctant Andrew followed Mark through the rusty iron gate and up the concrete path to Ellen's dark Lodge. Mark put his head round the door and smelt the musty, damp atmosphere. There was no sound, and he cautiously pushed the door open.

'Missus Biggs!' he called, and then as there was no reply, he called again, and this time Andrew joined in. 'Missus Biggs! Missus Ellen Biggs!'

'Told you—she's gone out, silly old bat,' said Andrew.

But there was something about the silence that gave Mark the shivers. He pushed the door open further and walked in, Andrew following reluctantly. Mark could see through to the kitchen, and there on the tiled floor, in

90

the dark, creepy silence, a shadowy hump moaned softly.

'Christ Almighty!' said Andrew Roberts, and he skidaddled out of the door as fast as he could. He was brought up short by Mark's voice, shouting urgently now from old Ellen's kitchen.

'Andrew! Quick—get help! Quickly! I reckon she's a goner!'

CHAPTER FOURTEEN

The School Governors, chaired by the Reverend Nigel Brooks, had had a difficult time sifting through the applications and whittling them down to a short list of four. Most of them were totally without experience of assessing a curriculum vitae and their protracted meetings had tested them in a way previously unknown in their time of office. They had guidance from the Governors' Guide, helpful hints on suppressing their own prejudices and advice on questioning the candidates, but still some felt inadequate and others distinctly rebellious.

'What's "discriminatory language"?' said Doreen Price, who had been affronted to read that 'traditional practice is not always good practice'. 'We did all right last time, didn't we,' she said. 'If we get another teacher as dedicated and all-round good for the village as Miss Layton, we shall be lucky. Not that I have much hopes,' she added gloomily, putting aside an application which smelled strongly of cigarette smoke. 'Suppose that would be called a personal prejudice,' she muttered to herself. But she left the smelly, closely-typed sheets where she'd put them, on her rejected pile.

The application of Sarah Drinkwater had been universally approved. 'This sounds like our kind of gel,' said Bill Turner. He liked her straightforward way of setting out her record of teaching so far. They all liked her reasons for wanting to come to Round Ringford, although Colin Osman wondered aloud why someone whose references showed a go-ahead, apparently ambitious achiever, should want to come to a tiny school in a tiny village, a school which might well come under review for closure in the near future.

'Did you say closure, Mr Osman?' Jean Jenkins had said, glancing sharply at Colin Osman, who looked at once as if he wished he hadn't said it. His new elevation to the District Council had made him privy to a number of confidential reports, and the need for saving money on the education budget had caused the old issue of village school closures to raise its ugly head once more.

'Oh, nothing of any significance, Mrs Jenkins,' he said hastily, and then added, 'I do just wonder if Miss Drinkwater would be using

Round Ringford as a stepping-stone to greater things. After all, a headship is a headship, however small the school.'

'Sounds like you don't think much of Ringford School,' said Jean Jenkins belligerently.

Colin Osman smoothed her down, and the discussion had continued. Finally they were agreed. Sarah Drinkwater was a must for the short list, and the other three were compromise candidates.

'I like the sound of that Mrs Jones myself,' said Jean Jenkins. 'She's a good sensible age, and got kids of her own. Be good for my Mark, that one would.'

John Barnett, Ringford farmer in his thirties, unmarried and living with his widowed mother, laughed. 'Couldn't have two Mrs Joneses in the school!' he said. 'And anyway, Jean,' he added kindly, 'it's not just your Mark we have to think about, you know. There're twenty-eight other children in the school.'

The Honourable Richard Standing was bored. He had been sitting on a hard chair in the vicarage all afternoon, his feet were cold and he desperately needed a drink. He had read quickly through the applications and decided on Sarah Drinkwater as clearly the most suitable. It had taken him about a quarter of an hour.

'Couldn't we just call her in for interview,

and if she's willing, go ahead without all this red tape?' he said. 'Did she send a photograph of herself?'

Bill Turner looked at his boss and guessed rightly that Mr Richard had listened to very little of what the others had said. He shook his head. 'No sir,' he said, 'but no doubt a good pair of legs will go in her favour.'

Nigel Brooks could see this leading up unfortunate avenues, and pulled the meeting together. The short list was agreed, and Sophie came in with a tray of tea and cakes, at which eyes brightened and differences were forgotten.

*   *   *

'That was a good afternoon's work, Jean,' said Bill Turner, stepping out along the empty road, the light going fast and the air cold and penetrating with flurries of snow. Jean was about to reply with a caustic criticism of Colin Osman, when they heard running steps behind them.

'Mr Turner!' gasped Andrew, as he grabbed hold of Bill's sleeve.

'What on earth ...' said Bill, and Jean Jenkins said immediately, 'What's happened to Mark? What is it, Andrew Roberts, where have you two...'

'Let him speak, Jean,' said Bill, peering through the gloom at Andrew's white face.

94

'It's old Ellen Biggs, Mr Turner,' he said. 'Please come, quickly. Mark says she's dyin'.'

Mrs Jenkins was a big woman, but under certain circumstances—and this was one of them—she could move very fast indeed. Bill Turner followed her equally swiftly, and in minutes the two of them faced a strange scene in the cold, scruffy kitchen of Ellen Biggs's Lodge.

Mark Jenkins sat on the stone-tiled floor, his chubby legs folded, and Ellen Biggs's tousled old head rested on his lap. Her eyes were closed, and her face an alarming greyish white. A rising lump on her forehead oozed blood, and she was still moaning. Mark was stroking her face with a grubby hand and saying in his mother's voice, 'Don't worry, Missus Biggs, they'll soon be here.'

*　　　*　　　*

In a warm, clean bed in Tresham General Hospital, Ellen Biggs finally opened her eyes, and saw the anxious face of Ivy Beasley staring at her.

'Ah, now then, Ellen Biggs, you've been causing a lot of trouble,' said Ivy, her voice cracking as she spoke, belying the sharpness of tone.

Ellen, in a very small, thin voice, said, 'I don't know what you're doin' 'ere, our Ivy.

And why're you all done up in that black outfit? I ain't dead yet, yer know.' She shut her eyes firmly.

Ivy swallowed a swift retort, and getting up from her seat by the bed, she gently adjusted the covers round her old friend, now apparently sleeping sweetly, whiffling a little as she breathed.

CHAPTER FIFTEEN

Sarah Drinkwater, of average height, with her mother's confidence and an amazingly small waist, sat on one of the four chairs placed in a line in the small classroom where Gabriella Jones took her babies every afternoon. They were not really babies, of course, but that is how Gabriella thought of them, some not much beyond the toddler stage, and all needing the occasional mothering.

Sarah's cat-green eyes took in every detail of this second classroom: not as lofty, warmer and more friendly for the little ones. It had been added to the original school building in the nineteenth century, when numbers had increased, and the crush of small children in summer, some of them infrequently washed, had been too much for the schoolmaster of the time.

'Good God, look at that!' whispered Sarah

to her neighbouring candidate, a middle-aged man who looked as depressed as if he had been told already he had no chance. A cottage harmonium stood against the wall under the window. It was still in good working order, and on rainy afternoons Gabriella Jones pedalled away and played old-fashioned hymn tunes for the children to join in. She knew it would not be approved by modern educationalists who came to the school every so often, 'just to observe, my dear'. They observed with their eyes out on stalks at the sight of Gabriella Jones, slender and blonde, pedalling away at a Victorian harmonium, whilst the children chorused, many out of tune, 'There's a Friend for little children, above the bri—hight blue sky . . .'

The four chairs were occupied by the short-listed candidates for the post of headteacher of Round Ringford Church of England Primary School, and in accordance with the Governors' every endeavour to be fair, there were two women and two men.

Sarah Drinkwater and the miserable man were joined by a friendly, motherly woman who embraced all of them with a warm smile and took out her knitting. And the fourth was a neatly-dressed young man in tweed sports jacket, grey flannels, and a rugby club tie. His wiry ginger hair had been well flattened for the interview, and his small blue eyes sized up the opposition, guessing accurately that Sarah

Drinkwater was his main rival.

In the big classroom, chilly in the evening without the combined body warmth of twenty-nine small children, the Governors sat nervously fiddling with their papers.

'It's worse for the candidates,' said Doreen Price, shoring up the flagging confidence of Jean Jenkins. 'Imagine facing us lot, a right assortment, we are.'

Colin Osman, who knew about these things, had said no self-respecting interviewing panel had more than three or four people these days. 'I could bring along my company's statement of acceptable recruitment processes,' he'd said to Nigel Brooks. Nigel had thanked him politely, but said he thought it would take them another six months to decide which of the Governors should be left off the panel, so they'd better proceed with everyone.

'Let's leave Miss Drinkwater until last,' said Bill Turner. He knew that Mr Richard had sent a message to say he'd been held up in London but would be along very soon, and was likely to be displeased if they began without him, especially if Sarah Drinkwater was first on the list.

'Right, then I suggest we ask Mrs Jones to come in,' said Nigel Brooks, sitting up straight and passing a hand through his wavy hair. Doreen Price glanced sideways at him and thought, not for the first time, that he had a profile just like one of them matinée idols of her youth.

'I can see Mr Richard's car pulling up,' she said, 'so we'll be complete.' It had worried her to think of the squire excluded, even for an unlikely candidate.

Everyone settled in their seats, except Colin Osman who bounded to the door which connected the two classrooms and ushered in Mrs Mary Jones. She was still stuffing her half-finished garment into a plastic carrier bag, and almost sat on an errant knitting needle. She smiled apologetically and said, 'Good evening, everyone. Very pleased to meet you all.'

It was unexpectedly easy. Nigel Brooks did most of the talking, but with scrupulous fairness made sure that each member of the interviewing panel had a chance to ask questions. Jean Jenkins had a tendency to stray into a comfortable conversation with each applicant, and had to be brought back into the fold by Nigel. Mr Richard appeared not to have read the relevant section in his Governors' Manual on avoiding personal questions unless related to the job, and repeatedly barked out dreadful embarrassments like 'Where do your people come from?' and 'What's that tie, then? Don't recognise it...'

Then it was time for Sarah Drinkwater to be brought in. She smiled at Colin Osman, meeting his eyes directly, without challenge but with no discernible nervousness. She nodded at the panel, accepted a seat with a polite 'Thank you,' and crossed her legs, not bothering to pull down her skirt which was in any case of a decent, but not too decent, length.

There's two of Mr Richard's requirements met with, anyway, thought Bill Turner, gazing at Sarah appreciatively.

'Good evening, Miss Drinkwater,' said the Reverend Nigel in a very friendly fashion. 'May I introduce my colleagues to you?' He went through the Governors' names and failed to remember those of the Local Education Authority representative, irritating him. He leaned back in his chair.

'Now,' he said, 'perhaps I may start the ball rolling by asking you why, with your record of achievement and results, you would like to be our headteacher here in Round Ringford?'

Sarah thought for a moment, unhurriedly, and then smiled with a flash of very even, very white teeth. 'From what I have seen of your school and the village, Mr Brooks,' she said, 'I cannot imagine anyone thinking twice about applying for such a desirable position.'

A feeling of gratified warmth ran through all members of the panel like an electric current. They relaxed, and waited for more of the same, and Sarah Drinkwater obliged. Without arrogance, flattery, or what Fred Mills would unhesitatingly call arse-licking, she gave a reasoned account of why she thought the headship of Ringford School would be good for her, and, equally, why she would be good for Round Ringford children.

The only slightly prickly moment was when John Barnett, his natural reserve holding him back from the general goodwill which was flooding the proceedings, asked his question. 'It says here in your papers, Miss Drinkwater,' he said, 'that the longest you have spent in any post since you left college has been a year and a half. Bearing in mind that we consider continuity in teaching a most important part of a child's education, can you assure us that if you took us on here in Ringford you'd stay a bit longer than that?'

In the slight chill that followed this, Colin Osman nodded wisely, wishing he'd thought to follow up his own earlier reservations with such a sensible question.

But Sarah Drinkwater was ready for him. 'I do see your point, Mr Barnett,' she said. She remembered everyone's name from the initial introductions. 'But I think it looks worse than it is.' She looked John Barnett in the eye, speculatively. He stared impassively back at her, waiting for her answer.

'The first school I taught in had its staff dramatically reduced, and as I was last in I was necessarily first out. And the second was a school of about the same size as Round Ringford's, and it was axed in a sweeping financial cost-cutting exercise in that county.

My present position is a temporary one, in any case, as I am filling in whilst the regular teacher is on maternity leave.'

The panel relaxed. Mr Richard glared at John Barnett. It was all going so well, with this girl clearly the outstanding candidate. Lovely hair, that, so shiny and brown, like a cap. They'd be bloody lucky to get her, in his view.

But John Barnett had not finished. 'I noticed you mentioned a school closure, Miss Drinkwater,' he said, 'and it must have occurred to you that the same could happen here. We are apparently still under review, and there are only twenty-nine children now. How do you feel about that?'

Sarah nodded seriously. She addressed herself directly to John Barnett. 'I did take that into account, Mr Barnett,' she said. 'And having been through the experience, I do know what a traumatic time it can be for the children and the village itself.'

What a marvellous girl, thought Richard Standing. Articulate, too.

Sarah leaned forward in her chair, now enfolding all the Governors in her sincerity. 'I would naturally rather not go through that again,' she said, 'but I did learn a great deal which would stand us in good stead, should we need to fight.' She grinned, this time at Mr Richard. 'I can promise you I'm a pretty good fighter,' she said.

My God, I bet you are, thought Mr Richard,

returning her smile.

With all questions satisfactorily answered, and a warm handshake from each member of the panel, including John Barnett, Sarah Drinkwater left the room. In the small classroom she collected her coat, and as she was the last one left, put out the light. Outside, she turned to look back at the steeply pitched outline of the school roof, black against a sky now hazily moonlit. She surveyed the empty breadth of the Green and ghostly strip of milk-white mist over the River Ringle. It was cold and dark, and not particularly welcoming, only one or two lights showing from uncurtained windows. But Sarah nodded briefly. 'It will do very well,' she said calmly, and drove off.

CHAPTER SIXTEEN

Joyce, newly married and now Mrs Davie, stood in the back garden of number fourteen, a large-pronged muck-raking fork in her hands, taking a rest from tidying up the compost heap. Whilst the house had been empty, stray dogs, cats, rabbits and probably foxes, had scrabbled and dug, and the result was a mess.

Donald was cutting back wistaria from the roof of the shed, where it had lifted up roofing felt and bent gutters, and he looked across to where Joyce stood with her back to him. He tried to see what she saw, and to imagine what she was thinking. He saw green, undulating pastures, with crows rising and falling, squabbling over small carcasses. He counted eleven heifers feeding round a big container of hay, and saw John Barnett driving away across the soggy grass field with his empty trailer. And looking the other way, he could tell where the Ringle ran through the valley by the line of willows, and by a sudden flapping of grey wings as a heron flew off from a successful trip to Flasher's Pool.

It was just as well he couldn't see what Joyce saw. Her vision was far away, across the ploughed field and into a scrubby wood known to her since childhood as Grumbler's Holt. She saw herself as a young woman wearing a light summer dress, pushing through green ferns and spiky brambles, to find Bill waiting to pull her to him hungrily as if he had been there for weeks. She, too, saw the willows, but there underneath them she laughingly spread a picnic cloth and emptied the basket of goodies, setting them out neatly and scolding Bill when he snatched a sausage roll and wouldn't wait for a plate. And she smoothed down her skirt as the twilight fell on another long summer day, and they packed up the picnic things and headed for home.

'Time for a cuppa, Joyce,' called Donald, not liking the droop of her shoulders and her fixed gaze into the distance. 'Come along, my dear,' he said. 'We've done enough for one day.'

*   *   *

Outside the Stores, Jean Jenkins was marshalling her troops. Warren had just got off the school bus, and competed for his mother's attention to tell her he was going on ahead. He didn't want to wait whilst the rest of his family spent hours deciding how to spend twenty pence. He was above all that kind of thing now, well established at Tresham Comprehensive and impatient to get home with William Roberts to see what was the latest on the football news. The Robertses had a satellite dish—to the scorn of everyone else in Macmillan Gardens—and their small, crowded front room, always permeated by kitchen smells of frying oil and cigarette smoke, was paradise to Warren Jenkins, with its unlimited viewing time, and packets of crisps always at the ready.

'Go on, then,' said Jean Jenkins, 'but don't forget your homework!' She grabbed a toy car from Eddie's hopeful grasp and banged it back on the shelf. Gemma and Amy were both rummaging in her capacious handbag, looking for loose change, and Mark kept up a kind of monotonous chant about sausages for tea.

With a generally applied clip round the ear,

Jean somehow got them all into the shop and instructed them to make their choices and be quick about it. The terrier had been left tied to a special dog hook on the shop wall, and he set up a piercing whine of complaint.

'Here, give me that, if that's what you want,' Jean said, taking two rolls of toffees from Gemma. 'I'll pay and you go out and see to that dog. One of these days he'll get stuck down a rabbit hole and I shall leave him there.'

The Jenkinses seemed to fill the shop, and Peggy tried her best to keep track of their various purchases. Hot coins from sticky palms were banged down onto the counter, and she held small white paper bags for each individual purchase. At last all had been served, and Jean opened the door, sending them all packing, with an instruction to 'get that dog back home and give him a biscuit'. She returned to the counter, with only small Eddie to consider, and breathed heavily in mock exhaustion.

'There are times, Peggy,' she said, 'when I envy my new neighbour. Well, my new old neighbour, you might say. That Joyce Turner, or as we should say, Joyce Davie. There she is, all quiet and peaceful, with her Donald lookin' after her as if she were made of fine china, her house newly decorated, and all the time in the world to do just what she wants.'

Peggy slipped Eddie a chocolate biscuit from a split packet under the counter. He beamed at her, darted a challenging look at his mother, and began to crunch happily.

'You spoil him, Peggy,' said Jean indulgently. She'd maybe been a bit tactless, going on about Joyce Davie, but then Peggy and Bill were married now and it had all been sorted out. Still, Peggy had gone a bit funny-looking, so she changed the subject.

'Looks like we've got a new headteacher,' she said.

'Bill was telling me,' said Peggy. Thank God Jean had changed tack. She was only too well aware of Joyce's return to Ringford, and the new contented housewife act she was playing all round the village. That's really mean, she corrected herself. Maybe she is a contented housewife. Poor woman had years of unhappiness to make up for. But then it was of her own making, wasn't it? More and more, she found Joyce's face intruding on her days and nights. Joyce standing at the bus stop, looking speculatively at the shop and waving to Bill as he cycled home, Joyce walking arm in arm across the Green with her Donald, glancing back to where Bill was sawing bits of dead branch off the chestnut tree. And, increasingly, Joyce standing on the other side of the counter asking for things she hadn't got, or reminiscing about old times in Ringford with Ivy Beasley as they waited to be served.

'Don't you think so, Peggy?' said Jean Jenkins loudly.

'What? Oh, sorry, Jean,' Peggy said, pushing a stray curl out of her eyes. 'I was miles away.'

'I could see that,' said Jean, 'and anyway, it weren't important. I should be gone by now, getting tea for Fox and the brood. God knows what I shall find when I get up home. Cheerio, my dear, and whatever you were thinkin' about, let's hope it was pleasant.'

The shop was quiet now, with only the constant hum of the cold display unit, and the measured ticking from the plain-faced clock that had been there since anyone in the village could remember.

And then the door opened with a jangle, and Bill came in, large and smiling, bringing cold air and a smell of bonfire smoke. She put up her face for a kiss, and hugged him tight.

'Hey, what's all this,' he said. 'You usually won't let me near you till I've had a wash. Not that I'm complaining ...' He put down his old khaki haversack and kissed her thoroughly. 'Yum,' he said, 'nearly as good as a nice cup of tea.'

Peggy locked up the shop and followed him into the kitchen, determined to banish all thoughts of Joyce for good. Or until the next time, she thought, and sighed.

CHAPTER SEVENTEEN

The small ward in Tresham General which Ellen Biggs shared with four other elderly women was being decorated for Christmas by three volunteers from the Further Education College. One of these was Octavia Jones, daughter of Gabriella, and currently devoting her life to good causes.

'Hello, Mrs Biggs!' she said. 'Fancy seeing you here. Mum told me you'd been brought in, but I didn't know which ward.'

'Well, if it isn't our Octavia,' said Ellen, with a small grin. She had not shared in the general disapproval of young Octavia's all-consuming crush on the village's most eligible young farmer. She could remember being hopelessly in love herself. Mind you, it had landed her in all sorts of trouble best forgotten, but she had watched with sympathy as Octavia languished around the village, her unrequited passion ending only when Robert Bates had married his Mandy and quickly produced two small children.

Octavia perched on the side of Ellen's bed, swinging a multi-coloured paper-chain in her hand, and idly helped herself to a stalk of grapes. 'Anything you need, Mrs Biggs?' she said. 'I could come in again any day after college.'

'Might need some more grapes,' said Ellen, pushing her fruit bowl out of Octavia's reach. 'No ta, dear,' she added. 'Ivy and Doris come regular, and bring me all sorts of things. You know our Ivy, everything has to be better'n anybody else's, so I'm doin' really well for cakes and fruit and that.'

'When are you coming home?' said Octavia, winding the paper-chain round the frame at the bottom of Ellen's bed. 'In time for Christmas?'

'Depends,' said Ellen. 'They say I could go 'ome today if I 'ad a decent place to go to, but the Lodge ain't warm or dry enough. Least, that's what they say, but I reckon if I got a good fire goin' it'd be all right.'

'Couldn't you stay with Miss Beasley?' said Octavia, and then the thought of anybody wanting to be a guest of Ivy Beasley sent her into a splutter of giggles.

'Now, now,' said Ellen reprovingly. 'Old Ivy's not that bad, Octavia. She can be very kind-hearted. Well, sometimes. Leastways, I 'ave known it once or twice.' And then Ellen began to laugh, and the other women in the ward looked at her with envy as she shook the bed with her guffaws.

'Heard the news about the school?' said Octavia, when they had both settled down.

''Ave they appointed?' said Ellen, keenly interested. Any scrap of gossip from Round Ringford was better than pounds of grapes.

'Yep, so Mum says. It's a woman, quite

young. Got a funny name—wait a minute, it'll come to me. I know it's Sarah...'

'That's not a funny name,' said Ellen. 'My old mother, God rest 'er soul, was called Sarah. Good ole name, that is—Sarah.'

'No, no, it's her surname that's funny. Something to do with water—yep, now I've got it—Sarah Drinkwater. The kids'll have fun with that,' said Octavia.

'A young woman, eh,' said Ellen. 'I don't know what our Ivy'll say to that. She were all for a man this time to keep proper discipline.'

'Mum's met this Miss Drinkwater, and she reckons she'll be good. Very confident, she says.'

'She'll 'ave to be to take on them little tearaways,' said Ellen. 'Well, that's a turn-up, my dear, ain't it. When does she start, then?'

'Next term. Miss Layton's keen to go, and this new woman can get away easily, Mum says. So next term.'

'Where's she goin' ter live?' Ellen's colour was good, and her eyes lively. The nurse came round to check on her medicine, and made a note to tell Sister that Mrs Biggs was looking much better. She could certainly be sitting out in a chair this afternoon. She had broken no bones and her bruises were fading.

'Well, that was a bit of a problem, apparently,' said Octavia, settling herself more comfortably on Ellen's bed. The other volunteers were exchanging looks about this skiving, but Octavia ignored them.

'She wants to live in the schoolhouse, but that horrible Welshman is still there, so they're going to give him notice, and then do it up nicely, so Miss Drinkwater can move in. Meanwhile,' she added, pausing to make it really dramatic for Mrs Biggs. 'Old Mrs Barnett has said she can have a room and meals at Walnut Farm.'

'Deirdre Barnett?' said Ellen, raising her bushy grey eyebrows. 'Well, you do surprise me, Octavia. Bit of a come down for 'er, ain't it, takin' in lodgers. What will 'er precious John say?'

'According to Mum, it's just as a favour to the Governors,' explained Octavia. 'Mrs Barnett's their clerk, isn't she, so I expect that's why.'

'Here, Octavia!' shouted a volunteer from the other side of the ward. 'Come and give us a hand with this holly!' Octavia smiled at Ellen, patted her hand, and said, 'If you're not home soon, Mrs Biggs, I shall come again.'

'That'd be nice, my dear,' said Ellen. 'But let's 'ope it won't be necessary.'

*　　*　　*

Ivy Beasley and Doris Ashbourne were determined that it would not be necessary for Ellen to stay in hospital for Christmas.

'I know she's an awkward old devil, but

112

we've got to stand by her,' said Doris, leaning against Ivy's kitchen table. She was muffled up in a thick tweed coat and two scarves, one round her neck and the other tied tightly round her head. It was very close in Ivy's kitchen, the only warm room in the house, and Doris was beginning to sweat.

'You'd better take your things off, Doris,' said Ivy, noticing. 'You'll not feel the benefit, otherwise.'

Doris had thought twice about coming out at all this morning. She'd looked out at a bleak Macmillan Gardens, and seen the east wind buffeting the small, bare trees which were so pretty in spring, almond blossom and laburnum alternating in splashes of pink and yellow, planted by the Council years ago, with no thought then of poisonous seeds for the Eddie Jenkinses who lived there.

But something had to be decided about Ellen, and Doris had wrapped herself up and set off. Her boots had slid dangerously on a slippery patch outside her front gate, and she grabbed the fence just in time. There was nobody about. Got more sense than me, thought Doris. Should be indoors by the fire on a morning like this.

But by the time she'd reached Ivy's front gate, the sun had come out, transforming the village. The east wind was still keen as a knife, but December's clear, cold sunlight lit up the ochre stone and wet slate roofs of the old houses. Bright red ribbons and holly berries shone from Christmas wreaths, already vying with one another from Ringford's front doors.

Now Doris took off her scarves and gloves, and laid her coat neatly over the back of one of Ivy's chairs. 'Thank you, Ivy,' she said, 'a cup of coffee would be very welcome.'

A scratching at Ivy's back door produced Gilbert, Peggy Turner's cat from next door, who lived a double life of self-indulgence and betrayal, eating in both houses, and receiving comfort and affection from both mistresses without scruple.

Settled in her spindle-back chair, Gilbert on her lap, Ivy tackled the problem of Ellen Biggs.

'She'll have to come here to me, of course,' she said reluctantly. 'There's the back bedroom doing nothing. Plenty of room in there, and there'll be no problem about Christmas Day. We can all be here like last year.'

Doris had seen Ivy's spare bedroom, and knew that she could not allow Ellen to be tucked up there between shiny, cold sheets, in a room with only that one-bar electric fire to heat it. Clean and tidy, as always, of course, but it was a house without real warmth of spirit, and that's what counted when you were old and frail.

'You've done more than enough, Ivy,' she said. 'All that toing and froing to Tresham, and baking for Ellen. No, it's my turn, and I'm only

114

too pleased. She can come to me. It's all on the one level, and the poor old thing is not good with stairs now, as you know, Ivy.' Doris waited. Ivy hated to be crossed, but she was struggling between duty and inclination. She did not relish the idea of Ellen in her silent house for any length of time. Ellen had no compunction about saying just what she thought. She alone in Round Ringford was in no kind of awe of Ivy Beasley. And, what's more, thought Ivy rapidly, once in, she might be difficult to get out.

'Well, if you're sure, Doris,' she said. 'But I shall cook the Christmas dinner, and bring it up to your bungalow.'

'Don't be ridiculous, Ivy. I am quite capable of cooking dinner for three. You can make the cake, though,' Doris added kindly. She breathed a sigh of relief. It had all been unexpectedly easy, and she began mentally preparing the room for Ellen. Some of those nice, fluffy blankets she'd hardly used, and lots of pillows to prop up the old thing. The heating was good in the bungalows, and Doris had thick carpets and bright, flowery curtains. Ellen would be very comfortable.

The sun was already past its best when Doris emerged into the cold midday. She turned up her coat collar and stepped out briskly. Then she remembered she needed teabags, and retraced her steps, past Ivy's clipped privet and up into the shop. On the top step, she turned.

The children were out to play, fuelled by their lunches, full of energy and life.

In the playground, Miss Layton stood, cup of tea in hand, talking to a young woman. The young woman was small and slight, wearing a long, dark blue coat to keep out the wind, though her smooth brown hair was scarcely ruffled. Her face was hidden from Doris, turned away, listening intently to Miss Layton. In a playground full of scarlet jerseys and flying scarves, lime green tennis balls and bright yellow netball markings, the soberly dressed young woman nevertheless commanded attention.

Who's that, then, wondered Doris. Could be the new headteacher. Yes, that'll be it. Miss Drinkwater. Something about her, though. Definitely something about her.

'Morning, Doris,' said Peggy Turner, pleasant and welcoming behind the shop counter. 'How's Ellen? Coming home for Christmas, is she?'

CHAPTER EIGHTEEN

The fitful sun had gone behind clouds again, and with it the transitory warmth, leaving a chill, sneaky little wind that lay in wait behind corners, ready to pounce. Sarah Drinkwater stood at the playground gate, a long blue scarf wound several times around her neck to keep out the cold. She smiled at the big woman who came to a breathless stop, recognising her from her interview.

'Good afternoon,' she said. 'Can I help you?'

Jean Jenkins was taken aback. This was her street, her playground, her school. It was for her to help others, not to be helped by this newcomer. 'Um, I was just looking for our Mark,' she said. 'I should've been here earlier, but Eddie was playing up. Mark's a big lad, untidy hair...'

'I know Mark,' said Sarah Drinkwater. 'I met him this morning. It's Mrs Jenkins, isn't it? Nice to see you again. Ah, there, look,' she added, pointing. 'There's Mark, just coming out of the shop.' With a polite farewell, she left Jean Jenkins puffing on the pavement, and walked off firmly in the direction of the vicarage.

*   *   *

'I left my car outside the school, Mrs Brooks,' Sarah said. 'After a whole day in that classroom I needed some fresh air. Miss Layton is not a great one for opening windows.'

'Do call me Sophie, my dear.' Sophie had made a large pot of tea, and set it out with scones and a pot of raspberry jam, seasonal with its Christmas paper cover, bought from

117

last week's Playgroup Bring and Buy. She and Nigel sat with Sarah around the big kitchen table, relishing the warmth from the vicarage's shabby Aga cooker and laughing at Sophie's old dog, Ricky, who was stretched out in front of it, closer than seemed wise.

I suppose I shall see quite a lot of these people next term, thought Sarah. What was it Mother said about them? Oh yes, everybody had thought Nigel was barmy to leave a lucrative solicitors' practice to be a vicar.

She glanced around the kitchen. Lovely old blue and white plates on the dresser, good wine glasses on shelves, a long row of well-thumbed cookery books, nice pieces of silver—sugar bowl, cream jug, mustard pot. Plenty of evidence of Nigel's former affluence. The Brookses would certainly be useful people to know. She wasn't sure how lodging at Walnut Farm would work out, and hadn't forgotten John Barnett's stubborn reservations at her interview. Could be a tricky one, farmer John.

'Thanks, Nigel, yes, I did have a very productive day with Miss Layton. She's a nice old thing, isn't she? The children were very quiet and well-behaved. A bit too quiet, perhaps, but we can soon fix that.'

And then a picture flashed across her inner eye: Mark Jenkins, caught unawares as she had walked from the room but turned back unexpectedly, Mark Jenkins with his tongue out and his fingers pulling his fleshy face into a hideous mask. And a rustle that could not be called giggling, but was discomforting all the same. Still, they were bound to try it on. Such a small group of children would be a doddle compared with some of the town classes she had taught.

CHAPTER NINETEEN

It might have been tempting for Dot Layton to coast to the end of term, doing only the minimum amount of Christmas preparation, allowing herself to wind down for her retirement. But that was not her way. She threw herself into the traditional and much loved rituals as if it were her first year in Round Ringford school.

'Right children,' she said one morning in early December, 'today we are going to make our decoration for the tree in the Green. Mark Jenkins, please give out the paper. Jody, you can help him.'

Jody Watts was a pretty ten-year-old from the new houses on Walnut Close. She had attended a town school until a year ago, and found it difficult to settle into such a small village class of mixed aged children. But under Miss Layton's gentle guidance, she had become confident and—said Andrew Roberts—bossy. 'Teacher's pet,' he said, pinching her leg under the desk.

'While Mark and Jody are doing that,' said Miss Layton, who missed nothing, 'perhaps Andrew Roberts will tell us about the custom of tree dressing.'

Andrew scowled. He thought he knew all there was on the subject. The first year the school had done it, his father said it was a stupid American custom and didn't look right in Ringford. And anyway, his mother said, agreeing, it only took one good rainy night to make the tree look like a waste paper dump.

'Stand up, please, Andrew, and be quick about it,' said Miss Layton. Andrew struggled to his feet, taking an unnecessarily long time about it.

'Tree dressing started in America,' he said, 'and now some schools do it in this country.'

Miss Layton looked at him in the eye. 'Thank you for that full and detailed description, Andrew. But it is not quite right is it? It is a custom found all over the world.' The literature had said it was a useful activity for schools of mixed cultures, not being allied to any particular religion. This hardly applied to Round Ringford, but Miss Layton had liked the idea, and so had the children.

Andrew Roberts looked mutinous. 'Well, my dad said it's just another thing we've copied from the Americans,' he said, staring at Miss Layton, daring her to contradict his father.

'Well,' she said diplomatically, 'that is a different matter. Sit down, Andrew.' She turned to the class

'We like to thank God for our lovely trees, don't we children.' A chorus of 'Yes, Miss Layton,' greeted this. Now they were on safe ground. 'So we make the tree look extra pretty once a year, to show how much we appreciate having it there, to give us shade in the summer and conkers to play with in the autumn, and beautiful bare branches for the snow to rest on in the winter. Isn't that right, Andrew Roberts?'

Andrew barely nodded. He wished she would just get on with it. All this soppy stuff about trees. He had an idea for ghost story, featuring his father and a headless soldier in the churchyard brandishing his sword, and he was impatient to get on to the next lesson to make a start on it. He had the ending already. His father would be so frightened by the ghost that he would stop drinking for ever. And his mother would give up crying.

'Andrew Roberts, are you with us?' Miss Layton was holding out a ball of string. 'Cut this into twenty-nine pieces, each one a metre in length. You can measure them on your ruler. And do look slippy, Andrew. You're half asleep today.'

And I bet I know why, thought Dot Layton. Renata Roberts had looked terrible when she opened up the school today, her eyes red and swollen, and her hands shaking as she fumbled with the locked door. Someone should do something about that Michael Roberts, Miss Layton thought for the hundredth time. But the village had closed ranks. He was one of their own, and so long as things did not get too noticeably bad, nothing would be done. Unfortunately, Renata Roberts would be the last one to complain.

The children bent their heads over silver stars and golden suns. Bright, shiny decorations blossomed under the busy scissors, and a quiet buzz of small voices commenting and criticising filled the classroom. Dot Layton moved around from one child to another, gently putting a crooked star back on course, reproving a smug Jody whose smiling sun outshone her neighbour's efforts. Eddie Jenkins had slipped from his chair and disappeared into a forest of small feet and legs to find the ball of string which had accidentally on purpose rolled off the edge of Andrew Roberts's desk.

'Eddie, will you get back in your chair at once,' said Miss Layton. The old clock had moved on, and it was nearly time for the next activity.

'Well done, children,' she said, as Jody Watts carefully gathered up the decorations and placed them neatly in a big cardboard box by Miss Layton's desk. Each had its tail of string tied on by Andrew Roberts—'With a reef knot, mind, Andrew'—and Jody skilfully avoided entangling them.

'And tomorrow,' said Miss Layton, 'shall we all go out and dress our special tree on the Green?'

'Ye-e-e-e-s, Miss Layton!' yelled the children, and Eddie Jenkins yelled louder than most.

The composition class resumed work, Dot Layton quietly reading a story to the small ones grouped solemnly around her chair. As usual, she managed without difficulty to keep an eye on the big children sitting at the playground end of the classroom, and saw Andrew Roberts writing busily and with complete concentration. Mark Jenkins, sitting next to him, tried once or twice to distract him, but Andrew took no notice. At the end of the lesson he looked up with a dazed expression, as if not sure where he was.

'Thank you, children,' said Miss Layton, taking in the books to mark. There were six pages of Andrew Roberts's handwriting, speedily done and difficult to read.

'All quiet now, ready for our going home prayer. Hands together and eyes closed.'

Calmed by Miss Layton's voice and the familiar comforting words, the children filed out to the cloakroom and their waiting mothers or fathers. It was not uncommon now for a mother to be working and the father the one who met the children out of school. Miss Layton took this in her stride, but was quietly amused when she saw the gaggle of young women on one side of the school gate, and a much smaller group of exaggeratedly nonchalant young men on the other. Now only Andrew Roberts was left, and he dawdled by Miss Layton's desk.

'Off you go, Andrew,' she said. 'There's nothing else, is there?'

'No, Miss,' said Andrew.

Dot Layton saw his eyes linger on the pile of books. 'I shall be reading your story this evening, Andrew. You have worked hard.'

A small smile flitted across the boy's dark face, and he scuffed his way out of the classroom.

Dot Layton leaned back in her chair. I'm really tired, she thought. Never used to feel so done in at the end of the day. Ah well, off home to a nice restoring cup of tea. She straightened the books ready to put in her bag, and then hesitated, lifting the top one from the pile. It was grubby and dog-eared. It was Andrew Roberts's. She opened it and began to read.

The handwriting was difficult to decipher, but the story unfolded in short vivid bursts, and Miss Layton had no trouble following it. Six pages later, she put it down on her desk. 'Oh, Andrew,' she said aloud, and sat without moving for several minutes.

*   *   *

The news of Miss Layton's retirement had

leaked out of the village and as far as the *Tresham Advertiser* offices in the town's Market Square. 'Might be good for a picture,' said the news editor. Photographs of children never failed, and this tree dressing business could provide a nice little story, married up with the headmistress's retirement.

Hoar frost clung to Ringford roofs and trees, and the low winter sun caught and held an array of sparkling icy fires on every surface. With the sun dazzling his eyes, in spite of dark glasses and a tinted windscreen, the reporter drove into the village and saw little of its theatrical beauty. He spotted a group of children on the Green already, and several adults—teachers, he supposed—talking to a line of parents around the chestnut tree. The great bare branches swooped low over the Standing seat, and one or two children were standing on the slippery wooden slats, reaching up to tie on silver stars and golden suns. The reporter parked his car, and walked over to the crowd. There were as many adults, if not more, than children, he noticed.

'Big ones help the little ones!' It was Dot Layton, well wrapped up in a dark wool reefer coat and headscarf. Her cheeks were red with the cold, but her eyes sparkled behind her steel-rimmed glasses. The children were excited, and she loved the heightened tension, the feeling of her school all working as one in the completion of a well-planned project.

'Excuse me,' said the reporter. 'Are you Miss Layton?'

'I am,' said Dot Layton, noting the camera and the notebook. She turned to Gabriella Jones and said, 'Would you take charge for a couple of minutes, Mrs Jones. When all the decorations are tied on, help the children to join hands in a big circle round the tree.' She turned back to the reporter.

'And when will the rest of the school be out to join the festivities?' he said. Surely there were more children than this couple of dozen? Don't know how these titchy little schools keep going, he thought.

Dot Layton stared at him, then smiled a little stiffly. 'This is the whole school. All the children are present, and many of the parents and other village folk as well. See for yourself.' Her waving hand took in a growing crowd, many with cameras, laughing and admiring the shining suns and stars as they quivered in the wind and sunlight.

The circle of children undulated back and forth like a snake eating its own tail. Gabriella Jones could see they wouldn't last much longer without breaking out into anarchy, and called across to Miss Layton.

'We're ready!' She looked at Jody Watts' long blonde hair swinging under her scarlet bobble hat, and wished for a fleeting second that her own troublesome Octavia was still at the village school, still malleable and not averse

126

to a cuddle before bedtime. Still, touch wood, Octavia had been remarkably trouble-free lately, with her passion for the environment and good deeds. Her thoughts were swiftly interrupted by a scuffle breaking out on the opposite side of the circle. Mark Jenkins and Andrew Roberts were hooking legs, struggling in combat to bring the vanquished one down to the frosty, cold ground.

Miss Layton marched over to them, removed Mark Jenkins by the scruff of his neck and put him between two small girls. 'There you are, Mark. Look after these two, please. See they go the right way—it's their first time.'

And then the children set off hand in hand, skipping round in a joyful ring, singing at the tops of their voices with the confidence of being well rehearsed in the lofty classroom every day for a week.

Thank you Lord for all our trees,
For leaves to give us shade,
Nests for birds, and flowers for bees,
What wonders You have made!
ALLELUIA!

This last enthusiastic shout echoed round the Green, and was taken up by bystanders until Miss Layton waved her arms to say that that was enough, she was sure God had heard them and was extremely pleased.

The reporter took many photographs, and some of the more aware children posed prettily. Eddie Jenkins, looking cherubic with his pale hair and bright blue eyes, waited until the last moment and then stuck out his tongue as far as it would go, transforming himself instantly into a village gargoyle.

'Brat,' muttered the reporter, and drove off at speed to get back to the safer world of Tresham scandal and mayhem.

'All into school now,' said Miss Layton firmly. 'And everyone is welcome to come with us for coffee. Children—take our guests back into the big classroom and make them welcome.'

*　　*　　*

Peggy Turner had joined the crowd, keeping a weather eye open for customers at the Stores, and now walked slowly back, chatting to Doris Ashbourne, agreeing once more that things would not be the same when Miss Layton had gone. As she turned to take a last look at the Green, now empty except for a few stragglers, she saw a trim figure in a neat tweed coat and soft beret disappear into the school gate, and at her side the stern shape of Ivy Beasley. Trust her, Peggy thought, trust Ivy to get that Joyce in on the act. She felt resentful, wishing she could be over there with the others. She was Bill Turner's rightful wife—and Bill a Governor, too. But the shop must be manned, and there was Mr Richard at the counter

128

already, tapping his fingers impatiently, waiting to be served.

CHAPTER TWENTY

Ivy Beasley sat stiffly on the edge of a chair, looking out of Doris Ashbourne's bungalow in Macmillan Gardens at absolutely nothing happening. She could see across the main street and over the Green, right down as far as the Ringle and further on, though now misty and indistinct, to the parkland of the Hall. Not a soul moved, not an animal, not even the Jenkins' terrier. Ivy cast about in her mind for something to comment on, some topic to discuss with Doris.

'I suppose you'll not be going to the nativity play, then?' she said.

Doris was in the small, clean kitchen, making tea for herself and Ivy. She had automatically put out three cups and saucers, and now returned to the cupboard the one that should have been for Ellen. It would soon be needed, Doris thought with some trepidation. Arrangements had been made for Ellen Biggs to leave hospital and be delivered at the end of the week by ambulance, like an unwieldy Christmas present for Doris Ashbourne. The bed in the tiny spare bedroom was already made up with crisp, clean sheets and fluffy blankets. Doris had put a pile of paperback romances on the bedside table, and under the bed, at the ready, she'd put her auction bargain, the large white china jerry with a design of pink roses on its bulbous sides. Save me getting her to the lavatory in the middle of the night, with any luck, Doris had thought. I knew it would come in useful.

'Depends on how Ellen is,' said Doris, settling down opposite Ivy with a cup of steaming tea in her hand. 'Here, have a piece of flapjack, Ivy. Freshly made this morning.'

'Ah,' said Ivy, 'the bits do get between the teeth, don't you think, Doris. Never make it myself. But still, if that's all you got...'

Doris restrained herself. She had other things to think about, what with shopping for Christmas and preparing for having another person in the house after all these years. And Ellen Biggs was not just another person. She was a very difficult old party, and Doris knew it was going to need all her patience and forbearance to make it work. She might as well get into practice with Ivy.

'The oats are quite soft, Ivy,' she said. 'I didn't leave it too long in the oven for that very reason.'

'Getting back to the nativity play,' said Ivy, taking the largest piece of flapjack, 'are you going to have to babysit our Ellen?'

'Probably not,' said Doris. 'Ellen's not ill. She's just too shaky to go back to the Lodge at

130

the moment. Especially in this weather.'

The crisp, frosty mornings had been replaced by mild, foggy days, when the sun lurked behind a layer of mist, ghostly and alien, never quite able to pierce the gloom. Bagley Woods were blue humps on the horizon, and the village was so silent and still that a sudden car passing through was a welcome reminder that life did exist out there beyond Round Ringford.

'Shall I save you a seat, then?' said Ivy. 'Miss Layton's invited the whole village, as it's her last term, and there's sure to be a crowd. Even them snotty ones who send their kids to private schools have got the nerve to turn up. "We like to support village events," I heard that Watts woman say in the shop.' Ivy's mimicry was deadly.

'But her Jody does go to the school, Ivy,' said Doris.

'I know that,' said Ivy. Doris reflected that of course Ivy knew all the children who spilled out of the school gates, laughing and fooling about in the pleasure of release at the end of the day. Ivy's vigil at her front window kept her excellently informed.

'Well, then,' said Doris, 'I do think you're being a bit hard, Ivy. It'll be a lovely send-off for Miss Layton. Who's going to be the Virgin Mary, do you know?'

Ivy did know, of course. 'None other than Miss Jody Watts,' she said. 'It's typical of those newcomers, taking all the best parts.'

Doris gave up. She abandoned the possible cast list and asked Ivy if she thought the new headteacher would be there.

'Doubt it,' said Ivy, reluctant to admit that this time she did not know. 'She'll probably be busy with her own school. Besides which, it'll be Dot Layton's evening, won't it.'

*   *   *

The big classroom had been cleared of desks, and chairs borrowed from the Village Hall were arranged in rows facing a stage erected from large blocks, stored for the rest of the year in the disused outside toilets at the bottom of the playground.

Bill Turner, with Peggy's help, had rigged up very presentable stage curtains, and the small neighbouring classroom had been transformed into a dressing room for the nervous troupe of small actors. Its door was firmly shut against the gathering audience, and inside Gabriella Jones, Miss Layton, and wardrobe mistress Jean Jenkins, gave final touches to costumes and last-minute rehearsing of lines not properly learned.

In the big room, slap in the middle of the front row of chairs, sat Ivy Beasley. She had made no concessions to people sitting behind, but sat up ramrod straight, the good grey felt hat set squarely on her strong, wiry hair. Grey gloves and scarf were on the chair beside her, saving it for Doris Ashbourne.

It was almost time for the performance to begin when Doris hurried into the school and scanned the audience to see where Ivy was sitting. Her face scarlet, she squeezed past Mr and Mrs Richard Standing—dutiful attenders—and sat down quickly beside a grim-faced Ivy.

'You made it very difficult, Doris, to keep your seat.' Ivy Beasley hissed this reproof out of the corner of her mouth, and Doris replied in a stage whisper that Ellen had taken a long time to settle in front of the fire with a flask of tea and the television on the right channel. Ivy's reaction to this was stifled by the curtains being drawn back by Mark Jenkins and Andrew Roberts, and Miss Layton stepping on to centre stage.

Her brief announcement drew an expectant round of applause, and then the nativity play, involving the whole school, got under way.

'What presents have you brought, then?' briskly enquired Jody Watts of the three bashful Kings hovering at the stable door. 'Oh God, bossy as usual,' a bearded Joseph, alias Andrew Roberts, said to the chubby Innkeeper at his side.

A small shepherd nearly stole the show. The striped blanket on Eddie Jenkins's head slipped further and further over his face until it obscured his blue eyes. He didn't move, but stood there blindly, dutifully holding a wobbling crook. Finally rescued by his mother's disembodied hand from behind the curtains, he received a small spatter of applause for courage in the line of duty.

After the nativity play, delivered as if for the first miraculous time and with innocent enthusiasm, came a change of mood. Andrew Roberts stood forward to announce a new version of Snow White, specially written by Miss Layton for the big ones. A great deal of funny business covered the absence of long speeches, and Mark Jenkins, unable to remember more than one line at a time, maintained his dignity as Grumpy by quick reference to the script left specially for him on a chair in the wings.

'Once in Royal David's city,' sang the entire school and audience in a final heart-warming singsong, and then Miss Layton stepped out once more.

Peggy Turner, holding Bill's hand in the back row, felt a lump in her throat as she watched Dot Layton, so much the pivot of this most important part of Ringford life, smile her neat smile at the waiting audience and begin to speak.

'Won't be easy for her, Bill,' Peggy whispered, and felt his hand squeeze hers in agreement. She looked round the room at the artwork on the walls, the old photographs and shields won at long-gone inter-school sports days. Her dear Bill, and many others in the audience, had sat there as small, scruffy children, had started their excursion into the wider world under Dot Layton's guiding hand. Here was the heart of the village, no doubt about that.

'Thank you, everyone,' said Miss Layton firmly. She had not rehearsed what she would say, certain that whatever words were necessary would come to her. I shan't say much, anyway, she had said to her sister. Nothing worse than a retiring teacher who won't retire.

'We are all grateful for your enthusiastic reception of our efforts this evening. The children have worked hard, and I must thank Mrs Jones and Mrs Jenkins for their help, also Mr Turner and Mrs Roberts for setting out the room for us.' She paused, looking straight at the small sea of faces.

'I promised my sister,' she added, in a different, softer voice that few had heard before, 'that I wouldn't make a long speech. But I do want to say this, just once.'

Peggy, always one step ahead in any plot, sniffed and felt for her handkerchief.

Dot Layton adjusted her spectacles and continued. 'This school, these children, and all the other children who have started their education in this little community, have been my life for the last thirty years. All kinds of children have been through my classroom, and

135

I just want to say that I have been proud of every one of them. Every one. My children.'

And then her voice broke, and she visibly collected herself together, smiling again apologetically at this once-only loss of composure.

The applause was deafening, and the children cheered on Eddie Jenkins in his stumbling approach to his teacher with a bouquet almost as big as himself.

*   *   *

'Did anyone else say anything?' asked Dot Layton's sister later that evening, as they sat by the fire admiring the amazing new music system that had been Dot's presentation from the Governors.

'Nigel Brooks went a bit overboard,' said Dot with a smile. 'And then Jean Jenkins rambled on a bit on behalf of the parents. They were really nice, though.'

Her sister looked at her shrewdly. 'Upset you a bit, hasn't it. Just as well there's only the Christmas party to go.'

Dot Layton touched her sister's arm gratefully. 'I shall go and make our cocoa. Early bed, I think, don't you.' Nothing more was said, but the understanding between them was more than adequate.

*   *   *

Tradition was that Mr Richard Standing from the Hall donned his Father Christmas costume on the last day of term, shouldered his sack of presents, and turned up unexpectedly on party afternoon around tea-time.

'And now one more present in the sack!' he said, having yo-ho'd his way through twenty-nine parcels.

The children played their part in looking anxious. Who had been missed? But no one put up their hand, and Richard Standing marched over to where Miss Layton was standing by the decorated tree, arms folded, watching happily as all went according to plan.

'Must be for you, Miss Layton,' he said, and she shook her head, laughing. But he insisted, and she took it, puzzled. 'Shall I open it?' she said hesitantly.

'Ye-e-s!' yelled the children.

Dot Layton was annoyed to find that her hands were shaking as she unwrapped the bulky parcel. As she tore away the Christmas paper, a smart black and red travelling case was revealed. Attached, a large card greeted her cheerfully with a picture of herself—quite recognisably herself—waving from an aeroplane taking off at an improbable angle from the school playground. Inside the card, every child in the school had signed his or her name.

'Oh, goodness,' she said. And finally it was too much, and she sat down on her own chair, with the smooth worn arms, and was unable to stop the rush of tears.

Now what, thought Richard Standing. He looked round at the worried faces and acted. 'Come on, children,' he said, grabbing the nearest hands, and made for Miss Layton. Then the others knew what to do, and Dot Layton was surrounded by loving hands and consoling voices, and Richard Standing walked quietly away. He took off his Father Christmas outfit, and drove home feeling—as he said to Susan that evening—quite moved.

CHAPTER TWENTY-ONE

Colin Osman, District Councillor and Newsletter editor, had come up with the idea one evening after supper, as he sat drinking coffee and sifting through the previous Sunday's newspapers before putting them out for the dustmen. His wife Pat had been filling him in on school news and he'd been only half listening. Although they had no children, Pat always volunteered when there was help needed at the school, and frequently regaled Colin with stories of the children's doings and sayings which he did not find as fascinating as she did. Lately, however, his community conscience had been pricking him into an uneasy awareness that everything in the village at the moment seemed to centre on the small group of children and their retiring head.

'Of course, Christmas is a time for the children,' he'd said, 'but as Nigel pointed out from the pulpit, it is for families in general. The Holy Family was an important unit, conveying a message much larger than just the birth of the infant Jesus.'

Pat had looked at him in astonishment. She'd never thought of the Holy Family as an important unit, for a start, and she had certainly not previously noticed Colin's interest in religious philosophy.

'What's this leading up to, Colin?' she had said. She knew him very well.

'I thought we might do something for the oldies,' he said.

Pat had winced. 'Elderly people in this village are very well taken care of at Christmas,' she said. 'Families and neighbours all make sure they have a proper dinner and presents, and are not left alone.'

'No, I mean a festive treat of some sort. I thought a New Year's lunch party in the Village Hall would be the kind of thing.'

Pat had sighed. How long had this bright idea been incubating? she wondered. Still, at least he was keen. Ringford seemed to have absorbed him without difficulty, and some even seemed to appreciate his efforts, which was more than could be said of other places they had lived.

'Is there time to organise it now?' she'd said, clutching at straws.

'Of course.' Colin was firm, and picked up the telephone.

It was not in his nature to waste time, and during the next few days he quickly persuaded the WI, under Doreen Price's capable leadership, to provide the lunch. A good hot roast, he said, feeling that this would be appropriate for a cold winter's day. 'We've got money left from Bonfire Night,' he'd said. Some WI members had thought it wrong to spend funds raised for fireworks on dinners for the old people, especially as they all did very well on Christmas Day anyway. But Doreen had not wanted to discourage him, and won over the dissenters with a promise to do extra fund-raising for fireworks next year.

Colin had given a lot of thought to the entertainment. A chap in the office did a very good comedy turn, but it veered towards the blue at times, so he'd rejected that. 'Home grown talent, that's what we need,' he said.

'Oh God, no, not Robert Bates again, with his guitar and his waggish songs,' said Pat. They seemed to talk of nothing else but the New Year's party since Colin made an action plan and set about carrying it out.

'There must be other people,' said Colin, determined now to pursue this. Old-fashioned songs, with Gabriella Jones at the twanging Village Hall piano. Maybe old Fred Mills could be persuaded to do his famous monologue once more. Poor old chap was looking very decrepit these days, but he could do it sitting down. A nice big rocking chair, and a glass of beer in his hand. Could look very good.

He sounded out these ideas to Pat, but she looked doubtful. 'I reckon they'd all be happier going home and watching the telly,' she said, and was then smitten with remorse at Colin's expression.

'The lunch is a really good idea, darling,' she said, 'but think carefully about the rest. They're a funny lot here in Ringford, they don't like being patronised.'

But Colin had the bit between his teeth, and was already mentally designing a set for the stage. Something warm and welcoming, lots of red velvet and plenty of lighting, he thought.

*   *   *

'I'd be a sight better off in front of me fire,' grumbled Fred, as Bill helped him on with his coat. 'I don't eat much these days, and you can be sure they'll sit me next to old Ellen Biggs. Thought she'd gone for good, but no, large as life and twice as much trouble, there she is at Doris's, runnin' the poor woman off her feet and queenin' it over everybody.'

'Come on, boy,' said Bill, locking Fred's front door and helping the old man into the

141

front seat of his van. 'We'll get you down to the hall in no time. I'm told there's a sherry welcome.'

Fred's eyes brightened at this, but he said he'd rather have a pint, and no, he didn't want no seat belt to go that short distance.

Bill looked at Fred's knobbly hands clutching his stick, and noticed that the tremor in the old man's body was worse. 'You sure you're going to be all right to do your monologue, Fred?' he said.

'If I remember it,' said Fred gloomily. He coughed. 'It's a long time since I did it, boy. Last time was when we 'ad them Silver Jubilee celebrations in Barnett's barn. D'you remember, Bill? A good feast, that was.'

Bill did remember, but chiefly because of the dramatic scene Joyce decided to enact. It was not part of the entertainment, but her sudden departure before the fresh-fruit trifle, screaming abuse at Bill, was the talk of the village for weeks.

'Yes,' he said grimly, 'I remember all right.'

They were silent until they reached the Village Hall, and then Bill helped Fred out and into his seat, surreptitiously exchanging place cards so that the old boy did not have to sit next to Ellen Biggs.

'There you are, Fred,' he said. 'Don't drink too much, else the Fireman will never get to his Wedding.'

'The Fireman's Wedding' was Fred's

speciality. He had delivered the monologue, with piano accompaniment from Miss Layton, at every social event in the village in living memory. Most of the older people knew it off by heart, and eagerly anticipated Fred's dramatic interpretation.

Colin Osman served thistle glasses of sweet sherry at the door, and Pat helped the old people off with their coats and scarves. Background music, a tape of Charlie Kunz playing old favourites softly on the piano, drifted over the tables. Pat had of course offered help once she had seen Colin was determined to go ahead with the party, and had recruited friends from the village—Mandy Bates, Caroline Dodwell from the new houses in Walnut Close, Gabriella Jones—to help decorate the hall and tables. It all looked very festive, and once the ice had been broken by Ellen Biggs launching into a rusty version of Jingle Bells, instantly suppressed by Ivy Beasley, the conversation had buzzed and Colin's smile of relief was plain to see.

The plates were cleared, cups of coffee served, and Colin mounted the stage, transformed by himself and Peter Dodwell into a miniature music-hall, complete with swaying chandelier.

'Friends,' said Colin, 'I must first thank all those, too numerous to mention by name, who have worked hard to bring about this party today.'

Cries of ' 'ear,'ear,' from Ellen Biggs.

'But all that hard work is rewarded,' continued Colin, 'by seeing you all tucking in and enjoying being together. However, we are not finished yet! You've all been waiting eagerly, I know, for our entertainment, and I promise you'll not be disappointed. We shall start with a song from our very own songbird, Octavia Jones, accompanied on the piano by her mother, who—' and he winked at Fred— 'looks more like her twin sister to me! I give you—Octavia Jones!'

Octavia had demurred at first. 'Oh God, no—not that, Mum, please!' But Gabriella had pointed out that charity begins at home, and if she was so keen to help the needy, she could start right here in Ringford and give some pleasure to the old folks.

'I've found the music for "A Brown Bird Singing"' she said. 'It's a very sweet old song, and I know they'll love it.'

They did love it. Octavia was wearing a blue and green tartan dress with a virginal white collar, and had tied her long blonde hair back with a black velvet ribbon. Her voice was true and clear, and she gave them her best, blushing and smiling with pleasure at the enthusiastic reception.

The build-up to Fred's monologue was suitably tense. Colin had helped Fred onto the stage and into the cushioned rocking chair, to tumultuous applause. He put the half-full tankard of beer into one of Fred's trembling hands, and the old man pulled his evil old pipe from his pocket with the other. He settled himself down, leered at the audience, and with a great sense of timing took a long swig at the beer.

'What are we looking at, Guv'nor?' began Fred, and there was more clapping as the familiar words were spoken.

The next few verses followed easily, and because Fred's voice was thin and quiet with age, the silence in the hall was complete. The old feeling of power over his listeners flowed through Fred, and he knew he had them where he wanted them. His old heart beat faster with the coming climax of the piece.

Ah Sir! T'was grand, but t'was awful!
The flames leapt up higher and higher;
The wind seemed to get underneath them
'Til they roared like a great blacksmith's fire!

I was just looking round at the people,
With their faces lit up in the glare,
When I heard someone cry, hoarse with
*   terror,*
'Look! There's a woman up there!'

Fred paused and peered down at the audience, getting his timing exactly right. He shifted in his chair, took another mouthful of beer, and continued.

'There was that face at the . . .' he began. And then he choked.

The glass of beer crashed to the floor, shattering everywhere and sending streams of foam trickling off the edge of the stage. Fred's pipe fell onto the red carpet and erupted into scattered ash and smoke. Octavia screamed, and Bill Turner, who had been chatting to Tom Price at the back of the hall, was on the stage in seconds.

Fred's head lolled back against the rocking chair, and his eyes were horribly open.

'He's dead,' said Ellen Biggs, gripping Ivy's hand. 'Fred's gone. Poor old bugger's gone.' The absolute certainty in her voice sent a shiver through Ivy Beasley. As she watched Bill Turner lift up the frail old body with infinite gentleness, and carry it off the stage and into the little dressing room behind, she knew that for once it was pointless to contradict.

CHAPTER TWENTY-TWO

On a cold, clear winter's morning, Frederick Albert Mills was laid to rest, next to his sister Elsie Maria, in the cemetery of St Mary's Church, Round Ringford. It was a small church, originally built and used by monks who had lived in an extensive priory, filling the baulk fields with prayer, Christian activity, and

146

finally corruption. Nothing remained of the priory, except for a few shadows in the growing corn, echoing foundations beneath the earth, one or two ancient houses reputed to be built of looted priory stone, and the church itself, squat and timeless, awesome in the huge span of historical events, great and small, which its rough, white-washed walls had witnessed.

The sun shone from a pale blue sky, the black yews in the churchyard swayed stiffly in the sharp wind, and Bill Turner tolled the funeral bell with a heavy heart. He should never have allowed Fred to do that monologue. It was his fault, not young Osman's. Colin was quick, thoughtless and brash, his only concern to make a success of his lunch party. But Bill had watched old Fred deteriorate, slowing up and letting things slide. Even his beloved garden was looking neglected.

Fred had lived in Ringford all his life, and the church was full. The sun shone through the bright stained glass above the altar, casting coloured shadows on the pale stone floor. The small coffin containing Fred's meagre remains stood in the chancel, surrounded by flowers. Everyone knew how much Fred loved flowers, and they had not let him down. Greenhouses had been raided, and the flower shop in Bagley had done a good trade in wreaths of chrysanthemums and carnations.

A handful of strangers sat in the front pew,

Fred's distant relations from Liverpool, and directly behind them, Ellen Biggs, Ivy Beasley and Doris Ashbourne. 'He'd have wanted you up here at the front,' said Tom Price, ushering them in.

Peggy Turner sat on her own, waiting for Bill to join her after the bell fell silent. She had noticed Donald Davie and Joyce sitting in a pew at the back. What's she doing here, she thought. Then she remembered that Joyce belonged in Ringford. She was a Ringford girl. And Peggy had moved to the Stores only three years ago. She glanced around again, and before she could turn her head away, she caught Joyce's eye, and saw a flicker of emotion. Dislike? Scorn? Oh, for God's sake, give it a rest, Peggy told herself, and then apologised silently to the Almighty for taking His name in vain in His own house.

Bill came and sat down quietly next to her and took her hand. He had a wonderful knack of knowing when she was feeling low, but this time was mistaken in the cause.

'Painful memories, gel?' he whispered anxiously. Peggy's husband Frank had been killed in a car accident in Ringford, and he, too, lay quietly under the blowing grasses of the cemetery.

Peggy thought it would be easier to pretend, and she nodded, squeezing Bill's hand.

The Reverend Nigel Brooks, who—in Ivy Beasley's words—knew how to do a good funeral, mounted the steps to the pulpit and addressed the congregation. He gave thanks for the life of Fred Mills, and told one or two little stories which made the congregation smile in fond recollection. He mentioned the dominoes school, where Fred was the champ, and the Horticultural Show, where Fred would be much missed for his onions and dahlias. He wondered how many remembered Fred in the church choir. Bill Turner silently recalled his own boyhood, when Fred had been a strong tenor and kept a firm hand on the lads in the front stall.

Nigel Brooks even managed to make Bill feel better about the party, saying that he knew if Fred had been given the choice, he would have elected to meet his Maker with a good pipe of tobacco and a pint in his hand.

'There, amongst his friends, basking in our love, Fred left us. We are the losers, and we shall not forget.'

In the quiet cemetery, surrounded by winter fields and the sparkling river where he had played and worked all his life, Fred was lowered into the earth.

'Forasmuch as it hath pleased Almighty God to take unto himself the soul of our dear brother here departed, we therefore commit his body to the ground . . .'

Ellen Biggs, who had insisted on missing no part of Fred's funeral, clutched Doris Ashbourne's arm.

'Ivy' whispered Doris. 'We'd better get Ellen home, or she'll be the next. Back me up, will you. She'll listen to you.'

The trio of women slowly left the graveside, and Nigel Brooks smiled kindly as they went.

* * *

'A nice hot cup of tea, that's what you need, Ellen,' said Doris, sitting her down in the best armchair in her front room. 'Put the kettle on, Ivy, while I get a rug for her knees.'

'I remember 'im when I first come to the Hall,' said Ellen, her eyes far away. 'He were a bit fresh once or twice, but I soon put 'im right. After that 'e were just a good friend.'

'I knew Fred from school,' said Ivy, her voice quiet, subdued. She turned to look down Macmillan Gardens, to Fred's house, cold and empty. 'He was always a bit of a squitty sort of chap, never made much of himself. But there was no harm in him, and he looked after that sister of his for years. Nobody could've done better.'

Doris refilled their cups, and sat down next to Ellen. 'I reckon he never really got over Elsie going,' she said. 'The heart went out of him, poor old Fred.'

They sat without speaking for several minutes, and then Ivy took her coat from the hook in Doris's narrow hallway, buttoning it up to the neck. 'Better be off, then,' she said.

150

'See you tomorrow.'

She seemed reluctant to go, reluctant to face her silent house, full of memories of the dead. At least there was life in Doris's bungalow, especially since Ellen had moved in there. Still, that couldn't go on for ever, thought Ivy. Doris was looking a bit peaky herself.

Fred's gate was hanging open, unheard of in his lifetime, and Ivy pulled it shut with a clang. She looked over the weedy vegetable patch to the small greenhouse, where Fred had spent so many contented hours with his trays of seedlings and geranium cuttings.

It's a funny business, growing old, she said to herself, walking on and turning the corner, hunching her shoulders against the cold wind.

Stop feeling sorry for yourself, Ivy Dorothy, said the voice in her head. Nobody's immortal, you know.

Except you, Mother, said Ivy bitterly.

*   *   *

Bill and Peggy wandered back down the lane and across the Green, hand in hand. As they passed the school, where Fred Mills had been a reluctant student, they could hear music. It was organ music, coming from the old harmonium. Bill remembered its strident tones only too well. 'Who's playing?' said Peggy. 'The children are not back from holiday yet, and Gabriella Jones is still up at the church.'

'Can't be burglars,' said Bill. 'They'd hardly advertise by playing the harmonium.'

He opened the playground gate and stood on tiptoe to peer in at the high windows. He turned back and looked at Peggy, standing by the railings, and raised his eyebrows. 'It's the new headmistress,' he said, 'all by herself, playing "See The Conquering Hero Comes".'

CHAPTER TWENTY-THREE

'Hands together and eyes closed,' said Miss Drinkwater.

Twenty-nine children, who had been shuffling nervously behind their desks, now relaxed. This was how every school assembly had begun since Miss Layton first came to Round Ringford. Sarah Drinkwater had done her homework well.

The children prayed for guidance and strength at the beginning of a new term, and Sarah assured God that they would all be working their hardest to make best use of the talents He had given them.

Mark Jenkins nudged Andrew Roberts, who made more of it than was necessary and crashed into his neighbour's desk. Closed eyes flew open, and the school held its breath. They knew exactly what Miss Layton would have done. Mark and Andrew stared at Miss

Drinkwater, Mark with a small challenging smirk. But Andrew regained his balance and closed his eyes piously.

Sarah Drinkwater's calm expression did not falter. She remained quite silent for a couple of minutes, looking fixedly at the two boys. Andrew Roberts did not meet her eyes, but Mark stared back at her. Then she turned away, smiled at the classroom in general, and spoke.

'I believe you usually have a reading now? Most mornings I shall ask for volunteers—which means preparation, you know—but on my first day at Ringford School I am going to choose someone. Mark Jenkins, I would like you to come out and read this little poem for me. It is one of my favourites.' She was very pleasant, smiling at Mark.

He looked startled, alarmed. Then his round face set into mutinous lines, and he cleared his throat.

'No,' he said.

'What did you say, Mark?' said Miss Drinkwater, still calm.

'No, I won't read it,' Mark said. His lower lip trembled.

'Oh yes, Mark,' she said, 'yes, of course you will. Come out here, please, so that we may all hear the poem.' She was no longer smiling, her green eyes cold and determined.

'Get going, stupid,' whispered Andrew Roberts.

The sun was high in the winter sky now, and rays of sunlight, cloudy with specks of dust stirred up by small feet, shone down on shining heads of newly washed hair. At the piano Gabriella Jones waited to play the morning hymn and wondered what on earth was going on. Whatever it was, the tension had mounted and she could see Mark Jenkins was near to tears.

'Out here, please,' said Miss Drinkwater. She held the open book towards Mark, and he slowly left his desk and shuffled forward to the front of the class.

'This is the one,' said Sarah Drinkwater, pointing to the page. Then she sat down, folded her arms and waited.

Mark looked down at the page, his face scarlet and his hands trembling, and he began to read. Everyone in the school knew that Mark Jenkins was a poor reader, had to have special help from a visiting teacher. As he stumbled from word to word, Gabriella Jones felt sick. This humiliation could not be right, not for such a small misdemeanour. She was searching desperately for some way of rescuing Mark, when he came to the end of the first verse and Miss Drinkwater stood up.

'Thank you, Mark,' she said. 'That will do. Not bad for such short notice. Next time we shall have more success, I am sure. Sit down, please.'

Mark did not look at Andrew as he returned

to his seat, but under the cover of his desk he kicked out at his friend's ankle and was a little comforted by the expression of pain on Andrew's face.

'And now we will have our hymn,' said Sarah Drinkwater. 'What shall we sing this morning, Mrs Jones?' Her smile for Gabriella was dazzling.

'Well,' said Gabriella, 'I wondered if you'd like to choose the hymn, Miss Drinkwater, as it is your first morning in Ringford School?' Gabriella had planned this little treat as a surprise for Sarah, but now she announced it grudgingly, not at all sure that little treats were in order.

'Oh, how lovely,' said Sarah, beaming at the children. 'Now, I wonder if we all know this one? Number four in the old hymn books, I think, Mrs Jones.'

Sarah had taken note of the hymns marked with a cross in the old Ancient and Modern on the harmonium. She was very thorough. Gabriella nodded, pleased that the tune would be familiar. All the children found their places and prepared to sing. All except for Mark Jenkins, that is, and he looked out of the window and across the fields, where he could see his dad moving through the river meadow on a tractor. Sarah Drinkwater was aware of this, but said nothing more. She took a deep breath, and began to sing with the children:

New every morning is the love
Our wakening and uprising prove;
Through sleep and darkness safely brought,
Restored to life and power, and thought.

The morning had had rather a shaky start, Sarah thought, but on the whole she felt she'd handled it rather well. She was a little sorry for Mark Jenkins, and not at all fooled by Andrew Roberts. His turn would come, no doubt. And anyway, now they knew exactly where they stood. Perhaps, after all, it had been a good beginning.

*   *   *

The bumpy lane leading to Walnut Farm shook Sarah's small car and did nothing at all for a sharp headache that had taken hold of her at the end of the school afternoon. Tension, that's all, she'd told herself firmly and swallowed a couple of tablets quickly, before Renata Roberts should come into the classroom. Without any water to wash them down, the tablets had got stuck, and Sarah coughed, making her eyes water. 'Not that bad, was it, Miss Drinkwater?' Mrs Roberts, waiting by the door with her broom, had looked innocently at the new teacher. 'Something caught in my throat,' said Sarah. 'No, no, everything's fine, thank you, Mrs Roberts. Absolutely fine.'

156

The yard at Walnut Farm was empty, except for a couple of cats staring balefully as Sarah got out of her car. The kitchen door stood open, and the interior seemed dark after the bright sunlight outside. 'Just in time for a cup of tea, Miss Drinkwater,' said Deirdre Barnett. Sarah had arrived at the farm yesterday, her car loaded with suitcases and books, and John Barnett had helped her unload. Once her belongings were carried up to the cool, dark-beamed bedroom that had been John's sister's, she had made her excuses and stayed upstairs to unpack. 'No, I'm not hungry, thank you,' she'd said, but Deirdre had knocked at her door and produced a tray of sandwiches and home-made fruit cake.

Now she noticed the table laid for tea. Oh Lord, they've decided to fatten me up, she thought. But she answered in her best friendly voice, 'Not Miss Drinkwater, please! Do call me Sarah.' John Barnett, sitting in an armchair by the window, reading a newspaper, looked up at her.

'Hello, Sarah,' he said, and went back to his paper.

Nice smile, thought Sarah. Perhaps he's not so bad.

'How was your first day, then?' said Deirdre, setting down a cup of tea and pointing to a chair. Sarah sat down gratefully and put her hands round the hot cup, comforted in spite of herself by Deirdre's motherly tone.

'Fine,' she said, and suppressed the thought of Mark Jenkins, stubborn and wounded. 'A nice bunch of kids.' Without thinking, she put her hands, hot from the teacup, up to her temples in an attempt to release the tight band of tension.

John Barnett stood up, stretching tall against the light from the window. 'Not always nice, not all of 'em,' he said, noticing Sarah's frown. 'Unless they've changed since my day.'

When was that? Sarah wondered, really looking at him for the first time. Difficult to tell how old he was. Big, certainly big. And in good shape, no doubt from all that farming or whatever. He was over by the telephone now, dialling a number. 'Some time tonight, then?' he said, and there was a chuckle in his voice. Girlfriend? thought Sarah. 'The lads'll be at the Bull later. Might catch up with you there. Cheers.' No, too casual for a girlfriend, surely.

'Right, then, mother,' John said. 'Bit more to do in the spinney. Back later.' He looked at Sarah and smiled again. It really was a very nice smile. 'Take it easy, Sarah,' he said.

'Thanks.' Sarah leaned back in the hard kitchen chair and took a deep breath, willing herself to relax. Perhaps he'd had a hard day, that time of the interview. He certainly seemed pleasant now. Reminds me of Dad. Well, not quite like Dad. Bigger, and—well—rougher.

'More shortbread, Sarah?' Deirdre demanded her attention. Sarah refused politely, and climbed the creaking staircase to her room. She sat down at the little desk Deirdre had placed for her next to the window, and took out her diary. Not a girl to confide in friends, Sarah never missed a day's entry, writing in her neat hand things that needed to be said.

CHAPTER TWENTY-FOUR

The low-ceilinged bedroom over the shop was cold and dark. Although Peggy knew it was time to get up—she'd heard the milk bottles chinking on the doorstep at least half an hour ago—she snuggled closer to Bill, stroking his back with a loving hand. He turned in his sleep and put his arms around her.

'Do you still love me?' Peggy asked. It had become a ritual, each morning the same question.

'Not this morning, thank you,' muttered Bill. He pulled her closer, and his bare skin was very warm and downy. Like a huge teddy bear, thought Peggy, succumbing to his sleepy advances with answering delight.

It was late when they finally tumbled out of bed and hurried downstairs to meet the post. The worst part of running a village post office was the early start. The two postladies, Maureen and Margaret, came in fully awake from the cold morning air, and with great efficiency sorted the letters ready for delivery. They divided Ringford between them, and the sorting didn't take them long. Maureen had another part-time job in Bagley, and Margaret helped her husband in a small market-garden along the Tresham Road, so their aim was to deliver the post as soon as was reasonably possible. Neither needed the small amount of money the job provided, but both enjoyed it, chatting to villagers who were awake, and occasionally in bad weather stopping for a quick warm-up, exchanging gossip, catching up on family news.

'Don't you miss him, Peggy?' said Maureen, as Peggy brought in steaming mugs of tea to send them on their way. Peggy stared at them for a moment, her heart lurching. Why should they suddenly ask if she missed her late husband Frank, after all this time, just now, so soon after she was back from her honeymoon?

'I miss the old bugger,' said Bill, getting his boots on in the corner of the kitchen. 'Old Fred had been there all my life. Tanned my arse when we knocked on his door and ran off, me and Tom Price. He was waiting for us the next night. Caught us red-handed, he did. Good old Fred.'

Of course, Peggy thought. They are talking about Fred Mills, not Frank.

'Ellen Biggs misses him most,' she said, rallying. 'I think she was fonder of him than she let on. Must be frightening for old people like Ellen when all their friends start popping off.'

'Just as well she's got old Ivy and Doris Ashbourne to look after her,' said Maureen, 'but I don't know how long that arrangement will last. Poor Doris took in a parcel yesterday—addressed to Ellen Biggs, of course—and I thought she looked worn out. Yawning her head off, she was.'

Margaret drained her mug and set it down. 'Very nice, thank you, Peggy,' she said. She looked out of the Post Office window and across the road. 'Seen the new headteacher yet?' she said.

'She popped in for a jar of instant,' said Peggy. 'Seemed a nice enough girl. Brisk, but pleasant.'

'She'll need her wits about her with that lot,' said Bill. He pulled on his jacket and departed, giving Peggy a noisy kiss and embarrassing her in front of the postladies. He saw this, and gave them each a peck on the cheek for good measure. 'Bye, gel,' he said, 'see you later.'

'That's a good man you've got there, Peggy,' said Maureen, laughing. 'Which is more than can be said of our Joyce's new man. Right little weed, that Donald Davie. No wonder she got Bill to help her with that great bag of compost yesterday. Weedy Donald just stood there, looking as if one puff of wind would blow him away. Bit of a liability that one, I reckon. What d'you think, Margaret?'

But Margaret did not answer. She frowned and shook her head at Maureen, as a scarlet-faced Peggy retreated with the empty mugs to the kitchen. The street was waking up as the postladies emerged, one or two cars going fast to catch trains from Tresham, an early-bird Mr Ross out with his little dog, Michael Roberts on a backfiring motorbike on his way to Hall Farm.

'Tact was never your strong point,' said Margaret to Maureen, as they set off on their Post Office regulation bicycles.

CHAPTER TWENTY-THREE

The work on the schoolhouse took longer than estimated, and in the weeks that followed, Sarah settled down comfortably at the farm. 'Always the same with builders,' said Deirdre, turning bacon in the frying pan. 'Got several jobs on the go, no doubt, juggling them all as it suits them.' She placed a piece of brown toast in front of Sarah Drinkwater, and once more pleaded with her to have a slice of bacon, or at least a boiled egg. 'You'll need it, Sarah,' she said, pushing back blue-grey hair from her round, hot face, 'to deal with those holy terrors at the school. Now how about a nice fresh brown egg, straight from the nest? John brought them in this morning, still warm.'

Deirdre Barnett was enjoying Sarah Drinkwater's stay at the farm. In fact, when she'd seen the decorator at the schoolhouse yesterday, and he said it would soon be ready for Sarah to move in, she'd felt a pang of regret. Although Sarah was not really her sort, much too cool and collected, she liked having someone to chat to over breakfast. She missed her husband, and her daughter Josie had been living in America for years. Deirdre had at one time entertained hopes of a match between Josie and Richard Standing. He'd been keen enough, but Josie had sent him packing, silly girl.

And now her afterthought son, John Barnett, bachelor farmer and School Governor, had taken his father's place on the farm calmly and efficiently, apparently quite content with his way of life, settled and sure of his place in the community. He could never fill the gap in Deirdre's life, of course, but he did his duty by her, and she had no complaints. Once or twice lately, she had absent-mindedly called him 'Johnnie', her pet name for his father. She was well looked after, the whole village knew that. She didn't know what she would do without him. But it was nice to have another woman around.

'Thank you, Mrs Barnett,' Sarah said, 'I'm sure they're the best eggs in Ringford, but I'm just not used to a big breakfast. You feed me so

163

well in the evening, it's enough to last twenty-four hours!' Sarah was the perfect diplomat.

The kitchen door stood open, letting in welcome spring sunshine. House martins were busy nest-building over the great barn doors, swooping back and forth, impelled by mysterious instincts which recalled them every spring to rear greedy, wearying families of noisy babies. Their appetites satisfied, the fledglings would grow rapidly and finally prepare to fly the nest, lining up at a hard-packed muddy nest edge to watch eagerly for their exhausted parents, fluffing out their wings in practice flutters. The scratty old farm cat, an ageing tabby seldom called anything but 'Cat!', sat gazing up at the birds, but she knew her limitations, and her eyes opened and closed lazily in the bright sunlight.

Lingering over her second cup of tea, Sarah listened to John's tractor idling in the yard, and heard above it his big voice giving instructions to William Roberts. William was Andrew's brother, still at school at Tresham but chafing against what he considered a useless education, impatient for the time when he could get a job and start earning money, leave home and have his own place somewhere. Perhaps he'd share his eldest brother Darren's terraced house in Tresham. Meanwhile, he had a day off school, and John Barnett had found some work for him to do.

'I expect you'll be looking for a farming job

when you leave school,' John had said. 'Follow in your father's footsteps, eh?' William had nodded, because it was easiest to agree. But privately he knew the last thing he wanted was to be like his father, Michael Roberts: rough, cruel to William's mother, frequently drunk, and yet tolerated by the village because he belonged.

'And don't leave that top gate open!' yelled John over the engine noise.

Sarah gathered up her school bag and prepared to leave. 'Shan't need a coat today, Mrs Barnett. It's wonderful out there, quite warm already.' She walked towards the door and turned to smile at Deirdre, now busy at the sink with her arms deep in sudsy water.

'I might be a little late tonight. We're having a gardening session after school for the big ones. I expect they'll be able to teach me a thing or two!'

I doubt it, thought Deirdre. It was the one thing she couldn't get used to with Sarah. She was always right, and knew everything about everything. And if there was some piece of information she could not supply, then it was not worth bothering with. Irrelevant, she would say. It was one of her favourite words.

Still, thought Deirdre, as she watched Sarah step out into the sunlit yard, I suppose she's got to know everything, her being a schoolteacher. She saw Sarah stoop to pat Nell's head. The old sheep dog was more or less retired now, but wherever John went, Nell was not far behind. He was her master and her life. She wagged her tail perfunctorily, and turned her rheumy eyes to where John had parked the tractor and was striding across the yard towards them.

'Morning, Sarah!' he said with a smile. He had admired the way she'd coped in these first few weeks, a young girl, a townie, thrown with little preparation to the roaring, shrieking lions who played three times a day in the old playground of Ringford School.

At least, that's how he had perceived her initially. But the last two months had opened his eyes. Sarah Drinkwater was tough. This was the first thing he learned about her, on discovering that she needed no rescuing from a posse of parents at the school gate. They were angry, shouting and waving the letters she had sent home with the children, stating that all long hair must be tied back neatly, and that toy guns were absolutely forbidden at all times, with no exceptions.

John had stood on the pavement outside the shop, clutching cans of lager, watching as Sarah calmed down the parents and had them nodding in sympathy and understanding in no time at all.

'Storm in a teacup,' she had said, when he brought up the subject that night at the supper table. 'Anything new or different in the school routine would have brought them there. Miss Layton warned me, so I was prepared.'

The second thing he learned about Sarah was that she was apparently unaware of the attention she attracted from the roving males of the village. And not just the local lads, ready for any new talent. John had seen Mr Richard dismissed like a naughty child when he had unwisely leaned too closely over her desk at a Governors' gathering in the classroom.

Not that John was all that interested. Goodness, that would be shitting on your own doorstep! One of his late father's best sayings, and never found wanting. No, John had no trouble in finding a partner for the Ringford Show Ball each year, and if anyone mentioned that it was time he started to think of settling down, he replied that he was a Ringford boy, and Ringford boys bided their time. 'No sense in getting the wrong ewe, when she's got to last a lifetime,' he said, and he seemed serious.

Still, he thought, seeing the sun shining on Sarah's silky brown hair, and her trim body moving easily inside a short red dress that was not much more than an elongated T-shirt, she's a good-looking girl, for a schoolteacher. 'Off now, then?' he said, smiling at her with his eyes.

'You going my way, John?' said Sarah absently, her mind on the history lesson she was preparing for tomorrow. 'I'm walking this morning. It's much too nice to take the car.'

'Will you be going home for Easter?' said John, as they set off down the lane. 'Not sure,' said Sarah, 'my parents are thinking about a cruise.' John put out a hand to steer her round a pot-hole, and although his touch was light, she felt the strength in his arm, and suddenly found she could not remember who came after Richard II.

The road from Walnut Farm ran along behind Walnut Close, the small development of new houses built in what had been the Home Close for the farm. Sarah and John passed back gardens bright with almond blossom and early daffodils. Yellow and purple polyanthus filled neat borders, and crisp white washing billowed gently in the warm wind. A small boy waved to them from his brightly painted swing, yelling, ''Lo, Miss Drinkwater!'

'There,' said John, 'you're one of us already.'

Sarah had recognised the child. His brother Charles was one of her brightest six-year-olds, from a family whose parents gave their children every chance, attended parents' evenings, helped with anything needing help, backed up Sarah's teaching with enthusiasm. This small one was likely to be a pleasure to teach, too. If they were all like that, teaching would be a doddle. She waved briefly at the swinging child, and turned to John.

'Not sure about that,' she said. 'I'm told you're not accepted in Ringford for at least twenty years. Peggy Turner was telling me in the shop. She says she still feels very much a newcomer, even though she's married a

Ringford man.'

'Nonsense,' said John. But he knew that there was a lot in what Peggy had said. Although incomers were soon accepted on one level quite quickly, provided they showed willing and were prepared to join in, there was still a real divide between the old village families and people who had lived lives elsewhere.

They turned into the Bagley Road, the lane which would take them into the main street of the village. As they passed the Tudor-style house belonging to the Rosses, John raised his hand to Mr Ross, busy in his immaculate garden already. 'Beats me what he finds to do,' said John.

'I'd hate to be a weed in that garden,' said Sarah, grinning. 'More a red rose than a weed,' said John gallantly, and then spoilt it by adding, 'and a very prickly one, at that.'

'Make a good pair, they would,' Mr Ross said to his wife, who stood watching as he bent over to pick out a young dandelion which had had the temerity to poke up through clumps of blue grape hyacinths.

'He's got the Barnett hair,' said his wife obliquely. It was true that John Barnett was a good looking man, with curly auburn hair and a narrow, slightly hooked nose inherited from his mother. He was tall and heavily built, and without the hard, physical work of the farm he would put on weight with maturity.

At the corner of Bagley Road and Ringford's main street, John whistled to Nell, who was investigating a scent in the playing fields. 'See you then,' he said, 'and be kind to the bad 'uns today, Miss Drinkwater.' He looked down at Sarah, and something teasing in his smile caused her to turn away, oddly confused.

'Don't worry,' she said lightly, 'I left the cane at the farm. Cheers, John.' She crossed with brisk steps into the school playground and disappeared.

Miss Ivy Beasley, crossing on the zebra outside the school, on her way to the Lodge to open the windows and give the deserted rooms an airing, saw John and Sarah, and wondered. What would Deirdre say if it came to that?

*　　*　　*

'Donald!' called Joyce from her back fence overlooking the fields. She was gazing with delight at five or six lambs playing leaping games on the big heap of muck John Barnett had piled up in the corner of the field. Joyce had seen him checking the lambs early that morning, and thought how much he reminded her of Bill when young—big and strong, moving heavy, mutinous sheep around as if they were puppies.

Donald Davie came quietly down the garden path and stood arm in arm with his wife, watching the lambs. A ragged-looking ewe stood about twenty yards away with a very small lamb. It bounded away from its mother and came right up to where the Davies stood. Joyce leaned over the fence and gently rubbed the black, velvety head, and the ewe, mad-eyed and alarmed, rushed up and stamped her forefoot. The lamb returned to her at once, nuzzling her udder, its catkin tail wagging from side to side in a frenzy of excitement.

'Aren't they lovely babies, Donald?' Joyce said. Donald squeezed her arm and smoothed down his thin hair, ruffled by the breeze.

'It is a perfect morning, Joycey,' he said.

She turned sharply and looked at him. 'You've never called me that before,' she said accusingly.

He was surprised at her tone, hurt. 'Why shouldn't I call you Joycey?' he asked.

'Oh, well, I suppose it's all right. I just don't like it much, that's all. Like you hate being called Don. It's not important, my dear,' she said, and kissed his cheek.

But Joyce heard another voice, a loud Ringford voice, calling her across the years. Joycey! Joycey! Look at these pheasants I shot today! You never saw such a plump hen as this, I bet you ... Joycey, come here and have a cuddle ... Joycey, don't look at me like that. It's not my fault, Joycey, please...

'Shall we go for a long walk today, Donald,' Joyce said, leading him firmly back up the

171

garden path. 'I'll show you the bluebell woods. If the sun lasts, we could take a picnic.'

'Won't it be damp underfoot?' said Donald. 'It's not summer yet, not even Easter. But a stroll would be lovely,' he added, seeing her face fall.

*　　*　　*

'Now we're wed,' said Peggy, gazing happily across the kitchen table at Bill, 'we never go for walks any more.'

They were relaxing at the end of the day, Peggy from a busy afternoon in the shop, coping with waves of schoolchildren and needing a dozen pairs of eyes and hands; and Bill from a vigorous spring-cleaning session in the Standings' kitchen garden, where he grew enough vegetables to feed the entire village.

'Well, now we've got a perfectly good bed upstairs,' said Bill, grinning at her.

'Don't be silly, Bill,' she said. 'You know perfectly well what I mean. I loved those walks in Bagley Woods, and times when we sat on the old tree stump and made plans. It was fun, wasn't it?'

'Could have been more fun,' said Bill, 'if you hadn't been so proper.'

She could see he was teasing, not prepared to be drawn into nostalgia. Well, he's right, I suppose, she thought, making plans is not nearly as good as the real thing, and she got up

172

to put the mugs in the sink.

'We could go now, if you want,' said Bill. 'It's light much later now, and the air's still warm. Shall we?'

Peggy fed Gilbert quickly, pleased that Bill had after all understood. 'Back soon, Gilbertiney,' she said, and followed Bill out of the back door.

The climb up Bagley Hill, between hedges full of celandines and young, bright green nettles, took away their breath, and they paused at the broken fence where the footpath led off into the woods.

'Just look at those snowdrops,' said Bill. 'They're late ones.'

He bent down, but Peggy was quick. 'Don't pick them, Bill,' she said. 'They never look so good in a vase. It's the old leaves and peeling bark, and all that ivy—you can never arrange them to look like that.'

'Don't mention Ivy to me,' said Bill, helping Peggy over a fallen tree, slippery with moss. 'The old bat never misses an opportunity, does she.'

'What now?' said Peggy.

'She stopped me by the bus shelter, and asked if I knew that Joyce and Donald were planning to take down the hedge in the front garden of number fourteen.' This thick privet hedge had shielded Joyce in her reclusion from the outside world. It was a symbol to Bill of all those unhappy years.

'I told her it was the best thing I had heard in months. That fixed the old devil. She stumped off looking very huffy.'

'But it's nothing to do with you now, is it Bill?' said Peggy. The sun had dipped below the trees, and she shivered as the air cooled.

'Nothing at all,' said Bill. 'Jolly good luck to them, that's what I say.'

They walked on in silence, stepping over the rapidly running streams which interlaced the woods, avoiding well known boggy patches. And then, suddenly, there were the bluebells, taking Peggy by surprise as she brooded about Joyce and Donald and high privet hedges. The clear, vivid, breathtaking colour stretched out between silvery birches, like a hazy, luminous forerunner of the summer sky.

'Bill, just look at that,' Peggy said. 'You can never hold that colour in your head, can you. It's the same every year, and yet it always seems so fresh and new. I wish I had the camera.'

'That blue doesn't come out on film,' said Bill. 'Some scientific reason for it. Do you want to pick some?'

Peggy shook her head. 'Best to leave them there,' she said.

Bill took Peggy's hand and led her along a footpath, until they were surrounded by bluebells, crossing a sea of heavenly blue. As they stepped out into the clearing by the track that led out of the wood and into Tom Price's top field, Peggy stopped.

'Someone's on our tree stump,' she said, frowning.

There was indeed a figure seated on the stump of an ancient felled oak, wide enough for two to sit comfortably. Peggy and Bill had sat there so many times in the past, gazing over the village and talking in the only private place they knew, that Peggy regarded it as their own.

'Mm,' said Bill, standing by Peggy. He took her hand again, and began to turn her round. 'And I know who it is,' he said.

He was too late. Donald Davie had heard voices, and looked round with a smile, pleased that he and Joyce were not the only ones mad enough to walk through a wild wood and sit on a soggy tree stump.

'Oh, shit,' said Bill. He and Peggy stood still and waited. Joyce stood up and turned to look at them. Her face was pale and set.

'Ah, sorry, Bill,' she said, ignoring Peggy. 'Have we got your seat? I remembered it was a favourite place. Many's the time we met up here, Donald, when we were young. Ah well, all water under the bridge now, isn't it, Bill.'

She took Donald Davie's arm and started off in the opposite direction, but turned again to deliver her parting shot.

'Seen the bluebells, Mrs Palmer—sorry, Turner? At least some things never change.'

Bill and Peggy watched until Donald and Joyce disappeared through the trees, and then they approached the oak stump. Bill looked

175

closely at Peggy, and said, 'Shall we sit down for bit, gel?'

Peggy shook her head. 'I'd like to go home,' she said.

CHAPTER TWENTY-SIX

'Cheer up, Peggy,' said Doreen Price, bouncing noisily into the shop, setting the old bell over the door jangling fiercely. 'Here,' she continued, handing over a large brown envelope to Peggy who was standing dejectedly behind the counter, 'here's news of a major dramatic event to take place in the village.'

'Dramatic events I can do without,' said Peggy, reaching into the envelope and drawing out a brightly-coloured poster. '*The Withered Arm*,' she read aloud, 'a wonderful evening's entertainment from the Royal Theatre Travelling Players, making a welcome return to Round Ringford Village Hall. Three absorbing stories by Thomas Hardy, guaranteed to have you shivering in your seats!'

'Sounds good so far,' said Doreen, looking shrewdly at Peggy. 'Just the job for taking you out for yourself. Better than the telly any day. They've been before, of course, and the hall is always full. Shall I put you down for a couple of tickets?'

'Are you serious, Doreen?' Peggy said, putting the poster down on the counter and straightening the already tidy display of Cadbury's Fruit and Nut. 'Can you see me and Bill settling down to an evening of Thomas Hardy?'

'Bet you went to see *Far from the Maddening Crowd,* didn't you?'

'Madding Crowd, actually, Doreen,' said Peggy irritably.

'There you are then,' said Doreen equably. 'Anyway, I'll just put two on one side for you, and you can consult with Bill.'

'Mm,' said Peggy. 'The air's a bit cool between us at the moment. I expect it's my fault, but sodding Joyce is getting on my nerves. And Bill seems to have a bit of a blind spot about his ex-wife. Oh, I don't know, Doreen, it's really all about nothing, but we don't seem to be able to put it right.'

So that's it, thought Doreen. 'That Joyce was always a trouble-maker,' she said. 'Just don't let her bother you, that's all. Ignore her. She never could abide being ignored.'

*   *   *

'Why can't I go, Ivy?' said Ellen Biggs from the depths of Doris Ashbourne's most comfortable armchair. 'It's only down to the Village Hall, and if you and Doris are goin' you can make sure I don't peg out on the way.'

177

Ellen was fed up with Ivy Beasley's efforts to restrict her movements. She was feeling very much better, and an evening at the play was just what she fancied. It had been very enjoyable that time the Travelling Players did a version of *Hamlet*. She'd not understood half the words, mind, but you could tell what was going on by the way they kept leaping around and killing each other.

'Well, I think it would be nice if we all went,' said Doris. 'Ellen could wrap up well, and it's always warm in the hall when the heaters are on and there's enough people to fill it.'

'Too warm, if you ask me,' said Ivy crossly. 'The silly old woman'll get pneumonia coming out into the cold night air. Still,' she continued, with a shrug of her shoulders, 'I can see you've both decided, so I might as well keep my mouth shut.'

'You can certainly say less about "the silly old woman,"' said Ellen angrily.

'Now, now,' said Doris the peacemaker, 'that's enough. We'll all go, and I'm sure it will be a very pleasant evening. That's if you two can stop bickering.' Time for a change of subject, she thought, and looking out of her sitting-room window down the Gardens, she saw Joyce Davie emerge from her gate and set off towards the main street.

'There goes Joyce,' she said. 'Who would have believed it, a couple of years ago, that a woman could change so completely.'

'Leopard don't change its spots,' said Ellen grumpily.

'What do you mean, Ellen?' said Ivy. 'Joyce is a new woman, and very happy with her Donald. Her house is as clean as a new pin, and she's beginning to take part in village life again. What more can you want?'

'I 'aven't forgotten the auction,' said Ellen darkly. 'And nor has Joyce. She'll be plottin' somethin' else, you can bet yer life. If I was Peggy Turner, I'd keep eyes in the back of me 'ead.'

Ivy exploded. 'Anything coming to Peggy Turner is fully deserved!' she said loudly. 'As for plotting, that's just your wicked mind, Ellen Biggs. It's gossipy remarks like that as causes all the trouble in this village!'

Ellen glared at her. 'You can talk, Ivy,' she said. 'Best case of the pot callin' the kettle I've heard for a long time. And yes, Doris, I would like another cup of tea, thank you.'

'And you, Ivy?' said Doris placatingly. Before Ivy could answer, Ellen jumped in again. 'Better put two extra spoonfuls of sugar in hers,' she said. 'Might sweeten her up a bit, though I doubt it meself.'

*   *   *

The Village Hall had been transformed by two young drama students and a clever carpenter from the Royal Theatre in Tresham. At one end a stage with dark green curtains had been erected, big bowls of chrysanthemums stood at either side, and an elaborate array of stage lighting had miraculously sprouted from the high ceiling. As Bill and Peggy, last to arrive, found their seats five rows from the front, the green curtains were drawn across, revealing a wonderfully painted nineteenth-century cottage interior. A spatter of applause went round the hall, and a tall, distinguished-looking man in breeches and waistcoat stepped forward to welcome the audience.

Doreen's promises were not betrayed. The young actors and actresses, two of each and adept at rapid costume changes, kept the sixty-odd villagers enthralled. In the heightened atmosphere of melodrama perfectly acted, tragedy, comedy and romance worked their magic spells. Peggy found herself laughing and gasping, only once looking round to see if Joyce Davie was sitting behind her, but not able to see in the dark. She grabbed Bill's hand as the tension rose, and he gave an answering squeeze.

''Ere,' said Ellen Biggs in an audible whisper to Doris, 'it's better than that *'amlet*, ain't it. Ooer, look out, ducky, 'e's right be'ind yer!' The last outspoken remark was addressed to a damsel in distress on the stage, who had trouble suppressing a smile.

It was during the third act that the lights suddenly went out, and several members of the audience screamed. Deirdre Barnett, who had reluctantly allowed Sarah to persuade her that an evening with Thomas Hardy would be a fun night out, was surprised as her lodger rose to her feet. However, the ever-ready Sarah was not needed, and subsided again as someone began to speak.

'Don't panic, ladies and gentlemen!' It was the voice of the distinguished-looking actor. 'Just a temporary hitch. Please remain in your seats, and we will have the lights on in a few minutes.' And then, in a sudden burst of theatrical fervour, he cried, 'Let there be light!' but there wasn't, and Tom Price shuffled his way to the front of the audience.

'Tom Price here,' he announced, as if anyone in the hall would fail to recognise his voice. 'Don't worry, Doreen's gone to see to it. She's got her torch, and all should be well in a minute or two. The meters have run out, she thinks.'

A couple of minutes passed, and a quiet buzz of patient conversation filled the darkened hall. Then Doreen's voice was heard. 'Oh, blast!' she said. 'I haven't got any. Have you, Tom?' Silence, then, 'Bugger it, neither have I, Doreen. Hang on, I'll ask around.'

A whispered message began to travel along the rows of waiting audience. It didn't have far to go, stopping at Joyce Davie, two rows in front of Peggy and Bill. She stood up and began to stumble over her neighbours' feet. 'I've got some, Tom,' she shouted. 'Always

181

keep some fifty-pence pieces in my purse for emergencies.'

'Them meters don't take nothin' else,' said Ellen Biggs. 'Ran out once when we 'ad that man with 'is 'oliday snaps come to talk to the WI. What a relief!—everybody pretended they 'adn't got no fifty p's, so he 'ad to stop. Bin goin' for an hour and a 'alf already, he 'ad.'

Just as Ivy was about to accuse Ellen of exaggerating as usual, the lights came on and everyone sat straighter in their seats, looking a little foolish as if caught out at something forbidden. A cheer went up as Joyce Davie walked out from behind the stage and made her way back to her seat. 'Good old Joyce!' shouted someone from the back, and everyone clapped.

As the performance began again, Bill turned to Peggy, reassured by the hand that had tucked into his. 'Off we go again, then gel,' he said, smiling down at her.

'Thanks to the very wonderful Joyce Davie,' said Peggy acidly, and put her hands firmly in her pockets.

CHAPTER TWENTY-SEVEN

For the benefit of Round Ringford's sick and ailing, Dr Russell from Bagley, near retirement but still active and alert, drove his big Rover down the middle of the country lanes and into the village to conduct his weekly surgery. He had been Ringford's doctor for thirty years, and several of the village families were into their third generation in his care.

He looked forward to Friday's surgery. The leisurely drive through farmland as familiar as his own garden was a source of quiet pleasure to him. He could read the landscape like a local newspaper, knew who was on the tractor swinging dangerously around the corner by Ringford bridge, could guess pretty accurately which farm had the red bull that week. And in the winter, he knew for sure when the hunt had found a fox in Grumbler's Holt, as he eased his big car past the roadside row of muddy cars and hunt followers with field glasses.

Dr Russell also knew roughly who would be waiting to see him in Ringford Surgery. He had his regulars, and he was always patient. Being a good listener, he was at once popular and effective.

On surgery mornings, the front parlour of Ivy Beasley's Victoria Villa doubled as a consulting room, and her immaculate kitchen served as waiting room. This morning, the spring sunlight had had a healing effect on Round Ringford, and there were only three patients for Dr Russell. Doreen Price had cracked a small bone in her foot. It was slow to heal, and gave her nasty jabs of pain, especially when she crossed a rutted field in her wellies.

Jean Jenkins was there with Eddie, who was having a day off school with earache. He had a bright red scarf tied round his clean blond hair, and looked very sorry for himself.

The third patient was not a regular. Doris Ashbourne, neatly dressed in a beige mac, her handbag clutched nervously in both hands, blinked a little as a shaft of sunlight penetrated Ivy's net curtains and fell on her spectacles. She had managed to parry Ivy's pointed questions when she'd arrived at the front door of Victoria Villa. 'It's nothing much, Ivy. I just need a prescription from Dr Russell, that's all.'

But Ivy was not fooled. She had seen Doris looking more and more tired as the weeks of looking after Ellen Biggs passed. It was worrying, and Ivy could not think of a neat solution. The Lodge was certainly not fit for Ellen to go back there, and anyway, she could no longer look after herself properly. Ivy had a lurking guilt that she should offer to have Ellen for a while, but she knew it would end in tears. I couldn't do it, Mother, she had said to her ghostly companion in the small wakeful hours. It wouldn't be good for either of us. For once, her mother agreed.

'You're next, Jean,' said Ivy officiously. She regarded herself as honorary doctor's receptionist on Friday mornings, and shepherded the villagers in and out briskly. She had been brought up not to waste the doctor's time, and had deep suspicions about some of

184

the newcomers from Walnut Close who had nothing better to do than moan to Dr Russell about their imagined illnesses. 'Not enough to do,' she'd said, 'that's the only thing wrong with them.'

Jean Jenkins led Eddie out of the kitchen, and they disappeared into Ivy's front room. Dr Russell sat at Ivy's oak drop-leafed table, behind a vase of bright polyanthus specially picked that morning, and smiled kindly at Jean.

'How's young Eddie, then?' he said.

'It's his ear again, Doctor,' said Jean Jenkins.

Dr Russell peered into Eddie's glowing ear, and nodded. 'It is inflamed, poor laddie,' he said. He sat down again and wrote out a prescription. 'Here, Jean,' he said, 'get this into him as soon as possible, and it'll clear up quickly. Soon be back at school, don't you worry, young Eddie.'

Eddie glared at him. 'Don't want to go to school,' he said.

'Don't you like school? Haven't you a new schoolteacher?'

'Miss Thirsty,' said Eddie. 'I hate her.'

'Eddie!' said Jean. 'He doesn't mean it,' she said apologetically. But Dr Russell laughed. 'What did you call her, Eddie?' he said.

Eddie was dumb, quelled into silence by his mother's warning stare.

'She's Miss Drinkwater,' Jean said. 'Seems

very good, so far. Not all the children get on with her, of course, but she knows how to keep them in order. Our Markie is not getting on as well as he did with Miss Layton, but it's early days.'

Dr Russell stood up and held out his hand. He knew from long experience that Jean Jenkins could happily chat for hours, and there was one other waiting to see him.

'Bring him back if it doesn't improve,' he said. 'Goodbye, Jean, my dear. Bye, Eddie.'

It was Doris's turn next, and as she was last, the nasty thought that Ivy might listen outside the door crossed her mind as she sat down on the chair in front of Dr Russell. It was bad enough knowing that some voices carried right through the wall to Ivy's kitchen, often causing a lull in the conversation there. She spoke in a low voice, just in case.

'I'm just so tired all the time, Doctor,' she said.

'Speak up please, Mrs Ashbourne,' said Dr Russell. 'We old fogies can't hear as well as we used to.'

Doris edged her chair nearer to the oak table. 'I don't seem to have the energy these days,' she said. 'And I don't sleep very well. Wake up every morning about five and can't get off again.'

'I see,' said Dr Russell, leaning back in his chair. 'Now, you still have Mrs Biggs with you, isn't that right?'

Doris nodded. He knew, of course. She could rely on him to know, without having to spell it out. Old Ellen woke early, and had to be helped to the lavatory. She had refused to use the flowered jerry, protesting that she could manage, but Doris had found her in a heap on the floor one morning, and after that she had insisted that Ellen call her.

Then there were the endless meals. When she was on her own, she often had biscuits and cheese at midday, and then something hot about six o'clock, eaten from a tray while she watched the news on the telly. But she felt duty-bound to cook a proper dinner for Ellen, and around four o'clock they had tea and cake, and after that a sandwich supper at nineish. And dozens of cups of tea and coffee in between.

She liked chatting to Ellen, of course, especially about the old days. But she also liked to be quiet, and doze off over the newspaper in the afternoon. Ellen seemed to need very little sleep, and no sooner had Doris's eyelids drooped than Ellen was barking some question at her which demanded an answer.

'Yes, I am very tired, Dr Russell,' she said. 'I think I need a tonic, or something.'

Dr Russell was silent for a few seconds, looking hard at Doris, twisting a pen in his fingers.

'I'll certainly give you something to help you sleep,' he said, 'but I think we might have to do

187

a bit more than that. Leave it with me, Mrs Ashbourne, and I'll be in touch.'

Doris walked past Ivy and out into the sunlit street. 'Must go, Ivy,' she said. 'It's time for Ellen's coffee, and she doesn't half grumble if it's not there on time. I shall see you later, shan't I. You bringing the cake today?'

Ivy confirmed that she had been baking, and though doubtless it wouldn't live up to that Mr Kipling that Ellen loved so much, she could safely say the chocolate sponge had risen quite satisfactorily.

Doris disappeared into Macmillan Gardens, and Ivy Beasley saw Dr Russell off in his car. He'll have to retire one day, Ivy thought, though not yet, I hope. He knows more about this village than most.

She stood in the sun, her arms folded and her legs planted firmly apart on her top step. The sudden eruption of children into the school playground shattered the peace of the village street. Shrieks and screams from the girls mingled with the boys' raucous shouts as they chased after a ball. Andrew Roberts demonstrated some nifty footwork as he outwitted the others with ease.

What's wrong with that Mark Jenkins? thought Ivy. She could see the bulky figure pressed up into a corner, his head down and shoulders hunched. Just the usual bullying, Ivy, said her mother's voice. Always the same, if you ask me. You were bullied, Ivy, don't you

188

remember. Four-eyes, they used to call you when you first wore glasses. Still, you could sort them out, as I recall.

Ah, yes, Ivy thought, but you don't know how I suffered, Mother. I learned the hard way, just like poor Markie Jenkins will. If you can't beat 'em, join 'em. Bullied Ivy Beasley turned into Ivy Beasley the bully. It's a jungle over there, Mother, you can be sure of that.

Her attention was caught by Maureen, the postlady, cycling along the street. She stopped at the school gate, propped her bicycle against the railings, and waved to Sarah Drinkwater, who was standing in the sun, watching the children and drinking coffee from a mug, a flash of scarlet in the sun.

'Now what does that Maureen want?' said Ivy to herself. It was too far away for her to hear, however, and she turned reluctantly and went back into the house.

CHAPTER TWENTY-EIGHT

Sarah Drinkwater saw Maureen waving and walked over to the gate. She also noticed Mark Jenkins in the corner, and a small shadow crossed her face. I shall have to do something about that boy, she thought. He hasn't forgiven me yet for not being Miss Layton.

'Sorry, Miss Drinkwater,' said Maureen,

'this letter was mixed up with post for Colin Osman. There's always a big bundle for him.' She handed a long white envelope to Sarah, and cycled off.

The envelope was postmarked Tresham, and Sarah turned it over a couple of times, wondering why she felt apprehensive. The school received dozens of letters from the Education Department, most of them unnecessary bureaucracy, requiring her to make graphs of this and collate statistics of that, and work out percentages of everything from classroom learning time to amounts of coffee consumed.

She didn't open it, waiting until the children were back in school and settled at their books. Then she slit open the envelope with Miss Layton's old paper-knife and drew out the letter. She was right to be apprehensive. She had not forgotten the school was under review, and occasionally wondered at the Governors' apparent lack of concern. But she had drifted along with them, never feeling a sense of urgency that anything needed to be done.

It was a long letter, and she read through to the end. So this was it. Miss Layton's retirement had brought to their notice that numbers were still small at Round Ringford, and they requested an up-to-date indication of pre-school-age children likely to be needing places in the future. They would subsequently be in a position to finalise the review and—

ominous word—rationalise the situation.

Sarah sat at her desk for a long time, thinking. The children were quiet, sensing from the expression on her face that something serious was afoot. At last she stood up, and Mark Jenkins quickly opened his workbook and pretended to be busy.

The rest of the morning proceeded as usual. Reading books were brought out, and Sarah helped each child in her expert way to master stories of Biff and Kipper and Chips, and Floppy the dog. Characters in books had changed, but the business of learning to read had gone on in this quiet classroom for generations of children. Sarah had a sudden alarming vision of a dusty, empty building, festooned with cobwebs, with damp books rotting away, old posters peeling from the walls. She shook her head and concentrated on Mark Jenkins, who stuttered and faltered, but Sarah waited patiently until he had his tongue round the words. He was finding it easier these days, but he would not admit it, not to Miss Thirsty. As he went back to his desk he knocked Andrew Roberts's pencil flying, and faced Sarah swiftly. 'It was an accident, Miss, honestly.' He waited, but was surprised at the absence of rebuke. He sat down, disappointed.

*   *   *

'Sarah!' said Deirdre Barnett, surprised to see

her lodger drive into the yard at lunchtime.

'I need to see John,' Sarah said. 'I've left Gabriella in charge.'

'He'll be in for his dinner any minute,' Deirdre said. 'You'd better have some too. You look a bit starved—feeling all right?'

John Barnett smiled at Sarah as he pulled off his boots at the door. 'Don't usually see you at this time of day,' he said. 'Nothing wrong at the school, I hope?'

'I need to talk to you, John,' she said, 'before I talk to the vicar.'

Vicar? Deirdre looked up sharply from mashing potatoes. But then Sarah went on to talk about a letter from the Education Department, and the need for an emergency Governors' meeting.

'What's the timing on this?' John had seen at once the seriousness of Sarah's unexpected appearance.

Sarah shook her head. 'Don't know. I'll ring up this afternoon, see what else I can find out. But we must tell Nigel and the rest. Fix a meeting. I know only too well how these things creep up on you. Closed before we know it.' Sarah's voice was grim.

'Blimey!' said John. 'Right-o, then, Sarah. Leave Nigel to me, and you get back and make that telephone call. And don't worry,' he said, smitten by the tension in her face, 'nobody pushes Ringford around.'

He stood at the kitchen window and

watched Sarah slip neatly into her car and drive off out of the yard. 'She's driving much too fast down that lane,' he said.

'She'll be all right,' said Deirdre.

'Hope so,' said John. 'Looks like we're going to need her now.'

'Maybe,' said his mother, and rattled the dishes in the sink.

CHAPTER TWENTY-NINE

Dr Russell had finished his calls in Ringford, and drove into the yard of Hall Farm to have coffee with Tom Price. This was a weekly ritual, and coffee was followed by a stroll round the farm, provided the weather was fine.

Tom Price and Guy Russell had been friends for years, and a natural warmth between them had deepened at the time of Doreen's second pregnancy. It was never talked about now, but Doreen had miscarried late. Nowadays, the tiny baby could possibly have survived, but then it might have been damaged. Lately Doreen had looked at Robert and Mandy Bates's little son, Joey, disabled with cerebral palsy, his future very uncertain, and comforted herself that at least she and Tom had been spared that dreadful, ongoing worry.

But at the time, Guy Russell had been a source of strength and consolation to Tom and

Doreen. They were not good at expressing their gratitude in words, but over the years had shown steady and generous friendship as the unhappy time had receded into its place in all their lives.

The two men had set off round the farm, heavy boots squelching through the mud at the Home Close gate. Guy Russell took a deep breath, drawing the clean, cold air into his lungs. Although the sun shone through high mackerel clouds, warming their backs as they walked out across the Close, the wind was keen, reminding them that it was not summer yet.

'Wheat's looking good, Tom,' said Guy. He'd wanted to be a farmer himself, but it had been taken for granted he would follow his father's footsteps into the medical profession.

Tom nodded. 'Those old beans are coming up again, though,' he said. Last year the field had been a mass of bean blossom, the scent sweet and cloying on warm spring days. A lark rose up yards away from them, its trilling song pouring out over the field, so strong and piercing that they could still hear it even when the bird had risen in bursts of flight, climbing invisible stairs, finally out of sight.

They walked in companionable silence, sniffing a new scent on the air. 'Foxy Jenkins is muckin' out this morning,' said Tom. 'Usually does on a Friday morning. That's his bonfire. They've got a new thoroughbred at the Hall, beautiful animal. Mrs Standing looks a treat, and by God, that can't half go!'

Tom's old spaniel, Bess, padded along in front of them, disappearing into the hedge and despatching protesting blue tits and a pale, spotted thrush. Hedge sparrows flitted through the budding hawthorn, always a few yards ahead of them, like hidden spies monitoring their progress.

'You got time to go on round the far pasture?' said Tom, standing by a stile which led to a tiny tributary of the Ringle. It was clear and full, with bright yellow puffs of pussy willow swaying at its margins.

Guy Russell nodded. 'But I do have to be at the vicarage soon. Sophie and Nigel are expecting me to call in, and I must talk to them about old Ellen Biggs.'

Doctors' business is confidential, but Guy Russell regarded this more as a village problem. What happened to Ellen Biggs concerned more than just the old woman. There was Doris Ashbourne and Ivy Beasley, and the Standings at the Hall. All those years as cook for the family meant that a certain responsibility was felt by Mr Richard; and Susan Standing, too, though she had been irritated by the autocratic ways of Ellen Biggs in her kitchen, could not but admire Ellen's courage and fortitude in old age.

Bess had vanished into a vast woodpile by the stream. Tom called her, but she did not reappear. 'Always bin foxes in there,' he said. 'We do some sawing there every so often, and that roots them out for a bit. But they always come back.'

At that moment, a small, reddish triangular face peered out between two horizontal ash trunks, surprise and fear in its black button eyes. It disappeared at once, and Bess shot out from the other end of the pile, deaf to Tom's shouts.

'She'll not get it,' said Tom comfortably. 'Crafty little devils. They've got dozens of ways out.'

The two men tramped back across the meadow, and Dr Russell changed his boots in the yard, throwing them into the back of his car.

'Cheerio, then, Tom,' he said. 'See you next week.' Doreen waved to him from the kitchen window and he drove slowly out of the yard and off towards the vicarage.

CHAPTER THIRTY

Nigel listened to Guy Russell's plea for help with the Ellen Biggs problem and felt flattered, but he couldn't concentrate. The news from John Barnett was too fresh in his mind, and he knew he had to get rid of old Guy in the nicest possible way, but soon. Then he could begin rounding up his troops. 'I'll talk to Sophie about it, Guy,' he said. 'She's awfully good at this kind of thing. Leave it to me, and I'll be in touch.' As soon as the old doctor had gone, Nigel set to work.

He decided on an immediate meeting of all the Governors, and then the whole village must be alerted. This was the most serious thing that had happened since he'd arrived in Ringford, and he welcomed the challenge. And now Guy asking for his help ... At last he began to feel that he was a necessary part of village life.

'Is it really urgent, Nigel?' Richard Standing wished he had not answered the telephone. He was collecting things together in his study ready to catch the Inter-City to London. With any luck he could be at Harrods before it closed. It was Susan's birthday on Saturday, and he'd left her present to the last minute as usual.

'Extremely urgent, Richard,' Nigel said. And then he told him of the letter from the Education Department, with its careful wording and sinister implications.

'Don't you think you're going over the top a bit?' said Richard. 'Could be another new broom at the Education Department, trying to make his mark.'

'That's possible, of course,' said Nigel, 'but the review's coming to a head, it seems, and it might be difficult to stop the consequences. We have to act now, Richard, pull out all the stops.

197

Perhaps we've been a bit too complacent, all of us.'

Richard Standing put down his document case and ran his hand through his lank, dark hair. He sighed. It sounded as if Nigel really meant what he said. A meeting tonight up at the vicarage, everybody present, no exceptions. Ah well, he supposed he could go into Tresham and see if Addenham's had anything suitable for Susie's birthday.

'Oh, all right, Nigel,' he said. 'It is very inconvenient, but if you're sure it's that important...'

'It is,' said Nigel Brooks firmly, and ran his finger down the list of Governors for the next telephone number.

*   *   *

'They couldn't, could they, Bill?' said Peggy Turner, putting clean blue and white plates back on the dresser. She had taken the call from Nigel Brooks, and relayed it to an alarmed Bill over tea.

'Village schools do close, Peggy,' he said. 'There's been a lot in the papers lately about the pros and cons of such small numbers. A lot of blather about peer group stimulus, and no proper teams for sport, and all that.'

'There could be something in it,' said Peggy.

'Maybe,' said Bill, 'but that's not the real reason. It's money, like always. Economies must be made, says the Chairman of the Education Department, when he's spent too much on yet more computers in the big schools. The village schools have always been the scapegoats, the first targets for so-called economies. The amount they'd save would be peanuts anyway, compared with what they waste in other places.'

Peggy looked at Bill, animated and angry at the idea of his school under threat. Pity he couldn't feel as much concern for his wife's problems, she thought grumpily. Still, she was impressed.

'You tell 'em, Bill,' she said. 'They're tangling with the wrong ones here in Ringford.'

*   *   *

Sophie Brooks stood by the big open door of the vicarage and welcomed the School Governors, one by one, as they marched up the path with purpose in their steps. Doreen Price had a worried frown on her pleasant face, and for once she failed to notice where Sophie had been planting the border with neat clumps of summer annuals—petunias, antirrhinums, asters. Normally Doreen would have commented, wondered if it wasn't a bit early, suggested covering them up if there looked like being a frost. But not today.

'Hello, Doreen,' Sophie said. 'Lovely

evening, isn't it?'

Doreen nodded abstractedly, and walked past her into the vicar's study. A sombre group greeted her.

'We're all here except Mr Richard,' said Nigel.

'He was off to London,' said Bill. 'It'd take more than the village school to keep him from the big city's delights.'

But Bill had misjudged his boss for once, and the sound of car wheels on the gravel outside the vicarage took Sophie once more to the door.

'Hello, Sophie my dear,' said Richard Standing. 'Seems we have an emergency on our hands, if Nigel is right.'

'It is certainly serious,' said Sophie, showing him into the study. 'I'll bring in some coffee in a while, Nigel,' she said, and gently shut the door.

$*$ $*$ $*$

'So what's it all about?' said Peggy, turning off the television as Bill returned from the vicarage. It was nearly eleven, and Peggy had begun to worry that Bill had been delayed by something or someone sinister. Especially by someone. 'I was worried,' she said. 'It's much later than usual.'

'It was a very unusual meeting,' said Bill, looking at her sharply. He sat down heavily in the armchair that had once been Frank's and was now his.

'But it's only a preliminary review,' said Peggy. 'Surely we needn't sound the alarm straight away?'

'They're a devious lot up at Tresham,' said Bill. 'We have to be one step ahead. Thank God Nigel Brooks seems to know what he's doing, and once he'd convinced Mr Richard, we really began to move.'

'So what's next?' Peggy folded up her tapestry and put it away in the workbox by her chair.

'A mass meeting. The whole village, in the Village Hall, this coming Saturday. Nigel is going to chair it, and Mr Richard's bringing as many influential nobs as he can muster. His brother, for one, he's on the Council, and knows all the right people.'

'What about Miss Drinkwater?' said Peggy.

'She wasn't there tonight,' said Bill, 'but that girl's a fighter. She's bright, and she's tough. It's why we chose her, partly. Sarah Drinkwater will not stand by and see her school closed down, you can be sure of that.'

*   *   *

'Saturday evening?' said Susan Standing. 'But Richard, it's my birthday!'

'Sorry, my love,' said Richard. 'I'll take you out on Sunday. We'll go over to that new place

201

on the canal. It's supposed to be quite decent, and open on Sunday evenings.'

'It's not the same,' said Susan, looking sulky.

'You'll be needed at the big meeting, Susie. Everyone has to be there. I want you with me, anyway. This is a matter for us all. Good God,' he added angrily, 'it was Great-Grandfather who built Ringford School. How bloody dare they!'

*   *   *

Sarah Drinkwater was in the kitchen when John Barnett returned from the vicarage. She was sitting in the old wheelback chair by the Rayburn, and had dozed off, her head drooping onto the worn cushion behind her. A wing of dark hair had fallen across her face, and her lashes flickered on her cheek as she slept. Wonder what she's dreaming about, thought John. She looked very young, and he started to walk towards her. His outstretched fingers almost touched her soft cheek when she stirred in her sleep and he backed away hastily. Old Nell struggled up and sent a small shovel flying. The clatter woke Sarah, and she sat up blinking, not sure where she was.

'Oh, John,' she said, smiling sleepily. 'How did it go?' Nigel Brooks had advised her not to be there, just this once. Less compromising for her, he'd said, and she had reluctantly agreed.

She sat up straight and waited for John to speak. He looked shaken. It couldn't have been that bad, surely?

'It's all systems go, Sarah,' he said finally, after clearing his throat and making a great fuss about getting a glass of water. 'There's a great deal to do. But there's also plenty of us to help, so I reckon we might even enjoy it.'

Sarah was fully awake now, and her eyes sparkled. 'Great!' she said. 'I've got so many ideas for what we can do from school.'

'I said I would help you with all that,' said John diffidently.

'Thanks,' said Sarah, leaning forward and touching his hand gratefully. 'And I was thinking of something else before I nodded off.' She paused, frowning with the effort of recall. 'Oh yes, now I remember. I have to move into the schoolhouse as soon as possible. The more established the whole school set-up appears to be, the more foolish it will seem to close it down. I think the builders have just about finished, anyway.'

John Barnett was taken unawares, not prepared for the pang he felt at the idea of Sarah not living with them any more. Of course she was right, and he would have to help her move in. But God, it would seem strange without her. Mum would miss her, too. She'd become quite a regular part of the place, coming and going in her little red car, holding forth on every subject under the sun, putting them right and arguing the toss when challenged.

'Right-o, then, Sarah,' he said briskly. This wouldn't do, this ridiculous sense of loss. He stood up. 'Time for bed, I think. You go first, and I'll lock up. We'll make some more plans tomorrow. Goodnight ...' Sarah felt suddenly chilly, like a naughty child shut out of a warm room. 'Night, John,' she said, and went slowly upstairs.

The curtains had not been drawn, and she looked out across the farmyard and the black, shadowy barns, to the moonlit fields. The trees and hedges could have been cut out of black paper against the silver light. Nothing moved, and there was no sound. She opened her window and leaned out. The air was sharp and she took a deep breath. Now she could hear the big bay stamping in his stable, pushing the straw about. She sniffed, and caught that unmistakable horsey smell. It reminded her of John. A couple of owls hooted to each other in the far woods. It was a lovely night, and Sarah stood quite motionless for several minutes. Better get to bed, she thought, and began to draw the curtains. It was then that she heard John's horse whinny, a strange, distressed sound that she had not heard before. It came again, louder this time. She heard the farmhouse door open and saw John's tall figure stride across the yard and disappear into the stable.

Sarah stood watching for several minutes, but John did not reappear. She was turning back the duvet when she heard him shout. 'Mother! Here, quickly!' Without thinking, Sarah pulled on her dressing-gown and slippers and went to the head of the stairs. She could hear Deirdre's snores coming loud and rhythmic from her bedroom, and so ran downstairs, tying her belt as she went.

The yard was now brightly lit, and Sarah screwed up her eyes against the brilliance. John had disappeared again, and she hurried across to the stable, now also lit, but with a softer, yellow light. She pushed open the half-door and went tentatively inside, acutely aware of her unsuitable pale pink dressing-gown dragging in the straw and the expensive satin mules her mother had given her for Christmas.

The horse was down in the straw on the stable floor, his beautiful long legs stuck out like knobbly sticks, and even Sarah could see that his big belly was huge, too big, outsize. John looked up and saw her, took in her night clothes and frowned. 'Sarah! For God's sake go and get Mother. You'll be no good here.'

'Deirdre's sound asleep and snoring,' Sarah said crossly. 'What's the matter with him? Can't I help?'

'Colic,' said John shortly, turning back and stroking the big belly with a gentle hand. 'That stupid William Roberts left a sack of chicken corn in the stable, and he's had half of it.' He got to his feet. 'I've got to get him to his feet,' he said. 'Go quickly and phone the vet—number's on the pad. Tell him to get here pronto. Then you'd better get back to bed.' He looked again at the small, straight girl, her shoulders squared, ready for anything. She leaned forward and patted the big horse's rump, and he caught a glimpse of smooth curving flesh. 'For God's sake go, Sarah,' he said, and turned back to the horse, who was now breathing hard, his eyes wild with pain.

Sarah made the call, but did not go back to bed. She put on the kettle, pulled on John's old jacket over her dressing-gown and quickly changed her slippers for a pair of Deirdre's Wellington boots which stood by the kitchen door. She poured tea into two big thick china mugs and, carrying them carefully, set out once more across the yard.

'Vet's coming straight away,' she said, pushing open the stable door. John had got the horse to his feet, and stood by his head, talking to him and stroking his velvety neck. 'Thanks,' he said. 'There was no need for you to...'

'Drink this tea,' Sarah said in her schoolteacher's voice. 'It'll buck you up. I'll stay until the vet comes. Just in case.'

Not much you can do, thought John, or me either, come to that. He'd had an old donkey once, and that'd done the same thing. Been in foal at the time, and it had been touch and go. But she'd survived, and the foal too. Once the vet had been and given the injection, he'd just have to wait.

'Thanks,' he said again, and stretched out his hand for the mug of tea. At that moment the horse swayed, and John turned in an attempt to stop him collapsing. Sarah was there too, her narrow shoulder up against the heavy animal. 'Christ!' said John, when the horse was once more steady. 'Don't do that again! Could've crushed you! He's a bloody big animal you know...'

He looked at Sarah, at his own jacket drowning her small body, at the muddy boots and dressing-gown streaked with brown stains. He remembered the glimpse of glowing skin and swallowed hard, turning away to soothe the horse, stroking the velvety flanks and neck.

Sarah watched John's hands, strong and long-fingered, with their fine fuzz of red-gold hair. They were dirty, but ... She imagined his hands, stroking, warm and gentle. 'John,' she said, and moved nearer to him.

He looked down at her, biting his lip. 'You're quite a girl, Sarah,' he said, and reached out.

'Evening, John!' said the vet, coming into the stable with a rush of cold night air. 'Now what's the big fella been up to?'

CHAPTER THIRTY-ONE

'Ellen!' Peggy Turner rushed from behind the counter to help the old woman up the steps and into the shop. 'What on earth are you doing? Does Doris know you've come out on your own?'

The good spell of spring weather was holding, and gateways and tracks full of mud and pools of water were beginning to dry up. The sun shone through the open door of the shop, and Ellen Biggs leaned against the counter, breathing heavily. 'I'm not weak in the head, Peggy Turner,' she said. 'Don't need a minder when I decide to take a walk. Anyway,' she added, gulping in draughts of air, 'I want to know what's goin' on. Our Ivy was very cagey about it all, and I decided to come and see for meself.'

Peggy fetched the chair from beside the Post Office cubicle and helped Ellen to sit down. 'See about what?' she said.

'The school,' said Ellen. 'What's all this about it closin'?'

Peggy went quickly into the kitchen, took the simmering kettle off the Rayburn, and reached for a teabag from the jar on the shelf.

'Here,' she said, 'drink this tea, Ellen, and I'll fill you in.' She wondered if she should telephone Doris Ashbourne, but Ellen

208

interrupted her thought.

'And you needn't try to get Doris on the 'phone, Peggy. She's gone into Tresham with Doreen Price, and won't be back till later. So you can just relax. I'm not plannin' on keelin' over yet, so get started and tell me what's happenin'.'

Peggy told her all she knew. Bill had sat for a long time last night, relaying what the Governors had decided to do. It was an ambitious plan, and all had to be put into action in a very short time.

'There's a review of village schools, Ellen, and Ringford is on the list. Apparently once a school is on the list, it's more or less bound to get the chop. Unless, that is, we can make it impossible for the Education Committee to close it.'

'How?' said Ellen, coming straight to the point.

'The Governors sat up in the vicarage until all hours working out their strategy,' said Peggy.

'Never mind about that,' said Ellen. 'How are we goin' to stop 'em?'

Peggy perched on a high stool behind the counter and tried to keep it simple.

'First a village meeting,' she said, 'and then all kinds of protests. There'll be a petition, and Mr Richard is going to get us on local radio and television through some of his friends, and he'll get in touch with Maurice Buswell, our

MP. Got to get him on our side, apparently. Seems he's a distant Standing relation, or something. Then Miss Drinkwater is making a plan of her own involving the children. John Barnett said he'd help her with that.'

'Did he just,' said Ellen.

'There'll be other things, of course, but we need to get the whole village working. That's why there'll be a meeting on Saturday.'

'Right,' said Ellen, 'I'll see that Doris and Ivy and me are there.'

Peggy looked alarmed. 'I'm sure no one will expect you to come out in the evening, Ellen. We all know you're dead against the closure. You can sign the petition when they go round with it.'

'From what I can gather,' said Ellen, 'this is goin' to be a meetin' not to be missed. I shall be there. Now dear,' she added, struggling to her feet, 'if you'll just help me down the steps, I'll be gettin' back to Doris's.'

Oh dear, thought Peggy, with a worried frown. But it is a lovely day, and I suppose the sunshine could do her good.

*   *   *

Ivy Beasley had earlier looked out of the window and seen the sunlight over the village, and decided to visit her mother's grave to give the headstone its weekly scrub. She sat on a tussock of warm grass for a few minutes,

210

looking out over the fields, watching the cows moving slowly across the pasture. It was very peaceful, and she had tried hard to empty her mind of everything, to relax and enjoy the warmth of the sun and the scent of flowers on the balmy wind. But even when she closed her eyes for a second or two, her thoughts went churning on, replaying what Joyce Davie had said to her about Peggy Turner, digesting the news about the school, worrying about Ellen Biggs and feeling guilty about Doris.

Might as well go home and get on with some work, said her mother's voice in her head. No chance of you relaxing, Ivy, when there's work to be done. Our sort don't relax, anyway. It's a sinful waste of time, if you ask me. And time is precious, as your father used to say. You soon run out of it, take it from me, Ivy.

Oh, shut up, Mother, said Ivy silently. She stood up, collected her basket from beside her mother's grave, and walked out of the cemetery and down Bate's End. As she turned on to the footpath which crossed the Green, she caught sight of a familiar figure moving slowly towards Macmillan Gardens.

'It can't be!' she said aloud, and began to hurry, nearly running as she got a clearer view of Ellen's bent old body making her way back to Doris Ashbourne's bungalow. She caught up with her just outside Fred Mills's old house, which was still empty and forlorn.

'Ellen Biggs!' she said. 'Just what do you

211

think you're doing? And where's Doris?'

'What question do you want answered first, Ivy?' said Ellen, leaning on old Fred's gate.

Ivy snorted, and took Ellen's arm. 'I'll get you back to Doris's, and then you can answer several more questions, Ellen Biggs,' she said, propelling poor Ellen faster than she wished to go.

'Now,' Ivy said, when she had settled Ellen into her chair and put on the kettle. 'You'd better explain, and make it good, else I'll have you put into Tresham House before you can say knife.'

Ellen had been fine until this last threat from Ivy Beasley. But this knocked her off balance, and she stared at Ivy, her old chins wobbling.

'What d'yer mean, Ivy?' she said. 'Nobody said nothin' about Tresham House.'

Later, when Doris came home and found Ivy still there, she wondered what on earth had been going on. Ellen looked worn out, and Ivy was distinctly shifty.

'I shouldn't have said it, Doris,' Ivy whispered in the kitchen, as Doris put away her shopping. 'But I was so angry with the old devil. She could have fallen, and caused a great deal of trouble.'

'Said what?' said Doris.

'Doesn't matter now,' said Ivy, withdrawing quickly. 'No doubt she'll tell you when I'm gone.' She walked into the hallway and put her head round the sitting-room door.

'I'm off, Ellen. For goodness sake, act your age and don't try any more excursions on your own.' She slammed the door as she left, rattling the frosted-glass panel and propelling the door key onto the mat.

'Ivy's dead against it, you know,' said Ellen, when Doris sat down opposite her with a fresh cup of tea.

'Against what?' said Doris, thinking she'd better not go out and leave Ellen for so long again.

'Against fighting for the school,' said Ellen. 'She says there's a lot to be said for lettin' it go. Miserable old bat. I reckon she'll be the only one in the village who don't fight. She'll wish she 'adn't, you know, Doris.'

'I think you'd better begin at the beginning, Ellen,' said Doris, slipping off her shoes and stretching out her aching feet.

CHAPTER THIRTY-TWO

It was there in the air, a tangible tension and excitement. Round Ringford had never witnessed anything like it, not recently, anyway.

'Might have been like this when them Roundheads came out from Tresham to get our Royalist vicar,' said Bill. He and Peggy were sitting either side of the kitchen table,

213

eating breakfast and talking about the only topic worth discussing in Ringford at the moment.

'Except the Education Department is not issued with pike or staff to drag Nigel Brooks to Tresham Assizes.'

Bill smiled. Peggy was the only one keeping cool about all this. The Arms was transformed every evening from a quiet village pub, where the only excitement was a run of luck for Michael Roberts at the dart board, to a hotbed of rumour and counter-rumour. Now the farmers, downing pints of Morton's best at the bar, were galvanised into arguments about education, every one in favour of the village school where they had all spent—or mis-spent—their formative years, but all disagreeing about the way the campaign to save it should be waged.

Colin Osman and Peter Dodwell, his friend from Walnut Close, spent long evenings over a couple of halfs with pads of paper and pens, drawing up charts and strategies. Tom Price, in his capacity as Parish Council Chairman, stood at the centre of it all with his pint, and tried to explain to a confused audience just exactly what was going on.

'Come to the meeting on Saturday,' he said finally, 'and then you'll know what it's all about, and what we've got to do.'

'We shall be there, boy, never fear,' said old Ted Bates. 'Me and Olive, and young Robert and Mandy—we'll all be there. It's the future I'm looking to. Little Joey, well, he'll have to go to a special school, no doubt. But young Margie—she'll be ready for Miss Drinkwater in no time. Kids grow so quickly these days, ain't that right, Don?'

Don Cutt nodded wisely. He did not feel particularly strongly about the school, but he did care very much about the success of his pub, and this new spirit of discussion caused dry throats and thirsty customers.

'Our William and Warren Jenkins are goin' round with notices, so nobody's left out,' said Michael Roberts. He'd offered to go and sort the buggers out up there in the Education offices, but Nigel Brooks had tactfully suggested he might be more usefully employed organising the distribution of notices announcing the meeting, urging villagers to attend.

'Maybe we could have one of those loudspeakers—like political candidates before elections,' said Peter Dodwell. 'I know a bloke at work who could put me on to one. What d'you think, Colin?'

'Great idea,' said Colin Osman. 'Good man, Peter.'

Mr Richard's car was seen turning regularly into the vicarage drive, and he and Nigel Brooks were closeted for hours in the study, making telephone calls, lists of useful people, talking to chums they knew from school.

'You never know, Sophie,' said Nigel, while his patient wife made yet another tray of coffee. 'You can't afford to neglect any possible contact. Do you remember that campaign in your folks' village to stop a chicken factory on the old recreation ground? It succeeded because every single person was against it. It'll be the same here, and the more support we get from outside the better.'

'Yes dear,' said Sophie, smothering a yawn. She whistled softly to the old black labrador to follow her into the garden for the last of his many short constitutionals each day. She did hope Nigel had not forgotten his promise to Guy Russell. The problem of Doris and Ellen Biggs concerned her more than the school. She had great faith in public common sense, and thought the fight would almost certainly be won. But sorting out a reasonable solution for Doris and Ellen was not so straightforward. She paced around the garden, waiting for Ricky to cock his leg, and breathed in the heady perfume of her tobacco plants, weedy and colourless in the daytime, but exotically alive at night.

'Come on, boy,' she said. 'Looks like the problem of Ellen and Doris is one for me. No doubt Nigel will take the credit if I think of a solution ...' Ricky made an attempt at an arthritic trot to catch up with her as she headed back towards the house.

'That was a nasty thing to say, wasn't it,

216

boy,' she said, as she helped him up the back steps. 'Forget I said it, Ricky.' But in the old dog's eyes she could do no wrong, and he rubbed his bony head against her hand in affection and admiration.

'Don't forget his bed-time biscuit,' said Nigel, beaming at her as she came into the kitchen. 'Do you know, Sophie, this whole thing has brought the village together in a way I wouldn't have believed possible.' He thought wistfully of his three-quarters empty church, but consoled himself that the Lord would be working with them, all the way.

CHAPTER THIRTY-THREE

Ringford schoolhouse had been built by Charles Standing in 1868, in the same style as his splendid new school. There had been a small educational establishment before this, of course. In fact, there had been two. It was hard to believe, but a Miss Brevitt had run a dame school in the two rooms over the Stores—'In our bedroom?' Peggy had said incredulously—and up the Bagley Road, behind the Village Hall and now used as a store, was the old school proper, a very small, plain rectangular building of red brick, with high windows and a shallow-pitched slate roof.

Something forbidding and correctional

about it had made the children glad when Squire Standing commissioned a pleasant Victorian design for his new school, with twin gables and large, airy classrooms. Huge windows admitted sunlight in summer and clear, white light on cold winter days. The children could still not see out, the windows being above their eye-level, but the atmosphere was much cheerier, as if education was now a thing to be enjoyed and not just endured.

The first occupant of the house was a schoolmaster, a Mr Thurrock, whose copper-plate handwritten records were kept by the vicar in the church safe. Jos Thurrock had ruled seventy-odd children with kindly discipline, but not enough to stop frequent absentees who were needed to pick stones, or scare rooks, or help with the harvest. His entries included irritated references to attendances being very small 'owing to Valentine's Day' and 'owing to the custom of going about with Garlands'. On 14 July 1873, he wrote without comment, 'Two girls left to work at the lace pillow for half a term.'

He would not have recognised the schoolhouse as Sarah Drinkwater opened the arched front door to check that the builders had at last finished. Pleasant pale shades of pink and cream decorated the walls, and a completely new kitchen had been installed. Miss Layton's Axminster stair carpet had gone and the oak stairs were stripped and polished.

Sarah's heels clattered as she went up and down, measuring rooms and making lists. The solitary Welshman had taken all his stuff, except for a huge wardrobe which stood in the middle of the floor in the main bedroom. He had presumably been unable to get it down the stairs.

'We can chop it up for firewood,' Sarah had said to John, who'd come to check measurements for her. She had teased him, saying she knew no Ringford man would ever chop up a perfectly good wardrobe. He'd pretended annoyance and made a grab for her, but at that moment Deirdre had come in with a large cabbage from the schoolhouse garden cradled in her arms. 'We can have this for supper ...' she'd said, her voice tailing off as she saw the look on her son's face.

Now Sarah surveyed again the wardrobe's massive bulk, and wondered if a good carpenter might split it, making a couple of smaller cupboards. The wood was sound, and that carving round the top fitted in well with the house. At least John would be satisfied.

It was a small house. The schoolmaster had never been a wealthy person, and his position in village society was relatively humble. One medium-sized parlour looked out on to the road at the front, and a second, smaller room to be used as a dining room, lay behind it, with a door into the kitchen and scullery. The back garden was a good size, big enough to grow

219

vegetables and flowers, and beyond its picket fence lay a small field with hawthorn hedges and then the water meadows, the River Ringle, and the chestnuts of the park. The high roofs of Ringford Hall, just visible above the trees, were a constant reminder to the first schoolmaster of his patron and mentor. Outside the back door, just across the concrete yard, was a sizeable shed, strongly constructed in shiplap timbers, and with a tiny window.

All very satisfactory, thought Sarah, as she crossed the yard and tried the shed door. I can keep a lot of my junk in here, looks nice and dry. But the door was locked, and she could see no key. As she turned back to the house, she stopped. Surely that had been a voice? A child's voice?

'Help...'

There it was again. It seemed to be coming from the shed. Some child must have got shut in there. Sarah peered through the small, dusty window, and could see enough to be sure that nobody was in there. A long wooden bench stretched the length of one side, and there were rows of shelves above it, all empty. As she stood uncertainly by the locked door, she heard the voice again.

'Help ...' This time it was behind her, and she whipped round.

'Who's that?' she said. The sun shone down benevolently on the yard and sparrows twittered under the eaves. Sarah could hear old

Nell in the distance barking her head off as she chased a car down the Bagley Road, It was all very normal, a perfectly average Saturday morning in Round Ringford.

Perhaps I imagined it, she told herself. But she knew she hadn't, and suppressed a shiver. Whatever or whoever it had been, it did not repeat its cry for help, and Sarah went back into the house to collect her bag and watch out for Gabriella Jones.

A shopping trip for furniture had been planned. Sarah was to move into the house next week, and Gabriella Jones had offered to help her choose some essentials. Sarah had accepted gratefully. She had always lived at home, in college, or in furnished flats, and had little real idea of what she should buy. Deirdre Barnett had offered her a bed that she was about to throw out, and Susan Standing had said vaguely that there were one or two pieces in the stables that might be useful. But Sarah needed a table and chairs, possibly a sofa for the front room, and a desk where she could work at the end of the school day.

A car horn sounded outside, and Sarah looked out the window. Gabriella's white Mini stood by the gate, its engine running, and she waved. 'Coming!' she mouthed to Gabriella, and hurried out, pulling the front door shut behind her and locking it with a pleasant feeling of ownership that was shadowed only by that strange childish cry.

'It's very nice of you, Gabriella,' Sarah said, fixing her seat-belt and relaxing in the passenger seat. 'Nice to be driven, too, for once.' She thought of telling Gabriella about the child's voice, but decided quickly against it, putting it firmly from her mind.

'No, I've been looking forward to it,' said Gabriella. 'Greg's off with the football team, and Octavia's taking library books to old people in Tresham. Still busy with her good works, our Octavia.' Old Ted Bates, trudging home after leaving his ancient Land Rover with his son at the garage, watched them drive past with an appreciative smile. Brighten up the day, them two do, he thought.

As Sarah settled into the new job at the school, Gabriella had found herself liking her more and more. There were times, of course, when she was reminded of that first humiliation of Mark Jenkins, and wondered if Sarah knew how harsh she had been, but she respected the changes she wished to make, and found that they were usually an improvement. Miss Layton had been wonderful to work for, always considerate and grateful for any extra time Gabriella might put in. But Sarah was nearer her own age, younger in fact, and they discovered plenty of things to talk about other than school. But it was school that occupied both of them this morning.

'All set for the meeting tonight?' said Gabriella, swerving round the Prices' old Bess as she wandered blindly across the road in front of them.

'Yep,' said Sarah. 'Should be well supported, from what John says. And Mr Richard's councillor brother is coming, and our MP—can't remember his name—and several other bigwigs Nigel and Mr Richard have managed to round up.'

'And the Education Department?' said Gabriella.

'Don't know,' said Sarah. 'Nobody's been invited, but they're sure to have got wind of it. Nigel said not to get them along until we'd had a chance to discuss it all with the village. The letter makes it quite clear that the review is to be immediate, and when I rang up, the office confirmed that Ringford is high on the list.'

They drove on in companionable silence for a few minutes, and then Gabriella said, not without a touch of mischief, 'Look, there's your John, up in the big field. Funny old life, isn't it, a farmer's. Out all day on his own. Must be a special kind of person to like that kind of life.'

Sarah looked across the fields to where John Barnett's Land Rover bumped over a grassy field, on his way to his herd of creamy Charollais cattle, a modern-day Lone Ranger.

'He's not my John,' she said, too quickly, and then added in a different tone, 'but he is a special kind of person, I suppose.'

CHAPTER THIRTY-FOUR

The weather on that epic Saturday evening in Round Ringford could not have been less encouraging for villagers to leave their homes and rush through a high wind and driving rain to the Village Hall. Heavy black clouds had masked the sun over Bagley Woods in the early afternoon. The temperature fell and great drops of rain splashed on the dry road and school playground, until the mottling had become a sheet of water across from the shop to the bus shelter, and umbrellas had had to be abandoned because of the strong wind.

In spite of this, the Village Hall was full to overflowing. There were not nearly enough chairs, and latecomers—not really late, but not there in good enough time to bag a chair—stood in a damp crush at the back of the hall. Jean Jenkins and Fox sat in the front row, as did Ivy Beasley, Doris Ashbourne and Ellen Biggs. Ellen had insisted, and Bill Turner had been urgently requested to fetch and carry her in Peggy's car.

'Otherwise,' said Doris darkly, 'I'll not be held responsible.'

A trestle table had been set up for Nigel Brooks, Chairman of the meeting, and by him sat Mr Richard, his brother James Standing, Maurice Buswell MP, a languid, middle-aged man with a narrow face and bouffant grey hair, Sarah Drinkwater, neat, soberly dressed, and lastly Deirdre Barnett, who, as Secretary to the Governors, had her shorthand notebook open at the ready.

'Shut the door, Bill,' said Tom Price, from the corner by the toilets, where he was trapped between Doreen and Peggy Turner, unable to move. 'We should make a start.'

Nigel Brooks's opening address was a model of conciseness. He stuck to the facts as they were known, and tried to avoid emotive expressions or obvious animosity towards the Education Department. It would be a matter of proving to those holding the purse strings that Round Ringford School was a viable concern, a cheaper and more effective way of educating the village children than any alternative likely to be proposed.

Jean Jenkins was the first on her feet when questions were asked for.

'I would like to ask, Mr Chairman,' she said, 'what our MP has to say about this disgraceful proposal.'

Nigel Brooks looked at Maurice Buswell, and nodded.

To the amazement of a great many people in the hall, their Tory MP was clearly not behind them. He stuttered and hesitated, and sprinkled his answer with 'buts' and 'ifs', but the upshot was that it was his duty to support government policy on the closure of non-viable village schools.

'And,' he added with more confidence than was justified, 'I am sure you will all come to agree with me that reviews and assessment of small schools in our county are more than overdue.'

In the shocked silence that followed this, one voice said firmly, 'Hear, hear!'

All eyes glared at Ivy Beasley, who did not flinch. She turned to Joyce Davie, sitting quietly beside her, and said in a loud voice, 'Never been afraid to speak my mind, Joyce.' Joyce nodded and tucked her arm through Donald's. But when her head turned to see what reaction Ivy's remark had had on the hall, it was Bill Turner's eyes that held hers. It was to him she directed a rueful smile.

'Old bat Beasley,' whispered Peggy, 'she only does it to annoy.' She had not missed the glance exchanged between Bill and Joyce, and despised herself for hating the narrow shoulders of his oh, so inoffensive ex-wife.

After that, in spite of Nigel's best efforts, it became a noisy free-for-all. There was no mistaking the strength of feeling. Round Ringford had been challenged, and had risen in fighting mood. Tom Price, his wife Doreen, Colin Osman and Peter Dodwell, Peggy Turner on behalf of the shop, Miss Layton at her stern best, all stood up with carefully reasoned arguments why it would be an act of folly to close the school. And finally Sarah

Drinkwater rose to her feet.

Her voice was quiet and clear, and her green eyes nobbled everyone in the hall, even Ellen Biggs, who was beginning to feel decidedly middling. Maurice Buswell had been writing furiously, planning to seek out Ivy Beasley and make as much as he could of her support.

He stopped when he heard his name pronounced in those clear, cool tones.

'Mr Buswell,' said Sarah. 'I have no doubt you will make much of a review that says twenty-nine children are not enough to make two decent football teams, that the old Victorian classroom echoes to the sound of children from five to eleven years old, all working on different subjects, with one teacher to supervise, books that are old and facilities old-fashioned and inadequate.

'No doubt you will gloss over the silver cup won every year by Ringford School Choir at the music festival in Tresham, the academic successes of generation after generation of Ringford children, the advances made by the slowest child, who forges ahead with a confidence born of being made to feel valuable in a small school by a teacher with time to give him.'

'That's it, Sarah,' said John Barnett quietly, glowing with pride.

When Sarah Drinkwater sat down, there was a spontaneous roar of applause, and Maurice Buswell looked down at his lap.

'Would you like to answer, Mr Buswell?' said Nigel Brooks, grinning like a cat with the cream.

Maurice Buswell shook his head and tried to gather some tatters of dignity around him. 'I have made my view quite clear,' he said, 'and I trust the sensible lady in the front row will not be the only one to come round to my way of thinking. I suggest you all go home and consider carefully when heads have cooled.'

This patronising remark received the cat-calls and derision it deserved, and Nigel Brooks had trouble in quelling the hall.

'Now to business,' he said, and in an atmosphere of indignation and determination a Protest Committee was formed, further meeting dates were fixed, and the hall slowly emptied. A small man in a grey suit and mac, slipped out unremarked. But his swift departure in a grey Ford Escort in the direction of Tresham was noticed by Doreen and Tom Price, walking back to the farm. 'Didn't recognise him, did you, Tom?' Doreen said. Tom shook his head. 'Spy in the camp, I reckon,' he said.

A sprinkling of people remained in the hall, talking desultorily, reluctant to abandon the exciting drama of the evening.

'After all,' said Maurice Buswell to Richard Standing, as they gathered their papers together, 'it is only a review, Richard. Nothing's been said about closure yet, you know.'

'Oh, come on, Maurice,' said Richard. 'You don't fool me. Typical way of going on, this is. Might cost the Party a vote or two, if you're not careful.'

Bill Turner was helping Ellen Biggs through the door at the rear of the hall, and nobody reckoned on her parting shot. She looked round and fixed Maurice Buswell with a baleful stare.

'Quite right, Mr Richard,' she said. 'And you're a traitor, Mr Member of Parliament Buswell. Yer won't catch me votin' for yer next time, yer great poof.'

*　　*　　*

John Barnett caught up with Sarah at the corner of Bagley Road. She was walking fast, head down into the wind, her boots splashing through deep puddles as she made no attempt to avoid them. She turned and nodded in acknowledgement as he wound down his car window and shouted through the storm rain, 'Get in, Sarah! You're soaked!'

Sarah stopped and blinked as the rain trickled off her hood into her eyes. 'I just wanted some fresh air,' she said. 'That Buswell man . . .'

John was out of the car now, walking over to where she stood. She's so small, he thought. Just a shrimp, but bloody good in a fight. As he put his arm round her shoulders and gently pushed her into the car, it occurred to him that he would hate to be in any kind of confrontation with Sarah. My God, you'd have to be strong.

'Went well,' he said, as the windscreen wipers threw off fans of water, barely able to keep the road visible. But John could have driven up to Walnut Farm blindfold, and he turned to look at Sarah's face, pale in the reflected light from the dashboard.

'Difficult to say,' she replied. She could still feel the pressure of his arm around her shoulders and found it difficult to concentrate. She shook her head a little, as if to dispel something unwanted, and smiled at him. 'At least the village is behind us,' she said. 'Except for Miss Beasley, for some reason?'

'Take no notice of old Ivy,' he said. 'She's just cussed. Takes the opposite view from force of habit. Mind you, she might regret it this time.' He turned into the lane leading to the farm, and slowed down to a crawl. Huge puddles had collected in the rough surface, and as the car lurched through with great splashes of muddy water the engine spluttered and cut out.

'Shit!' said John, and looked apologetically at Sarah. 'Bloody thing's stalled.'

'Oldest trick in the book, John,' she said. 'Next to running out of petrol ...' There was a fraction's pause, and then John began to chuckle, just like he had on the telephone that first day at the farm. 'Well,' he said, 'since you've brought up the subject ...' But Sarah had slipped away from his reach, opened the car door and was stumping off down the lane. John slammed out of his seat and ran to catch up with her. 'Sarah!' he yelled over the storm. 'What's up?' He was irritated, sure that he'd read the signals accurately. None of his other girls had played so hard to get, for Christ's sake.

'Nothing's up!' shouted Sarah. 'Except that I'm wet and cold, tired and hungry, and your bloody car has broken down.' John stopped, sighed deeply, and returned to his car. Sarah opened the kitchen door of the farm and allowed Deirdre to take her wet clothes, make her a hot drink and see her off upstairs to bed. As she sat at her desk, sipping Horlicks and staring at the blank page of her diary, she heard the car splutter into the yard. Then the kitchen door banged shut, followed by Deirdre's voice chiding and consoling, with John's gruff replies.

'Good meeting,' wrote Sarah. 'A long fight to come, but we stand a good chance, Rotten weather. Very wet coming home. John's car broke down, and he ...' She hesitated, chewed the end of her pen, then crossed out 'and he'. continuing, 'Poor John!' Couldn't be too careful in this house, she thought, grinned, and closed her diary with a snap.

Wet feet and a drip on the end of her nose did not improve Peggy Turner's low spirits as she unlocked the door and nearly tripped over Gilbert, who was sitting on the door mat waiting for her mistress's return. 'Do get out of the way!' she said sharply, then relented and picked up the little cat, hugging her and apologising. 'Not your fault, pussy,' she said, 'it's that nasty Joyce Davie.'

Peggy had come home alone, leaving Bill to see that the hall was secure after the last stragglers had gone. It had been a good meeting, she supposed, though all she could think of was that look. I must be going mad, she thought. They only looked at each other. Can't expect the man to go about with his eyes averted. It's pure jealousy, she told herself, and put on the kettle. Best to have a nice hot cup of tea ready for Bill, and certainly say nothing about it.

Bill came into the kitchen shaking his wet hair and stamping his feet. 'What a night, gel!' he said. 'Still, it didn't keep people away. Reckon it went really well, don't you.' He took off his wet jacket, put his shoes by the Rayburn to dry. He pulled Peggy towards him for a cuddle.

'One person I could have done without,' said Peggy, slipping out of his arms. Oh God, why did I say that? And now it's too late.

Bill frowned and turned away from her. 'You making tea?' he said, and his voice was cold. He poured boiling water into the pot and set it down on the kitchen table. Peggy reached for two mugs from the dresser, and took out a bottle of milk from the fridge. They sat down facing each other, their eyes not meeting.

'It's no good, Peggy,' he said, finally.

'What's no good?'

'You being so silly about Joyce.'

'It's not me that's silly.'

'You've no cause. You know that.' Bill put down his mug, and reached across the table to take Peggy's hand. 'Can I say something you might not like?' he said.

Peggy's heart sank. Why the hell had she brought up the subject when she'd decided to let it lie? She nodded. 'If it will help,' she said.

'Well then,' began Bill with a sigh. 'I've known Joyce since we were both kids at the village school. We went out together for two years before we got married, and everyone in the village was happy. We were happy. It looked like the perfect marriage. We had a nice little council house, I'd got a steady job, and we were in love.' Peggy winced, felt real pain and wished he would shut up. She knew all this, anyway.

'What's all this got to do with anything?' she said, taking her hand away from his.

'Wait, let me go on,' said Bill. 'Maybe it should've been said before. You know the bit about the miscarriage and Joyce getting ill in her mind. And those awful years that were hell for both her and me.'

'Of course I know,' said Peggy. She'd witnessed some of it, hadn't she?

'The fact is, gel,' Bill said sadly, 'that you can't just rub out a big part of your life, pretend it didn't happen. Joyce and me were happy as kings for a while. There was a lot of love and affection, and good times we spent together. You'd find it hard to believe, but Joyce was a very attractive person to be with, then.'

I don't know that I can stand much more of this, thought Peggy. And then Bill said something which went straight home, making her more ashamed than she'd thought possible.

'Fact is, gel,' he said, 'you spend a lot of time telling me about things you and Frank did together. And when he was killed, you still loved him. Had no reason not to. And if you can love a dead person, you love him now. I could be jealous—no, fair's fair, I *am* jealous sometimes. Seems we'll never be just us. There's Frank in the graveyard. Most Sundays we walk up and put flowers on the grave. And there's Joyce in Macmillan, always about, always putting in a mischievous word if she can. Don't think I don't know, Peg. She's a clever woman.'

Peggy had never heard Bill talk like this. She was not liking any of it, but had a sneaking feeling that he was right. It should all have been said before. Maybe before they got married.

'Are you telling me you still love Joyce?' she said in a very small voice. Might as well be hung for a sheep. She never forgot his answer.

'Yes, I suppose I do. In a way.' Bill put his head in his hands. His voice was muffled as he continued. 'There is still the old Joyce that I married, somewhere in my mind.' He looked up at Peggy and was smitten at the horror on her face. 'Don't get me wrong, gel!' he said. 'I don't love Joyce Davie. She's someone else now. I just hope that the old Joyce will comfort Donald and love him like she once loved me. I don't want her, I really don't. But nor do I hate her, and I won't be cold and nasty to her just to please you.'

He just has to say one thing more, thought Peggy. Please, Bill, say it. But he didn't, and they went to bed in silence. After a few minutes, Peggy spoke. 'Bill,' she said, 'I'm very sorry,' but as he gently snored and snuffled beside her, she knew he had not heard.

CHAPTER THIRTY-FIVE

The man in the grey suit lifted up his telephone and dialled his news editor.

'Who wants him?' said the news editor's wife.

'Phil—Phil Summers,' said the reporter.

There was a short interval, during which the reporter heard his news editor roaring down the stairs, 'What the hell does he want?' Then he came on the telephone, and Phil Summers explained.

'Another of these village school closures,' he said. 'But looks like being a fight, this time. Round Ringford. Remember the tree dressing? Small village, but they mean to make a big noise, that was very clear. Old Madame Maurice was there, and got a good rollicking for his pains. Usual thing about following government policy. They didn't like it one bit.'

'Nobody on his side?' said the news editor, reluctantly interested.

'One old battle-axe. She agreed with him. But it looked like the rest were going to lynch him at one point.'

'Who else was there—anyone from the *Gazette*?'

'Not that I could see. Your favourite Councillor, James Standing, was there. His brother's the village squire, on the Protest Committee.'

The news editor was hooked. 'Ah,' he said, 'our James, eh. Right, Phil old son, better get back there. See the old battle-axe for a start, and then if there's no joy there, we might get a David-and-Goliath out of it.'

'I'll be on my way,' said Phil Summers. 'Should find most of them at home on a Sunday.'

'Dead right,' said the news editor, and he hung up.

*   *   *

Ivy Beasley crammed her new black straw hat firmly on her head, and looked at the effect in the long mirror. She saw a square, solid figure in pleated check skirt and lightweight grey jacket, pale beige stockings, summer's colour, and sensible shoes that did nothing for her sturdy legs. She sighed. 'Nobody'd look at that twice,' she said aloud.

Just as well, said her mother's voice in her head. What'd you want people to look at you for, Ivy? At your age? Neat and tidy, that's the best you can hope for now.

You made sure nobody ever looked at me, Mother, said Ivy sullenly.

That's enough of that, Ivy Beasley. And don't forget what talking to yourself means.

What does it mean, Mother? said Ivy.

Going off your head, that's what, said her mother.

Ivy slammed the front door behind her and set off for church. As so often, her mother's voice had put her in a black mood, and she scarcely acknowledged Doris Ashbourne, who fell in with her outside the pub.

'Morning, Ivy,' said Doris. 'Not feeling well?'

Ivy grunted. 'I'm all right,' she said.

237

'Cheer up,' said Doris, 'it's a lovely morning.' She could have done without a gloomy Ivy Beasley. Ellen had been more difficult than usual this morning, and getting her out of bed had been a real struggle.

'Still, the poor old thing's very brave,' said Doris, hurrying to keep in step with Ivy. 'It's just first thing, before she's had her cups of tea and pills, she's a bit scratchy. Then she's her old self, more or less.'

This was intended to remind Ivy that there were people a lot worse off than herself, but it had the opposite effect. Ivy immediately felt guilty all over again at Doris having to bear all the burden of Ellen Biggs. She knew she should take a turn. Maybe she should offer now. Instead, she changed the subject.

'Lot of excitement last night, Doris,' she said. 'Hot heads and hot air never got nobody anywhere.'

'It was a good meeting, I thought,' said Doris, 'and your "hear, hears" weren't a lot of help, Ivy.'

'Somebody's got to be sensible,' said Ivy. 'That school's been hanging on by a thread for years. Not enough children in the village now, and some of them newcomers send their kids to schools in other villages. Did you see Fletching was advertising for pupils in the Parish Magazine, Doris?'

Doris shook her head. Ivy was off on her hobby-horse, and she wished desperately she could forestall her. She needed cheering up and turned to look across the Green, determined to change the subject. 'Just look at that Eddie,' she said.

The sunlit Green was alive with children. Mark Jenkins and Andrew Roberts were kicking a football, with the Jenkins terrier fruitlessly chasing it. Small Eddie screamed with exaggerated terror as his sisters pushed him higher and higher on the swings. Doris smiled to herself. And there was—was it?—yes, Octavia Jones pushing little Joey Bates along in his new, shiny wheelchair. Jody Watts, crisp and fresh in a new dress, wandered along the footpath by the river, eyeing the footballers and hoping Andrew would notice her. A lark rose from a scrubby patch by the bridge, chortling into the blue sky.

'It *is* a lovely day, Ivy,' said Doris, but Ivy was not deflected.

'And that new teacher,' she said. 'No wonder people are sending their kids to other schools. Can't keep her mind on the job, if you ask me. Always making eyes at that John Barnett. And those kids screaming and shouting three times a day in the playground. Can't hear myself think sometimes. I certainly shouldn't miss that row if they do close the place down.'

'Miss Drinkwater's very good, they say. And Deirdre's fond of her, never mind John. She likes the children to let off steam in the playground,' said Doris mildly. They were passing Ellen's Lodge house, quiet and empty. She thought wistfully of the days when the three of them met for tea, and Ellen had been too independent to allow Ivy and Doris to help her wash up.

'Steam!' said Ivy. 'Sounds like a riot to me. It'd be a right fool who couldn't sort out twenty odd kids.'

'You'd best be careful, Ivy,' said Doris, as they turned into the churchyard, 'who hears you say all this. The powers that be only need one person to say what they want to hear, and before you know where we are, there'll be no village school. And not long after that, there'll be no village shop, either.' Doris Ashbourne spoke from experience. She remembered how the schoolchildren's daily purchases of sweets and drinks had swelled the takings.

But Ivy snorted. 'Huh!' she said. 'You won't catch me feeling sorry for Peggy Palmer—I mean Turner—whatever happens.'

They walked into the cool church porch, and took their prayer books from Mr Ross.

'Morning, ladies,' he said, and was surprised at their stony faces. They walked into the church, where the usual sprinkling of worshippers was already seated, whispering quietly, admiring the flowers. It had been Doreen Price's turn this week, and she was a genius with flowers, everyone agreed. As always, all heads turned each time footsteps

240

sounded on the red tiled floor.

'One of these days, Ivy,' whispered Doris, as they knelt to greet their Maker, 'you'll cut off your nose to spite your face.'

'You sound just like my dear departed mother,' said Ivy Beasley, and shut her eyes tight.

*　　*　　*

The grey Ford Escort drew up outside the Stores, and Phil Summers got out. He looked up and down the street, and saw Mark Jenkins and Andrew Roberts passing a football between them, heading his way.

'Hey!' he shouted. 'Can I ask you something?'

Andrew veered off towards Macmillan Gardens, but Mark Jenkins stood still and looked at the stranger. He said nothing. He remembered that afternoon when he and Andrew were small, and Andrew had almost got into a strange car at the offer of sweets. Mark had his mother's warnings fresh in his ears, and he'd hauled Andrew out of the car, yelling at the top of his voice. The car had driven off at speed, and Andrew had rounded on Mark. 'Why don't you mind your own business!' he'd spat. 'Your dad would give you a good going over if he knew,' Mark had defended himself, and to save his friend, had agreed to keep it a secret. But he had not forgotten.

'I'm looking for a middle-aged lady,' said Phil Summers. 'Straight grey hair, specs, shortish. Wears a hat. Do you know her?'

Mark Jenkins still said nothing, but did not move away.

Oh God, thought Phil Summers, trust my luck to get hold of a dimmie. 'Never mind,' he said. 'I'll ask someone else.'

'It's Miss Beasley,' said Mark, judging the stranger harmless. 'Lives over there, Victoria Villa.'

'Thanks,' said the reporter, and crossed the road. He knocked at the door of Victoria Villa and waited. He knocked several times, and there was no reply, and when he turned away, Mark Jenkins was still standing there, watching him.

'Nobody in,' said Mark.

'I've gathered that,' said Phil Summers irritably.

'She's at church. Won't be back till twelve,' said Mark stolidly.

The reporter took a deep breath and asked God to give him strength. Then he went back to his car to wait.

*   *   *

'Who's that then, Ivy?' said Doris Ashbourne, as they walked back from church. Ivy had cheered up considerably. The Reverend Nigel

Brooks had taken her hand after the service, and complimented her on her new hat. She had gone quite pink, and now her step was definitely springier.

'Search me,' she said. 'Don't get visitors on a Sunday. Nor any other day, come to that.'

'Except Robert,' said Doris quickly. She certainly did not want Ivy's spirits sliding again so soon.

'Except Robert,' agreed Ivy, with a smile. Robert Bates was the son of old Ted, ran the motor repair workshop in the village, and had a soft spot for Ivy, who had helped to bring him up. Now that Robert had his own family, little Joey and Margaret, and a good wife, Mandy, Ivy did not see so much of him. But they all remembered her birthday, and Robert popped in when he could.

'There's someone getting out,' said Doris, as they approached the car.

'Good morning,' said Phil Summers. 'Miss Beasley?' He put out his hand.

'That's me,' said Ivy, not taking it.

'Ah, good,' said the reporter. 'I wonder if you could spare me a few minutes. Phil Summers, *Tresham Advertiser*.'

Doris drew in her breath noisily. 'Told you so, Ivy,' she said.

But Ivy did not bat an eyelid. 'On a Sunday?' she said, her dark, thick eyebrows raised. 'Certainly not, young man.' She took Doris by the arm and marched her firmly across the road and into Victoria Villa, shutting the door with a bang.

CHAPTER THIRTY-SIX

Joyce Davie walked along the footpath behind the playing field pavilion, her footsteps quick and erratic. She was almost running. Finally, a stitch in her side slowed her up, and she paused, gasping for breath. She looked round to see if anyone followed. There was nothing on the path but the usual screwed up cigarette packets and empty beer cans, tossed aside by kids breaking the rules out of sight of home. Joyce set off again, and came out into the Bagley Road. She needed time to cool off. For the first time since their marriage, she and Donald had had a row, and it had upset Joyce more than she would have thought possible. She had also seen a new side of Donald Davie.

It had all been so stupid. They had walked back from the school meeting with Ivy Beasley, and after she had disappeared into Victoria Villa, Joyce had said with a laugh to Donald, 'Good old Ivy, trust her to take a stand against the rest.'

He hadn't replied at the time, nor said anything yesterday. But this morning, when she had said Ivy would be coming up for a coffee, Donald had said he'd make sure he was

244

out, then.

Taken aback, Joyce had defended Ivy, pointed out that she was the only one, apart from Bill, who had visited her in the hospital all those weeks. 'I owe her my friendship, at least,' she had said, shaking the tablecloth vigorously out into the back yard.

'She's trouble, Joyce,' Donald Davie had said simply. 'She's full of prejudice and bitterness, and she's not the friend I would choose for you.'

At this, Joyce had exploded. Almost, she thought now, in the old way, as she had so many times with Bill. I lost control, she said to herself, her hands shaking as she leaned against a field gate and looked blindly across the fields. It was raining now, a fine mist rather than real raindrops, and the valley was grey and flat. The river had lost its sparkle, and a sudden angry squawking of distant ducks, disturbed by a predator, sent a shiver down Joyce's spine.

She walked away from the village, up Bagley Hill, and as she came to the gap in the fence that led to the path through the woods, she saw Bill. He had his gun, and a knapsack on his shoulder. He had not seen her, and came through the trees whistling.

For one moment, Joyce thought of running, but then what would be the point. Here was the person she knew best in the world. Who better to talk to, to help her sort it out?

'Joyce,' said Bill. He stopped at the fence,

245

and looked at her. 'Hello, Bill,' she said. And then she burst into tears, and after hesitating for a couple of seconds, he put his arm round her shoulders and waited until they stopped shaking.

'Better tell me what's up,' he said.

They walked slowly back down the hill, unaware that the mist had turned to real rain, and Joyce told him most of what had happened. Bill listened attentively, but then he laughed and said that Ivy was an old bat, Donald was quite right. But Ringford was used to her, and Donald would soon get used to her, too. And it wasn't anything important enough to quarrel about, so she'd better go home straight away and make it up.

Just before an unspoken agreement caused them to separate, Bill heading for the main street and Joyce taking the path behind the playing fields once more, a car came up behind them, slowing down as they went into single file to allow it to pass.

It was Robert Bates, waving cheerily, and beside him sat Ivy Beasley, her shopping basket firmly clasped in stubby hands, her eyes astonished as she saw Joyce and Bill.

'Bloody hell,' said Bill, appalled. But Joyce giggled, and walked off down the footpath, a skip in her step, like a naughty schoolgirl.

*   *   *

'Joyce,' said Donald, as she came through the door. He had cleared the kitchen, done the washing up and was busy making a salad. 'Joyce, my dear,' he said, 'I am sorry. God knows I'm sorry. Please forgive me.'

Joyce went into his open arms, noticing for the first time that he was a mite shorter than she, and kissed his cheek. 'Dear Donald,' she said, 'it was my fault. Ivy can be a pig. But she did stick by me, and I can't just ditch her now.'

'It wasn't Ivy, not really,' said Donald slowly. Joyce pulled back from him and looked at his miserable face. 'What do you mean, Donald?' she said.

He took a deep breath, and then said in a rush, 'I'm a bit jealous, that's really it, Joyce. Saw you look at Bill Turner in that special way, and it made me mad.' Joyce said nothing. 'I know it's ridiculous,' Donald continued pathetically, 'but it's because I love you.'

Joyce's pale face was suffused with colour, and she sat down suddenly at the kitchen table. She grinned at Donald.

'Do you know, Donald Davie,' she said, 'that's the first time you've said that to me. Like that.'

'Said what?' said Donald.

'That you love me. Properly, like that,' said Joyce.

*   *   *

The shop was full when Bill walked up the steps and through the open door. His hair was misted with rain, and there were dark patches of wet on the shoulders of his jersey.

Over the heads of customers, Peggy looked at him. 'You're wet,' she said. 'Better go up and change your things. There's coffee on the Rayburn—help yourself.'

Typical, she thought to herself. Shop's been empty all morning, and now, just when Bill comes home, everybody's shopping at the same time. She was serving Mrs Ross, assuring her that the teabags were not full of dust, but made a good strong cup. Jean Jenkins and Pat Osman had gone into a huddle over by the frozen food cabinet. Mandy Bates had parked Margie's pushchair by the cereals, and Doris Ashbourne was leaning over to reach the cornflakes, laughing at Margie's outstretched hand, and asking anxiously after little Joey's progress.

Into the middle of all this stepped Sophie Brooks. And because she was the vicar's wife, an immediate silence greeted her arrival, in spite of her friendly 'Morning, everyone,' as she took a tube of toothpaste off the stand.

'You go first, Mrs Brooks, if you're in a rush,' said Jean Jenkins deferentially.

'No, no,' said Sophie, 'no hurry. I'm quite happy to wait. I need a little word with Peggy, when she's attended to you all.'

Oh no, thought Peggy. So, no cup of coffee

with Bill, that was quite obvious. Damn. She had been waiting for the right time for a talk with him, to put her side of this stupid thing with Joyce. She wondered if he knew this and was deliberately stalling her. He'd seemed so busy lately. Oh my God, she thought, why did that stupid woman decide to come back to Ringford. Did she know how much trouble it would cause? Of course she did. Peggy was now in no doubt that this was the prime reason for her return.

At last Sophie Brooks was the only one left. She'd listened to the resumed gossip about the meeting and the school, and had confirmed that they would soon be hearing about plans made by the Protest Committee. 'Everybody's help will be wanted,' she said encouragingly, and they'd shied off a bit, muttering about busy families and demands on their time.

Now she smiled, and paid for her toothpaste. 'Can you spare me a minute or two, Peggy?' she said. 'I'd like to talk to you about Ellen and Doris.'

'Ah,' said Peggy, 'I had a feeling it would be that. Why don't you come through, Sophie, and have a cup of coffee with Bill and me.' Sophie was a good friend, and needed help.

It was a difficult one, they all agreed. Doris was clearly exhausted, and something would have to be done.

'Couldn't Ellen go back home now?' said Bill.

'No, not with the Lodge in its present state,' said Sophie. 'And anyway, even if it was fit for habitation, Ellen still needs a lot of help. She couldn't manage completely on her own.'

'What do Social Services say?' said Peggy.

'They just pop in to Doris occasionally, say she's doing a great job, and pop out again,' said Sophie. 'She did say something about them offering help from a care assistant, but she'd refused. You know our Doris! So it's up to us to think of something.'

Peggy poured out more coffee, and then sat down opposite Bill, looking at him speculatively. He was relaxed and smiling. I suppose he feels safe with Sophie here, she thought meanly.

'Bill,' she said, 'if the money could be found, could you have a go at the Lodge, with the Standings' permission, of course? Make it dry and safe. Then we—you and me, Sophie— could put in a few better bits of furniture, warm blankets, that kind of thing.' Her eyes brightened with enthusiasm for this possible solution.

Bill nodded. 'Course I could,' he said. 'It wouldn't take all that much, and Mr Richard is very worried about the old girl, difficult as she is.'

'That would be marvellous,' said Sophie, 'but it would still leave us with the problem of help. She'd need help, quite a lot of it.'

They sat in silence, the bubble of excitement

collapsing.

'Well,' said Peggy, 'perhaps that offer of a care assistant would apply to Ellen on her own. We could ask, Sophie. See what there is going?'

Sophie stood up. 'Peggy,' she said, 'you're a marvel. We shall have to put it all tactfully to Doris and Ellen first, of course, and Mr Richard, and the Social Services. But now we've got something practical to suggest, I'm sure we'll succeed. Bless you both. Nigel will be most grateful. He's got more than enough to think about at the moment, with the school business.'

She turned to leave the kitchen, and saw that someone had come very quietly into the shop.

'Miss Beasley,' Sophie said, 'we didn't hear you. Peggy's just coming.'

'People often don't hear me,' said Ivy Beasley. 'Or see me, either,' she added, looking at Bill, who appeared at the kitchen doorway with Peggy. 'You'd think I was invisible at times, Mrs Palmer—I mean, Turner—but it's quite extraordinary what I see and hear.' She paused and continued to look straight at Bill. 'Bag anything good up in the woods this morning, did you, Bill?' she said, and then asked for her usual Monday morning box of matches.

'Dreadful morning, Miss Beasley,' said Sophie pleasantly, filling an awkward silence.

'Indeed, Mrs Brooks,' said Ivy. 'Raining quite hard now. I met Mrs Davie and she was

251

soaked, looked like a drowned rat, poor thing. Where had she been, to get so wet, I wonder?' She picked up her matches, proffered the exact money, and left, the door bell jangling violently in her wake.

It seemed to Peggy that the temperature in the shop had dropped several degrees. She turned to Bill, ignoring Sophie, who was looking puzzled, and said, 'Now just what did she mean by that?' She was alarmed to see that Bill did not meet her eye, but turned back into the kitchen.

'Nothing at all,' he said, 'it's just old Ivy up to her usual tricks.'

Sophie had remembered that she needed more butter, and by the time she had gone over once more their plan for Ellen and Doris, Bill had disappeared out of the back door.

'Let me know what happens, then, Sophie,' Peggy said, with an effort to concentrate. Sophie stepped out on to the pavement feeling something had been going on which she knew nothing about, but she dismissed it as none of her business and turned for home. It was then that she saw Ivy Beasley outside Victoria Villa, talking to a man in a grey suit. As she approached, she heard Ivy say, 'You'd better come in, then,' and they both vanished through Ivy's front door.

CHAPTER THIRTY-SEVEN

The *Tresham Advertiser* appeared every Thursday, but did not reach Ringford until Friday morning, when a small string-tied bundle was dropped off at the shop for Andrew Roberts to pick up and deliver.

Colin Osman, however, had been in Tresham on Thursday afternoon, taking his typescript to the printers for the latest edition of Ringford Newsletter—a fat one, full of the school dramas—and he bought an *Advertiser* from the news stand by the station. He didn't open it until he reached home, and then it was Pat who leafed through it quickly over a cup of tea.

'Good God, Colin, look at this!' she said. She handed over the paper, and Colin's eyes widened.

'Oh Lord,' he said, 'Ivy's gone and done it now.'

The centre spread was devoted to the proposed review of Round Ringford Church of England Primary School, and the news editor had decided to give the story a prominence Phil Summers had not dreamed of.

VILLAGE RESIDENT
DEFIES SCHOOL PROTEST

The headline across two pages was in big, black type. Underneath was a picture of Ivy Beasley glaring at the camera, with the village school in the background and its children whooping it up in the playground. The text was uncompromising. ' "There used to be seventy children there once," said Miss Beasley. "It's been shrinking for years, and now there's not enough to make a proper school." '

Phil Summers had reported what Ivy Beasley had said, but he'd led her on to say it, gently prodding her about noisy children and the new headmistress. 'Too small, now, is it, Miss Beasley?' he had said. 'Looks more like a nursery playgroup to me,' he'd smiled, and Ivy had agreed. In the paper, it said Miss Beasley had complained that the children had no discipline and behaved like babies with their new headmistress. 'Young, isn't she?' Phil Summers had enquired, and in his report Miss Beasley said, 'Not long out of her cradle herself, if you ask me.'

'Wait till Nigel sees this,' said Colin Osman. 'He's not going to be at all pleased. Nor is Mr Richard, or Sarah Drinkwater.'

'Nor anyone else in the village, I reckon,' said Pat. 'I'd not be in Ivy Beasley's shoes, that's for sure.'

Colin was reading on down the page. 'It does give the other point of view, though,' he said. 'There's a big chunk of what Sarah Drinkwater said at the meeting. And he's got a good quote from Councillor James Standing. That's Mr Richard's brother, you know, Pat.'

'I do know,' said Pat.

'Seems he's behind us. And that's important, because all County Councillors are on the Education Committee, you know.'

'I do know,' said Pat.

Colin frowned at her, and handed back the paper. 'All right,' he said, 'read it for yourself.'

*   *   *

This particular Friday in May was a holiday for the village school, always had been since the death of Charles Standing, the school's founder. It had been his birthday, and the Governors agreed that the custom was a nice one, and should be perpetuated. It had to come off the grand total of holidays, of course, but none of the parents had complained. Not yet, anyway.

'It'll be a good day to move into the schoolhouse,' Sarah had said, and noted that John's face fell. Deirdre, who had earlier tried to persuade Sarah to give up the idea of the schoolhouse, to stay on as their lodger, with perhaps a sitting room of her own, had lately said no more on the subject, and had switched to grumbling about the length of time builders took these days to do quite simple jobs. Sarah had begun to feel Deirdre was easing her out.

It was a perfect day, promising to be warm,

and Sarah woke up early. She heard John moving about in the kitchen downstairs, and pulled on her cotton wrap. He'd have made tea, and she hoped there'd be one in the pot for her.

He had the *Farmers Weekly* propped up against the sugar bowl, and looked up as she came into the kitchen, her hair tousled and her face still full of sleep. She looked no more than eighteen years old, and he knew right there and then that he loved her. Oh my God, he thought. Things like this don't happen to me. I'll fall when it suits me, take a wife when I feel the time is ripe. It's impossible—she's not my type, and her mum and dad come from a different world. All these things flashed through his mind, and he knew that they'd been lurking there for some time. He also knew that they made no difference to the way he felt.

'Morning, John. Looks like a nice day. Nothing worse than moving house in the rain.' She sat down opposite him, and he poured her a mug of tea. The kitchen door was open, and the farmyard beyond shone in the early morning sunlight. Deirdre's old bantam cock strutted around his wives, scratching with his lethal talons and pecking up insects and dried grains of split corn. Old Nell snoozed in the sun, her tail flailing lazily at flies already busy in the empty, muck-smelling stables.

'I'll miss the farm,' Sarah said suddenly, surprising herself. She looked at John, and his expression was odd.

'Just the farm?' he said.

'And you and Deirdre, of course,' she said. 'But I shan't be far away, shall I?'

'Too far,' said John, and he leaned across the table and took her small, warm hand. 'I don't have to spell it out, do I?' he said.

She shook her head, and said, 'I'd rather you didn't. Not now, anyway.' He couldn't go on, not when she looked like that. But he noticed she didn't take her hand away until Deirdre's heavy footsteps were heard on the stairs.

CHAPTER THIRTY-EIGHT

Barnett's trailer, swept clean and hitched to the back of the Land Rover, trundled up and down the lane a couple of times, loaded with large cardboard boxes and several tea-chests. Sarah's mother had enjoyed collecting up household items for her daughter's new house, and Sarah had had difficulty in preventing both parents turning up to help her move in.

'I'll be fine, Mother,' she had said on the telephone. 'John will cope with everything. He can lift a ton weight with no problem, so don't worry.'

'John who?' her mother had asked sharply.

'John Barnett—he's the farmer where I've been living. You know that perfectly well,

Mother.'

'Oh, yes. Well, take care, dear, and don't overstrain yourself.' And then there had been her father's voice in the background.

'Hello, Dad?'

'Good luck, my angel,' said her father, in his nice, slow voice. And then he'd whispered into the telephone, 'Just as well your mother's not with you. She does love to take control. Anything you need, Sarah, money, or anything at all—just ask me. Bye, my darling.'

Sarah stood in the little front garden of the schoolhouse, resting her aching muscles and warming herself in the sun. Should be John's last trip. He'd gone for the brand-new bed, still crated up from the supplier, a surprise present from her dad, and saving her from Deirdre's chuck-out.

A small crowd had gathered to watch the exciting proceedings, and offer help and advice as John and Sarah carried in all her belongings and arranged them around the house as she had planned. Mark and Andrew, at a loose end on a day when the bigger children were at school in Tresham, leaned over Sarah's front fence and conducted a running commentary laced with witty remarks which they alone found hilarious. Occasionally Mark Jenkins verged on being unacceptably cheeky, but Sarah couldn't be bothered with him today.

'You could be doing some homework, Mark,' she said mildly. 'Go over that difficult bit of reading. I'm sure your mum would help.'

'It's a holiday, ain't it,' he'd said. 'Don't see why I should work when nobody else is.' He and Andrew sloped off after a while, heading for the river. Sarah did not notice them go.

The Land Rover and trailer came out of the Bagley Road and past the Village Hall. Sarah's crated bed rocked from side to side, but stayed put until John pulled up outside the schoolhouse.

'There we are, Sarah,' he said, leaping out, full of energy and finally infected with the excitement of moving house. 'Get this set up, and you'll be able to sleep the sleep of the virtuous tonight.'

'Very funny,' said Sarah. John peered at her more closely. She looked dog tired, big shadows under her eyes and her shoulders drooping.

'You've done too much,' he said, and for the first time heard his father's voice in his own. 'Come on inside, and we'll have a break.' He shut the garden gate and glared at the bystanders. 'Now, my girl,' he said, 'in we go.' He moved her gently inside, and shut the front door firmly. Sarah noticed the 'my girl'. Very masterful, she thought, and walked through to the kitchen. She couldn't remember ever having felt so tired.

The remains of the small crowd, Jody Watts and small Eddie, old Ted Bates, pushing his little disabled grandson in his wheelchair, and, most recently, Ellen Biggs, all finally drifted off.

'Show's over,' said Ellen. 'Better get back to Doris. She'll be worried about me.'

Inside the house, Sarah sat down on a kitchen chair and looked around at the chaos. 'Oh God,' she said, 'I wish I'd stayed at the farm.'

John stood still and looked straight at her, frowning. 'Do you mean that?' he said.

Sarah stared at the floor. 'Right now, yes, I do mean it,' she said. 'But I've not forgotten why I had to move.'

'The school,' said John.

'Yep,' said Sarah. 'My school.'

'And that's all that matters to you, isn't it.'

Sarah looked up, surprised at the vehemence in John's voice. She had a sudden picture of him striding across the farmyard, jumping up into his tractor, herding the cows, whistling to Nell ... caressing his horse ... his voice always there, around the farm, greeting her when she came home from school, arguing over supper, teasing her out of her bad moods. None of that, she thought, not any more, from now on.

'Don't,' she said, 'don't be cross.' And she, Miss Drinkwater, tough headmistress and fighting campaigner, began to cry.

'Poor little Sarah,' said John, half teasing, and then his arm was round her. He smoothed her hair and wiped the tears from her cheeks with a confident touch. She stopped crying, sniffed, and looked up at him. 'God, you're the sexiest man I've ever met,' she said, and standing on tiptoe, could just manage to put her arms around his neck and tangle her fingers in the thick red curls.

A great deal was said later that Sarah, on reflection, thought would have been better left unsaid. She blamed her exhaustion. I am not at all sure about all this, she thought, not yet. But she hadn't the strength left to think clearly. And anyway, she was enjoying herself too much.

Before John left for home, he touched her cheek and said, 'Nearly forgot, Sarah. I've got a house present for you. Shan't be a minute.'

He went out, and she heard the Land Rover door open and shut. He returned with an old shopping basket, something small and white curled up inside. She peered in, and two blue-black eyes looked at her apprehensively.

'Jemima,' said John, lifting out a small, fluffy white and grey puppy. 'Least, you don't have to call her that. She's nothing special, I'm afraid, just an old farm terrier. Mother a Cairn, father unknown.'

He put the tiny puppy into Sarah's outstretched hands. Jemima was so small that she fitted in the warm hollow perfectly. She yawned, a huge, jaw-splitting yawn that frightened her and she began to tremble. 'What a darling!' Sarah said. 'My very own guard dog!' She laughed and held the puppy close.

'That's it,' said John. 'Give her a few months, and she'll send your mystery voice packing.' Ah, thought Sarah, so he did notice I was upset about that. She'd mentioned it back at the farm, and he'd dismissed the story with a derisive snort.

After the Land Rover and trailer drove away, the house seemed very quiet. Jemima went to sleep in her basket, and Sarah rinsed the glasses under the tap. I'll just sit down for a bit, she thought, take a break. She wanted to think about John. A few seconds later she, too, was asleep in her chair.

It was dusk when Sarah woke, sure that she had heard someone call her. She stood up, stiff and chilly now, and listened. There it was again. The voice of a child in trouble. 'Help...'

It seemed to come from the shed in the yard, and Sarah took the key from a hook by the back door and went to look. Her small white protector followed closely at her heels. But there was no one in the shed, or in the garden, or anywhere else that Sarah could see. She bent down to pick up Jemima.

'Must have dreamed it,' she said, rubbing her face against the silky white fur.

'Help ...' The voice was thin but insistent. Sarah looked down to the bottom of the garden now. But only shadows of trees and bushes moved in the light breeze. Jemima's ears were back, and she growled, a small, grating sound.

'Oh, go away!' Sarah said loudly, but her voice shook a little, and her hands trembled as she took Jemima back into the house.

CHAPTER THIRTY-NINE

The early weather forecast predicted a hot day for the whole country. In fact, with an air of faint surprise, the weather man said it looked as if we were in for quite a spell of hot weather. Sarah Drinkwater, awoken by her radio alarm and this cheering information, for a moment could not remember where she was. Then she heard a little whining noise from the foot of her new bed and knew that she was now not only the rightful resident of the schoolhouse, but the brand-new owner of a small dog.

'Jemima!' she said, and got out of bed. The puppy pounced delightedly on her bare feet and nibbled her toes.

'All right, all right! I know you're hungry. Please don't eat my toes, Jeems, let's go downstairs and find you something more suitable.'

She picked up the warm little body and went over to the open window. It was still cool and the air clean and refreshing, and the Green sparkled with dew not yet drawn up by the sun. In the angle between the wall and the eaves, a huge spider travelled quickly across her web to a trapped fly. Sarah drew back hastily, but continued to look out, round the village. She stood for several minutes, watching a blackbird pulling worms from her front lawn, and the milk float calling at each house around the Green, the red-haired milkman conducting his business at the trot. Probably has another job, once he's finished the milk, she thought.

The kitchen cupboards yielded only a tin of tuna fish, and Sarah worried that this would be too rich for a puppy. 'Trust John not to think of bringing you some food,' she said. John. Yes, well, she had some thinking to do about that. 'Never mind, you shall have some of my scrambled egg. There,' she added, putting Jemima down by a bowl of water on the floor, 'at least I remembered to give you a drink last night.'

And then it came back to her, that pitiful cry. She had heard it on two occasions now, and needed some explanation.

She had breakfast, sharing her egg with a ravenous Jemima, and pulled on some old clothes. It was strange, not seeing John at the other side of the table, not being waited on by Deirdre, not hearing the cows, old Nell, and the bantam cock. Still, she reminded herself, she was better off without the heaps of strawy muck to step in on her way to school, and the ripe smell of confined turkeys, with their unlovely gobbling.

This is all mine, she encouraged herself. I can

264

do exactly as I please, and I shall soon get used to being alone again. 'And anyway,' she said, 'I'm not alone, am I, Jeems.' She scooped up the wriggling puppy and walked out into her back garden, just to get the feel of her domain.

The shed looked solid and innocent. John had put several boxes and bits of garden equipment in there for her, and she opened the door to check on them. All exactly as he had left them. No trace of a child, crying for help.

Perhaps I should ask someone, thought Sarah, sitting on the old wooden bench outside her back door. Jemima settled in her lap and closed her eyes. The little dog's short bursts of activity quickly exhausted her, and she needed frequent naps to restore her energy. The sun was very warm in the sheltered yard, and Sarah leaned her head back against the wall and closed her eyes.

'Sarah!' It was a man's voice, and she looked round eagerly. Goodness, it would be nice to see John right now.

But it wasn't John Barnett. It was the Reverend Nigel Brooks, and he was carrying the *Tresham Advertiser*.

'Morning, my dear,' he said, coming round the side of the house. 'All settled in, are we? Oh, my, what an enchanting puppy!'

He sat down beside her, and stroked the top of Jemima's silky head. Then he opened the *Advertiser*, and folded it back. 'Don't know if you've seen this,' he said. 'We decided not to worry you with it yesterday. You certainly had enough to occupy you. Though I'm sure John was a tower of strength.'

Nigel had been walking old Ricky through the meadow at the back of the schoolhouse yesterday evening. It was Ivy Beasley's field, let out permanently to Tom Price, who grazed a few young heifers on it, and in spring put out a few sheep and lambs for the children to see at playtimes. Neither Tom nor Ivy objected to Nigel walking old Ricky there, and it had become a favourite route for them. Nigel had been pleased to see a light again in the schoolhouse, and on looking through Sarah's kitchen window had been delighted at what he saw. But heavens, he'd thought, I wonder if Deirdre knows?

Now he handed the *Advertiser* to Sarah, and she read through the centre pages with growing amazement. 'How could she!' she said. 'The old devil! What's the school ever done to her?'

'Um, well,' said Nigel, shifting about uncomfortably. He knew he should try to defuse this potentially explosive situation. There were good things to be said about Ivy Beasley. He knew that from past experience. But for the moment, he couldn't think of a single excuse for her traitorous behaviour.

'She is entitled to her point of view, I suppose,' he said lamely. 'There may be others in the village who agree with her, of course, though no one else has said anything of the

266

sort.'

Sarah Drinkwater put Jemima down gently, and stood up. 'Right, Mr Brooks,' she said. 'If the old bat wants a fight, she shall have one. Come in and have a cup of coffee, and tell me about Miss Ivy Beasley. And,' she added, 'before I forget, do you know if anything bad ever happened to a child in this garden?'

'Nothing more than a good telling-off from Miss Layton, I imagine,' laughed Nigel Brooks. 'But if you mean further back than that, you'll have to ask Ted Bates. Poor old Fred Mills was the expert on village history, but Ted's next best. You have to get him on a good day, though.'

*   *   *

It was mid-morning before Sarah walked over to the Stores to get a tin of dog food for Jemima. She carried the puppy in her arms, and Peggy said she would turn a blind eye for once. Dogs were not allowed in the shop, but, as Sarah said, you could hardly call Jemima a whole dog, not yet.

'There's these small tins, Miss Drinkwater. They're specially for pups, several flavours. Try them out and see which one she likes.' After some minutes of cooing and stroking, Sarah and Peggy smiled agreeably at one another, and Peggy said how delighted she was that Sarah had a home of her own now. She put

267

the tins in a flimsy plastic carrier, and handed them over the counter.

'We shall see more of you, we hope,' she said. 'And maybe John, too,' she added, and laughed at Sarah's frown. 'Can't keep anything secret in Ringford, you know, Miss Drinkwater,' she said. Then she remembered Ivy's hints of possible secrets between Joyce and Bill that had not been revealed, and was immediately depressed.

As Sarah left the shop, Jemima suddenly wormed her way out of her arms and plummeted to the ground. Sarah made a grab for her, and the plastic carrier burst with the strain, scattering tins of puppy meat all over the pavement. They rolled down into the gutter and came to rest by the big drain.

'Oh, shit!' said Sarah loudly. An old man getting down from a battered tractor looked at her suspiciously.

'' 'Ere,' he said, 'you're in a bugger's muddle there. It's the new schoolteacher, isn't it? Should know better than to use that language.'

Sarah apologised stiffly, said yes, she was the new headteacher, and had been in the village for several months now, and that she could manage, thank you.

'Looks like a bloody cat, that does,' said the old man, looking disparagingly at Jemima. Taking no notice of Sarah's refusal of help, he bent down and gathered up the tins, tying them securely inside the bag.

'Thank you very much, Mr er . . .' said Sarah. The old man didn't introduce himself, but barked at her, 'You'll be gettin' my little grand-daughter one day. Margie Bates. There's another, but he's handicapped. Our Joey—goes to a special group Jean Jenkins set up in the Hall stables.'

This was quite a speech for Ted Bates, but for all his taciturnity he was not proof against a pretty girl in jeans and T-shirt, especially one who seemed to glow in the sun. She turned to him with interest. 'Mr Ted Bates?' she said. He nodded.

'You're the one who knows all about Round Ringford, aren't you,' she said.

Ted nodded again. 'Born and bred,' he said. 'Lived here all me bloody life. And my father before me.'

'Ah,' said Sarah, reflecting that he was a fine one to criticise her language. 'Then I wonder if I could ask you something.'

'Ask away,' said Ted.

'Well,' said Sarah, 'it's difficult to know how to explain it, but twice now, round at the back of the schoolhouse, I've heard a voice, and there's been nobody there.' She expected the old man to laugh. But he didn't. He pulled at the belt securing his trousers, hitching them up over his scrawny hips.

'A child's voice, was it?' he said. 'Yes, well, that'd be little Daisy.'

'Daisy who?' said Sarah. 'There's nobody

called Daisy in the school.'

'No, there wouldn't be,' said Ted. 'Not a popular name for girls now. But when Daisy Causewell were a little girl, it were a favourite.'

'Were a—I mean, *was* a little girl?'

'She died in 1926,' said Ted, as if it was yesterday. 'I remember me dad talking about it. Upset the village, that did. She were only eight, poor little mite. Run over, she was, coming back to school after her dinner. Weren't many cars in them days, but one of 'em got young Daisy. Killed outright. They laid her out in your shed, on that long bench. Cobbler worked in there for a few years. Old George. He'd been wounded in the Great War and couldn't get a bloody job nowhere. Made good boots, according to my dad.'

'Oh, no,' said Sarah, feeling her eyes smart, 'how sad! What happened to Daisy's parents?'

'Ned Causewell was out of work, too. Hard times, they was. And Betty, her mother, had two other kids. That's why they laid Daisy out in your shed overnight. Their house was too small. Things were bad in them days, you know.' Ted's eyes were misty, too, and he looked away across the Green at another, grimmer time in Round Ringford.

'Has anyone else heard Daisy?' said Sarah. She was not at all sure that this explanation was going to make it any easier to cope with those cries for help.

'Nope,' said Ted, to Sarah's surprise. 'Not

270

for years. Could be you're sympathetic. They say ghosts only appear to certain people. Looks like you're one of 'em.' And with these dubiously flattering words, he disappeared into the shop.

CHAPTER FORTY

Colin Osman had offered straight away to do the petition.

'I think it would be appropriate, Nigel,' he said to the Protest Committee. 'In my capacity as District Councillor, I need to be in constant touch with my ward. Wonderful opportunity—and I flatter myself not many will resist my powers of persuasion!'

'Not many want to,' said Doreen Price. 'You're on a good wicket there, Colin. There's only Ivy Beasley, as far as we know. And I reckon she's only doing it to be awkward. That's Ivy all over.'

'Nevertheless, Doreen, I shall go prepared. Perhaps I could run through our case once more, Nigel? Make sure I haven't overlooked any salient points.'

Nigel sighed. It was all so straightforward, really. The village school had been in Ringford for more than a hundred years, doing a good job, a better job than could be done any other way. It was still doing that, and as far as he could see, there were no preferable alternatives. If they could convince the Education Department that it was also the cheapest option, they couldn't lose.

'Fire away, then, Colin,' he said. 'But make it snappy.'

'Right,' said Colin, leaning back in his chair. They were in the vicarage dining room, their papers spread out on the long mahogany table, and in spite of open windows and the cool evening air outside, the room had become stuffy. Richard Standing shifted restlessly in his seat, and Sarah Drinkwater found herself constantly distracted by John's presence beside her. He took her right hand under the table, and rather than snatch it away she made fumbling notes with her left, feeling Deirdre's eyes on her from across the room.

'One,' said Colin. Richard Standing groaned audibly, but Colin ignored him. Squire he might be, but he had no hereditary influence over Colin Osman.

'One: Ringford is situated in an isolated, rural part of the county. The village, although remote, is a growing one. The number on the school roll at present is twenty-nine, but within the catchment area there are sufficient children of preschool age to give a firm indication that in three years' time the number is expected to grow to fifty plus.'

So many words, thought Nigel, but he nodded encouragingly. 'And two?' said

272

Richard Standing, shuffling papers impatiently.

'Two,' said Colin, not in the least discomforted, 'should our school close, the nearest alternative is Fletching, ten miles away. It is entirely unsuitable for four-year-old children to travel ten miles in an unsupervised bus twice a day in all weathers.' He was actually not too sure what four-year-old children could put up with, but he was well briefed by his wife, Pat.

'Often gets snowed up,' said Doreen.

'Our Eddie'd be sick,' said Jean Jenkins. 'Always is, on coaches.'

'The educational development of children has been seen to suffer when they spend long periods away from home at such an early age,' said Sarah Drinkwater, making a big effort to concentrate.

'There's something nobody's mentioned,' John Barnett said, apparently having no difficulty in doing two things at once. 'What is it they're always going on about—the edge that private schools claim over state schools? Small classes, more individual tuition. Results are always better with a smaller pupil/teacher ratio. If that's true, then our kids have got it made. Best kind of education any child could have. Small numbers, excellent teacher,' and he gave Sarah's hidden hand an extra squeeze, 'wonderful environment. How many kids sit under a great sycamore tree for shade on a hot summer day, eating their sandwiches and throwing bits of bread to the school sparrows?'

'Quite right, boy,' said Bill, and the others beamed. As Doreen said to Tom later, if it'd been John Barnett going round with the petition, he'd get a hundred per cent, including old Poison Ivy.

'Now to other matters,' said Nigel firmly. That was quite enough priming for Colin Osman.

Deirdre Barnett, taking the Minutes, glanced over at John and Sarah with growing dismay. Something definitely up, there. People don't look at each other like that unless something's up. My Johnnie. She'll take him for a ride, and drop him when it suits her. That sort always do. You can tell. Deirdre was beginning to forget that she had not so long ago been quite fond of Sarah.

'Letters asking all parents to write to County Councillors have been sent home with the children,' she said, checking off a list in her notebook, 'with a specimen letter for them to follow.'

'Radio Tresham are giving us a slot next week,' said Mr Richard. 'And that idiot, Tim Bingley-Smith—*Gazette's* editor—has promised brother James that he'll give us a big spread. A chance to answer Ivy Beasley in print. Can't think what came over the ridiculous woman.'

'Ivy had a rotten time when she was a child,'

said Bill Turner. 'She told my mother she was sick every morning before going to school, she was that terrified of the bullies. And her old mum was no help. Fight your own battles, Ivy. That was her watchword.'

He caught Colin Osman's sceptical eye, and added, 'Oh, no, I'm not making excuses for old Ivy. Just telling you, that's all. There's usually a reason for these things.'

A short silence followed this. Then Sarah cleared her throat and said, 'Well, there's no bullying in my school.'

'Huh!' said Jean Jenkins, seeing again her Markie, white-faced, pinned into a corner of the playground, out of sight of Miss Drinkwater.

'And we do have to live in the present, Mr Turner,' continued Sarah. But she had heard Jean Jenkins, and thought guiltily that she really must do something about Mark Jenkins. 'Perhaps I could give a quick run-down on what the children are planning?'

'I must go in a few minutes,' said Richard Standing, looking at his watch.

'It is, after all, the children who are our main concern.' Sarah directed her cool, green-eyed gaze at Mr Richard. He sat back, smiled feebly at her, and waited. She felt John's grasp relax and managed to extract her hand before she continued.

'The Children's Crusade, we are calling it,' said Sarah. She had seen it all in her imagination. 'On the day of the review presentation to the Council, we shall march with placards designed by the children, through Tresham pedestrian precinct. A protest song is being composed by the bigger ones, directed by Gabriella Jones. We shall assemble outside County Hall and ask to be present at the meeting as observers.'

'Gracious,' said Doreen Price.

'You'll not be allowed,' said Deirdre Barnett.

'Great stuff, Sarah,' said Colin Osman.

'We'll be there,' said Jean Jenkins, forgetting her Markie for once, carried along by Sarah's enthusiasm. 'I'll make sure all the parents come too.'

'Splendid!' said Richard Standing. 'Great-Grandfather would be proud of you, Miss Drinkwater.'

John Barnett scribbled something on a piece of paper, and pushed it along for Sarah to read.

'I love you, Miss Drinkwater,' it said. Smiling, Sarah screwed up the message and stuffed it deep into her skirt pocket.

CHAPTER FORTY-ONE

Jean Jenkins had been the one to suggest it. 'It'll raise a few funds,' she said. 'We're bound to need a pound or two. Can't expect the vicar

276

to make a load of phone calls at his own expense. And you bet Mr Richard will be keeping count of what he spends. The likes of him didn't get rich by bein' generous.'

'I doubt if Mr Richard would claim to be rich,' said Fox Jenkins. He was weeding a row of lettuces in his productive back garden, and patiently listened to Jean at the same time. She had brought out a cup of tea, and was sitting on an old kitchen chair on the concrete path at the end of the lettuce row. She loved to chat with Fox when he was gardening. It was the only time she could catch him in one place long enough.

'Won't a barn dance take a bit of time to organise?' Fox said, chucking a dandelion into an old galvanised pail at his side.

Jean shook her head. 'All we need is a barn, a decent band and a caller who knows what he's doin'. Don Cutt'll provide a bar, and the WI can always rustle up some good food. Peggy can put a poster up in the shop, and young Octavia Jones will round up some friends. Gabriella said she's into country pursuits at the moment, so barn dancing should be just up her street.'

'I can see you've got it all worked out and don't need my advice,' said Fox. His tone was mild. He was proud of his Jean and her undoubted organising capabilities. She'd had those babies like shelling peas, and they were all a credit to her. Even Markie, though he

277

seemed to be going through a bad patch at the moment.

'There's only one thing, my duck,' Fox said, straightening up and squinting up at Jean. The sun was high now, and he could feel the heat on the back of his neck. 'You have remembered who masterminds refreshments produced by the WI, I suppose?'

'Ah,' said Jean. 'I see what you mean. Our Ivy is the one, and she's more against us than with us at the moment. Still, we might bring her round, don't you think?'

Fox shook his head. 'Never bin known,' he said.

*   *   *

Might as well tackle old Ivy this morning, thought Jean, as she waved the twins off to school and turned back to ginger up Mark and Eddie. Around coffee time, she set off for the shop, thinking she could call in at Victoria Villa on the way and hope to catch Ivy in a good mood.

'Difficult,' said Doris Ashbourne, who joined up with her as she walked down the Gardens. 'Ivy's moods are very unpredictable. Depends what you want, Jean.' Jean explained, and Doris was doubtful. 'Can be very stubborn, our Ivy,' she said. 'It doesn't make her many friends, but to give her credit, she does stick to her guns once she's made up her mind ... unfortunately ...' Doris looked depressed. She could smell trouble coming for Ivy, and although her old friend irritated her beyond measure at times, she did not wish to see her hurt.

Ivy's little iron gate was swinging open when Jean Jenkins approached. Oh damn, she thought, looks like she's out. But then the familiar square figure emerged from the shop and marched into her garden, shutting the gate firmly behind her.

'Miss Beasley!' shouted Jean, quickening her pace. 'Have you got a minute?'

Ivy turned. 'What for, Mrs Jenkins?' she said.

'Perhaps I could just come in to explain. Won't take a second,' puffed Jean.

'In that case, it can be said here, can't it?' said Ivy. 'I'm busy baking and haven't got time for even one of your seconds, I'm afraid.' Ivy held Jean Jenkins responsible for all the transgressions of her children over the years: cheeky remarks, balls kicked into Ivy's front garden, crisp packets thrown over her privet hedge, giggling insults at the bus stop. She was polite, but cool.

'Oh, very well,' said Jean, feeling she'd lost the battle already. 'It's about refreshments for the fund-raising dance. You know, the Fight for the School Fund.' Shouldn't have mentioned that, Jean, she thought. 'We thought the WI might help with food, and bein'' as you're the best baker in Ringford, wondered if you might organise it … like …' Jean tailed off, daunted by the ice in Ivy's eyes. Not even creepin' is going to help me now, she thought.

Ivy retreated backwards up her path until she reached her steps, and then said in a very loud voice so that the queue at the bus stop, and the chatterers outside the shop, could all hear perfectly clearly.

'You have always had a great deal of cheek, Jean Jenkins,' she said. 'No doubt why your Mark is such a thoroughly ungovernable child. But in spite of your feeble attempts at flattery, the answer is no, no, NO! I do not approve of fighting for the school. If its time has come, then that's that. So please go away and let me get on with my work.'

The door of Victoria Villa banged shut, and Jean Jenkins slunk away, taking refuge in the shop and Peggy Palmer's sympathetic ear.

*   *   *

Finding a venue, as Colin Osman called it, was also more difficult than Jean had anticipated. Tom Price had an old brick-built barn which would have been ideal, but it was full of machinery and sacks of feed and fertiliser. After several abortive approaches to farmers in the village, Jean had a rethink and announced that the dance would now be a Square dance, and would be held in the Village Hall. 'It's a lot easier, anyway,' she said bravely to Sarah Drinkwater in the school cloakroom, 'what with the kitchen and that.'

'Right,' said Sarah, impressed by Jean's dogged persistence, so far all on her own. 'We don't need a Committee for this dance, do we. You and I can organise this one, without a lot of red tape and unnecessary blather.'

Jean was under the impression that she had more or less organised it already, but agreed with Miss Drinkwater, and suggested getting together one evening to make the final arrangements. And Sarah did, after all, prove useful. Her eye had been caught by an advertisement in the *Tresham Advertiser* for a Square dance over at Waltonby. 'Be there! Be Square!' it had said, and Sarah had winced. It got worse. The band was called 'Sunday Suits and Muddy Boots', and a good time was guaranteed 'for oldies and youngies alike'. But now she swallowed hard, and suggested to Jean that they try to get a booking. 'After all,' she said, 'it's very short notice, and we may have trouble finding a band with that evening free.'

A mild, light voice answered the band's telephone, when Jean had finally located it through her sister in Bagley, and to her relief said that yes, they could make it for the Ringford dance. They'd had a booking, but it had fallen through. It had been a wedding reception, and the whole thing had been cancelled and the bride-to-be run off with her

281

fiancé's best man.

'There we are then,' said Sarah, 'couldn't be simpler. I don't see why people make such a fuss about organising these events, do you, Jean?'

Jean thought of all the time she had spent on the telephone, and the most unpleasant conversation she had had with Ivy Beasley. Oh well, it wasn't worth saying anything. And anyway, for her Mark's sake, she was determined to keep on the right side of Miss Drinkwater.

*   *   *

The Village Hall had once more been transformed. This time it was rustic simplicity. The chairs had been stacked and stored, and instead, clean straw bales pushed up against the walls, with Doreen's gingham tablecloths she kept for Open Gardens Sunday spread over to keep the worst of the prickles from those who sat out the dances.

The band knew what they were about, fiddler, guitarist and a girl in long skirt and pigtails who played a huge accordion that all but obscured her from view. The man who had been so mild on the telephone turned out to be tall and willowy, with round shoulders, a wispy beard and a huge calling voice. But his real genius was in getting everyone on the floor, even Doreen and Tom, who hadn't danced for years, and Bill Turner, who had never square danced before and had little or no sense of rhythm.

'Nice to see the old people here,' said Doris to Jean Jenkins in the kitchen. 'Old Fred would have loved it. Great one for square dancing, he was. And his sister. Even old Ivy was light on her feet once, though you'd not believe it now, the way she stumps around. Her dad had her taught properly, much to her mother's disgust.'

'Ivy'd not be here anyway,' said Jean. 'Gave me an earful when I asked about refreshments. The school can close down and she for one would be glad to see the back of it, she said, more or less. Still, we've managed quite well without her, haven't we.'

Doris looked worried. 'She can be a bit of a fool, sometimes, our Ivy,' she said. 'She's got herself stuck into this ridiculous position and don't know how to get out of it. She doesn't really mean it, you know. Just her usual habit of taking the opposite point of view and being cussed about it. I bet she wishes she'd never opened her mouth to that reporter.'

Jean Jenkins looked sceptical. 'You'd have thought she meant it if you'd been in my shoes, Doris,' she said. 'The air was blue when I left Victoria Villa. Still, you may be right. Nobody in the village is talking to Ivy now.'

*   *   *

Clearing up next morning was not such fun. There were bits of straw everywhere, and just as Fox and Jean had brushed up the last of it, their terrier, who had followed them down from Macmillan Gardens, fancied he could smell rats in a straw bale and began scratching it all to pieces with his furious sharp claws, sending clouds of chaffy straw and dust everywhere.

'Get that dog out of here!' yelled Jean, and Fox vanished, the terrier in tow. Jean sat down heavily and surveyed the scene. They had spent hours sweeping and collecting up paper cups and plates, scraps of trodden-in food and cigarette ends. There was the scarlet rose Octavia Jones had tucked behind her ear, now wilted and flattened. She'd had a good time, though, thought Jean. Turning out all right after all, that Octavia. And John Barnett and Miss Drinkwater! Couldn't have prised them apart by the last dance ... Ah, love's young dream ... still, we've all had our day. Jean got to her feet, danced a few steps partnered by her broom, and got back to work.

CHAPTER FORTY-TWO

The small sitting room in Doris's old person's bungalow was even more spick and span than usual. Her bits of brass twinkled in the sunlight streaming through the big window. Every surface had been dusted, every square inch of carpet hoovered until not even a house mite could survive.

Ellen sat in the comfortable chair she had made her own, at her elbow a table with magazines, the television remote control, and a cup of coffee. Her ratty grey hair had been neatly combed, and she was wearing a fresh white blouse. 'Don't suppose you'll object to wearing one of mine, seeing as your entire wardrobe consists of other people's cast-offs,' Doris had said.

Ellen had grumbled, nevertheless. 'Don't know what all the fuss is about,' she said. 'Social Services have been here before, and you've never bothered. And what's old Ivy comin' this mornin' for? She's not due till termorrow.'

'It's a different one coming from Tresham Social Services,' said Doris. 'They want to talk about your future. Vicar's wife is coming, and Ivy, so you can just be nice, Ellen Biggs.'

'I ain't got no future,' Ellen had said grumpily. 'We're gettin' on all right, anyway, Doris, ain't we? Why do they need to come pokin' their noses in?'

Doris hadn't answered that one. She knew she couldn't go on with Ellen much longer, but still felt ashamed. She would be letting down the old woman. Ellen hadn't known such comfort for many years, and had bloomed.

Sometimes Doris thought Ellen was the fitter of the two of them.

*   *   *

At Victoria Villa, Ivy Beasley put down a saucer of top-of-the-milk for Gilbert, Peggy Turner's fickle cat. 'There you are, puss,' she said. A quick look round to make sure all was well, and then she left by her back door, locking it behind her. She wouldn't be gone long, she was sure, but you never knew. The sky was clear, the run of hot weather still holding, but Ivy collected her grey cardigan from the front room. You never knew. Rain could come over Bagley Woods without warning, and many's the time she'd been caught.

She stepped out of her neat front garden, and shut the iron gate with a click. Jean Jenkins was talking to Olive Bates by the bus stop, and Ivy gave them her usual chilly smile. She was taken aback by the hostile looks received in return. She shrugged, anchored her handbag firmly under her arm, and walked on to Macmillan Gardens. This morning might be tricky. She realised that the time had come for Doris to be relieved of Ellen Biggs, and though she knew the obvious next step was for Ellen to be moved to Victoria Villa, she also knew that she couldn't face it.

Joyce Davie was in her front garden,

clipping the hedge, keeping it down to its new, sociable height. 'Morning, Joyce,' said Ivy, lifting her hand in salute. Joyce turned away, and Ivy stopped. Maybe she didn't hear me, she thought.

'Morning, Joyce!' She shouted this time, so that nobody could have missed it. But Joyce did not turn round, just scuttled down the passage at the side of the house and disappeared. A moment's real fear pierced Ivy, but she was reassured by Doris's warm welcome.

'Come on in, Ivy,' she said. 'The others are all here.' And then she whispered into Ivy's ear, 'We need you, Ivy. Ellen's dug her toes in.'

*　　　*　　　*

Sophie Brooks climbed the steps to the shop, thanking Heaven that Peggy did not shut at lunchtime. There was no one else in there, and she greeted Peggy with a brave smile. 'How're the aching muscles this morning, Peggy?' she said. 'You were nimble as a goat at the dance, my dear.'

'A foolish old goat,' said Peggy. 'I could hardly move next day. Still, it was good fun, wasn't it, and Jean made over a hundred pounds.' Then she remembered where Sophie had been. 'Goodness, I forgot to ask,' she said, 'how'd the meeting go?'

'Well,' said Sophie, 'how long have you got?'

287

'Oh dear,' said Peggy. 'Bad as that, was it. Well, give me the expurgated version.'

'No,' said Sophie, 'it wasn't too dreadful, and in the end I think we've come to quite a good solution. But Ellen Biggs is no fool. She's extremely comfortable with Doris Ashbourne, and is not going to give it up lightly.'

'I saw Ivy setting off,' said Peggy. 'Was she any help, or just her usual obstinate self.'

'As a matter of fact,' said Sophie, perching on the edge of the chair reserved for pensioners who had to wait for the Post Office cubicle, 'Ivy Beasley was the one who shifted Ellen in the end. She was quite stern with her. The rest of us had been pussy-footing around, treating her like fragile china, but Ivy took her in hand with no ceremony.'

'Mm,' said Peggy. 'She's used to getting her own way, is our Ivy. It will be all right for old Ellen, won't it? What exactly has been decided?'

'Your idea of Bill doing up the Lodge was agreed. There'll be some kind of grant, and they hope Mr Richard will chip in, it being his property. They'll make sure it's not damp, and easier to run for Ellen, then move her back in. Some kind of Care Package—sorry, Peggy, but that's what they called it—will be put together, and Ellen will be monitored and helped with what she can't manage herself.'

'And all this from Tresham?' said Peggy, looking doubtful.

'No, we've all got to do our bit. It's a pity there's still nobody living in Robert Bates's old cottage, but the vicarage is very close to the Lodge, and we shall make sure we check on Ellen every day. The Social Services woman did say that Ellen would probably be better in the long run with a few of her own jobs to do. She's made great strides, you know, Peggy, since that fall. Doris has done a grand job.'

'How does Ivy fit in to all this?' said Peggy. She hated to think of the old bat getting off scot-free. Trust her to have wriggled out of any responsibility for her old friend.

'She's offered to cook Ellen a good meal.'

'What, every day?'

'Yes. Every day. That's what she said, and I get the impression Ivy Beasley does not offer such things without meaning it.'

'Oh,' said Peggy. 'Oh, well.'

'I know you have every reason to dislike her, Peggy, but she really was quite helpful. She looked a bit odd, sort of shaken up, when she first arrived, but soon settled down to the usual abrasiveness. But, as she said, an ounce of help is worth a pound of pity.'

'Well, I'm very glad. You've done extremely well, Sophie,' said Peggy magnanimously.

'Nigel will be pleased,' said Sophie. 'Brownie points for him all round, when he tots up his good works for the month.'

'Sophie!' said Peggy, laughing.

'Well, you know our Nigel,' said Sophie, and

with a grin she turned to go. 'He's been a different chap since a couple of real problems came his way. All we've got to do now, Peggy dear, is prevent the school from closing, and he'll feel his ministry has been worth while.'

'Do you ever wonder why you married him, Sophie?' said Peggy. They were very good friends.

'Not 'arf,' said Sophie. 'But then, I didn't marry a vicar, did I? I married a solicitor, and there's nothing in the marriage contract that says a change of career entitles either spouse to ditch the whole thing.'

'Unfortunately?' said Peggy.

'That'd be telling,' said Sophie, and waved her a cheerful goodbye. Perhaps I should have asked her about Bill, she thought as she walked back up to the vicarage. Still, they seem fine now, and I'm sure Peggy would tell me if anything was seriously wrong.

*　　　*　　　*

'Did you hear how it went?' said Bill, after they'd had supper and were sitting in the long, quiet room. Nothing more had been said about the day Bill and Joyce had got so wet, nor about Ivy's heavy hints in the shop as a result. Peggy and Bill had square danced together with every appearance of devotion, and Bill had side-stepped neatly when the Ladies' Request had sent Joyce in his direction.

Everything seemed perfectly normal, on the surface. But Peggy still felt unsettled. It was as if a thin, chilly mist had descended between them. Sooner or later, she was sure, something would have to happen to clear the air properly.

Now she twisted in her chair, rearranging cushions. 'The meeting about Ellen?' she said. 'Well, Sophie came in at lunchtime. Poor thing had had a basinful, I reckon. But they finally worked something out, much as we'd planned. You'll be hearing more about the work to be done later, I expect.'

'Good,' said Bill. 'Sooner Ellen gets back there the better, from Doris's point of view. I thought Doris looked very poorly in her garden yesterday. She could hardly bend over to do a bit of weeding.'

'What were you doing in Macmillan Gardens?' said Peggy quickly, and immediately wished she hadn't.

Bill looked at her with irritation. 'I'd just been calling on my ex-wife Joyce while her new husband was out. We had a quick bunk up in their bed, and I managed to get away before Donald returned.' His voice was harsh, and Peggy winced.

'I only asked,' she said, and her chin wobbled.

'I thought we'd had all that out,' said Bill. 'I don't know what else I can say.'

'There's something I'd like to say...'

'Hang on a minute,' said Bill. He leaned

forward to switch on the television. 'The results are just coming up—must check them off. Then I'll listen all night, gel, if that's what you want.'

By the time Bill had finished checking, Peggy had opened her book. How to start? She'd made several attempts in her head, and they all sounded terrible, pompous. It's not that I'm jealous, Bill ... But she was. I do understand how you feel, Bill ... But she didn't, not wholly. How could anyone have any affection left after constant animosity for all those years?

'Now then,' said Bill, settling back in his chair, 'I'm all ears.'

'Doesn't matter,' Peggy said. 'Not important.'

CHAPTER FORTY-THREE

'You're not looking very cheerful this morning, Peggy,' said Richard Standing. He was not feeling so good himself. Susan had gone on and on this morning about all the time he was spending on the village school.

'It's not as if we shall be sending Poppy there,' she had said. 'I've put her name down provisionally at that dear little school in Fletching. You know, where the little boys wear knickerbockers.'

'Poppy's not a little boy,' said Mr Richard.

'Oh, Richard. Don't be difficult. You know perfectly well what I mean.'

Richard Standing did know, but he felt uncomfortable and could not account for it. He found the meetings of the Protest Committee tedious, Colin Osman deadly boring, and Sarah Drinkwater totally impervious to his advances. And yet when he got home to Susan's tales of coffee mornings and the lovely day she had spent at the Cordon Bleu demonstration over at the Flemings, he had an odd feeling of having left the real world behind. He had not attempted to explain to Susan, but muttered something about Great-Grandfather Charles, and perpetuating his philanthropy.

Now he thought not for the first time what an attractive woman Peggy Turner was. No wonder old Bill had got his feet in under the table there. He wasn't to know poor Frank Palmer would have a fatal accident, of course, but he had certainly been at the ready with strong arms and soft words when Peggy had been widowed.

'It's a dreadful morning, Mr Richard,' said Peggy.

'Absolutely,' said Richard. 'It's raining, and the wind is cold. Even the children haven't come out to play, and Sarah Drinkwater is a stickler for fresh air unless there's a monsoon.'

Peggy looked at him. He's really quite attractive in a sloppy sort of way, she thought.

'Ah, well,' she said, 'it's warm and dry in here, Mr Richard. Now, what can I do for you?' She twinkled at him. Well, why not? she thought resentfully. Have to cheer myself up somehow.

Richard Standing knew an overture when he saw one, however small. 'Save my life, Peggy, my dear,' he said, leaning over the counter. 'A small sliced brown will do it. If Poppy doesn't get her Marmite soldiers for tea, I shall be running to you for sanctuary.'

Oh blimey, thought Peggy, that's quite enough of that, and reached for the loaf. She saw a roll of paper in Mr Richard's hand and swiftly changed the subject.

'A poster for the board?' she said.

Frank had fixed up a noticeboard for village posters, and it vied with Colin Osman's Newsletter for details of events and meetings.

'Open Gardens Sunday,' said Richard Standing. 'Thank you so much.' The game was over, and he retreated gracefully.

'Goodness,' said Peggy, 'is it time for that already? There's been so much going on with the school ... Which Sunday is it this year?'

'Second in July,' said Mr Richard. 'There'll be one more garden open this year. The Wattses in Walnut Close have offered. They're quite new—have a girl at the school, I believe—and should be encouraged, we thought.'

Peggy pinned up the notice, and Mr Richard still stood there. He seemed in conversational mood this morning. Might be a good time to sound him out.

'What are the chances for our school surviving, d'you reckon, Mr Richard?' she said. Everyone was aware that in the higher echelons of the County Council and the Education Department there were the right people to know, and Mr Richard knew many of them.

'Oh, a good chance, I should think, Mrs Turner,' he said. He picked up the bread and walked towards the open door. The rain had settled down to a steady downpour, and he pulled up his coat collar. 'But I did have one thought this morning. Don't know if it's important, but it occurred to me that the school holidays begin in three weeks' time. That could be a very major factor. Is Nigel Brooks at home this morning, d'you know?'

Peggy had been in Ringford long enough not to think this an odd question to ask the village shopkeeper.

'Yes—he's making notes for his debut on Radio Tresham,' she said. 'You should find him there all morning.'

*   *   *

What on earth made me decide to live in this godforsaken village? Sarah cursed as she walked straight into a deep puddle between the school and her own back door. She had left

295

Gabriella in charge of playtime, a structured playtime with games and activities to be done quietly in the classroom. Rainy days were a sod, she thought gloomily. The children needed that burst of freedom halfway through the morning. Now they'd be difficult all day. And if that Mark Jenkins didn't stop kicking his feet on the underside of his desk, she would probably give him twenty lashes.

She stood in her kitchen munching biscuits, and reflected on Mark Jenkins. He had still not forgiven her for replacing Miss Layton, and persisted in his subtle campaign to disrupt her classes and generally wear her nerves to a frazzle. There was nothing really bad enough to punish, just annoying interruptions, like the desk kicking. Perhaps she should have a word with Miss Layton about him. She'd called once or twice on the retired headmistress, and found her friendly and helpful. No wonder Mark Jenkins missed her. Sarah felt a pang of sympathy for him. Mark was lumpy and slow. But why can't he just forget Dot Layton and co-operate?

Irritated with Mark, she took another biscuit. She'd not been able to get down to schoolwork properly all day. She'd woken early and stayed in bed trying to decide whether she was really in love with John, a young farmer whose world scarcely overlapped hers, or just overwhelmed by the powerful physical effect he had on her. Since that moving day, when she'd discovered just how loving John could be, they had seen each other most days. John would tap at the schoolhouse kitchen window, grinning at her alarm. He'd stay for tea, and supper, and nearly to breakfast, and they grew easier in each other's company. After a disastrous evening at the Rugby Club, where Sarah tried hard but couldn't join in the badinage and local references, their outings were mostly to the cinema or for meals out at pubs and nearby restaurants. There was a small difficulty with Deirdre. Sarah no longer felt welcome at the farm. Deirdre was sharp with her, finding fault and digging into her family background. Sarah knew exactly what was up with Deirdre, and didn't much care. It was John she wanted. Or did she want him? And how much and how far? And what would her life be like if she took him on?

Reaching no real conclusions, and feeling cross with herself, Sarah got up late and missed breakfast in order to be in school on time. Now she took another chocolate biscuit, looked at the clock and prepared to go back into school. Poised to leap the puddle, she heard her telephone ringing. Might as well answer it in the house, she thought, in case it's John. She opened the door again, and rushed to the telephone.

It wasn't John, but a familiar voice, one she hadn't heard for some time. 'Sarah?'

'Jeremy!' Sarah's smile broadened. Jeremy Griffiths had been at college with her, and they'd been inseparable for a couple of terms. Then he'd decided teaching was not for him, and had left to join his father's stockbroking firm.

'Sarah, darling, how are you? Now listen. I have to be in—what's it called?—yes, Tresham, tomorrow. Please say you're free. I'm longing to see you.'

Sarah had a fleeting thought that Tresham was not that far from London, and the telephone lines worked perfectly well, if he was that keen. But she said that yes, she was free. Her diary in Round Ringford was not often completely full, she said, and she'd love to see him again.

It was only after she put down the telephone that she remembered John had suggested they went to see that new movie everyone was talking about. Well, quite new. It was on in Tresham now, until the end of the week, and tomorrow was the only night John could manage, what with the Rugby Club and a Farmers' Union meeting, and another get together at the vicarage.

'Damn,' said Sarah, forgetting to jump, and getting the other foot wet. 'Now what am I going to do about John?' She realised that she had no telephone number for Jeremy, and short of standing him up, she'd have to be there, at the Saxon Hotel, as arranged.

*   *   *

'Well, there you are,' said Deirdre. 'I told you you'd be better steering well clear of that one.'

'Don't be silly, Mum,' said John Barnett, putting down the telephone. He could not completely disguise his disappointment that Sarah had cancelled their outing, and his mother's interference irritated him. He was increasingly aware of his mother's animosity towards Sarah. It had been all right, he thought, before she knew I was interested. She'd been quite fond of Sarah then. Now it's claws out, protecting her cub against predators.

It was more than that, of course. Deirdre was jealous. She'd had John around for a long time now, looking after her even better than his father had, always there when she needed him. Without realising it, she had more or less taken it for granted that he would not now marry. He'd be one of Ringford's bachelor sons, banding together for visits to race meetings and rugby football matches, finding partners for the Show Dance and Hunt Ball, but on the whole preferring a night at the Arms with the blokes to coping with the intricacies of the female mind.

'You'd not have spoken to me like that, John,' said Deirdre, stung, 'until that Sarah came along. I'm not silly. I know what I'm talking about. She's just filling in time with

299

you. She doesn't belong to the country, however much she likes the idea of being the village school headteacher. Her parents come from Harrogate, they're posh, and she's an only. They'll want more for her than a farmer's boy from Round Ringford.'

John sighed, and sat down at the kitchen table. 'Sorry, Mum,' he said. 'But it is my business, you know. Me and Sarah just enjoy going out together. She's good company, that's all. There's nothing more.' Liar, he thought to himself. Bloody liar.

His mother sat down opposite him, and he looked at her with affection. She'd been a good mother, and he knew he was her favourite, her last, late son, and a comfort to her when his dad had died. And she wasn't an old woman, not by any means. Not ready for Tresham House for many years. Couldn't be much fun for her here at the farm, with just the other old women to go out with.

He made an impulsive offer. 'Sarah's got too much work to do, she says. Head Office want some more information for the school review. Urgent, she says. So would you like to come to the pictures, Mum?' he said. 'It's my only free evening this week, and it's supposed to be a really good film.'

Deirdre smiled. 'Well, yes, I would, John. Thanks.' That'll teach her, she thought.

CHAPTER FORTY-FOUR

Sarah Drinkwater sat at a table for two in the softly lit dining room of the Saxon Hotel in Tresham, a glass of champagne in her hand. She wore an elegant brown silk jacket over a pale cream dress which did a lot for her trim figure. Her dark hair shimmered in the light like the silk of the jacket, and other diners turned to look at her as she laughed at Jeremy Griffiths's ridiculous jokes.

'You've changed, Sarah,' he said.

'Of course I have,' she said. 'You've changed, too. We're neither of us the spotty students who held hands in the back row of the Goldwyn Cinema in New Cross.' She felt a sudden pang at the thought of herself and John Barnett, holding hands in the back row of the County Cinema in Tresham, but suppressed it at once.

'Bit more than holding hands, wasn't it, darling?' said Jeremy. His grin was as appealing as ever, in spite of his stockbroker uniform of well cut grey suit, striped shirt, tastefully abstract tie, and monogrammed cuff-links. Sarah remembered his shock of black curls, and looked regretfully at the neat haircut. Still, he had a good head, and you could see the shape of it now.

'You look wonderful,' Jeremy said, reaching

out his hand. Sarah put hers into it, willingly. She hadn't felt so cool and sophisticated for months. It was as if the claustrophobic affairs of Round Ringford, the mud and puddles and Mark Jenkins, and the piteously crying Daisy, had never been.

'You will come to see me in London, won't you, Sarah,' he said. 'Don't let it go again. I think we may have something precious here.'

A smart reply, pointing out that he was the one who 'let it go', rose up in Sarah, but instead, she took another mouthful of champagne and nodded.

'Absolutely,' she said. How lovely. An evening out in London, maybe dinner in Jeremy's flat...

Jeremy was there before her. 'Now, my darling,' he said. 'Are you going to show me your little country nest? You lead the way, and I'll follow in the BMW. And I shan't lose you again, never fear!'

*   *   *

John and his mother emerged from the County Cinema, blinking under the bright sodium lamps.

'That was really good, John,' said Deirdre, and tucked her hand through his arm. 'Haven't been to the pictures for so long. Thank you, son.'

'Glad you liked it, Mum,' he said. 'I enjoyed

302

it, too.' But he lied again. He had no idea whether it was a good film or a bad one. He couldn't even have related the plot. All the time, in the stuffy darkness, he had thought of Sarah. Was it a genuine reason, or had she just given him an excuse? Maybe she was tired of him. Perhaps Mum was right.

They walked down Tresham High Street to the short-stay car park. At the crossroads by the Saxon Hotel, the lights were against them, and they stood on the island between the dual carriageway and waited. Deirdre's grip on John's arm suddenly tightened.

'John!' she said. 'Isn't that Sarah's car?'

'Where?' said John, his heart lurching.

'Look, there, waiting in the queue.' Deirdre began to feel that things were definitely looking up.

John looked across the line of cars, and there, without question, was Sarah's smart little car, and inside, a very smart Sarah. A stab of fearful nausea made him turn quickly away. And then the lights changed, and Sarah's car, closely followed by a dark red BMW, moved off and disappeared down the road in the direction of Waltonby and Round Ringford.

*   *   *

'Oh, bloody hell,' said Sarah Drinkwater, suddenly quite sober. She had seen John and Deirdre, and had prayed for the lights to

303

change. But she knew they had seen her, and had had to go on sitting there, trapped.

She looked in her driving mirror, and there was Jeremy, the grin still lingering. Sarah drove out of Tresham, and put her foot down. On the unfamiliar, unlit roads, Jeremy Griffiths had trouble keeping up with her. She knew every bend, every narrowing of the road, and when she had lost sight of his lights at the notorious cuttings outside Waltonby, she took a quick right turn and made her cautious way down a narrow muddy lane that was more of a track than a road.

Another look in the driving mirror, and there was no sign of Jeremy. Sarah knew this was an alternative route, very narrow and tortuous, but if she went slowly, she would come out just beyond Round Ringford on the Fletching Road, and could go home that way. She sighed with relief, and meant to spend the next half hour working out a convincing story to tell John in the morning. It was a strange, transitional half hour.

By the time she had negotiated a fallen branch from an overhanging oak, and steered carefully round a huge mound of muck with trickling streams of brown slurry, her speed and her thoughts had slowed down to something more appropriate for the countryside at night. This was fortunate for a hare which appeared suddenly and magically in her headlights. Mesmerised, it loped off in front of the car, zigzagging wildly, but unable to escape the beam of Sarah's headlights. She began to laugh. It was such a comic creature, with its long, stringy legs and signalling ears.

But it's not comic at all, she thought, slowing to a crawl. It is absolutely terrified. She stopped the car and turned off her lights. It was perfectly dark under the overhanging trees, quite still, and silent.

She opened her window, and took in a deep breath of night air. It wasn't silent, of course, or still, once she began to listen. She was gradually aware of rustles and snaps of undergrowth as little creatures retreated, soft chirrups of roosting birds disturbed by her presence, the feathery sound of wings as an owl swooped to have a look at her.

I wonder if it was a good film, she thought, and started her engine. I do hope Jemima hasn't been too lonely. She wanted to get home now, and when she switched on her lights the hare had vanished. She drove on slowly and thoughtfully.

Turning into Ringford's main street, Sarah saw that it was dark and, as far as she could see, deserted. There was the usual orange puddle of light outside the shadowy pub, left on all night for security. It was late, and the Turners' bedroom window glowed softly. Victoria Villa was in complete darkness. Whew, thought Sarah. And then she put her foot on the brake, hard.

Outside the schoolhouse, side lights dimly on, was the dark red, shiny BMW.

CHAPTER FORTY-FIVE

Once Bill Turner had got the go-ahead, it did not take him long to do the necessary work on Ellen's Lodge house. Richard Standing had been as helpful as his bank balance would allow, as he put it, and with a damp course, new doors and floors, a proper bathroom and the roof repaired, the cottage was warm and dry. Peggy and Sophie Brooks had spent hours searching second-hand shops and linen sales, and refurbished Ellen's little sitting room until both of them said they wouldn't mind living there themselves.

Doris had not looked forward to this day of moving. Ellen had spent the last few days dropping heavy hints about how much she would miss her cup of tea in bed, and Doris's cooking, and the morning sun across her flowery counterpane.

'You'll be getting a good meal from Ivy every day,' Doris said now, helping Ellen on with her new pink cardigan.

'So I shall,' said Ellen. 'But that means a good helpin' of Ivy Beasley's conversation as well.'

'Then you'll not be lonely,' said Doris

sternly. She was determined not to let Ellen's little campaign get to her. Today, Ellen would be back home at the Lodge, and Doris's life would be her own again.

'Depends what you call lonely,' said Ellen gloomily. 'It's in the middle of the night, when I can't sleep, that your ole snorin' comin' through the wall seems a comfort. Must have driven your Jack out once or twice, when he were alive.'

'There's gratitude!' said Doris. But her soft heart was sore at the thought of Ellen alone in her Lodge, with nothing but the eerily hooting owls in the avenue of dark chestnuts for company. 'Here, Ellen,' she said, with sudden inspiration. 'Take this little radio—you can switch it on in the night if you can't sleep. There's always something on.'

Ellen's eyes brightened. 'Don't you need it no more, Doris?' she said. 'Well, that's very civil of you, I'm sure. Show me how to find the stations.'

They were still fiddling with wavebands when Bill Turner arrived in Peggy's car to fetch Ellen. Macmillan Gardens was looking its summer best. Donald Davie, a newly enthusiastic gardener, had offered to take on the central flower-beds which old Fred Mills had lovingly maintained for so many years. 'I'll help you, Donald,' Joyce had said. And if Bill comes up the Gardens when we're working on the beds, we can ask his advice, she thought with a secret smile.

'African marigolds and blue lobelia, I think, Joyce,' Donald had said. The rich, bright orange flowers had grown tall and strong, and delicate little blue blooms had bushed out into luxuriant masses. Clumps of white alyssum interspersed at regular intervals emphasised the singing, sunny blocks of colour in Donald's beds.

'Looks more like the Municipal Park in Tresham than our ole village,' Ellen said caustically, casting a look around the Gardens. But she was feeling more generous now, looking forward to having a lie-in in the mornings with her own bedside radio. 'That Donald do keep the grass nice,' she said, as she stood on the pavement outside Doris's bungalow, her old bones soaking up the warm sunlight. 'He's worked hard. You have to give 'im that, even if 'e don't look no more'n a skinned rabbit.'

'Joyce helps him,' said Bill absently. He wanted to get Ellen into the car and away down to the Lodge as soon as possible. Mr Richard had gone up to London this morning, taking in a quick meeting with Maurice Buswell MP at the club, he'd said, and had left Bill a list of jobs that would take him well past teatime.

'Oh God,' said old Ellen. 'Here comes Ivy. Let's get goin', Bill. I can do without a lecture on keepin' meself clean.'

'That was yesterday, Ellen,' whispered Doris

conspiratorially. 'Today is how to get your sink unblocked with an old dishrag.'

Ellen cackled, and got into the car with surprising agility.

*   *   *

'Well, I must say this is a bit more like it,' Ellen said, leaning back in her new comfortable armchair. 'Don't I remember this chair in the Nanny's room?' she said.

Doris and Ivy sat opposite her on the rejuvenated sofa, and relaxed. It had been a tricky moment when Ellen stepped across the threshold of her Lodge once more. But the bright vase of flowers on a newly steadied table, the fresh paint and new carpet and curtains, worked miracles. Ellen could not sit down at first. She went from one improvement to another, marvelling at her new bed, the handy rail around a new lavatory, the hot water that gushed out when she turned on a tap.

'Blimey,' she'd said, 'are you sure we're in the right 'ouse, Ivy.'

Ivy and Doris had stayed on after Bill left, and now all three women felt unexpectedly emotional. Here they sat in Ellen's house, as before, except in considerably greater comfort, sipping tea and eating slices of Ivy's excellent lemon sponge.

'Quite like old times, ain't it,' said Ellen,

wiping crumbs from her mouth with the back of her hand.

'Very true,' said Ivy, handing her a paper serviette.

*   *   *

Doris stepped into her bungalow with a sigh of relief. It was quiet and peaceful. She went into the sitting room and turned on the television for the local news. The stories were all of accidents and burglaries, and a child had been abducted from a housing estate in Tresham. She turned it off, and went through to the kitchen. Every surface was perfectly clean, and she picked up the kettle. Then she put it down again. She'd had three cups at Ellen's. Any more, and she'd be up all night.

Might as well do a bit of knitting, she thought, and went back to the sitting room. But it was a difficult cable pattern, and she couldn't concentrate. A few weeds need pulling out, she said to herself, and walked out into the back garden. It was beginning to rain, and the wind whipped at her hair. She returned to the kitchen, and began to stuff the sheets from Ellen's bed into the washing machine. But I can do that tomorrow, she thought. Don't want that row going all evening.

She reached for the bread. She'd make a cheese and tomato sandwich for her supper. I'll leave it ready for later on, she thought. And then she realised she had taken out of the cupboard two plates and placed them on two trays for two laps.

'Oh dear me,' she said. 'That Ellen Biggs.' Sniffing hard, she fumbled for her handkerchief and wiped her tear-filled eyes.

CHAPTER FORTY-SIX

Nigel Brooks had been downstairs, made a tray of tea, and returned before Sophie woke up. Now he drew back the curtains of the big room, with its long windows overlooking sloping lawns and an ancient cedar tree, this morning shrouded in mist. Here his predecessor had slept in bachelor state for many years before passing away peacefully in the night. Nothing but pleasant echoes of old Cyril Collins remained, and Nigel and Sophie had happily chosen this for their bedroom when they moved in.

'Wake up, Soph,' Nigel said, and handed her a cup of tea. She sat up, arranging pillows behind her back, and was quickly immersed in her book, slowly sipping hot tea.

'Soon be the end of term,' said Nigel conversationally.

'Mm,' said Sophie. She was almost at the end of a book about a vicar's wife who goes off and has an affair and works in a supermarket, and generally behaves like no vicar's wife Sophie had ever known. Still, it was a good read, and Sophie hated to be interrupted, especially on the last chapter.

'There'll be children all round the village every day,' said Nigel, 'up to no good, getting in the way, annoying Ivy Beasley. I shall miss my weekly visits to the school to convert the heathen, you know.'

'Mm,' said Sophie.

Nigel leaned over and kissed her warm cheek. 'You're not listening to me, are you, Soph,' he said. He reached out and took her book away, putting it down on the bedside table. 'Hey, Nigel! I'd nearly finished it!' Sophie frowned at him and tried to wriggle free.

'Hard luck,' he said. 'Dear little Soph...'

*   *   *

'Anyway,' continued Nigel, as they sat over breakfast in the big kitchen 'at least we can have a pause in the Protest Committee activities. Sarah will be off on holiday somewhere, and presumably the Education Department will have some kind of moratorium during the summer break.'

'What makes you think that?' said Sophie. 'Probably busying themselves so they can drop their bombshell while everybody's in Spain.'

'Or Scotland,' said Nigel. They'd fixed a

walking holiday in the Cairngorms for a couple of weeks in August, and Nigel had promised nothing should stand in their way.

'Exactly,' said Sophie. She was about to caution him against any thoughts of cancelling because of the school crisis, when she heard the letters thud onto the doormat in the hall. Old black Ricky followed her to collect them, and she put them into his open jaws, ever hopeful that one day he would take them to his master. Ricky looked at her pityingly and let the letters fall back in a heap on the mat.

'Here, Nigel!' called Sophie, as she gathered them up. 'There's one from the Education Department.'

'Good,' said Nigel. 'I expect it'll be a date in the autumn for the Education Committee's decision on the Department report. It'll give our Sarah plenty of time to get her Joan of Arc costume ready.'

'Now, now, Nigel, our Sarah is just what's needed right now. Can you imagine Dot Layton leading the entire school through the pedestrian precinct of Tresham Town Centre?'

Nigel reached for the letters. 'You're right, Sophie. But that young lady is just like her self-opinionated mother. Never in the wrong, our Sarah.'

*   *   *

But being in the wrong is exactly what Sarah

Drinkwater suspected of herself, and with an increasingly sinking heart. Since that evening with Jeremy at the Saxon Hotel, John Barnett had been avoiding her. There was no question of that. Although he made one excuse after another for not seeing her, Sarah knew that he had drawn his own conclusions at those traffic lights in Tresham.

What she did not know, was that Ivy Beasley, in conversation in the shop with Deirdre Barnett, had spoken in an undertone of a dark red car she had seen parked outside the schoolhouse late at night. 'Nobody in it, Mrs Barnett,' she had said. 'I was quite worried that Miss Drinkwater might have a burglar. But then I could see a light in her bedroom window. Burglars don't put the lights on, do they, Mrs Barnett.'

This information had been faithfully relayed by Deirdre to John, who had reacted with such dismay that Deirdre had felt unexpectedly ashamed. And because she loved John very much, she also knew that she should have kept Ivy's malicious gossip to herself, but it was too late.

There was still half an hour or so before school, and Sarah wandered about her comfortable little house, plumping up cushions on her bright, chintzy sofa, straightening piles of books and papers on the new desk, adding water to a vase of white and yellow daisies from her garden. She went

314

upstairs and pulled the duvet over her new bed, wide and comfortable, plenty of room for more than one. Oh, to hell with Jeremy Griffiths, she thought, I wish he'd never surfaced, with his precious worldly charm. Dear old John. He looks so hurt.

Her father had telephoned as usual last evening, and found her gloomy and pessimistic, talking of an approach made to her by a special school in Tresham. 'Saw me on the telly. Said they were impressed.' Sarah's voice was flat, giving nothing away.

'But Ringford School won't close,' her father had reassured her. 'And as for being a fish out of water in the village, what do you mean, darling? You're so good at organising things around you. What's gone wrong?'

Sarah had not told him about John, but her father was a perceptive man, and when he put down the telephone he turned to Sarah's mother and said that he had good news. 'Good news? Tell me quickly,' she had said, looking apprehensive. 'I think our Sarah has found she's got a heart, after all,' he'd said, and shut his ears to his wife's scornful tirade.

It was a grey, colourless morning in Ringford, like a punishment for all the lovely June days that had gone before. Sarah looked across the Green and over the rooftops to where she could see the hazy line of walnut trees leading to the Barnetts' farm. I wonder what John's doing, she thought. Probably ringing up some Young Farmers' bimbo to be his partner for the Show dance. 'Well, what do I care?' she said to Jemima, lifting her up and extracting a ball of choking fluff that had entwined itself round the puppy's needle-sharp teeth. And then there it was again, the familiar voice, floating in disturbingly through her bedroom window.

'Help! Help!'

It was tremulous and full of tears. Sarah banged the window shut, ran downstairs and out into the yard, where the heavy mist had turned into drizzle. Jemima followed her at speed, missed her footing on the stairs and tumbled headlong, but righted herself and caught up with Sarah as she stopped outside the shed door.

'Right!' Sarah wrenched open the door and marched inside. Nothing. No small girl's thin, undernourished body laid out on the cobbler's bench. No weeping mother, no beaten, despairing father. Nothing. Sarah shut the shed door and slumped heavily down onto the damp wooden bench, her heart thumping. Jemima licked her bare leg, anxious to put right whatever was troubling her beloved mistress.

Sarah looked around the garden, across the water meadows and into the playground. Nobody. Nobody, except Renata Roberts picking up discarded sweet papers, and Mark Jenkins sloping in through the playground gate, pigeon-toed and lumbering, his trousers at half-mast as usual and his school bag slung untidily over his shoulder.

Jemima rushed across to the fence and barked, a high-pitched, warning bark.

'Come here, Jeems,' said Sarah wearily. 'Come on, it's time for school.'

*   *   *

The school cloakroom steamed gently. Residual warmth from yesterday's glorious sun lingered inside, and damp anoraks and macs would be dry by playtime. Sarah stood at the porch door, greeting the parents and children as usual. Maureen, the postlady, pushed her way through the crowd and handed a pile of letters to Sarah. 'Morning, Miss Drinkwater!' she said. 'Hope the weather bucks up again for the holidays...'

'Make way, children,' said Sarah. Maureen returned to where she had propped her bicycle against the fence. She waved cheerily and pedalled off, her postbag considerably lighter now she had delivered the catalogues and junk mail that arrived every morning for the school.

Jean Jenkins, helping Eddie off with his jacket and embarrassing him in front of the girls with a smacking kiss on his cherry red cheek, turned to Sarah. 'Just think, Miss Drinkwater,' she said. 'If all this goes, Ringford won't know the day's begun, will it.'

Sarah took her letters into the big classroom,

317

asked Gabriella Jones to hold the fort for a few minutes, and went to find Renata Roberts. 'Ah, Mrs Roberts,' she said, 'I just caught you in time.' Renata had been about to leave, an old cardigan her only protection against the now steadily falling rain.

'Tell me,' said Sarah, 'when you were in the playground before school, did you hear anyone calling for help?' She looked closely at Renata's face, hoping for clues. But Renata shook her head.

'Nothing, Miss Drinkwater,' she said. 'But then I'm a bit deaf in one ear this morning.'

Because your loving husband clipped you one, no doubt, thought Sarah angrily. She put her hand on Renata's arm and smiled. 'Don't worry,' she said, 'it doesn't matter at all. Here, take my umbrella—bring it back this afternoon.'

Renata stared at her, surprised at this unusually warm gesture from tough Miss Drinkwater. 'Could'a been little Daisy,' she said, trying to help. 'She's not been heard for a long while, but she might've turned up again for some reason.'

'What reason?' said Sarah quickly.

Renata Roberts shrugged. She was already worrying how she could creep into the house without disturbing her hungover husband. But she saw that Sarah looked upset, and tried to reassure her.

'Daisy never done no harm,' she said. 'They

say she comes back when the school's in trouble. Or someone in the school. Could be the closing down business, Miss Drinkwater. I shouldn't take no notice, if I were you. It's probably a pigeon in the trees, anyway.'

'Someone in the school?' repeated Sarah to herself as she returned to the classroom. Me? Am I in trouble? Or in love? Oh, for God's sake. Gabriella had the children waiting quietly, and took her seat at the piano.

'Thank you, Mrs Jones,' Sarah said lightly. 'Now children, hands together and eyes closed...'

It was not until break that she had time to deal with her letters, and she was just slitting open the envelope from the Education Department when she saw Nigel Brooks coming past the window.

*   *   *

'I don't believe it!' Sarah sat down in Miss Layton's chair and threw the letter on to her desk.

'Same as mine,' said Nigel. ' "The Education Committee will meet on the twenty-seventh"—next Friday—"to consider a recommendation from the Education Department that Round Ringford Church of England Primary School should be closed." '

They stared at each other, white-faced, shocked. 'But so little notice!' said Sarah.

'It says here that should the Committee approve the recommendation, there will be a period of two months for appeal before ratification by the Secretary of State.'

'That doesn't mean a thing!' said Sarah. She stood up and began pacing up and down, oblivious to the escalation of noise in the playground as an unsupervised Andrew Roberts flew into a rage with his best friend, Mark Jenkins. 'I saw you!' screamed Andrew, and his voice carried into the silent classroom. Sarah took no notice. She was remembering the campaign to keep her previous school open. They had been so brave and confident, but once the County Councillors had put their seal on the recommendation, it had been a lost cause. Their appeal had been dismissed.

'The lovely Maurice,' said Nigel suddenly, forgetting his collar and cloth. 'Our delightful Member of Parliament has to be nobbled. I must get up to the Hall and speak to Mr Richard straight away.'

Sarah stopped her pacing, and looked Nigel in the eye. 'Right!' she said, 'Round Ringford School is on the march! Look out, Tresham, here we come!'

CHAPTER FORTY-SEVEN

'Emergency meeting, says Nigel.' Bill replaced the receiver and turned to Peggy. It was lunchtime, and they were both in the shop, stacking new supplies on the shelves.

Every week, and sometimes twice a week, Bill drove in his old van to the wholesalers in Tresham with Peggy's shopping list. He was pleased to see that each week the list grew longer. Since they had returned from honeymoon, business had steadily increased, and Bill liked to think it was partly thanks to him. He had announced his willingness to deliver an order, however small, and numbers had doubled. Although he was often tired at the end of a long day at the Hall, he never minded putting the boxes of groceries in the back of the van and setting off round the village. It was a change from working on his own, and he enjoyed chatting to people he wouldn't otherwise have met. Had he chosen to accept the offers, there were plenty of opportunities for a cup of tea and perhaps more at several of the houses. Bill knew that Peggy now felt more optimistic about the shop, and this rubbed off on the customers. People liked coming in. It made all the difference.

'Not another emergency,' said Peggy. She was beginning to think Nigel Brooks thrived on emergencies. Now Ellen was settled comfortably and off his hands, Nigel must have turned all his attention to the school.

'This time it sounds serious,' said Bill. 'Seems that the Education lot have fixed a date for submitting their report to the Committee, and it recommends closure of Round Ringford.'

'Closure!' said Peggy. 'But Mr Richard said...'

'Well, he was wrong,' said Bill. 'I reckon he's taken too much for granted, the silly sod. Perhaps he'll lean harder on Maurice Buswell now. Nigel thinks our MP has to be the best hope.'

'How long have we got?'

'Report is presented next Friday.'

'Next Friday! But that's no time at all! Oh Lord, Bill, looks like we've been caught napping.'

The telephone rang again, and Peggy's face changed. 'Just a minute,' she said stiffly. She turned to Bill. 'It's Mrs Joyce Davie,' she said frostily. 'For you.' She walked out of the shop into the kitchen, and punctiliously shut the door.

'Peggy—you needn't ... Oh, bugger it,' Bill said, and picked up the telephone. 'Joyce?' he said.

'Hello, Bill ...' Joyce's voice was croaky and faint. 'Afraid I have to ask a favour. Donald's gone over to his mother for a couple of days—

poor old girl's on the blink—and I've got this flu bug. Came on suddenly this morning, and now I ache all over and can hardly speak.' Bill had to strain to hear her, and felt a pang of sympathy.

'What can I do, Joycey?' he said. Unfortunately the kitchen door had bounced ajar again, and his voice carried.

'Could you possibly pop up with some LemSip?' said Joyce. 'I've got nothing in the house at all, not even an aspirin ...' Her voice tailed off, and Bill assured her he'd be round straight away. 'You'd better get straight to bed and stay there,' he said.

When he went into the kitchen, he found it empty, and through the window he could see Peggy at the bottom of the garden, leaning over the fence and stroking the velvety nose of John Barnett's big bay, quite restored from his bout of colic and turned out to grass for the summer.

*   *   *

'So I shall have to give the WI a miss for once.' Doreen Price had walked up through the Home Close to find Tom, who was moving an old oil drum away from a gap in the fence. He'd decided to repair the broken posts properly and had been talking to the old donkey who kept him company and didn't answer back.

'Don't suppose the sky will fall,' said Tom. He was feeling irritable and impatient. His back hurt and he suspected he shouldn't have heaved those bales yesterday. He'd have to get something from Guy Russell, though he knew it was really inexorable old age and there was nothing to be done about that.

'What's Nigel's hurry this time?' he said.

'I told you,' said Doreen. 'They've recommended closing the school.' She threw a handful of corn to the flock of hens which had followed her hopefully across the close. The donkey stamped its foreleg, scattering the hens, and began hoovering up the corn. 'Bracken! You evil old donk,' said Doreen, shoving the shaggy grey animal out of the way. 'I don't know why we have to keep this useless creature,' she said.

'Expect you'll want to get rid of me, too,' said Tom, 'when I'm old and no good to anyone.'

'Tom Price!' said Doreen. 'Just stop this at once. You brought backache on yourself, quite unnecessarily. A couple of days' rest and you'll be right as rain.' She reflected, not for the first time, on the paradox of a great strong farmer who could operate in all weathers and conditions, and yet turn into a self-pitying child at the least little ailment.

Tom straightened up, both hands across the small of his back. He drew in his breath to indicate considerable agony, and smiled pathetically at her. 'A nice cup of hot tea would do it a power of good, Doreen,' he said, 'and then you can tell me all about it.' He knew there

324

must be some mistake. Round Ringford School would never close. It was ridiculous. Nigel Brooks must have got hold of the wrong end of the stick somehow.

*   *   *

Richard Standing took Nigel's news very seriously. He had not, as Bill suspected, neglected to keep Maurice Buswell's attentions fixed on the disaster that could soon befall the voters of Round Ringford. Lunch at his Club, with plenty of the best claret, had elicited a firm promise from Maurice that when the time came, he would be thoroughly involved. Richard was aware, however, that woozly as Maurice might have been, he had not committed himself to being thoroughly involved on the side of the save-the-school brigade.

Now Richard was reminded that Maurice would need gingering up on the subject, and he went off to find Susan with a suggestion he knew she would not welcome. He found her in the drawing room, and approached her with a smile that immediately aroused her suspicions.

'Could you bear it, Susan,' he said, 'if I asked the lovely Maurice to come down this weekend?'

'Oh, God,' said Susan. 'Just him?'

'Well, there's not much point in matching him up with the neighbourhood's eligible girls, is there. And anyway, I want to make him feel

325

he's our very best personal friend and has a moral obligation to help us out.'

'Help us out how?' said Susan. She sat at her rosewood desk, writing invitations for a charity fund-raising picnic she was organising with Jean Jenkins for the special nursery group. Set up originally for the benefit of Joey Bates, multiply handicapped and owner of the most heart-warming smile in Ringford, the group had flourished and been commended by the authorities for its good work. Susan had occasional visions of herself standing outside Buckingham Palace, her MBE displayed for a press photograph, with a beaming Richard at her side. Only good sense and a modicum of humility prevented her from suggesting her name be put forward.

'Back us on the school, of course,' said Richard, frowning. Susan was not making it easy for him. 'The review recommends closure, in no uncertain terms, and we have very little time.'

'Seems like you've been banging on about it for ever,' said Susan, licking the last envelope. 'By the way, they've phased out knickerbockers at the Montessori.'

'Great,' said Richard, pouring himself a gin. 'What a relief. It's really been worrying me.'

'All right, all right! Maurice can come for the weekend. Perhaps you'd like me to do my best to straighten him out? I'll wear my sexiest dress...'

'That's enough, Susan,' said Richard. He lifted the lid off the ice bucket, found it empty, and set off for the kitchen.

'Oh, and something else,' said Susan. Richard turned at the door with a resigned expression.

'Seems Ringford's not the only school in trouble. Fletching is down to thirty-five children, and for all their trendy advertising, numbers are still dropping.'

'Fletching will have to fight its own battles,' said Richard. He looked up at the portrait of Charles Standing, upright and proud. 'I have a duty to my ancestors, Susan,' he said, with a soppy smile.

'Just my luck to marry a man whose duty includes entertaining the lovely Maurice,' said Susan. Then, suddenly relenting, she crossed the room and took Richard's glass. 'Here, I'll get the ice,' she said. 'You sit down and make a plan. Looks like we have to be very organised and sharp for the next few days.'

*   *   *

The last person to get a call from Nigel was Colin Osman. He had just got in from a business trip and heard from Pat that Nigel had sounded very strange when he rang earlier. He picked up the telephone on his way to take a cooling shower.

'Saw you go past in the car,' said Nigel. 'Sorry to bother you straight away, Colin, but we've got a crisis.' He gave Colin a succinct and vivid account of the situation, and asked if he could manage an emergency Governors' meeting at half past seven.

'Tonight?' said Colin, his voice firm and decisive. 'Right then, Nigel. See you later.'

CHAPTER FORTY-EIGHT

Ivy Beasley woke early. She pulled on an old grey cardigan over the top of her white cotton nightdress, one of her mother's, trimmed with white eyelet embroidery and worth more in the antique market in Tresham than Ivy would have believed. Pushing her feet into dilapidated carpet slippers, she set off for the bathroom at the back of the house, head down, eyes still cloudy with sleep.

Might as well get up, Ivy. Her mother's voice, always lying in wait in Ivy's thoughts, greeted her every morning in the same way, sharp and admonitory. Ivy hesitated, then continued along the landing. She was in no mood for her mother's scolding tone. There's not a lot you can do, Mother, if I want an extra half-hour, she said.

What on earth for? A lovely morning like this you should be up and doing, Ivy Beasley!

Oh, shut up, Mother. It was always the same. The least little self-indulgence invoked the familiar critical response. But Ivy had to admit that this morning it was more than a little self-indulgence. She felt an overpowering urge to crawl back under the covers, close her eyes, and shut out the world. For ever, if necessary.

Ivy! That's quite enough of that! Your father and me didn't work hard for you all our lives, and leave you well provided for, so that you could feel sorry for yourself at the least little set-back.

The old wall clock in the hall chimed six, and Ivy shivered. The lino on the landing floor was cold and penetrated through a hole in the bottom of one of her slippers.

What's up with you, then? Her mother's voice accompanied her to the bathroom, and as Ivy pulled up her nightdress and sat on the cold wooden lavatory seat, she shook her head as if to shake out the unwelcome intruder. She pulled the chain and started back along the landing, where the low rays of the sun slanted in through the narrow window. The thought of a dry, sunny day would normally have been enough to get Ivy Beasley dressed and down in her kitchen, whites on the boil, teatowels out on the line, and a list of jobs to do in the garden. But not this morning. She retreated to her bedroom, still dark with heavy curtains drawn across, and shut the door.

She stood by her bed, crisp and virginal with its white crocheted cotton bedspread that had taken her mother three winters to complete. There they were, Mother and Father, standing side by side in the porch of Victoria Villa, unsmiling and stiff. The photograph had slipped a fraction to one side, and Ivy stretched out a hand to straighten it.

Had to stand there for hours, said her mother's voice. No wonder we're not smiling.

A sudden impulse made Ivy reach up and touch her mother's face. I had a nightmare, Mother, she said. Can't get it out of my head. They were pelting things at me. I was sitting in the old stocks on the village green, in my nightie, just like now. This nightie, that you worked yourself. And there was this great crowd of people, all from the village, chucking things at me. Wet, rotten things.

Nightmare? You haven't had nightmares since them bullies at the school got at you. Stick up for yourself, Ivy. I said it then and say it now. And anyway, there's never been stocks on Ringford Green.

I know, said Ivy. But they were like them stocks over at Waltonby, nasty old creosoted things. Anyway, I couldn't get away, and I woke up yelling and screaming.

Just as well you're not semi-detached, said her mother's remote, unsympathetic voice.

'What do you mean?' Ivy spoke aloud in surprise at her mother's odd remark. Then she understood, and backed away from the photograph. As in life, her mother's first thought had been what the neighbours would think. Now the possibility of Ivy being overheard, yelling in terror in the middle of the night, was all that concerned her ghostly mother.

Ivy climbed into bed. 'That's it then,' she said. 'I might as well talk to the chickens. There's nobody to listen, nobody who cares tuppence. The entire village has turned against me for having my own opinion about the school, and you, Mother, are just something I dream up to keep me company. Except it's usually more of a nightmare than a dream,' she added with grim humour. In the silence that followed, she pulled the covers over her head and shut her eyes tight.

Minutes later, she shot out of bed again. She looked at herself in the mirror and set her mouth in a determined line. It was a face to be reckoned with. Don't forget you're a Beasley, she told the face. A good, solid house of your own, secretary of the WI, trustee of the Poors Lot charity, landowner. Well, the small field at the back of the school was land, wasn't it? There you are then, Ivy reassured herself. A person of note, as they say.

Stand up to them, Mother said. She was right, of course. If Ivy didn't defend herself, nobody else would, that was certain. Besides, no one understood the reasons why she'd be glad to see the back of the school. None of these pushy new people remembered what she remembered. They didn't have to clear up all the sweet wrappers and crisp packets every day, nor put up with the kids' cheek when they go by. And they're not deafened every time the school comes out to play.

Well, you couldn't expect them to understand, I suppose, Ivy thought with uncharacteristic tolerance, and began to dress. She drew back the curtains, and smiled at the sun streaming into her chilly bedroom, warming the air and dazzling the stony gaze of her mother and father.

Ivy Beasley had had an idea. It would need some thinking about, but on the face of it, it looked as if it might be the answer.

'If all goes well,' she said, 'they might even let me out of the stocks.' She addressed the little cat Gilbert, there at the back door for her morning snack. Ivy took a deep breath of morning air that was like nectar. 'Here,' she said, putting down a saucer on the mat. 'I saved this for you from last night. It's the best bit, puss.'

*   *   *

Nothing would keep John Barnett in bed later than six o'clock, and he was often up earlier on perfect summer mornings like today. He'd done a couple of hours in the clear morning sunlight, getting in the last of the hay in the far fields, before coming back to the house for

332

breakfast.

It had looked like being a bad season, with sporadic heavy rain just at the wrong time. But lately there had been enough really hot days to get the sweet-smelling grasses and clovers baled up and stacked in the barn ready for the winter. Not that they made much hay these days. It was mostly silage, and there was nothing sweet-smelling about that. Because her mother, and her grandmother, had done it, Deirdre Barnett always brought tea up to the field. Sitting in the lee of the hedge, shaded from the hot afternoon sun, she loved to talk of the old days, and John hadn't the heart to tell her he'd rather skip tea and get finished.

John stopped his tractor in the yard and set off for the house, greeted by the incomparable smell of frying bacon issuing from the open kitchen door. Deirdre was standing by the cooker and turned to smile at him.

'Hungry, boy?' she said, and dished out rashers of curling bacon, a slice of golden fried bread, two sausages and a perfect, frilly egg.

There was no answering smile from John. It seemed to Deirdre that he hadn't smiled for weeks. A cloud of misery had descended on her beloved son ever since that night in Tresham. And she hadn't improved matters by passing on Ivy's malicious story about the BMW. If only she knew how to put it right, Deirdre would have moved heaven and earth to do so. But short of going down to the schoolhouse and accosting Sarah Drinkwater on the subject, she had no idea what to do. What could she say to her? Stop breaking my son's heart? She could imagine Miss Sarah's reply to that. And anyway, she had taken dozens of calls from Sarah, anxious to speak to John, and it had been he who had pretended to be out, waving at his mother to put the telephone down.

'There's a message for you,' she said, and her heart turned over when she saw his face brighten in spite of himself. 'From the vicar,' she continued. John looked down quickly at his plate, and mopped up the golden yolk with a piece of fried bread. 'What's he want now?' he said.

'Can you go with the protest group to Tresham on Friday next?' Deirdre said. Well, at least Sarah was sure to be there. That should cheer him up.

'I told him I couldn't go,' said John. 'We're too busy on the farm. They've got plenty of folks without me. The whole village is going, from what I hear.'

'But he specially asked for you to go,' said Deirdre. 'Seems he thinks you'd represent the real village people. Farmers and that.'

'Bollocks,' said John, and stood up. He took his plate to the sink, and without saying another word stalked out into the yard, started his tractor and roared out of sight.

Deirdre stood at the window and watched

him go. So much for John's famous straightforward common sense, she thought. He's behaving like a spoilt child. Plenty more fish in the sea. All them girls at Young Farmers. They'd give their eye teeth to get hold of my John. And he has to go and fall for a stuck-up schoolteacher. I wish his father was here to tell him straight.

She scraped the bacon rind and bits of sausage skin on to the cats' plate and took it out into the yard. Scrawny cats appeared as if by magic, and a couple of black and white kittens that Deirdre hadn't seen before approached cautiously. 'That old cat!' she said. 'Still at it at her age!'

John Barnett, lonely and isolated in his tractor cab, spent the morning thinking gloomily about next Friday's protest in Tresham. The Governors' emergency meeting had planned a major demonstration. Everyone who could manage it would be transported by bus to Tresham, and there they would march behind the schoolchildren to County Hall, led by Miss Drinkwater, bearing placards and banners, and singing the special song. Press and television had been alerted, and Maurice Buswell MP kept fully informed. He had still not committed himself to the cause, but he had greatly enjoyed his weekend with the Standings, felt quite one of the family. Richard had been so charming, and Susan too, of course.

They'll not miss me, thought John, as he swung the tractor round the corner of the field. Specially Sarah. She'll be so taken up with her crusade she won't notice the absence of John Barnett, local hick.

The sun was hot now, and John stopped the tractor and climbed out of his cab. He walked over to the neighbouring field and checked the wheat. Should be an early harvest, with luck. Phew! He took off his shirt and felt the full blast of the midday sun on his bare skin. He scratched his chest where the hair prickled in the heat, and turned to get back to work. Soon be dinner time, he thought. His eye was caught by something moving across the field, something small and white. He stared, trying to make out what it could be. An animal of some sort. Then he heard a sharp, high bark, and knew it was Jemima.

He stopped dead, transfixed by a moment of ridiculous excitement. Sarah had come looking for him. She would explain it all satisfactorily, and they would be reconciled. Life could begin again. But as he looked round the field and down the track leading back to the farm, he could see nobody. Jemima was getting closer, still barking with delight at having found a friend.

She'd run away and got lost. John reluctantly came to this sensible conclusion, and walked forward to meet her. He picked up the hot, panting little dog and held her close.

She smelt of Sarah's perfume, and he buried his face in her fur. 'Hello, Jeemsie,' he said, and his voice broke.

*   *   *

Sarah Drinkwater was very busy. All the children were busy, too, making big placards saying, 'Save our School', and 'Don't let Ringford School Die', and 'Ringford Children say No!' Sarah had set the big ones to write their own slogans, and Andrew Roberts had come up with 'Only Fools Close Schools'. She knew that this was much the snappiest, but felt that it erred on the side of belligerence, and knew from experience that it was no good insulting people whose minds you were out to change.

On the other hand, she had allowed the other big ones to use their own slogans. Mark Jenkins had come up with 'Ringford School Rules OK!' and she'd reluctantly permitted that. 'See if you can think of something else, Andrew,' she had said, 'something not quite so hard-hitting.' Andrew had sulked, and muttered that his dad believed in hitting hard, and it seemed to get him what he wanted. Sarah had turned away, unable to face the look in Andrew's eyes.

'Time to clear up, children,' she said now. 'Will you collect the paints, Jody, and Andrew, you can peg up the placards to dry.' She watched curiously to see what Andrew had produced as his second attempt. Whatever it was, she would have to let him use it. He pegged up everyone else's first, and then his own. She held her breath, unable to believe that he could have done it in so short a time. He'd taken the biggest piece of cardboard in the cupboard, and painted in thick, bold strokes the old, arched door leading into the school. On it, a roughly torn sheet of paper said CLOSED! in hard, bright red letters. Underneath, a small boy stood, school satchel on his back, lunchbox in his hand. His shoulders drooped, and in a few deft strokes of his paintbrush Andrew had communicated all that the Protest Committee, Miss Drinkwater and the school Governors had been trying to say.

'That's very good, Andrew,' Sarah said. 'Very good indeed.'

The schoolroom emptied, and Gabriella Jones came in to supervise the children who had lunch at school. 'Look at that, Gabriella,' said Sarah, pointing to Andrew's placard. 'Goodness,' said Gabriella. 'it makes you want to weep, doesn't it.' Sarah nodded. 'That should get them right between the eyes,' she said, and went on her way to snatch a quick lunch.

'Jemima?' Sarah opened the kitchen door and was surprised that no bouncing little dog greeted her as if she'd been away for weeks.

'Jemima?' She was sure she'd left her in the kitchen, asleep in her basket. The door to the hall stood ajar, and Sarah went through, still calling. No delighted headlong rush, no skittering paws on the wooden stairs. She began to feel panic rising, and rushed out into the back garden. 'Jemima! Jeems, Jeemsie, where are you?'

She ran back into school, but nobody had seen Jemima. 'I shall have to ring the police,' she said desperately to Gabriella. 'Poor little thing might be caught in a trap—she might be anywhere!' And she rushed out again, thinking that perhaps Jemima had got shut in the shed. 'No!' Sarah shouted as she ran, 'don't let Daisy get her!'

Gracious, thought Gabriella, has our Sarah popped her cork? Dogs escaped all the time, and seldom came to any harm in Ringford. Jemima would probably come back in her own time. That terrier of the Jenkins was always out on the loose, but could be seen trotting purposefully in the direction of Macmillan Gardens at nightfall, or whenever his dinner was due.

'Don't put that sandwich in your mouth all at once, Eddie,' she said, and as she got up from Miss Layton's desk to pick up a fallen crust, she saw the bright orange Barnett tractor pull up outside the schoolhouse. John Barnett got down from the cab, carrying something small and white in the crook of his arm, and opened Sarah's front gate.

'Ah,' said Gabriella, 'that's all right, then.' She smiled with more than relief, and was especially kind to a new infant who had managed to spill her acid yellow drink all over her clean dress.

*   *   *

Sarah went to answer the door and did not bother to wipe the tears from her hot, flushed face. If it's the Reverend Nigel Brooks wanting yet another progress report, I shall ... I shall ...

John Barnett looked at her standing in her narrow hall, small, crushed and weeping. Without a word, he handed Jemima over, and Sarah clutched the little dog close to her breast, crying and laughing at the same time. John turned on his heel and started up the garden path to the gate.

'John, don't go!' said Sarah. 'Please don't go. Please.'

John turned and looked at her, frowning.

'Please come in for a minute. I have to thank you properly ... and I do have something else to say.'

'Well,' he said, and paused. After what seemed like hours to Sarah, he began to walk back towards her. 'Just for a minute, then,' he said. 'We're very busy on the farm.'

'I know,' said Sarah humbly, and stood aside for him to pass.

CHAPTER FORTY-NINE

It was very quiet in the small sitting room of the schoolhouse. John Barnett sat on the edge of one of Sarah's chintz chairs, and she, still holding Jemima close, stood by the fireplace looking down at him.

'Would you like a coffee?' she said.

John Barnett shook his head. 'I've not got long, Sarah.' The way he said her name made Sarah want to cry all over again.

'All right, then,' she said. 'I'll try to explain. I know it's that night in Tresham. I saw you and Deirdre at the traffic lights. It is that, isn't it?'

'Your life's your own,' he said. He wouldn't look at her, but stared down at his hands. Sarah looked at them too, those lovely big hands she knew so well. Jeremy Griffiths had small hands for a man, neatly manicured and soft. Sarah moved across to the sofa and sat down. 'I'd been to dinner at the Saxon with an old friend. We were at college together. He was in Tresham on business, and telephoned on the off-chance that we could meet.'

John lifted his head and looked her straight in the eyes. 'Why did you lie to me? There was no need to lie.'

Now's my chance, thought Sarah. She had been through her story so many times, making it convincing enough to bring John back to her.

All she had to do was put on a bit of a performance, and she knew she was good at that.

'Well,' she began, at her most beguiling, her cat-green eyes warm. But John interrupted her. 'No, Sarah,' he said quietly. 'Not that. All you have to do is tell me the truth. Not that you *have* to, mind. But it'll never be any good if you don't.'

Sarah bridled. She was not used to this. Had she really committed such a crime? Nobody talked to her like this. And then she looked at John, at his serious face with a streak of grease down one cheek, and his ruffled red hair bleached at the front by the sun. Why couldn't he just put his arms round her and forget about Jeremy Griffiths?

'All right, then,' she said. If it was plain speaking he wanted, he should have it. 'I just hope what I'm going to say won't hurt you, because I don't want that.' Though I have hurt him, she thought. I knew it might, and I went ahead.

'Jeremy phoned one lunchtime when everything had gone wrong. Mark Jenkins was being awkward—all the kids were difficult—and then I stepped straight into a deep puddle outside the back door.'

The ghost of a smile flitted across John's face.

Sarah continued, 'I was fed up, fed up with teaching, fed up with the weather, the school,

Round Ringford, poor little Daisy ... I was fed up with myself. I felt dull and old and unattractive. When I heard Jeremy's voice, it was like salvation. I got out my most elegant clothes—which I hadn't worn for months—and went off determined to enjoy myself.'

'And did you?' said John.

'Yes,' said Sarah honestly. 'I had a lovely evening. Jeremy was charming and attentive, and we drank champagne.'

'And you drove back,' said John. 'You might have had an accident, with all that booze inside you.'

Sarah sighed and was silent. How can I explain to him that I was high, not on booze, but on the wonderful, warm candlelight, the flattery and flowers, me in my sexy silk dress and high heels? Will John Barnett, bachelor farmer, one of the lads, ever understand that at the time I loved Jeremy's light, suggestive banter and his lordly way with the waiters? Not in a million years, Sarah.

'I wouldn't have minded,' said John. 'We could've gone to the pictures another time. I really wouldn't have minded. If you'd told me.'

But that wasn't enough. He wanted to ask her about the BMW. That was what really mattered, and he couldn't ask. And Sarah, not knowing that Ivy Beasley had seen it, and had made capital of it, was unaware that this was what had to be explained. So John stood up and took Sarah's hand, gave it a squeeze, and

343

said he'd see her around. She followed him to the front door and closed it behind him, and as she heard his tractor roar its way back to the farm, she went dismally into the kitchen to boil an egg.

CHAPTER FIFTY

The coach, sparkling white and newly cleaned for the occasion, bearing proudly 'Geoff Jacobs Travel—Tresham—England' along its gleaming length, drew up in the park behind the multi-storey and the shopping centre, already thronged with market-day shoppers and gangs of unemployed youths looking for a bit of action.

Excitement was running high inside the coach. There were children and villagers mixed, and Sarah Drinkwater had trouble keeping order as mothers handed out sweets and crisps. Ah well, she thought, today is special, and accepted a minty toffee from Jean Jenkins. Many more people had left Ringford by car earlier, making their way to Tresham to join up with the coach party. A queue formed to join the main road. Car windows were lowered and encouraging remarks exchanged. There was an undeniable atmosphere of anticipation of a day to be won. Round Ringford had come together in a crisis, and many of them saw the battle with the Education Department as war. War had been declared, and the battalions were on the march.

'Get into two's!' shouted Sarah, and the children, bearing their placards, neatly nailed to smooth broom handles by Bill Turner, formed up in a line. 'Hold hands and keep together!'

Sarah caught Andrew Roberts' eye. 'How can we hold hands *and* our banners?' he said innocently.

'Be quiet, Andrew,' said Sarah firmly.

Mark Jenkins trailed his placard along the ground, scraping Jody Watts's leg. She screamed and appealed to Gabriella Jones for justice. 'Not now, Jody,' said Gabriella. 'And Mark Jenkins, behave yourself, or you'll wait in the coach.'

'Don't care,' said Mark Jenkins, and surreptitiously dug the end of his broomstick into Andrew Roberts's narrow back.

'Are you ready then,' said Sarah, and they set off through the wasteland of coach station and multi-storey car park, until the snaking crocodile reached the warmth and light of the shopping centre. She saw Jean and Fox Jenkins, Mr and Mrs Ross, the rest of the Macmillan Gardens contingent, and Mandy Bates pushing Joey in his wheelchair with little Margaret on his lap, all standing in an uncertain group, waiting for instructions.

345

There was no John Barnett. Sarah suppressed her disappointment and looked round at the shoppers and checkout girls staring at them. She waved, smiled and turned to the children.

'Off we go!' she shouted. 'Don't forget, keep singing until I tell you to stop.'

Everyone knew the tune of 'Old MacDonald had a Farm', but the words were new, written by the children, and sung shakily at first, then with gathering confidence.

Old Round Ringford's had a School,
For Years and Years and Years!
And in this School we've Worked and
*   Played,*
For Years and Years and Years.

With Reading here, and Writing there,
Here a word, there a word, everywhere a
*   new word*

Old Round Ringford's had a School,
For Years and Years and Years!

And on they marched, two of the recorder group playing the tune, and the rest chanting the words they had practised so often, and knew were true.

And in this School we've Worked and
*   Played,*
For Years and Years and Years!
With Arithmetic here and Arithmetic there,

346

Here addition, there subtraction,
everywhere the answer's right!

Old Round Ringford's had a school
For Years and Years and Years!

They streamed out of the shopping centre and into the pedestrian precinct, parents and friends joining in the song, photographers and television cameras following them, Sarah Drinkwater, like the Pied Piper, stepping out with purpose at their head.

Outside County Hall, the rest of the village waited. Colin Osman stood, petition in hand, sheaves and sheaves of it, and Pat bobbed up and down excitedly at his side. Doreen and Tom, stolid and respectable, had positioned themselves by the double doors and kept the entrance way clear. 'Don't want to get moved on by the boys in blue, do we,' Tom said sensibly. A police car was stationed on the opposite side of the road, and a grinning police constable saw that the road was not obstructed, waving on cars which slowed down to take a look at the growing crowd.

Round the corner, into Guildhall Road, came the children.

And in this School we've worked and played
For Years and Years and Years!
With a painting here and a drawing there
Here some art, there some craft, everywhere
we're busy bees!

347

Old Round Ringford's had a school,
For Years and Years and Years!

At last everyone had arrived, and the Reverend Nigel Brooks, authoritative in the black suit and white collar of his trade, stood forward and called for silence.

'We all know why we're here,' he said, his pulpit voice carrying easily over the crowd. 'But for the benefit of people who don't, we are here to save our village school. There's a proposal to close it, and we don't intend to let it happen. It's as simple as that. Now, if everyone will be patient, a small group of us will go inside and present the petition to the meeting of the Education Committee, and one of us will come back immediately and report.'

The double doors opened, and Nigel Brooks, Colin Osman, Tom Price, Bill Turner and Sarah Drinkwater, disappeared from sight. Peggy Turner and Doreen Price moved into action. From enormous picnic baskets they produced dozens of flasks and paper cups and began to hand out coffee and biscuits. Along with these went leaflets, devised and printed by Colin Osman, giving a further explanation of Ringford's fight. The core of villagers and children were now surrounded by a large number of curious bystanders. Several of the groups of unemployed lads from the shopping centre had followed for a bit of fun, and were now enthusiastically drinking the free coffee and shouting 'Save Ringford School!' in hoarse voices, not in the least bothered that most of them had never heard of Round Ringford before this morning.

When the double doors opened once more, and Nigel Brooks appeared, a cheer went up. He raised his hand, like Moses on his descent from the mountain. 'Not yet, friends,' he said. 'We've presented the petition, and the Chairman has said the children may go in, provided they are very, very quiet.'

Inside the Council Chamber, with its impressive coat of arms and dark oak panelling, the meeting was in session. Here was a place where for many years the ancient rights of a democratic people had been administered faithfully, on the whole for the right motives, and with much serious dissent, manoeuvring and pitting of wits. In spite of arguments which sometimes neared a pitch of hysteria, the solemn atmosphere invariably had a sobering effect in the end, and the Councillors maintained a sense of dignity and responsibility. If they did not, they were apt to find their days were numbered.

Into the public gallery of this temple of local government filed the children, overawed and silent, but with their placards still held high. Gabriella Jones manoeuvred them into their seats. She gave a thumbs-up sign to Sarah, anxiously waiting for them at the far end of the gallery.

Unprecedented as this was, the Councillors took the children's entry in their stride. The Chairman of the Education Committee was a woman of great experience and not inconsiderable heart. She smiled up at the gallery, and spoke slowly and clearly.

'Welcome children,' she said. 'We all know how important this day is for you, and you can rest assured that whatever is decided will be in your best interests.'

The children were like mice. They froze into silence, and even Mark Jenkins sat biting his nails and frowning with the effort of trying to understand what was going on.

With professional fluency and a dry, emotionless tone, the man from the Education Department presented his report to the Committee of councillors, all voluntary, worthy members of their community, giving up their time for a variety of motives, but all with a sense of serving their fellow men. The Review of Ringford and Fletching Schools had been exhaustive, he said. Here Sarah looked at Gabriella in surprise. Fletching? No wonder there had been a crowd from the neighbouring village round the County Hall entrance. Hoping to come in on the coat-tails of Round Ringford, no doubt.

For endless minutes, during which big ones and little ones of Round Ringford School sat if mesmerised, a list of reasons why these small

350

schools were not viable for future budgeting was put before the Committee. And then, as if sentence of death weren't enough, the man from the Education Department proposed his alternative plan.

'Each of these schools cannot survive on its own,' he said. 'But together they could be a useful, viable entity, meeting the demands of the National Curriculum, and fulfilling all the requirements of modern education. Therefore ...' He paused to clear his throat. The temperature had risen in the Council Chamber, and the high, old-fashioned windows were difficult to open. 'Therefore it is proposed,' he continued, 'to close Round Ringford School and transport the children to Fletching, where there are good facilities and, very important, space for extension when necessary.'

This, of course, was too much for the children of Round Ringford Church of England School, who had years of rivalry with their enemies at Fletching in their bones. Ringford had always beaten Fletching at inter-school sports, in music competitions, in the netball league. And when they left the village school, Ringford children had continued to outshine the Fletching lot, persistently making their way up to receive prizes for every subject under the sun. Known for it, they were. Ringford children were tops, and they weren't going to stand for it.

'It was dreadful, really,' said Gabriella to her husband Greg, as they sat over a cup of tea when he came home from Tresham. 'After the chap from the Department sat down looking smug, they had a debate. Only Mr Richard's brother James spoke up for Ringford. All the rest were for closure, in spite of all those letters we wrote. They thought the idea of teaming up with Fletching was great. You could see it was going against us, and Sarah's face was as black as thunder.'

Greg poured more tea in to Gabriella's cup, and then into his own. The cool sitting room with its neutral tones and vases of dried grasses and seed-heads, was an oasis of calm after the day's hectic goings-on.

'There was a rustling at first,' Gabriella went on, 'and I thought it was Mark Jenkins again. Then I realised it was Andrew Roberts. He was stamping his feet up and down, not very loud, but in a kind of drumming rhythm. Everything was very quiet, and the Chairman looked up at the gallery.'

'What about the chap from the Education Department?' said Greg.

'He was still looking smug. Then Jody Roberts—she's a bit sweet on Andrew, I think—started banging her feet in time with him, and gradually all the rest joined in. It was like an army on the march, and the Councillors were furious. Sarah just stared straight ahead, and then I realised she was stamping too.'

'Did Nigel join in?'

'Yep—everyone did. Me too, Greg.'

'Not very grown up,' said Greg.

'You weren't there,' said Gabriella.

'What happened next?'

'The Chairwoman stood up and raised her hand, like a traffic cop, and we all stopped, and waited. "I have to ask for the Gallery to be emptied," she said. You could see she was livid, and I don't really blame her. I suppose we'd made her look a fool.'

'So how did you get to hear the Committee's decision?' said Greg.

'Maurice Buswell,' said Gabriella. 'Our beloved MP was somewhere there, though we hadn't spotted him. Suppose he didn't want to be seen taking sides. Anyway, we'd all been waiting for some while outside County Hall, and the crowd was huge. Maurice came out and everybody was quiet.'

'And?' said Greg. But he knew what Gabriella would say. She'd blurted out the bare facts the minute she got home. 'What did our Maurice have to say?'

'He was his usual pompous self,' said Gabriella. She got up and began to wander around the room. 'He said that the report was thoroughly debated by the Councillors, and had been approved by a majority vote.'

'So,' said Greg. 'After all our efforts. What a

let down.'

'Fletching were cock-a-hoop, as you can imagine,' said Gabriella.

'So everybody went home?' said Greg.

'Yes, it was awful. But it was worst for the children. Lots of them were crying, and Sarah and the parents did their best to comfort them. Made a great story for the reporters and the cameras, of course.'

'It's not the end, though, is it?' said Greg.

Gabriella shook her head. 'We've got two months before it is ratified by the Secretary of State for Education,' she said. 'But he very seldom upsets a recommendation made by one of his Departments.'

'Well, this'll need a lot of thought,' said Greg. 'But just now, how do you fancy a meal at the Bull this evening?'

'At Fletching?' said Gabriella. 'Not likely! But I wouldn't say no to a jumbo sausage at the Arms. The rest are having a wake there later on, so we can drown our sorrows.'

She put the empty teacups on the tray, and stood up to take them to the kitchen. 'There was one odd thing, though,' she said, turning back to Greg.

He put down his evening paper and looked at her. 'Odd?' he said.

'Yes. When most of the people had gone off, Maurice Buswell was talking to Richard Standing and his brother James outside County Hall, and I saw Ivy Beasley go up to them. It was the first I'd seen of her, and I was surprised. I thought she'd be keeping her head down for safety.'

'Well, that's not very odd,' said Greg.

'No, but the three blokes stopped talking and listened to her as if she'd brought news of the Abdication.'

'What are you talking about, Gabbie?' said Greg.

'Whatever it was she said, they nodded and smiled, and our Ivy was handed into Maurice's car like she was royalty, and off they went. What do you make of that, Greg?'

But he could offer no explanation, and agreed with Gabriella that it was after all very odd indeed.

CHAPTER FIFTY-ONE

It was as though a pall had descended on Round Ringford. The main street was empty, and everywhere seemed uncannily quiet. Families had gone to ground to lick their wounds and re-live the day, its light-hearted, confident beginning, and its crushed and miserable end. The sun had retreated behind a big black cloud looming over Bagley Woods, and in the dismal evening light Peggy Turner looked out of her sitting-room window across to the school.

'I could swear it knows,' said Peggy. The old building, with its twin eaves and tall windows looked grey and downcast. The brave banners proclaiming so optimistically SAVE OUR SCHOOL, drooped and stirred in the light wind. At the schoolhouse, Peggy could see the curtains still drawn across from the previous night. Sarah had set out so early and in such haste that she had not had time to draw them back. 'Looks blind, poor little house,' said Peggy, a catch in her voice.

'They're just buildings, Peggy,' Bill said. He was sitting in Frank's chair, watching television, waiting for the local news. They were sure to be on, and he was curious to see how it all looked from the camera's-eye view.

'Oh, no they're not just buildings, Bill. I should have thought you'd know better than that, you having been to school there. Buildings absorb what's going on in them. I'm sure of that. All those years and years of children inside the classrooms, laughing and crying, little lives just beginning. Any old building has memories stored in its walls, just like people.'

'Fanciful nonsense!' grunted Bill. Peggy's sentimental ruminations were beginning to irritate him. He hadn't felt comfortable with her since that day Joyce telephoned, though she'd said nothing more. Why couldn't they get back to the way it was before Joyce came back? Surely Peggy could get used to it, if he could.

Still, give her time, he told himself. She'll come round. He looked at her standing by the window and willed her to turn round and smile at him in the old way.

'I suppose you'd say little Daisy was fanciful nonsense,' Peggy said, still staring out at the schoolhouse. 'How do you explain little Daisy's voice?'

'A load of—ah, there we are! Look, there's Sarah!'

Peggy sat down and looked at the screen. She felt like crying. There were the children, marching and singing, Sarah stepping out in front. And Mandy and little Joey in his wheelchair. And there was Nigel, speaking to the crowd, smiling and waving. And then, inevitably, the bad news, the children looking bewildered and their parents comforting them, and Nigel saying bravely to the camera that Ringford would fight on, never fear.

'But what's the good?' said Peggy. 'Looks to me as if it's all signed and sealed. What can we do?'

Bill stood up and turned off the television. 'Go for a pint, gel,' he said hopefully. 'That's what we can do. That's what Ringford has always done in times of crisis. Come on, put your bonnet on and let's go.'

*   *   *

Up at Walnut Farm, in the dark sitting-room—cold and comfortless with no fire and no lights turned on—John Barnett was also watching the local news. Hunched up in the corner of a sofa he smiled faintly at the children's singing. Then Sarah was on screen, and his smile vanished. She looked wonderful, almost shining with courage and enthusiasm. Like some bloody Saint Joan, thought John.

Another news item took over the screen, and John got up, snapping off the television and leaving the room. In the kitchen, Deirdre heard him slam the door and go up to his room. She knew exactly what he'd been watching, and decided to say nothing. It was a muddle, this Sarah Drinkwater business, and she had no idea how to help John out of it.

'Going for a beer, Mum.' John walked quickly through the kitchen, and was out in the yard before she could reply. She heard his car roar off down the lane, and sighed. 'That boy needs his father,' she said.

*   *   *

The Arms was full. Although much too early for regulars to be there on normal nights, everybody had had their tea, watched the news, and set off for consolation.

'Only good outcome, I reckon,' said Don Cutt, as he pulled pints one after the other, 'it's certainly good for business.'

Colin Osman and Pat stood at the bar with

358

Tom Price and Nigel Brooks, and Bill and Peggy joined them. 'What'll you have?' said Tom.

'No, I'll get them,' said Bill. 'A pint of Morton's and half of Guinness for Peggy.' Gabriella and Greg Jones arrived at the same time as John Barnett, and John insisted on buying the drinks. He hovered at the edge of the group, feeling left out because he'd not been there in Tresham with the rest.

'John and Sarah have quarrelled,' whispered Gabriella to Greg. 'Something to do with Deirdre, I reckon. Sarah's really upset.'

'Too old to be tied to his mother's apron strings,' said Greg. 'Time to grow up, silly bugger. He couldn't do better than Sarah.'

'Sssh!' said Gabriella. But John had already heard Greg's remark, and moved further away, his face glummer than ever.

The conversation was desultory. They were all in a state of shock, and re-ran high points of the day to keep themselves from descending into total gloom.

'It was a grand sight,' said Tom. 'You have to hand it to Sarah. She put on a great show, with the children and their song, and all them placards.' There was a general murmur of agreement, and John Barnett took a big gulp of beer.

'Did you see Andrew Roberts's?' said Peggy.

'It was on the telly,' said Pat Osman. 'They brought the camera close in on it. D'you reckon Sarah helped him with it? It was really good.'

'That song was clever,' said Colin. 'People were joining in all along the route. If the County Councillors could have seen all that, instead of being cooped up in their stuffy Council Chamber, I reckon they might have thought differently.'

Tom shook his head. He had been Parish Council Chairman for too long to expect County Councillors to be swayed by such things. They were proud men and women, and often said on such occasions that they dealt in facts, not emotion. Still, he was proud too, proud of his village and the fight they'd put up. He hadn't really believed the school would be closed until Maurice Buswell had come out and announced it in his measured, melodious voice.

'Wasn't much help to us, was he?' he said. 'Our MP might as well not have been there for all the good he was.'

'We may yet make use of him,' said Nigel. The others turned to him hopefully. Did he know something they didn't? But he shook his head. 'It's just possible he could sway things our way, but only if he was convinced our case was the right one. And I have to say that Maurice Buswell is a political climber. He's not going to lose his footing on the ladder just to save one small village school. Government policy, he keeps saying.'

'Government policy my arse!' said Colin, suddenly and unexpectedly. 'As old Fred Mills would have said,' he added apologetically, seeing his wife's face. Possible plans for continuing the fight were mooted back and forth, but nobody had any real heart for it.

'Truth is,' said Bill, when discussion of the day's events had petered out and silence fallen. 'Truth is, what they say is right. The two schools together will work better. And Fletching has a bloody great football field big enough for three teams right next to the school, where they can extend with no trouble at all.'

'Does it belong to them, though?' said Colin Osman.

'Always been part of the school to my knowledge,' said Bill. 'Lord Bailee set up Fletching about the same time as Charles Standing built ours. Expect it was the fashion in them days.'

'Still,' said Nigel Brooks. 'Colin has an interesting point there.'

The pub remained full until closing time, and a crowd stood talking outside for some time in the cool, dark evening. John Barnett slipped by the others and drove off unnoticed. An owl hooted up in the woods, the sound carrying across the valley. Peggy and Bill walked home along the street, calling goodnight to others on the way, and crossed the road by the bus shelter. Mellowed by Mortons Best, Bill took her arm. 'Another day tomorrow, gel,' he said. Peggy nodded. Now, she told herself, now's the time to explain, put it right. But Bill was looking up at the lighted window in Victoria Villa. 'Ivy's still awake,' he said.

'Probably can't sleep,' said Peggy, opening the side gate. 'Serves her right. I hope the old bat's awake all night.' She walked round to the back door, leaving Bill still staring up at Ivy's house.

Ivy Beasley was not awake. She had been sitting up in bed, pencil and paper in hand, making lists of things to do, people to see, and had fallen asleep with the light on. Her head, neatly encased in a hair net, had drooped to one side, and there was a smile on her lips.

CHAPTER FIFTY-TWO

Open Gardens Sunday had never been less heralded. The school had taken up so much of the villagers' time and thoughts that the usual run-up of doubts and fears had been put aside. No one had bothered about the weather forecast. Colin Osman had not said a word about dandelions, and Pat had forgotten to turn on the sprinkler, leaving the lawn a parched yellow.

Not all gardens had been neglected, of course. The Rosses' neat, geometric beds were like the flags of all nations, with dwarf orange marigolds and white lobelia, scarlet salvias and geraniums, silver, furry lambs' tongue and hanging baskets dripping all colours of the rainbow around his mock-baronial front porch. In the Hall grounds, tranquil as always, the lavender walk between well-clipped box hedges was as restrained and scented as when it was laid out in the eighteenth century, and the stone shepherd boy at the end of the walk still piped his pastoral with unfeeling joy. Doreen Price's garden of acers and conifers and creeping ground cover was as cunningly pruned and fertilised as in every other year.

Only Fred Mills's garden was heartbreakingly weedy and unkempt. It was all Doris Ashbourne could do to walk by it without choking with tears. She took to going down the other side of the Gardens, so as to avoid seeing the ragged privet hedge and the swinging gate. I wish they'd get another family in there, she thought. You'd have expected with all the homeless and that, it would have been taken straight away. Still, they'd have a good bit of redecorating to do after old Fred had let it go in his last years. Doris's own garden, small and weedless, was not open in the official sense, but as people would be walking past, she had found time to dead-head the roses and tidy up at the front.

Nigel Brooks had pulled a few tufts of grass from his gravel drive, but the vicarage was not on the route for visitors, and not being a natural gardener, he had given little thought lately to Open Gardens Sunday. Unsmiling and depressed by his campaign's reversal, he even forgot to pray for good weather in his nightly address to his Maker. 'Help us, O Lord,' he said, 'in our fight for what is right and Your Will.' He did hope it was not God's policy, as well as the Government's, to close down small village schools. If that was so, then all was lost. Nigel firmly believed this, and spent some time making out a good case for Ringford School, until his knees hurt and he left matters in more ominipotent hands than his.

Open Gardens Sunday, however, was not overlooked by the Almighty. It dawned bright and clear, not a cloud in the sky, and the Ringle chuckled and sparkled over its stony bed at the far side of the Green. Robert Bates had been out early hammering in direction signs to the gardens on show, and to Doreen's Tea Rooms at Hall Farm. The Standing Arms had an 'Open All Day' sign, and Renata Roberts had offered—in spite of conspicuous lack of encouragement from her husband—to run a cut-flower stall on the Green. Andrew had said he would help her, and so had Mark. She was not sure about this, but Warren Jenkins had said he would keep an eye on his young brother, and so she was not too worried. Anyone could bring flowers for sale, and

Renata had a good show from the Hall greenhouse and from the Dodwells in Walnut Close.

The cheerful day was not appreciated by Joyce Davie, who was first woken by a blackbird singing at the top of its voice from the cherry tree in the Jenkins's garden next door, and then blinded by strong sun penetrating through the thick cotton of her bedroom curtains. She tried to open her eyelids, but they were gummed together. She rubbed them, and shaded her painful eyes from the brightness.

'Oh God,' she groaned. 'I wish Donald was here.' But Donald's aged mother was dying slowly, and she had encouraged him to stay by her side until the old lady slipped away. Joyce hoped it would not be much longer. With Donald around, she felt safe, able to conduct her life in the complicated and sometimes devious way she loved. Now this wretched flu would not go, and although she urged Donald each night on the telephone not to come home, saying she would be perfectly all right, she began to think that perhaps she needed some help.

Pushing back the rumpled bedcovers, Joyce put her feet out of bed and attempted to stand up. The room swam, and she sat down heavily. Damn, she thought. Better get to the telephone. She managed to struggle downstairs, feeling faint and grabbing at the banisters to stop herself falling. About to call Donald, she hesitated. He's got enough to worry about, poor Don, she thought. She began to dial.

*   *   *

'Hello?' said Peggy, lifting the telephone in the sitting room. She supposed it was Bill with some urgent message. He had left early, anxious to put the finishing touches to the already immaculate kitchen garden at the Hall. 'Hello? Bill?'

A croaking, faint voice answered her. 'Mrs Turner? Is Bill there, please?'

Peggy froze. Bloody woman, today of all days, when everyone was so busy with a myriad of tasks involved in organising this special Sunday. 'No, he's not,' she said shortly. There was a silence, and then to Peggy's horror she heard a sob. Oh, Lord. Now what? She distrusted every inch of Joyce Davie. 'Are you all right?' she said grudgingly.

The sob was followed by a spasm of coughing which even Peggy had to admit sounded serious. Then Joyce managed another sentence. 'I think I need some help. Could you phone for the ...' And then another fit of coughing followed, during which Peggy made up her mind. It was Sunday, after all.

'Get back to bed, Mrs Davie,' she said. 'I'll be round in about ten minutes. Have you used up all the LemSip? Yes, well, I'll bring another packet, and see what else needs doing. Just go back to bed and keep warm.'

'Sod it, sod it, sod it!' Peggy's angry exclamation as she banged down the telephone frightened the little cat, who fled through the cat flap with a clatter and vanished into the old washhouse in Peggy's back yard. It was sanctuary for her from both Ivy and Peggy when things got too hot.

*   *   *

Early visitors, anxious to have the open gardens to themselves, had begun to arrive and park around the Green. Peggy scowled unreasonably at an old Rover which had blocked her driveway. She had no intention of taking her car anywhere, but it was a good excuse to scowl. She banged her garden gate and set off up the streets towards Macmillan Gardens. In her basket were LemSip and cough linctus from the shop, and a large box of tissues. In the short walk between the Stores and number fourteen she went through a turmoil of wild thoughts. What was she doing? She could easily have phoned for the doctor and left it to him. Or got hold of Bill somehow, and sent him up there. Maybe that's why she was on her errand of mercy to the person she disliked most in the world. Maybe she would do even that to prevent Bill entering Joyce's bedroom.

'Morning, Peggy! Lovely day for it, isn't it?' Jean Jenkins was halfway down the Gardens, laden with home-made cakes for Doreen Price's improvised tea rooms in a scrubbed out stable. Jean was startled at Peggy's expression, and turned to look back at her. She was astonished to see her turn into number fourteen and disappear through the gate. 'Well, that beats all!' she said to Eddie, who trotted by her side, his mouth full of filched chocolate cake.

It was cool in Joyce's hallway, and the light dim. Peggy's eyes adjusted slowly, and she stood at the bottom of the stairs, uncertain what to do next. Joyce had left the back door unlocked for her, and she suddenly felt panic, like a fly enticed into a spider's web. Her heart thumped and her palms were wet. She shifted the basket from one hand to the other, and cleared her throat loudly. A very small voice reached her from above. 'Come up, please,' croaked Joyce.

The pile on the new stair carpet was thick and absorbed the noise of Peggy's footsteps. She paused outside the bedroom door, and then knocked lightly. Good grief, she thought, taking a deep breath, the woman's ill. What can she do to me?

Joyce's bedroom was hot, and full of the unpleasant odour of sickness. Peggy surveyed in one quick glance the bright curtains, new carpet, light pine furniture and pleasant landscapes on the walls. Joyce was lying on her back with her hands covering her eyes. Her hair was damp and clung in dark strands around her face, and her skin was like parchment.

'Oh dear,' said Peggy. 'You are in a mess.'

There was no answer, and then Joyce turned convulsively away from Peggy and began to cry, her thin shoulders heaving. The crying set her off on another coughing bout, and Peggy's soft heart took over. Her soothing words and gentle hands straightening the bedclothes calmed Joyce, who finally stopped coughing. 'It's only flu,' she said, 'but I can't seem to shake it off. Better not come too close,' she added. Bit late for that, thought Peggy.

She tidied the room, spooned cough linctus into Joyce's birdlike mouth, and went downstairs to heat water for the LemSip. She felt very odd, moving about the house which had for so long assumed the identity of a witch's lair. This was the kitchen where Bill and Joyce had sat over their joyless meals, where Joyce had thrown a saucepan full of hot potatoes at Bill and caught him on the back of the neck. The scar that Peggy had felt under her fingers was the result, evidence of the violence in Joyce that had ended in mental breakdown and divorce.

The kettle spluttered and boiled, and Peggy took the steaming lemon liquid back up the stairs. She helped Joyce to sit up, wondering at her own ability to support this woman who tried so hard to cause injury, not physically now, but in a way that was much worse. Joyce drank in thirsty gulps, and then flopped back on the pillows. She closed her eyes, and Peggy saw great black smudges under them, extra black against her pallid skin.

'Right,' she said. 'I'm going now, but I'll be back later to give you another drink. And I'll phone the doctor. They don't usually do much for flu, but he'll probably call in tomorrow.' She looked down at Joyce, and had an odd feeling of being six feet tall. Picking up her basket, she reached the bedroom door, hesitated, and turned back to the slight figure lying neat and tidy in the big bed. 'One more thing,' she said. 'In future, just leave Bill and me alone, will you? I think you know what I mean.' Joyce's feverish eyes stared at her, but she said nothing. As Peggy left the room, went downstairs and out into the fresh air, she was overwhelmed by a sense of relief.

*   *   *

'I don't believe it!' said Doris Ashbourne to Ivy Beasley, as they sat drinking coffee in Doris's sunny front room. Ivy's garden was not open this year. She pretended not to mind that she had not been asked, but in her heart she was deeply wounded. She knew the reason, of

370

course, but considered it an unnecessarily cruel punishment for speaking her mind.

Doris and Ivy were waiting for Ellen Biggs to hobble up from the Lodge, and then they would set off on a gentle perambulation round the gardens, making pointed comments and critical remarks, and not hesitating to take a peek into open windows when the opportunity arose. Ivy had had serious doubts whether Ellen would be able to make it this year, but the tough old bird had insisted, and so Ivy and Doris looked fixedly out of the window, neither of them admitting to anxiety for their stubborn friend's safety.

It was while they were watching so steadfastly that they saw Peggy Turner walk out of Joyce Davie's garden gate and turn off down towards the High Street.

'What on earth was she doing there?' said Doris. Ivy Beasley appeared to have lost the power of speech. 'That Joyce is still down with flu, isn't she, Ivy?' Ivy gulped, and drew in her breath sharply. Her reply came like a fusillade of bullets.

'She was, last thing I heard,' she said. 'Nasty thing, flu. I've kept away until she's rid of it. Can't be doing with flu just now.'

'Call yourself Joyce's friend, Ivy!' said Doris. 'The poor woman could've been at death's door. Her Donald's away, you know, waiting on his dying mother.'

Ivy bridled. 'Well,' she said harshly, 'come to

371

that, Doris Ashbourne, you're a neighbour here in the Gardens, so why haven't you been over there with a bowl of broth and a helping hand?'

Doris was saved from having to reply by the sight of Ellen Biggs stumping round the corner, and stopping for a rest at old Fred's gatepost, where she clung on and caught her breath. Ivy and Doris rose to their feet and hurried out, down the path and quickly along to where Ellen stood. 'All right, all right!' she said, waving away their supporting arms. 'I'm not finished yet. Just 'avin' a bit of rest. Give me a minit or two an' I'll be fine. Got the kettle on, Doris? I could do with a cuppa before we start.'

In the flurry of getting Ellen Biggs up to the bungalow and settled down for a cup of tea, Ivy and Doris temporarily forgot about Peggy's mysterious visit to number fourteen. But when Ellen had stopped complaining and was noisily gulping down the hot tea, they asked her if she had met Peggy.

'Yep,' she said. 'I did meet her, and what of it?' Ivy and Doris filled her in, and she cackled loudly.

'That's a turn up,' she said. 'Bill 'ad better look out, if 'is two wives are on friendly terms. Could cause a great deal of bother, that could!' She cackled again with unholy mirth, and spilt the remains of her tea over Doris's pristine pale grey carpet.

Peggy Turner put ham, tomatoes and bread on the kitchen table, ready for when Bill called in for a quick break. Mr Richard was taking over the Hall gate money for an hour, and Bill came grinning through the door dead on twelve thirty.

'Going well, gel,' he said, sitting down at the table. 'You off to help Doreen this afternoon?'

'Bill,' said Peggy. He looked up at her, surprised by her tone of voice, which was steady, serious. 'I went to see Joyce this morning,' she said.

It took a few seconds for Bill to register what she'd said, and then he rounded on her. 'What did you say?' he spluttered. 'Went to see Joyce! What on earth for?'

Peggy told him of her errand of mercy, and did not spare him the gruesome details of Joyce's unlovely appearance. 'Never seen such a mess,' she said, watching him out of the corner of her eye. 'I'll call in again later, just to check.'

'Well,' said Bill grimly, 'you are certainly not going back there this afternoon. No reason why you should catch flu. In fact, I forbid it, Peggy. I'll look in myself, but you stay well clear. And that's an order.'

Now Peggy was smiling. What was she up to? thought Bill. He wasn't sure about that smile. 'What did Joyce say, anyway?' he said, putting down his piece of bread, his appetite gone.

'Said Donald was away, waiting for his mother to die, and she couldn't manage. I phoned for the doctor, and he's coming tomorrow. Meantime,' Peggy continued, and though the smile was still there, her voice was very firm, 'meantime, I shall go in as promised, and there'll be no need for you to interfere. It'll be all right now, Bill.'

She took a load of washing out of the machine, put it in a basket, and approached the back door. 'Better get this out while the sun's hot, Sunday or no Sunday, and Ivy Beasley notwithstanding,' she said. 'Good luck for this afternoon, love, if you're gone before I come in.' And she disappeared.

Bill stood up, rinsed his hands quickly at the sink, and went out through the shop. He stood at the door looking round at the unaccustomed sight of crowds in the village, the parked cars and strolling visitors. 'Women!' he said, and took a step outside. Then, like a man who has forgotten something important, he turned quickly and went back to the kitchen. He could see Peggy struggling to anchor a flapping white sheet to the line, her mouth full of pegs, and he marched purposefully out into the garden.

* * *

Next door, in Victoria Villa, Ivy Beasley stood

at her landing window. She had deserted Ellen and Doris for a few minutes, saying that there was nothing like your own toilet seat. They stood waiting patiently for her on the pavement outside, agreeing that nobody could be more irritating than Ivy when she was on form.

Her toilet seat duly warmed, Ivy was returning along the landing when something in Peggy Turner's garden caught her eye, and now she watched, transfixed by what she saw.

'Well! In broad daylight!' she muttered, seeing Bill approach Peggy and remove the pegs tenderly from her mouth. You shouldn't be spying, said her mother's voice, but Ivy didn't move. She saw Peggy lost in Bill's bear hug, witnessed the healing kiss that contracted her solitary heart, and continued to watch until they vanished from sight. Unloved and unpopular, Ivy Beasley had never felt so alone.

'Thought you said it was goin' t'be a quick one,' said Ellen crossly. Her legs were hurting, but she was not going to admit it.

'Oh, be quiet, Ellen,' said Ivy, banging her garden gate. 'Come along, Doris, step out! We'll never get these gardens done if we spend all this time hanging about.'

CHAPTER FIFTY-THREE

John Barnett stood by the five-barred gate that led to the Home Close. He looked across his sunlit fields, at the ripening corn and neatly trimmed hedges, the old oaks and the new spinney he and his dad had planted in the corner of the baulk field. The farmhouse behind him shaded the yard, and a few of Deirdre's hens scratched and clucked. Old Nell nosed around in the stable, turning over scraps of straw and dung in the hope of finding something edible.

I should be the happiest bloke in Ringford, he thought. My own farm, good health, plenty of girls looking for an eligible bachelor like me, all my creature comforts taken care of. Why do I feel so bloody fed-up, then?

He knew exactly why, of course. It was Sarah. Sarah Drinkwater. Miss Thirsty. Not so long ago he'd never heard of her. He looked back on those carefree years when the bitterest blow he could imagine would have been exclusion from the rugby team. And now he was finding life without her more painful than he thought possible. He'd contacted one or two old girlfriends, but they had seemed shallow and easy compared with Sarah. Got in too deep, he told himself. I know her too well, now. Probably better than anyone.

Old Nell came over to him and pushed her nose into his hand. 'Good girl,' he said, stroking her head. He climbed up and sat on the gate, looking back towards the house. Nell sat beside him, waiting for his next move. 'Fact is, Nell,' he said, 'she's got me hooked. Can't get away from it. You've seen her, Nell, twisting me round her little finger. Good moods, bad moods, I've seen them all. And I still want her more than anything else.'

John jumped off the gate and set off back towards the yard. Head down, he addressed an imaginary Sarah. 'It's like this,' he said, 'I've made you laugh, seen you cry, mopped up your tears. You've said I turn you on like nobody else. You can have it all. But no more buggers like Jeremy Griffiths, no matter how low you feel!'

Nell, trotting along at his side, looked up apprehensively. But her master said nothing more. He was walking fast now, and she pricked her ears and wrinkled her nose as cooking smells wafted out of the farm kitchen door.

'Mum?' shouted John. 'I'm just off. Should be back for lunch, and then I expect they'll need me again this afternoon.'

He started up his car and drove slowly out of the yard, down to the road. As usual, there were children out playing in the back gardens of Walnut Close, and one or two waved as he went by. He remembered the fuss over the new houses. Always something to protest about in villages, he thought. Folk who think they're coming here to live a quiet life get a rude awakening.

He drew up outside the school, headquarters for the day of the Open Gardens Committee. He'd promised to help with all the paperwork, counting money and tickets, checking off the rota of helpers, being on hand for emergencies. Colin Osman was over by Sarah's desk, talking on his mobile phone to Pat who'd been left in charge of their own open garden.

'Just give them a leaflet at the same time as their ticket,' he was saying. 'It really couldn't be simpler, Pat.'

John settled down at the desk, sitting in Sarah's chair, her faint, lemony perfume a lingering presence. As soon as Colin had finished his call, John's attention was totally taken up with a barrage of instructions and information. Helpers came and went. Nigel Brooks, having banished the school campaign from his mind with superhuman effort, strode in, big smile in place, and said the village was full of people, everything was going well, and wasn't it a perfect day?

'The Lord looks after his own,' said John. Nigel Brooks's relentless good humour irritated him, and he wandered away to look out of the classroom window. The playground was empty. Only a pair of white doves—fugitives from the Hall—sat in close intimacy on the ridge of the old school lavatories. Used now as a store for broken chairs and stage blocks, and anything else that couldn't be pushed into the cupboards in the school, the long, low building belonged to another age, when children were smaller and often undernourished. The mellow red brick was beginning to crumble and at Sarah's garden end a rough blue slate had slipped drunkenly sideways, leaving a bleached wooden slat exposed to the wind and rain.

Nice little building once, that was, thought John. Them lavs have seen some fun. The tiny cubicles with wooden latched doors had always been a risky source of amusement, with the low brick wall in front barely concealing what was going on inside. There was a strong chance that a teacher would march down and peer over the wall, and then you'd had it. John grinned to himself as he recalled the day he'd wedged a door shut on himself and Melanie Price. She'd yelled and screamed, 'I'll tell teacher if you don't let me out, John Barnett!' He could hear her angry voice now.

He turned round and saw Colin Osman wandering around the classroom, staring absently at the bright paintings pinned to the wall, at the weather charts and the maps of foreign lands, lists of wild flowers and childish interpretations of historical events. Small minds were being expanded here all right. Had been for over a hundred years.

'Colin,' he said. 'What happens to the building if the school closes down?'

'Depends who owns it,' said Colin. 'Probably still belongs to Standings. Or it might be Church property. Sometimes they can't find the deeds when a school closes, and then there's an almighty rumpus.'

'It'd be awful to see it knocked down,' said John.

'It's not likely,' said Colin. 'The building is probably listed. It could be used as a village community centre, or a youth club, or something like that.' His phone rang. 'Right, Pat,' he said with a resigned expression. 'If John can hold the fort here, I'll be home in a few minutes.' He switched off and pushed the phone into his pocket. 'Sorry, John,' he said. 'Pat's in a spot of trouble with some yobs from Tresham. Can you cope? Shouldn't be long.'

After Colin had gone, it was quiet. Deirdre wandered in to see if John needed anything, got a cool response, and left in a huff. John could see groups of people strolling in the sun, families with skipping children, couples with sun hats and arms entwined. He could hear the doves cooing softly, and somewhere a baby screamed, but not for long.

'This is bloody boring,' he said aloud. He could be getting some work done on the farm. There was always something to be done. His eye was caught by three or four Guernsey heifer calves in the little field behind the playground. Their spindly legs and mild faces might have come straight from a child's picture book. Tom Price must have put them there for the children. He was a family man, of course, and a grandad now. It'd be nice to have a little chap to take an interest in the farm...

'Oh my God,' he said aloud. 'It'll be the electric train set next.'

He wished Colin would come back, and then he could get away for a bit of lunch. Although he'd been pleased to offer his help, it really didn't warrant the two of them. And he needed to check on that cow. She wouldn't be long now, from the look of her. He heard Jemima bark in the schoolhouse garden, and wondered what Sarah was doing.

* * *

In her kitchen, Sarah Drinkwater was washing up her breakfast dishes. She'd stayed in bed late, feeling depressed and unwilling to face the day. With little appetite, she'd nevertheless eaten a bowl of cereal, a boiled egg and an apple. 'A good breakfast,' her mother was fond of saying, 'is the answer to most ailments, Sarah.' Whether it worked for ailments of the heart was another matter.

'I suppose I'd better have a walk round the gardens,' she said to Jemima, who cocked one ear at the magic word. 'Oh, sorry, Jeems,' said Sarah. 'I didn't mean walkies. I don't think you'd be allowed, even on a lead. I'll take you out later, Jeemsy.' The little dog looked crestfallen and curled up again, her sharp nose resting on the edge of her basket. Sarah swilled the sink with cold water, and then as she turned off the tap Daisy was there again.

'Help! Help me!'

Sarah stood motionless for a moment, her shoulders hunched and tense. Then she willed herself not to turn round, but shouted at the top of her voice, 'Go away, Daisy! Go away at once!' It was her schoolteacher's voice, harsh and authoritative, and was followed by silence, except for Jemima whimpering and shivering in her basket. That's it, then, thought Sarah. I must do that every time. Perhaps she'll get the message.

And then there was another, more sinister noise, a thin scratching sound, like something sharp against glass, from the direction of the window. Sarah whipped round, her back against the sink. Jemima leapt from her basket and stood on her hind legs, trying to reach the window, barking repeatedly in ear-splitting terror.

The scratching was not repeated, but Sarah had had enough. Too much, in fact, what with the school disaster, and John's coolness, and never knowing when wretched Daisy would be pleading for help. She dropped the dripping dishcloth and fled, Jemima at her heels, out of the kitchen and through the yard, into the sunlit garden. She stopped by the row of peas that John had helped her plant, clamped both hands over her ears and yelled, 'Shut up, shut up, shut up!', then ran, still screaming, out of the little gate at the bottom of the garden into the field with the heifers.

*   *   *

'Christ! What was that?' said John to Colin, who had just returned from sorting out the hooligans.

'Sounds like Sarah,' said Colin. 'Perhaps she ...' But he was talking to himself. John had disappeared in seconds through the school cloakroom and out into Sarah's garden. He could see no one, but immediately noticed the swinging gate and charged out into the field, scattering the heifers and calling as he ran.

He finally caught up with Sarah a couple of fields further on, where he found her crouched down with her back to a willow tree with Jemima whining and pushing her nose into Sarah's screwed up fist. She seemed not to notice John, but looked at her mistress's blank face.

'Sarah?' John knelt down on the short turf beside the willow. A shallow stream ran noisily behind them, and the sun penetrated the shifting leaves, dappling the ground and softening the shade. 'What's up?' My God, thought John, she looks terrified. He'd seen shock before, that awful night his dad had died with a choking rattle that had sent Deirdre

383

screaming down the stairs to find John.

Very quietly and gently, John twisted round until he was sitting next to Sarah against the broad tree trunk. He put his arm around her shoulders, softly, with no pressure. With his other hand he touched her clenched fist, slowly stroking until the fingers relaxed. He said nothing. He could feel the tension in her shoulders, and very carefully lifted her hand to his lips, kissing the damp palm.

The sun moved round, until John and Sarah, still having said nothing, motionless, were in full sunlight. It was warm, and beads of perspiration now stood on Sarah's forehead. Her colour had returned, and she was breathing more easily.

'It was Daisy,' she said finally, her voice breaking.

'I know,' said John.

'It's not my imagination, you know.'

'I know.'

'Why don't you love me any more?'

'I do. I do, really. I never stopped—it was just—oh well, you know all about that.'

'What am I going to do about Daisy?'

'I love you so much. I'll do something. Come on, give us a kiss and let's go home.' Well, thought John, so much for telling her straight. But what did he care, with the sun warm on his back and Sarah in his arms?

*　　　*　　　*

'I think we could call it a day, John,' said Colin. 'Thanks a lot for all your help.' He speculated idly on the cause of John's marked improvement in mood, and arrived at roughly the right answer.

John strolled out into the cooling sun, and went down the passage by the house to look at Sarah's kitchen window. Might find a clue, maybe. He could see nothing out of the way. As he turned, he stepped on something, crunching under his shoe. It was a pencil, and where it had split John could see smudged initials in blobby blue ballpoint. They were indecipherable now, but John Barnett knew a school issue pencil when he saw one.

'Right,' he said. 'Now we're getting somewhere,' and walked off whistling, his head held high and a spring in his step.

*　　　*　　　*

'Funny, ain't it?' Ellen said to Ivy and Doris, as they sat on a stone seat outside the mellow golden walls of Ringford Hall. 'Sittin' 'ere like Lady Muck, takin' our refreshment on the terrace. Lord knows what old Mr Charles would have said. Still, he'd never've 'ad all this 'oi polloi trampin' round his precious gardens in the first place.'

'Things've changed, Ellen,' said Doris. 'Mr Richard knows he's got to keep up with the times or go under.'

'Huh!' said Ivy Beasley. 'I wouldn't mind having what he's got. Not my idea of poverty, Doris.'

'No, well, it's all relative, isn't it,' said Doris.

'Come again?' said Ellen.

'Ignore her,' said Ivy to Doris. 'She knows exactly what you mean.'

The three friends walked slowly down the chestnut drive back to Ellen's Lodge. Ellen had been truculent and stubborn all day. 'I paid good money, and I'm goin' to see all them gardens,' she said. They'd had a break for lunch, a magnificent picnic put together by Ivy Beasley, sitting on comfortable canvas chairs in Doreen Price's garden. Doreen had brought them complimentary cups of steaming tea from her stable café, and given them special dispensation to sit there as long as they liked. In the shade of an ancient mulberry tree, they had rested and cooled themselves, fortifying Ellen for the afternoon ahead.

'It's funny, though, ain't it?' said Ellen.

'You said that before,' said Ivy. She was tired, too, having been up half the night planning and plotting.

'What's funny, Ellen?' said Doris. She sighed. Why was it always her who had to keep the peace? Anybody'd think the two of them would be glad to have had a lovely day, and Ellen still more or less upright and healthy.

'Well, it's funny spendin' the whole day goin' round your own village as if you was on an outin' with the WI, or somethin'.'

'That's the best bit,' said Ivy. 'No long coach ride, no dirty toilets in car parks. And you get to see a lot you'd never have seen otherwise.'

'Such as John Barnett and Sarah Drinkwater!' chortled Ellen. 'Did you see the way they were sittin' in the sun on that little wall outside her house, holdin' hands and drinkin' coffee?'

Ivy sniffed. 'Must be hard up, that John Barnett. If you ask me, he'd be much better off with a local girl, not one who knows nothing about farming and couldn't care less.'

'You used to say that about Mandy Bates,' said Doris Ashbourne. 'But you've changed your tune about her. Maybe Sarah Drinkwater could adapt. People do, you know, Ivy.'

Ivy bristled, and seemed about to say something, but pursed her lips and opened Ellen's garden gate. The little garden, overrun by old-fashioned sweet roses and orange lilies, clumps of cat-mint and self-seeded columbine, welcomed them with warm scents and soft abundance.

'Reckon your garden is the best we've seen today, Ellen,' said Ivy, with sudden generosity. 'This is how a cottage garden should be. My mother used to say they were all like this when she was little. All them gardening books, Dad said, they told folk more than they needed to know. Work of the devil, he'd say.'

Ellen opened her front door, and collapsed

387

gratefully onto her new sofa. 'Ah well, Ivy,' she said, 'your dad was a hard man.'

But a good one, thought Ivy. They wanted what was best for me, both of them. Wonder what they'd say if they knew what I was up to now?

It was not until Ivy was in her own kitchen, watching the light fade outside her window and listening to the twittering, settling song of roosting starlings under her eaves, that she was answered.

We know what you're up to, Ivy Dorothy, don't you worry, said her mother's voice. If you ask me, I think you've gone stark raving mad.

Well, I haven't asked you, Mother, said Ivy, and she got up to switch on the light and fetch her library book from her bedside table.

CHAPTER FIFTY-FOUR

Ringford School broke up for the summer holidays knowing there was a good chance it would never open up again. The annual sports day, with lines of yelling children in white T-shirts and red shorts, to all appearances was the same as ever, but there was a major element missing. There could be no optimistic looking forward. In every other year, a child who didn't win his race would always have another chance next summer, but now he probably wouldn't. And extra humiliation was heaped on the sports team at the inter-schools sports meeting, when Fletching beat them into second place in the relay event.

There were notices posted on notice boards and on telegraph poles in Ringford and Fletching, announcing the Education Committee's decision to close Round Ringford Church of England Primary School, and one dark night nameless ones went round tearing them all off. They were replaced two days later.

Sarah Drinkwater's parents urged her to come home for a week or two, but she refused. She realised that even two weeks without John would now seem a terrible waste of time. In too deep, Sarah Drinkwater, she said to herself. Time it was sorted out before it's too late.

'John,' said Sarah, as he reluctantly kissed her goodnight on the schoolhouse doorstep. He still dare not risk Deirdre's ire if he'd not slept in his bed at all. 'Yes, my darling,' he said.

'We should talk,' said Sarah.

'We do talk,' said John.

'Yes, but seriously.' Sarah looked up at him in the porch light and tried not to be distracted by his smile.

'Ah,' said John. 'I don't like the sound of that.'

'Don't worry, it's nothing to do with Jeremy Griffiths!' They'd finally been able to talk amiably about that momentous evening. Sarah had made it easy for John by laughing at Jeremy's townie ways, mocking her ex-boyfriend in unfavourable comparisons. John stopped short of a direct question—did Jeremy or did he not? It didn't really matter now.

'What is it about, then?'

'The future, I suppose,' said Sarah, looking down at her bare feet.

Alarm bells rang in John's bachelor head. Delightful as things now were between them, there was clearly more to be said. 'Right-o, then,' he said lightly. 'Tomorrow night? Let's go to the Partridge over at Fletching. Nice and intimate they say...'

*   *   *

The Fletching Partridge was a restaurant with a reputation. It was new to John Barnett, who'd previously seen the menu and the prices and backed away instinctively. More for the incomers, that one was. But something in Sarah's voice had made it clear that this was going to be an evening out of the general run.

They arrived in the car park, and John slotted his big Ford between a Mercedes and a Volvo estate. He adjusted his tie and on impulse went round to open the door for Sarah. 'Crumbs,' she said. She was wearing the cream silk dress and smart shoes that had so impressed Jeremy. They crunched over the gravel park and into the side door of the restaurant.

It was interior decor gone mad. Swathes of pink brocade anchored with bunches of dried flowers, soft pink shaded lamps, frilly tablecloths and matching napkins, tall thin glasses on wobbling stems, a posy of pink carnations on every table.

'Would you care for a drink in the bar first, sir?' said a smiling waiter. 'And then you can consider the menu and decide on your dining delights for tonight.' Sarah giggled. But John frowned, and put his hand under her elbow.

'Better do what we are told,' he muttered, and they went through to the bar. Sarah asked for a dry sherry, and John hesitated. He wanted a pint of Morton's Best more then anything else in the world, but was unsure. He settled for a gin and tonic, and Sarah raised her eyebrows. 'Not like you, John,' she said. 'Thought you were a pint man.'

They were given a huge menu, so big that they could scarcely hold it steady between them. 'Oh my God,' said Sarah. 'Morning-gathered mushrooms.'

'What?' said John.

'Well, you know...'

John shook his head. He felt more and more depressed. This was all wrong. It wasn't him at all. He began to feel as if the ghost of Jeremy Griffiths was taking over the evening. Still, better try for Sarah's sake. There's this talk we're going to have.

They ordered their meal and sipped their aperitifs. Conversation was stilted, and by the time they were ushered into the pink dining-room, John's spirits were in his boots. He looked at Sarah, lovely and calm, sitting opposite him, and felt even more dismal. She belonged here, and he did not. Nothing to do with class or money, he thought. Just different worlds.

They'd ordered soup, and when it came with a thick circle of cream and a coy nasturtium nestling in the centre, John leaned over to Sarah, his face darkened. 'Never eaten a bloody flower in my life,' he said.

'Just put it on the side of your plate, then,' said Sarah, and her voice had sharpened. She knew now—had known ever since they walked into the place and John had ordered that gin—that this was a mistake. Nothing was ever going to make him relax now. No chance of a real talk. Intimate my foot, she thought angrily. How the hell are we going to get out of it.

They got through the meal quickly. Service was good, and the waiter seemed permanently at their side, offering more wine, petit fours, brandy and eventually not troubling to disguise his scorn as they refused even coffee and got up to leave. They drove home in silence, and John drew up slowly outside the schoolhouse. 'Sorry, Sarah,' he said.

'My fault,' she said. 'See you tomorrow?' He leaned over and kissed on her cheek.

'Love you,' he said. Sarah nodded, touched his cheek with her fingertips, and then got out of the car, disappearing through her door without looking back.

*   *   *

The village's summer events proceeded in an orderly fashion. Ringford Show was unlucky this year. It rained most of the day in a steady downpour, turning the field into a soggy quagmire through which Bill Turner and Fox Jenkins squelched in a determined effort to keep the programme to time, but classes were delayed, and dripping wet children whined and wanted to go home. And then, about three o'clock, the sun came out and set all the raindrops on ringside ropes and tent roofs sparkling. Susan Standing, elegant and perfectly turned out, swept the board in the classes she entered on her beloved mare, and little Poppy, blonde curls bobbing about under her riding cap, stuck to her fat Shetland pony as if by superglue. Richard Standing led her up and down the tinies' obstacle race at a fastish trot, and when he stumbled and fell on a tussock of grass, Poppy chortled with delight and screamed 'Come on, Dad!'

'Chip off the old block, that one,' said Ted Bates, standing at the ringside with his grandson Joey, Poppy's number one fan. It hadn't been easy pushing the wheelchair over the rough muddy field, but Ted was not having Joey left at home.

Donald Davie's mother had died peacefully in her sleep, and Donald had returned to find Joyce restored in health but in a strange, clinging mood. Peggy Turner had kept her word and made sure Joyce was looked after until the flu had gone, and then she avoided number fourteen as before. But Joyce's spell was broken. Peggy no longer worried if Bill was late home, and was polite to Joyce in the shop. It was not true to say they were friends, but an indefinite truce had been declared.

Holidays had emptied the village, and the Green was quiet. Only the Jenkinses played in the children's corner, as Jean and Fox were saving up for a new car and had decided against a holiday this year. 'We shall have days out,' Jean had said to Doris Ashbourne over the fence. 'The kids are fed up, o'course, but mostly because all their friends are away. Still, we're taking them to the pictures tomorrow. That'll set us back a fair old bit, but we agreed on one or two treats. It's only right, Fox says.'

The shop takings were down, but Bill said not to worry, they'd soon buck up when term started again. Has he forgotten, Peggy wondered, that term may not start up again as far as Ringford is concerned? They went for long walks on Sundays, and sometimes Peggy took a picnic over to Flasher's Pool where Bill sat fishing and dozing. The grassy bed by the pool was just as fragrant and springy as that wonderful afternoon last summer, when their love was settled once and for all.

The ice-cream van came round most days, and Peggy fumed at the cheek of the man, parking right outside the shop and taking away her business. His best customers were a small group of teenagers, mostly from Walnut Close, who played netball in the school playground every afternoon. They'd been given permission by Sarah Drinkwater, who was glad to have some young folk around.

They were not, however, so well received by Ivy Beasley, whose nerves were shattered by the constant 'thud thud' of hard ball on asphalt, and the cries of triumph at every goal scored. More than once she had serious doubts about what she had set in motion.

*   *   *

The lofty black and white-tiled entrance to Ringford Hall was cool, and Ivy, hot and sticky from the walk up from the village, smiled gratefully at Susan Standing. 'We could do with a drop of rain, Mrs Standing,' she said, as Susan ushered her into Richard's oak-panelled study. It was a serious, dark room, with books from floor to ceiling along one wall, and shaded lamps on Richard's large, business-like desk. It had been his father's study, and he had deliberately done very little to change it. From the long, heavily curtained windows, Ivy could see the yellowing, dry grass of the park, and groups of cattle shading themselves under broad oaks and beech.

As her eyes became accustomed to the gloom, she saw that others were there before her, and she nodded to each one, taking her chair by Richard's desk, and folding her hands over her handbag, her feet in their well-polished brown shoes placed neatly together on the worn Chinese rug.

Her companions were Richard Standing, perfectly relaxed behind his father's desk, his brother James, small and pear-shaped, peering through thick-lensed spectacles, Maurice Buswell MP, languid and affable, the Reverend Nigel Brooks, Tom Price, and a tall, slim young man Ivy had never seen before.

'Welcome, Ivy,' said Richard Standing, beaming at her with such bonhomie that she blinked in embarrassment. 'You know everyone here, I think, except Simon Hawkins. He's from Hawkins, Jones and Varley in Tresham. Been our solicitors for donkeys' years, so you can trust young Simon absolutely.' Ivy nodded again, and pursed her lips. 'Good afternoon, Mr Hawkins,' she said.

'Perhaps I might sum up our thoughts on your proposal, Ivy, just so that we all know what we're talking about? Simon has, of course, been briefed, but just a reminder might be useful.'

'Please carry on, Mr Richard,' said Ivy. 'I shall interrupt where necessary.' Her dignity was immense, her self-confidence unshakeable. At least, that's how it looked from the outside. Inside, Ivy was quaking.

'Well then,' said Richard. 'As you all know, Miss Beasley owns a small field adjacent to the school playground, and for many years now, ever since her excellent father died, the field has been let for keep to Tom here. He's grazed stock on it and kept the grass in order, and it's been a little nest egg in rent for Ivy, which is just what her father intended. Right so far, Ivy?' He smiled at her benevolently. He'd noticed her hands fiddling with the handbag clasp, and guessed that her outward calm belied inward anxiety.

'Quite right, Mr Richard,' said Ivy. 'Please carry on.'

'Now, one of the reasons Ringford School lost the battle against closure, and Fletching won, was that there is no available space to extend our school for the extra children who would be bussed in from Fletching.'

'Whereas,' interrupted James Standing, his glasses twinkling, 'Fletching School has a large field at the rear of the playground which they use for sporting activities. Rented from me,' he added, and looked extremely smug.

Simon Hawkins nodded wisely. His father

had schooled him well in the ways of village procedure, and he knew he had to wait for the crux of the matter.

Ivy cleared her throat. 'Perhaps I could take over here, Mr Richard,' she said. Richard Standing smiled encouragingly, and Ivy turned to address the young solicitor.

'My father, the late Mr Beasley, thought a lot of Ringford,' she said. 'And his father before him. We've been here for generations, and Beasleys have always done their bit for the village. Now,' she continued, her voice firmer, 'it is well known that I have reservations about Ringford School, mostly because of the noise and cheek I endure from today's badly brought up children. And my schooldays memories are not particularly happy ones. But I am not stupid.'

Not stupid at all, thought Tom Price, with something like affection.

'I can see that this village will die without the school,' continued Ivy. 'It's not a real village without a school, or a shop, or a church.'

'Or a pub,' put in Tom mischievously.

Ivy ignored him. 'Ringford School needs land for extension,' she said firmly. 'I've got land right next to the school, and I intend to make it available. I want you, Mr Hawkins, to arrange it so that the school can have it for as long as is needed. And if there are new buildings to be put up, so be it.'

Simon Hawkins' eyebrows were raised. This

398

was going to take some sorting out. First time he'd encountered anyone quite like Miss Ivy Beasley. He was about to speak, when Nigel Brooks said mildly, 'But the rent, Miss Beasley. As Chairman of the Governors, I have to say we are stretched to the absolute limit now on the budget, and couldn't possibly afford rent.' He hated pouring cold water on Ivy's plan, but he and his fellow Governors had done sums far into the night and couldn't see any way round it.

'Rent?' said Ivy. 'Who said anything about rent?'

Richard Standing beamed, as if he had personally orchestrated Ivy's long deliberations. 'Your father would be so proud, Ivy,' he said.

'But, Ivy,' persisted Tom Price, 'what about your income? You're not telling me that rent hasn't been more than useful.'

'None of it's been spent, Tom Price,' said Ivy with a sniff. 'You can rest assured I shan't starve. Unlike today's spendthrifts, we were brought up to save for a rainy day. Well, I reckon that day's arrived.'

The chorus of gratitude and genuine good feeling was interrupted by Susan easing open the study door and appearing with a laden tea tray.

'Time for refreshment,' she said. 'I can see from your faces we have something to celebrate.'

'You'd better come in, Ivy,' said Doris Ashbourne, standing at the door of her bungalow. 'Did you say you were coming round? I know I'm forgetful, but I don't think...'

'No, no,' said Ivy. 'There wasn't no arrangement. I just need to sit down a minute and...'

Something's up, thought Doris. For one thing, Ivy prided herself on her grammar. She did look a bit peculiar.

'I'll put the kettle on, Ivy,' Doris said, 'then we can have a chat, and that.'

Over a good strong cup of tea, Ivy unburdened herself. She'd meant to keep it a secret from even Doris, but found she had to tell somebody, and her mother's ghostly presence wouldn't do. Doris was so amazed as the story unfolded that she allowed her tea to get cold, and forgot to refill the pot.

'I'll thank you to keep all this to yourself, Doris,' said Ivy, winding up. 'And no hints to that Ellen Biggs, whatever you do.'

'What do you take me for, Ivy?' said Doris. 'All those years in the Post Office were good training, I can tell you. Nobody can keep a secret better than me.'

The tense lines on Ivy's face slowly disappeared, and she leaned back in her chair, feeling a lot better at sharing her gigantic decision with someone as down to earth and sensible as Doris.

'Even so, Ivy,' continued Doris, leaning forward conspiratorially, 'it doesn't really alter the Committee's decision. After all, Fletching does have its field already.'

'Ah,' said Ivy. 'Now this is a nice one, Doris. You'll like this. You know James Standing, Mr Richard's brother?'

'Course I do,' said Doris. Ivy did like to spin it out. Still, so did they all.

'Well, the Fletching field is his. Rents it to the school on a short let, with proviso that he can reclaim it at any time. Seems that's just what he intends to do. Going to build a couple of posh new houses there. And what with him being on Planning at the Council, he don't anticipate any problems.'

'Well, I never,' said Doris, and as she could think of nothing more to say, she got up and boiled more water for the cooling teapot.

From the sitting room, Ivy's voice followed her. 'Now remember, Doris,' she said loudly, 'not a word to anyone.'

CHAPTER FIFTY-FIVE

In roughly twenty-four hours, the entire village knew Ivy's secret, and it was not Doris's fault. Nigel Brooks had been so excited he had rushed home and told Sophie, who, on the phone to Peggy, couldn't help mentioning it—

obliquely, of course, but Peggy guessed most of it—but cautioned Peggy not to say a word. Bill came in, weary and fed up with Susan Standing constantly changing her mind about which herbs she wanted in her new herb garden, so Peggy told him just the bare outline to cheer him up.

In the Arms, later that evening, Bill indicated to Tom Price that he knew something about what was being hatched, and Tom assumed he knew it all and began to discuss it enthusiastically. Many people were in the bar, and Tom's voice was loud. And so it was that out of the whole village population, only a few people in Walnut Close remained in ignorance. But though almost everyone knew of Ivy Beasley's charitable act, they also knew she wanted it kept secret, and so far as she would be aware, only the small cabal at the Hall, and, of course, Doris, were privy to the plan.

Deirdre Barnett had not welcomed the news. All she could see in it was the certainty that Sarah Drinkwater would be staying on in Ringford. It didn't take much intelligence to see the way things were heading. She spent sleepless nights wondering what would happen to her. It was well known that you couldn't have two mistresses in one kitchen. Cast out in the snow, that's what I'll be, she said to herself.

'Fair waved the golden corn,' sang John Barnett, as he shaved in front of the spotty mirror of the farm bathroom. He'd always loved the hymns at school, and although he was seen in church only at Christmas, Easter and Harvest Festival, he could still remember whole verses they'd sung in the lofty classroom. The harvest was nearly all in, and the frantic race against weather and the vagaries of man-made machinery was slowing down to a more peaceful rate. But although he'd worked all hours God sent, surrounded by clouds of dust in his lumbering combine, he had also had plenty of time to think, isolated up there in the glass cabin.

Since that evening at the Partridge, he and Sarah had resumed their routine, and he'd deliberately not brought up the subject of The Talk. His mother's sharply expressed doubts about Sarah's suitability to be a farmer's wife went round and round in John's head, and he came to no conclusions. He knew his mother was right on many points. Farming could be cold, dirty, boring and repetitive. You never knew whether it would be a good year and you could afford a few treats, or if the bad weather would ruin crops, delay ripening and kill off weakly lambs, cutting income drastically and imposing a pulling-in of horns.

But then, every time, he came back to the one sure and lasting fact. He loved Sarah, wanted her, and knew that there'd never be anyone else he would want so much.

He had been told, of course, about Ivy's generosity, and this had hastened the need for some action on his part. If, with the new information, the Secretary of State decided to reverse the closure decision, he presumed Sarah would stay. But not for long. She was ambitious, and had already mentioned the offer from the school in Tresham. If the closure was confirmed, then she'd go anyway. After years of jogging along happily with no sense of urgency about his future, John Barnett was on the rack.

*　　　*　　　*

Maurice Buswell MP hurried down the platform at Euston Station, only just in time for the train which would take him to god-awful Tresham, where he hoped Richard Standing would be waiting to meet him. He'd had a hard day. A great stack of letters piled in his in-tray greeted him as he walked into his office, and then he'd had that difficult session with the Secretary of State for Education. If it hadn't been for Richard and that charming James Standing, he wouldn't have been so determined to get over his case for Round Ringford. After all, the proposed closure of one wretched little village school was not a major world-shaking event. But he had prepared his brief like a barrister, marshalled every fact and figure he could extract from the bulky file the vicar had given him, and presented the new aspects with all his considerable charm.

He struggled into the crowded train and looked in vain for a seat. He'd missed the Inter-City, which had a restaurant car, and fought his way through hot, smelly rush-hour commuters until he finally found somewhere to sit. He put his bulging briefcase on the rack, and collapsed gratefully.

'Maurice! What a lovely surprise!' He looked across and saw, first with pleasure and then with some reservation, Susan Standing and little Poppy, grinning at him from the opposite seats. 'We wondered if you might be on this train,' Susan said, 'didn't we, Poppy?' The small girl nodded violently, spraying soft chocolate ice-cream across the space between them. A few small drops fell on Maurice's immaculate pale beige trousers, and he rubbed at them ineffectually with his handkerchief, spreading the stain, making it worse.

'How nice,' he said. 'We shall be quite a family when Richard meets us at Tresham.'

'Oh, no,' said Susan, 'I left the wagon there, so we can pick it up and go straight home.'

Maurice shuddered at the thought of sharing 'the wagon' with sticky little Poppy, but he smiled bravely, and embarked with faked enthusiasm on *The Tale of Pigling Bland*, reading it upside down as Poppy looked at the pictures and pulled him up short when he tried to skip a paragraph or two.

Fortunately for Maurice Buswell's ego, the

wagon turned out to be a very smart four-wheel-drive monster, and he climbed in with a sigh of relief. Richard Standing was waiting for them at the Hall, large gins and tonic at the ready, and took Maurice into the drawing room while Susan bore Poppy away for her tea.

'Well, Maurice,' he said, 'how'd it go?'

Maurice Buswell did not give a straight answer. He had suffered in the heat and pollution of London, he had given of his all to the Secretary of State for Education, and he meant to make Richard suffer a little, too.

'I was extremely lucky to get an audience, as we say,' he began. 'Only because my sister married his cousin, you know. He has very little time, and the closure of a village school in the middle of nowhere doesn't usually get very high priority.'

Richard Standing nodded understandingly. He knew exactly what Maurice Buswell was up to, and obligingly played his part. 'Jolly lucky to have you as our MP,' he said, his face bland.

'Well,' said Maurice self-deprecatingly, 'I don't know about that. But at least we'd met before, at the wedding. Anyway, he listened very attentively—I have to say I'd prepared the ground very well—and all I can tell you, Richard, is that he seemed quite convinced by our case. We shan't know officially, of course, until the Department informs us. But I do honestly think we have cause for optimism.'

'Great! Well done, Maurice!' said Richard.

He strode to the door and called loudly down the passage towards the green baize door, 'Susan! Susan! Come here, darling! Good news!'

'It isn't absolutely definite,' said Maurice cautiously, but he smiled broadly and accepted a glass of bubbly white wine with alacrity, sending it fizzing down his throat in celebratory pursuit of the gin and tonic.

*   *   *

''S'like bein' in the condemned cell,' said Ellen. 'Waiting on a reprieve. Poor devils—now I know what they felt like.'

She was sitting comfortably in Ivy Beasley's front room, her feet on a little tapestry stool worked long ago by Ivy's mother, the woolwork basket of flowers faded now from their original vibrant colours. Holding out her plate, she accepted a second slice of coffee cream sponge.

'Best yet, this sponge,' she said. 'Bein' on tenterhooks 'asn't spoilt yer bakin', anyway, Ivy.'

Ivy smiled briefly. She was confident that Doris hadn't broken her pledge of secrecy, and thought that Ellen was merely infected with the forlorn hope prevalent in the village that some miracle would happen before the start of next term.

'Another piece, Doris?' she said, and cut a

generous slice.

'It's Deirdre Barnett I worry about,' said Ellen, shaking her tousled grey head.

'What now?' said Ivy. 'Thanks to a lot of folk in the village, you've nothing at all to worry about, Ellen Biggs. So there's no need to go making something out of nothing.'

''S'not nothing,' said Ellen, grinning broadly.

'You're not worried, Ellen,' said Doris, with a sideways look at Ivy. 'You just glory in a bit of gossip. Come on then, I can see you're bursting to tell us.'

'Well,' said Ellen, 'I were in the shop, and Deirdre were there, talking to Peggy Turner, and she were nearly in tears. Really! Nearly in tears, she were.'

'Huh,' said Ivy. 'Must be something to do with her John, then. Only thing Deirdre Barnett would weep over.'

'Right first time, Ivy,' said Ellen. She took her feet off the stool and leaned forward to pick up her cup. She slurped down her tea with no pretence at politeness, and banged it back in the saucer. 'Her John it is. She's in a panic about that Sarah Drinkwater, and don't know how she can stop it. Serve her right, I say. Taken young John for granted for too long. Long past time he took a wife, I say, so good luck to 'im.'

'He'll have to be quick, then,' said Doris.

Ivy smiled knowingly.

'Yep,' said Ellen. 'Too right, Doris. Miss Thirsty'll be off to pastures new if our school ain't opened up again. She'll kiss goodbye to Round Ringford, and prob'ly think good riddance, if we did but know. At least she'd be rid of that Daisy child, callin' and callin' and frightenin' the poor girl out of her wits. You watch, our schoolteacher'll be up an' off in no time.'

'I don't think so,' said Ivy, and surprised Ellen with her benevolent air.

'Oh, well,' she said, 'if you don't think so, Ivy, then it ain't so. No more to be said, our Doris.'

'Now, now,' said Doris. 'We'll all just have to wait and see. Shall we give you a hand with the washing-up, Ivy?'

This ritual question received the usual ritual refusal, and Doris helped Ellen down the step and watched her set off painfully for home.

'Home help still coming in, Ellen?' she called after her.

Ellen stopped and turned around slowly, leaning on her stick. 'Home hindrance, more like,' she said. 'I stopped them nosy parkers comin' in a week or two ago. I can manage,' she said, and hobbled away.

CHAPTER FIFTY-SIX

'Gotcha!' John Barnett's voice from outside Sarah's back door was triumphant. They had been lingering over supper, finishing a bottle of red wine between them, and a companionable silence had fallen. Relaxed by good food and drink, John had made a decision. If Sarah wanted to talk, the way they hadn't been able to that awful evening at the Partridge, he would encourage her, and knew now what he had to say in return. And then, just as he'd leaned over and taken Sarah's hand, Jemima had whined and looked up at the window, one ear cocked, her head on one side.

'Help! Help me! Please, help!' The cry had been muffled this time, and stumbled, breaking with heartrending sadness as it pleaded in the warm air of the summer evening.

Sarah had frozen, but John was on his feet like lightning. He was out of the back door before Jemima could leap out of her basket, and returned looking grim.

'Here she is, then,' he said to an astonished Sarah. 'Here's little Daisy.'

'Ouch!' said Mark Jenkins. 'Let go my ear, or I'll tell my dad!'

'We'll have more than that to tell your dad,' said John menacingly. He felt in his pocket, and brought out the crushed pencil. 'Yours, I

410

believe?' he said grimly.

'It weren't me!' said Mark Jenkins, beginning to blub. 'It were Andrew's fault. He thought of it. Just to pay 'er back, an' that.'

'You'll pay her back, all right,' said John, reaching for his jacket. 'Thanks for supper, sweetie,' he said. 'I'm off to Jenkinses with this brat—Fox and Jean'll be home. I'll see you tomorrow.' And finish what hardly got started, he thought.

But Sarah was on her feet now, her hand on John's arm. 'Hang on a minute,' she said. 'This is really for me to sort out. Between me and Mark. It's nice of you, but I think it's best to leave him to me now. I'll be OK—he's not a very dangerous character—look at him!'

Mark Jenkins certainly looked far from dangerous. He had slumped down on one of Sarah's kitchen chairs, and tears were streaming down his fat cheeks. He rubbed at them with his fists, leaving great muddy smears all over his face.

Uncertain what to do, John pulled on his jacket. 'Well, you're the schoolteacher,' he said reluctantly. 'Just don't let him off lightly, that's all. Little bugger deserves a good hiding.' He kissed Sarah on the cheek, glared at Mark Jenkins, and left.

It was very quiet in the kitchen, and for several minutes Sarah sat and looked at Mark Jenkins without saying anything. Then she tore off a piece of kitchen paper and handed it to him. 'Clean your face, Mark,' she said, 'and then you'd better explain.'

It was a pathetic story, incoherently told, and when Mark had finished, Sarah stood up and went to the window, looking out into the dark garden and the starry sky. 'Do you think it was fair, Mark?' she said. 'I made you look a fool, once, in front of your friends. It wasn't very kind, I admit that, but you did ask for it. And for that, you've terrified me, over and over again. Was that fair?'

Mark Jenkins shook his head dumbly. 'Sorry, Miss,' he said. He looked at her, weighing up his chances. 'Do you have to tell my dad, Miss? He'll tan the arse off me.'

'You know he won't, Mark,' said Sarah. 'Lucky you've not got Andrew's father, isn't it? But your dad would be very upset to know that you've been so stupid.'

Mark nodded humbly. Were things going his way?

'We'll make a bargain, then,' said Sarah. 'I'm off to Spain for a week with Mrs Jones, just a short break, and I want you to look after Jemima, take her for walks and see she gets properly fed. She's very precious to me, and I have to trust you.'

Mark's grin made it quite clear that he regarded this as more of a treat than a punishment. Blimey, he'd got off lightly. Miss Thirsty had certainly changed. Probably somethin' to do with John Barnett. Very snug,

412

they were. Still, p'raps Andrew would leave him be, now. 'She'll be great with me, Miss,' he said. 'I'm an expert on dogs.'

Sarah saw Mark out of the front door and watched him disappear into the darkness. She thought of the Jenkins terrier, very old and very spry, and knew that Jemima would be in good hands. 'We shall be all right now, Jeems,' she said, picking up the little dog and giving her a big hug in sudden blissful relief that Daisy would trouble her no more.

* * *

Next morning was sombre, heavy rain pouring down the gutters of the schoolhouse and overflowing on to the concrete path with noisy splashes. The previous day's warmth lingered inside Sarah's small sitting room, and she sat on the arm of a chair talking to her father on the telephone. In her hand she held a new letter from the special school, urging her to make a decision.

'Well, darling,' said her father, 'have you decided?'

'Not really,' she said. 'They want me to start at the beginning of term, so they say. An emergency. It's a department with problem kids and would be quite a challenge.'

'But you couldn't leave Ringford, just when you've won the fight, surely?'

'Now would be a good time, in a way,' said

Sarah, absently stroking Jemima's head and looking out at the lashing rain. 'I've done all I can for them, and the future looks good. They'll easily get someone else.'

'Well, I don't know I'm sure,' said her father, which is what he always said when at a loss. He knew Sarah too well to mention John Barnett, although they'd met him one afternoon when visiting the schoolhouse. 'How soon do you have to make up your mind?' he said.

'Straight away, more or less. They've been on at me ever since they heard the school might close. And then I'm off to Spain with Gabriella, you remember, and they need to know before I go. Anyway, Dad, don't worry—I'll sort it out.'

There was something about Sarah's tone that caused her father to report back to her mother that in his view Sarah had made up her mind already. 'Always was a close one,' her mother said. 'No doubt we'll be the last to know.' Her father just smiled, and said he hoped it would clear up before lunch, otherwise he'd not get a decent round of golf before the weekend.

*　　　*　　　*

At exactly one o'clock, John Barnett clumped into Sarah's kitchen, very wet and muddy, and was roundly told off for leaving lumps of evil-smelling muck on her clean floor. He took no

414

notice whatsoever, and grinned at her broadly.

'It's no good,' he said. 'If I don't do it now, I'll never get round to it.'

'Do what?' said Sarah.

'This,' he said, fumbling in his pocket and producing a small, square box. 'Will you marry me? Please say yes, and let's stop buggering about. I love you so much I can't think of anything else. Please?'

Sarah dried her hands and took the little box. 'John Barnett,' she said. 'That is the most unromantic proposal I could possibly imagine.' She looked him straight in the eye.

'Right-o, then,' he said, and went down on one sopping wet knee. 'I love you more than life itself,' he said, 'and implore you to be my wife.'

'Oh, John!' said Sarah. She grabbed his hands, pulling him to his feet and putting her arms tight around him. 'I do love you best when you're being silly—and yes, please, I do want to marry you. Very much.'

Jemima danced and barked around them, and none of them noticed that the rain had stopped and a weak sun was shining through the clouds. The small box was opened, and the sapphire and diamond ring found to fit perfectly.

'Well, that settles it,' said Sarah, as she and John walked through the garden hand in hand. 'I shan't take the job in Tresham.'

'What job?' said John.

'The one I wanted to talk to you about,' said Sarah. 'I can see I'll have my work cut out here, what with my little school and my big husband.'

'Well I'm damned,' said John, and he kissed her again.

CHAPTER FIFTY-SEVEN

It was to be quite a party. Ringford had agreed to celebrate the reprieve of their school with a bloody good knees-up, but because many people were still away on holiday they planned the party for the beginning of term. 'We want a hundred per cent turnout, Doreen,' Tom Price had said. 'This is something for the whole village, and by God, we're going to have a do that'll be heard as far as Fletching.' Doreen had thought that would be tactless, to say the least, but she gathered together her ladies from the WI and menus were discussed for a feast such as had never been eaten before.

From the day when the Reverend Nigel Brooks was seen running full-pelt through the village, cassock flying, waving a piece of paper like some latter-day Neville Chamberlain, the clouds had lifted from Round Ringford. The flag flew from the school flagpole, waving bravely in the freshening winds. As the village turned from summer's verdant green to the yellow and bronze of approaching autumn, and the first curling leaves floated from the Hall avenue of chestnuts on to the damp ground, meetings of the School Feast sub-committees met in front rooms, and ambitious plans were laid.

Mark Jenkins had lost his hunted look, and gained in confidence as he smashed Andrew Robert's champion conkers three times in succession. Sarah Drinkwater and Gabriella Jones returned from Spain, full of secrets and confidences, and Sarah had found that Jemima, though overjoyed to see her again, was now deeply attached to Mark. She'd agreed with a light heart that Mark could regularly walk the little dog alongside the Jenkins terrier, who, although old enough to know better, made it clear he fancied Jemima rotten.

This time, Nigel Brooks had not forgotten to pray for fine weather. The only space big enough to seat the entire village was Tom Price's big barn, which he emptied with a will. Big metal barns can be cold, echoing places, but blow heaters had been hired, and given reasonable weather, Tom was confident that with a thorough sweeping and hosing down, the whole place could be transformed.

The schoolchildren were given Friday off, provided each one helped in the general activity of preparing the Feast. 'No sneaking off to Tresham on the bus, mind,' Sarah had cautioned them, not missing the look exchanged between Andrew Roberts and Jody Watts. 'I want everyone—and that includes you, Andrew Roberts—working hard to give thanks for being here in your own school.' The Fletching children had looked glum, but Sarah had cheered them up with a promise of a special project on the history of their own village. 'Not really much consolation,' she confided to John Barnett, 'but it was the best I could do.'

Gabriella Jones was now working full-time with the extra children, and advertisements were out for a further half-time teacher. Drawings were ready for the school extension, and Ivy Beasley smiled with quiet pride when she saw the architects in conference in the playground.

The only person in Ringford who was totally miserable amongst all the rejoicing was Deirdre Barnett. She looked sadly around the farmhouse, her home for nearly forty-five years, at the big kitchen where she had presided over her family, the low-ceilinged bedroom with its creaking boards and sloping floor, where her children had been conceived and her husband had choked his last. She called her hens each morning and watched them running towards her, lurching in ungainly haste, like drunkards after a good night at the Arms. 'It'll be the pot for you lot,' she said to them. 'Can't see Miss Sarah bothering with hens. John'll have to get used to supermarket eggs, I shouldn't wonder. And that's not all he'll have to get used to.' Like many a mother in her situation, Deirdre couldn't see that true love would more than compensate for the lack of new-laid eggs.

*　　　*　　　*

'Sun's shining!' yelled Nigel Brooks, as he leapt out of bed like a youth, bouncing Sophie out of sleep and setting old Ricky barking in the kitchen below. He hurriedly dressed and gobbled down a plate of corn flakes, ate half his toast, and threw the rest to his grateful old dog.

'I'm off, Sophie! See you later!' It was a morning for exclamation marks. Nigel grabbed his bike from the garage and rode off down Bate's End, swerving dangerously round by the Arms. He scorched into Prices' yard and skidded to a halt by the stone steps that led up to the back door of the farmhouse, where Tom stood, deep in conversation with Colin Osman. Colin had a clipboard in his hand and was riffling through a sheaf of papers with the air of a man with important work to do.

'All in hand, Colin,' Tom was saying. 'You can relax, lad. The women have got it all in hand. Why don't you see if Don Cutt needs some help at the Arms? He's staying open, though I doubt he'll get many customers today. I expect you got a list somewhere of the booze we'll need.' His smile was warm, and Colin did not notice the wink Tom directed at Nigel.

After Colin had disappeared, Tom and Nigel went into the house. 'Come through, Nigel,' said Tom. 'It's in here.' Nigel followed him through to Doreen's cool sitting room where the scent from the great vase of white roses mingled with the faint smell of woodsmoke and ancient timbers. Tom led Nigel over to the corner of the room and pointed. Peggy Turner's not entirely selfless suggestion had been acted upon.

'Oh, yes. Oh yes, Tom, that'll do very well,' said Nigel, and crouched down with a soft look on his face.

*   *   *

By twelve o'clock, most of Ringford was assembled. Every place had a name card, and the barn was indeed transformed. Streamers, balloons, flowers, scenes of school life on old sheets painted by the children, bright tablecloths and napkins, bottles of wine, baskets of home-baked rolls, huge bowls of salad. An army of helpers had worked all morning, and having rushed home to change, were back with their families in their Sunday best.

Peggy and Bill Turner had made a dozen journeys to the food wholesalers, and—against

Bill's better judgement—had asked the Feast Committee for no profit on supplies. 'We shall never be rich, gel,' Bill had said sadly to Peggy. 'No, but we shall certainly be happy,' she countered, grabbing his arm as he got out of their warm bed, collapsing him back into her loving embrace.

Mountains of cold roast beef, home-cooked ham, whole salmon, great wedges of cheese: all were consumed with the greatest of enthusiasm, and washed down liberally with bottles of red and white wine and foaming pints of Morton's Best. Ivy Beasley, Ellen Biggs and Doris Ashbourne sat together in a warm, draught-free corner. 'Don't want you being a bother with pneumonia, Ellen Biggs,' Ivy had said. More than once Ivy had looked around the packed barn with a feeling of satisfaction. She had been momentarily mystified by people being nice to her lately, in the street and in the shop. Quite different, they'd been. But Doris could be relied on, and Mr Richard and the others were all trustworthy men, surely. Must just be relief that the school wasn't closing after all. She had no more dreams about being put in the stocks.

A whisper began around the table where Jean Jenkins and her brood were sitting. Speeches? Weren't nobody going to make a speech? And then up got Nigel Brooks, a smile from ear to ear on his handsome face. He banged on the table with his spoon, and there were cries of 'Silence! Silence for the vicar!'

'Ladies and Gentlemen,' he began. 'Turn right, first on the left,' shouted some well-oiled wag. But nothing could stop Nigel smiling today. He sat flanked by Richard and Susan Standing, with Poppy up and down like a yo-yo, and on his other side Maurice Buswell MP. Nigel Brooks, Chairman of the School Governors and hero, looked around the barn with pride and reflected that this was probably the best day of his ministry to Round Ringford so far.

His speech was clear and straightforward. He thanked everyone, left out nobody who mattered, including God, and offered his congratulations to the Protest Committee in particular. 'Worth all those meetings, eh, Mr Richard!'

Doreen and her WI members were praised for the excellence of the feast, and the schoolchildren had a round of applause for their decorations. And then, in the small silence that followed Nigel Brooks's final words, John Barnett got to his feet.

'Good old John! You tell 'em!' shouted one of his cronies, who had helped carry the beer crates up from the pub and duly slaked his thirst before the festivities began.

'Um, ladies and gentlemen,' began John, his colour rising. 'I don't know if this is in order, but what I have to announce is directly connected to the school. That is, to the schoolmistress.'

Roars of applause, cat-calls and fists banging on wooden trestle tables.

'Well, you've not heard what I've got to say yet!' said John, his confidence growing. 'Now then, as you all know, we had a very good schoolteacher for years in Miss Layton, and all of us were sorry to see her go.' Nods and 'hear hears' towards the retired teacher, who had come back to celebrate her old school's reprieve.

'It'd not be right to say I was pleased to see her retire, but I have to admit that I was very pleased to see Miss Drinkwater take her place.'

'John!' whispered Sarah, pink with embarrassment.

'Very pleased indeed,' said John, turning to Sarah with a look so brimming with love that his mother felt a real pain, right in her heart. 'I am proud to announce that Miss Sarah Drinkwater—dear Sarah—has done me the honour of agreeing to be my wife.'

The barn echoed for many minutes with cheers and shouts, and Sarah leaned across and gave John the softest of kisses on his flaming cheek. 'Very nicely done, John,' she said. 'You shall have a gold star for that.'

Ellen Biggs, her eyes on Deirdre Barnett, leaned across and whispered to Doris, 'Looks like a squeezed lemon, our Deirdre,' and cackled with unholy glee. Peggy Turner, sitting close by, heard Ellen's whisper, and felt sorry for Deirdre. Jealousy was an evil thing, and destructive, no doubt about that. She looked across to where Joyce Davie sat and saw her smile at her Donald. There you are, she told herself, all's well with the world. Then she saw Bill lean over and fill up Donald's glass. She watched Joyce turn her face up to him, and at that moment he looked across the tables, caught Peggy's eye and blew her a kiss. She smiled. Now he knew, and it was going to be all right. She noticed that John Barnett had his arm around Sarah's small shoulders. Love and marriage, she thought. How different it is the second time round. But no regrets, Bill, none at all.

Coffee was circulating round the long tables when Richard Standing rose to his feet. A respectful silence fell, and only little Poppy dared chortle and screech at the antics of the Jenkins's terrier under the table. 'Hush, darling,' said Susan, 'listen to Daddy, there's a good girl.'

Richard Standing looked round the room, found the object of his search, sitting placidly with her friends. 'Friends and neighbours,' he said, with a very pleasant smile, 'And especially Miss Beasley. There is just one more speech to be made.' Ivy sat bolt upright, very alarmed. He wouldn't, not after he'd promised!

'I think you will all know what I mean when I say we owe a great debt of gratitude to Miss Ivy Beasley for what we are celebrating here today. She has typically forbidden any reference to her generosity, but Ringford is not the place for keeping secrets. If anyone is mystified so far, please put up your hand ...' Not a single hand was raised.

'To mark our great appreciation of Miss Beasley, a true villager and loyal friend of Ringford School, I would ask you, Ivy, please to come up and receive a small token of our thanks.'

Ivy Beasley looked in utter fury at Doris Ashbourne. 'Never again, Doris Ashbourne!' she said, 'never again will I ask you to keep a secret.' Doris's protests of innocence were drowned by more roars of approval, and shouts of 'Good old Ivy!' She stood up, and was annoyed to find that her knees wobbled, but she made her way steadily to the top table.

Richard Standing reached down and lifted up a wicker basket. He put it on the table in front of Ivy, and she stared inside. A very small, chocolate-coloured kitten with wide open eyes looked fearlessly back at her. Then its tiny mouth opened and a sharp yowl startled her. Ivy Beasley had met her match. She reached in and gently picked up the kitten. With a smile that she could not suppress, she lifted it high and showed it to the assembled company.

'If you ask me,' she said, 'this little mite's hungry. So thanks very much everybody, and I'll go and get it something to eat.'

'What will you call it, Ivy,' said Susan Standing, stroking the aristocratic little head. 'Something really grand?'

'Tiddles,' said Ivy Beasley, holding the little scrap to her hot cheek. 'A proper cat's name, that is. Come on, Tiddles, let's go and have it out with your Auntie Doris.'

EPILOGUE

A thick mist shrouded Round Ringford, remnant of the last days of winter, and in the front room of the little Victorian schoolhouse, a middle-aged woman peered out, but could barely see across the road.

Goodness, she thought, I do hope the children will be all right. Her daughter-in-law, the headteacher, and a small group of staff and parents, had taken every single child in the school, barring none, on a coach trip to London to the Science Museum. They had set off early, and the coach driver was reassuring. He said he could find his way blindfold, he had done the journey that often.

The woman left the window and returned to her warm kitchen, where she put on the kettle, popped a biscuit into the little white dog's mouth, and assured her that her mistress would be back later that day.

It was very quiet, the eerie quiet of countryside under a pall of mist. 'It would have been like this,' said the woman to the little dog, 'if we'd lost the school. No children about at all. Dead, it would have been.'

The white dog snuffled into her blanket and went to sleep, retreating from a day without her beloved mistress.

Behind the school playground, scaffolding and

427

piles of bricks filled the little field. Can't even see Tom's calves, thought the woman. She missed the farm all the time, but tried to make the best of it. It had been the logical thing, when her son married the headmistress. They would live at the farm, and she would move to rent the schoolhouse, newly renovated and furnished by her daughter-in-law before her marriage. It had been a dreadful wrench, but she'd tried not to show it. She had recognised the inevitable, and resolved to try to love the prickly young schoolteacher as much as her precious son. Well, it could never be quite the same, but she would do her best.

'They must be nearly there by now,' she said, and the little dog opened one eye, cocked one ear. 'Forecast said fog in the Midlands, so perhaps they drove out of it.'

She went out to the shed to fetch a basket of clothes waiting to be ironed, and returned to the house. Not a bad little house, really, she told herself. Nice dry shed for storing things, and easy to keep clean. But she longed for the sounds of the farm in the early mornings, the feel of a warm, new-laid egg in her palm, straight from the nest. She shrugged. Get on with some work. No good brooding.

The iron winked at her, ready to be used. She smoothed sheets and pillowcases, folded tea-towels and hung crisply-ironed blouses on hangers to air. Soon be lunchtime, and then it would be afternoon, and the children would be

428

back, *full of their outing, tired and fractious.*

And then the little dog was out of her basket, whining, and the woman heard it too. It was a little girl's voice, thin and trembling, tailing off in despair.

'Help! Help me ... please ...' it said.